Demons. It sounded ridiculous even to her ears, and she knew the truth. She shook her head. "We found out about this place because thieves stumbled onto a gold goblet here. Right about where you're standing. One of them was murdered in the forest when they left. The other turned himself in after his friend died at his feet."

His fingers slipped through hers, twining their hands together intimately. Chloe gained strength from his firm hold. He turned and guided her hand to his hip. He caught her other hand, did the same. When her palms rested on his belt loops, he slid his arms around her waist. One half step brought his body close to hers. "I will keep you safe, Chloe," he murmured as he gazed into her eyes. He dipped his head to brush his cheek against hers. "I promise I will keep you safe."

She closed her eyes, longing to believe him. He used the right words, the confident comforting tone of voice. No one had offered anything of the sort, not even her brother. And yet, little could truly convince her. Lucan had no idea what he spoke of. No clue what lurked there in the trees. He couldn't defend her any more than she could protect herself. No one could.

Immortal Trust

The Curse
of the Templars

Claire Ashgrove

A TOM DOHERTY ASSOCIATES BOOK • NEW YORK

This is a work of fiction. All of the characters, organizations, and events portrayed in this novel are either products of the author's imagination or are used fictitiously.

IMMORTAL TRUST: THE CURSE OF THE TEMPLARS

Copyright © 2013 by Valerie M. Hatfield

All rights reserved.

A Tor Book
Published by Tom Doherty Associates, LLC
175 Fifth Avenue
New York, NY 10010

www.tor-forge.com

Tor® is a registered trademark of Tom Doherty Associates, LLC.

ISBN 978-0-7653-6760-0

Tor books may be purchased for educational, business, or promotional use. For information on bulk purchases, please contact Macmillan Corporate and Premium Sales Department at 1-800-221-7945 extension 5442 or write specialmarkets@macmillan.com.

First Edition: April 2013

Printed in the United States of America

0 9 8 7 6 5 4 3 2 1

To the two most important men in my life, my children,
Garrett and Pierce. I love you, boys.

Acknowledgments

To my family, who has remained constant in their support and encouragement, especially my children, who would much rather Mommy play cars than work! Thank you for understanding. Thank you for everything.

To my friends Dyann and Dennis Barr, without whom I could not have done so many of the things I have. I hope, someday, I can return everything tenfold. You are as close as family and loved every bit as much.

To Heartland Romance Authors and Midwest Romance Writers, my siblings in this crazy journey, thanks so much for the lessons you've taught and the mentoring you've given. You're simply awesome, a better bunch of authors I can't imagine!

To my agent, Jewelann Cone, thank you for all your dedication. And to my wonderful editor, Whitney Ross, thank you for making everything that much better.

To Jason . . . you already know all the words. They come from my heart, where you've set down thick, unmovable roots. Now, if only you'd get over this cat thing, you could honestly call yourself perfect. Hee! Thank you, sweetheart, for everything.

The Curse

In 1119, nine knights rode with Hugues de Payens to the Holy Land, becoming the Knights Templar. All were bound by marriage or by blood. Eight were recorded over time. The ninth vanished into history.

Beneath the legendary Temple Mount, the knights uncovered holy relics, including the Copper Scroll—a document written by Azazel's unholy hand. For their forbidden digging, the archangels exacted a sacrifice. The knights would spend eternity battling the demons of Azazel's creation, but with each vile death they claimed, a portion of darkness would enter their soul. In time, they would transform into knights of Azazel, warriors veined with evil, destined to fight against the Almighty.

Yet an ancient prophecy remained to give them hope. When darkness raped the land, the seraphs would return. Female descendants of the Nephilim would carry the light to heal their dying souls.

Centuries have passed. Azazel's might grows to intolerable limits. With the acquisition of eight holy relics, he will gain the power to overthrow the Almighty.

Six Templars stand above the rest in duty, honor, and loyalty. But each is haunted by a tragic past, and their darkened souls rapidly near the end. As they battle both the overwhelming power of evil and the nightmares of lives they left behind, the seraphs are more than tools to victory.

They are salvation.

Prologue

Whence comes the teacher, she who is blind shall
    follow.
The one who digs in dust precedes the finding of
    the jewel.
And she who understands the sword precludes the
    greatest loyalty.
When darkness rapes the land, the seraphs shall
    purify the Templar
And lead the sacred swords to victory.
    —Ancient Prophecy of the Knights Templar

Ornes, France
January

Julian Broussard glanced out the frosty window at a
distant mound of rock and cursed his sister's ridiculous fear of the dark for the hundredth time. If she
weren't such a goose, he'd have someone to share the
nightly rounds. Another pair of hands to pick up tools
their team of student archaeologists left lying in the mud.
Another set of eyes to check the waterproofed markers
that identified bits and pieces they'd chiseled out of
frozen ground.

But no, as usual, Chloe and her imaginary demons managed to find sanctuary in the hotel's ample warmth before the last student left the site. Leaving Julian an hour's worth of work with only a flashlight to guide his way around the exposed medieval structures.

He muttered and thumped open the mobile trailer's lightweight door. A frigid northern wind whipped across his face, stealing his breath. The scent of snow lingered in the air. With luck, it would skip over Ornes and carry on into Paris. Now that they were finally into the guts of what they'd come to find, a snowstorm would only piss him off further. He'd had his fill of melting ice, moving snow, and needing a jackhammer to break through frozen soil.

Pebbles crunched beneath his feet as he trudged down the steep path that led to the excavation site. Hunkered down in his coat, muffler about his ears, he followed the bold white beam of light. His breath billowed out before him, and he wished once more that they could transport the whole damn project to Arizona. He despised the cold.

His light caught on the narrow shelf of stones that marked the boundary. Forty-two days of excavating ground, moving aside the crumbled remnants Hitler's bombs left behind, and at last, the feudal castle rose from the depths of the earth. With every exterior nuance recorded, tomorrow they would begin scaling off the interior. Rebuilding walls. Laying out stones and whatever else they found in the fortified enclosure.

If luck was on their side, they'd locate the stash vagabonds reported at the start of the year. Damn shame he couldn't force the man who'd been jailed for stealing artifacts into identifying the exact location. Even more damning, the other thief died out here. Supposedly of fright.

Fright, my ass. They probably fought over the take.

In any case, the rumor fueled Chloe's paranoia to exceptional heights. She hardly ever neared the forest's edge, day or night. Locked away in the field trailers, she catalogued bits of pottery, fragments of stone, and detailed their discoveries in their required logs.

A glimmer of gold halted his walk. He swung the flashlight before him and cocked his head as the light glinted off a jutting fragment in the earth. Julian stepped over the remnants of what had once been a thick stone wall and squatted before the golden chip. With the butt end of the flashlight between his teeth, he plucked his trowel from his back pocket. Using the point, he loosened the ground around the object. Chunks broke free. He brushed them aside with his thumb.

A handle? He frowned at the exposed scrollwork design. The thieves had brought in a golden chalice with a similar design. Could this be a serving pitcher? In gold? Julian scraped at the earth with the flat edge of his tool.

The breeze picked up, stirring the overhead branches. He tucked his chin deeper into his coat, determined to ignore the near-freezing temperature. A few more carefully placed wedges of the point, and he'd have . . .

His hand stilled as the gravel crunched behind him. Though thick clouds obscured the sky, an even thicker shadow descended over his shoulder. The hair at the nape of his neck lifted, and an unexplainable shudder rolled down his spine. His heart stuttered into an unnatural cadence.

Closing his fingers around the trowel's wooden handle, he poised the weapon to defend himself and turned.

A hand shot out. Fingers dug into his shoulder. Julian lifted his gaze across a blackened chain-mail-clad chest, up a thick neck, and onto a coif-covered head. Shadows marred the man's face, blocking all features save for his eyes. But the eerie green light that filled a malicious gaze closed Julian's throat.

Not human.

The illogical thought drifted across his mind seconds before the hand on his shoulder tightened and dragged him to his feet. Despite the utter lack of heat in the air, sweat broke over Julian's skin. He swallowed hard, told himself ghosts only lived in his sister's mind.

"Azazel sent for you."

The hollow empty laugh that issued from the ebony-clad man's throat silenced the feeble protests of Julian's mind. Nothing *living* made that sort of spine-chilling sound.

"Wh-who?" he croaked.

"You will bring him the Veil."

"The veil? What veil?" Julian twisted his shoulders, attempting escape.

The man's grip clamped into bone. Pain shot down Julian's arm, wrenching a pitiful cry from his throat. As he stumbled against a rush of dizziness, a fist slammed into his face. Pinpricks of light burst behind Julian's eyes. Distantly, he recognized he was moving. Leaves crunched beneath the being's boots. Chain mail clinked in the stillness. The revolting stench of death assaulted his nose.

Grasping at the last of his strength, Julian fought off the pull of unconsciousness and opened his eyes. What stood before him justified every irrational fear his sister possessed. Red-orange eyes gleamed with wicked hunger. Yellowish fangs protruded from an unholy face.

The thing that had brought him into the forest thrust him into a deadly embrace. Claws raked across his back, slid between his ribs. Agony lanced through his body. An anguished cry tore from his throat.

"Yes, scream," the creature murmured. "It is so much better when you scream."

Tendrils of darkness fingered at Julian's mind. He grasped at them, desperate for the promised escape. But seconds before he succumbed to blissful oblivion, he felt the invasion. The foul, horrific, *glorious* presence of death pressed against his mind. A whisper of command more comforting than any cessation of his heart.

Then nothing.

CHAPTER I

Ornes, France
February

Winter cast a gray pallor over snowcapped fields as the SUV wound down a narrow country lane. Lucan reclined in the passenger seat, outwardly the picture of perfect knightly composure. Inside, however, naught remained at peace. In the passing of nine miles, he would set his eyes upon his seraph. The weight of her identifying serpentine torc pressed into his palm. Though he kept his hand tucked into his coat pocket, his anxiety seeped out through the clench of his fingers. Would she welcome him? Or would he face the trials Merrick and Farran had when they found their eternal mates?

He shifted in his seat, crossed the opposite ankle over his knee. His right hand tapped against the passenger door's armrest. Four days' travel, and he had never known a more indefinite passing of time. Even after centuries of existence, when he had become accustomed to the never-ending setting suns, the short span of time was unbearable. Salvation came with this

Chloe Broussard. Escape from the eternal suspicion that plagued his wakefulness.

Love too might grace his life—if the archangel Gabriel paired him appropriately. Though, in truth, Lucan cared little about the sentimental bonds. 'Twas the tie to brotherhood, the knowledge his fate would remain in the Almighty's hands that mattered most. All else was naught but fancy. A trifle enjoyment of comfort the Templar cast aside long ago.

He breathed deeply to quell the rapid beat of his heart. If they did not arrive soon, he would rather shove open the door and walk. Whilst a foot journey would delay his inevitable meeting further, his mind would not be preoccupied with questions. Nor would he suffer this unexplainable hope he could not seem to cast aside.

"Rest easy, brother, we have but a few more miles." Caradoc shifted behind the wheel. The grimace that crossed his face as his aching bones settled into the leather seat belied his own suffering.

For a heartbeat, guilt swamped Lucan. He should not be so eager to embrace healing when those he cared about suffered. As a former commander and the second unto Merrick, Caradoc deserved his soul pairing far more than Lucan. Merrick and Farran each found theirs—Lucan had become convinced Caradoc would follow. But nay, Gabriel came to him. Bade him to take Caradoc, enlist Gareth from Europe, and deliver the serpents to Chloe before Azazel could ensnare her.

Laughter in the backseat washed away Lucan's brief unease. He glanced over his shoulder to find the younger Gareth grinning broadly. "Bah, Caradoc, you expect him to rest easy when he waits to discover whether his mate bears the face of an old crone or that of an angel's grace?"

Caradoc shrugged, but the hint of a smile fringed his grim expression. "'Tis naught more than a betrothal. We have all been down such paths. Tell me, Gareth, when you were pledged as a lad, did you pause to consider what the maid would look like?"

Gareth's laughter deepened. "Nay. She would bear me sons. More comely wenches were made for my pleasure."

The reminder of lives left behind tightened Lucan's chest. Banter that should have lightened his heart only brought bitterness. Scenes of the family he had once known, and their violent demise. The maid he would have wed had killed those who shared his blood. Or rather, the forbidden love she gave to a man Lucan believed capable only of generosity and kindness. She brought that man, the one he had called brother, to an early grave as well.

As if Caradoc sensed Lucan's discomfort, he murmured. "Leave Enid behind, Lucan. She has no place in this."

Lucan nodded long and slow. Enid resided in the grave. Next to her beloved. He had thought little of her through the centuries. He would not make the mistake of allowing her to rise from the dead. Yet the irony of circumstance did not escape him. Chloe posed the same risks. She held the same power to bring brothers to blows. To shred ties that ran deeper than blood and destroy families. For he would kill for her, as he had killed to avenge his murdered father.

She was his seraph. His to protect against all others, including his Templar brethren, should jealousy override sense and oaths. Already the fierceness of his preordained bond filled his blood.

The road curved around a sharp bend, then flattened out once more. Tall pines sheltered the asphalt from the recent snows. Ahead, a row of vehicles tucked into the landscape marked their destination. Caradoc slowed the SUV and eased into the gravel parking lot. He shut off the engine, then swiveled in his seat. His gaze flickered between Lucan and Gareth.

"Whilst we are here for Chloe, we cannot forget the Veronica. With it, Azazel can decode the angels' language. Once Chloe uncovers the reliquary that protects it, he will stop at naught to obtain the sacred cloth."

Lucan met Caradoc's heavy stare, understanding all he did not say. If Chloe were oathed by that time, she would remain untouched. If Azazel discovered her seraph's blood before she spoke her vows, a fate far worse than death awaited. The previous attempts on Noelle's life lent credence to the archangels' belief Azazel wished to replace his lost lover, Lilith. Worse, should he possess a seraph, should he break the prophecy by claiming this one, Azazel's ascension to the Almighty's divine throne would all but become guaranteed.

Gareth broke the heavy silence by opening his door. Cold air washed into the comfortable heat. Caradoc winced as the gust cut through his heavy coat, and Lucan braced himself for the wintry outdoors. He stepped out into the snow.

Two mobile trailers sat beyond the memorial stones that marked this tiny village as a casualty of Hitler's greed. Bits of rubble, chunks of buildings that once stood straight and proud, edged the gravel path to the trailers' doors. Lucan surveyed the protruding rocks, sadness filling his heart. Such unnecessary destruction. Ornes could have become a great city like its sister, Verdun. 'Twas a good thing the European Templar commander, Alaric, deigned to accompany their quest. He would hate to see the nothingness his homeland had become. But like so many other strongholds that had once known glory, the le Goix legacy crumbled beneath the fist of time.

Like Lucan's beloved Seacourt.

He shook off the momentary melancholy and fixed his gaze on the smaller trailer's front steps. With purpose, he strode for the door. His brothers followed behind, their distance respectful.

Halfway down the path, the door burst open. Dressed in a coat so large it dwarfed her, a woman bounded out. Her long auburn hair caught in the breeze and streamed out behind her. She approached at a determined pace, arms folded across her chest.

Lucan's pulse jumped as Chloe Broussard marched directly toward him. 'Twas time. Four days finally came to fruition with this moment. He found his smile, hoped it did not falter like the anxious stuttering behind his ribs. Letting go of her torc, he withdrew his hand from his pocket and extended it in greeting. "I am Lucan. 'Tis a pleasure to meet you."

She came to an abrupt halt two feet before him. Her gaze dropped to his hand, before lifting to his face. Amber eyes widened for an instant, then narrowed just as quickly. "You were supposed to be here this morning. It's almost five, almost dark, and my team's sat idle all day waiting on *the Church's* representatives to supervise what we're perfectly capable of not only excavating, but also documenting, cleaning, and preserving for shipment. But it seems *the Church* didn't trust our integrity."

Lucan clamped his teeth together, silencing a defensive bark. God's teeth, for once 'twould be nice if Gabriel made the bonding of seraphs easy.

Lucan's eyes hardened like steel and clashed with Chloe's annoyed scowl. She turned her back on the three imposing men, unwilling to let Lucan's handsome face sway her into better spirits. Held back by the insistence from the Vatican that she wait until their representatives could be present, her team had missed a full day. A delay that would cost them dearly if the overcast sky made good on its threat of snow.

She stomped inside the trailer, letting the door bang shut behind her. Determined to ignore the twinge of guilt her unprofessional attitude brought, she dropped into her desk chair and folded her arms across her chest.

As expected, Lucan and the other two blocks of stone ducked through the doorway and entered the single-wide's makeshift office. They formed a triangle in front of her desk—two blond corners at the rear, with Lucan as the point man. She let her gaze wander across the masculine faces. At Lucan's right, the slightly taller, sandy blond wore a haggard expression. As if he had seen more from life than his midthirties warranted. He regarded her with subtle curiosity. Like a colleague who assessed a competitive peer. Beside him, the other blond's expression brimmed with humor. Soft brown eyes crinkled at the corners, as if he enjoyed some inside joke.

Her gaze shifted to Lucan, and a strange tightness

possessed her skin. Her work took her to the four corners of the world. She'd seen, spoken to, and even worked with handsome men. For that matter, her brother had been known to make women titter stupidly when he walked into the room. But this man . . . His broad shoulders screamed strength. His narrow waist said he knew the meaning of a hard workout. Yet, the way he looked at her, as if he could read her very thoughts, made her wholly uncomfortable. Behind the unmistakable sharpness of annoyance, interest fringed his unusual gray eyes. And the raven hair that fell almost to his shoulders suggested an uninhibited nature that contradicted his neat attire.

A shiver raced down her spine as the word *naughty* flitted through her thoughts.

He quirked a dark eyebrow. One corner of his mouth threatened to yield to a self-assured smile.

Heat crept into Chloe's cheeks. She quickly averted her gaze and shuffled a stack of papers from one side of the desk to the other. Handsome maybe. Cocky she could do without. Particularly if she had to work beside him for the next several months. She'd had her fill of trying to prove herself among her colleagues.

Fixing her stare on the less threatening face to Lucan's left, she cleared her throat. "Is there a particular reason you decided to show up today?" Sarcasm crept into her voice. "Why not tomorrow? By then we might have a foot of snow to dig through and three extra pairs of hands would be welcome."

With the smoothness of brandy, Lucan's deep British accent washed over her. "I fear we are both victims of miscommunication. We were instructed to arrive this evening, milady."

Milady? Chloe blinked. The antiquated title prickled her arms with goose bumps. She left her chair to give herself a bit of breathing room and drifted to the long countertop behind her. Picking up a printed copy of the Vatican's communication, she flicked the corner of the paper. "It says here *Sunday* the nineteenth. I assumed we'd start the week promptly this morning." Turning, she strode back to the group of men and thrust the paper at Lucan's wide chest.

He pushed it gently aside. Reaching into his coat pocket, he withdrew a folded square of paper. As he pressed the creases smooth, Chloe groaned inwardly. She didn't have to look to know what that sheet of paper would say. Inevitably, his copy would read *Monday* the twentieth. Her luck wouldn't have it any other way.

She accepted his outstretched offering and scanned the paper, confirming her suspicion. Her angry sails deflated, she let out a heavy sigh. "I apologize."

"No apologies are necessary." Lucan's mouth lifted with a smile. His eyes sparkled with the gesture, not unlike silver beneath bright sunlight. "'Tis understandable you would be upset."

For a moment, Chloe could do no more than stare. If he'd been handsome moments ago, that warm smile made him breathtaking. Her gaze skipped down to his boots, making note of the thick expanse of his thighs, the way the denim fitted snug. As she again met his discerning stare, and that dark eyebrow quirked as it had before, her cheeks heated once more. Good grief, he wasn't the least bit uncomfortable by her appreciative appraisal. If anything, she half suspected he'd have no qualms mentioning it aloud if his friends weren't present.

He took a confident step forward and extended his hand a second time. "Shall we try this again? I am Lucan."

Swallowing hard, Chloe slid her palm into his. His fingers tightened just enough to make the strength in his hands obvious, but his grip came nowhere close to painful. Pleasant almost. If it weren't for the overwhelming masculine presence that flooded her awareness. She tugged on her hand, anxious to be free of the unsettling sensations that accompanied the scrape of his skin.

The pressure around her fingers strengthened, trapping her in place. Lucan nodded over his left shoulder. "This is Caradoc." He tipped his head at the other man. "And Gareth."

Chloe offered the other two men an uncomfortable smile. "A pleasure, gentlemen."

Lucan's thumb brushed across the back of her hand. The light gesture carried entirely too much intimacy for her liking. She pulled back, and this time, Lucan's fingers let go. Her palm slipped free, but his gaze imprisoned her. Suggestion glinted in those steely depths. A silent, yet bold statement that invited her to enjoy a bit of wickedly sinful abandon.

She broke free from the rush of heat that infused her blood by returning to her desk. He might be drop-dead gorgeous, but colleagues and sex didn't mesh. She'd learned that lesson the hard way. Nothing short of absolute desperation would let her entertain the notions Lucan's eyes conveyed. And she hadn't reached desperate yet. Two years without a man left her a bit hungry for physical satisfaction, but the lack of orgasms hadn't erased all sense from her head.

Determined to communicate strict professionalism, she summoned her no-nonsense business demeanor. "So, gentlemen, since it's so late, what do you say to an early start in the morning—assuming the weather co-operates?"

Lucan glanced toward the door. "There is nothing you require of us this evening?"

Chloe shook her head and forced her irritation aside. "No, we've done nothing today. I was instructed to wait until you arrived before we excavated any more relics that could belong to the Church."

Caradoc gestured at the closed crates stacked on the countertop. "We would like to see the artifacts you've already unearthed."

"Those?" She chuckled softly. "Those aren't what you're here for. Anything that could possibly carry religious significance is in the other trailer. My brother, Julian, already left for the hotel. He has the keys, I'm afraid."

Lucan's gaze narrowed with suspicion. "But the cars outside—no one is here with you?"

At the reminder she'd have to close up the field office alone, Chloe's chest tightened. Out here, especially at night, the presence that had hounded her the last eight years intensified. She didn't know what, exactly, it was, but she understood one thing clearly—it didn't like her.

She ignored the chill that inched down her spine. "I've been doing paperwork all day. I'm used to working alone." Just not at night. Never at night.

A slight frown pulled at Lucan's brow. "Do you have much work remaining?"

"Oh, not much." She gestured at the open record book

on her desk. "I need to transfer notes on three more artifacts into the computer. Then I'll head on back." Forcing brevity, she laughed. "Just me and the trees. The quiet's nice."

The tight downturn to Lucan's mouth evidenced his disbelief. He twisted to address Caradoc. "Go on. I will stay with her."

"No!" Chloe blurted out. Lord no, not alone with him. She'd take the presence in the darkness over ten minutes alone with him. He posed a far greater risk. "I mean, thank you, but that's not necessary. I've been here for a full month. I'm quite capable of locking up on my own. Rest assured, I won't be fiddling with anything that would interest you."

Lucan eased out of his coat and draped it over the back of a nearby chair. "'Tis not the Church's interest that concerns me, milady, but your safety." Leather creaked as he sat down.

"Till morn then," Gareth chimed, his eagerness to be free of the trailer evident. He exited swiftly.

Caradoc clamped his hand on Lucan's shoulder in a brotherly gesture of support. "I shall inform Merrick we have arrived."

To Chloe's horror, he too vanished out the door. Unable to look at Lucan, she stared at her blank laptop screen. "Maybe work can wait until tomorrow."

Her feeble excuse met a wall of determination. "Nay. Do what you must. I will . . ." Trailing off, he glanced around the trailer. On spying Chloe's coveted, specially shipped from Tucson, latest edition of *Cosmopolitan*, he picked up the magazine and scanned the cover. A smirk drifted across his sensual mouth. "I will learn how to turn a weekend getaway into an erotic paradise."

Sheer mortification scalded her face. With a fierce push, she swiveled her chair around so she wouldn't have to look at him and pressed the button to bring her laptop out of sleep mode. Torture. Not only did the Church seek to insult her ethics by demanding she cease excavation until their representatives arrived to oversee her work, they sought to torture her with a man who could define *erotic paradise*.

CHAPTER 2

✝

Lucan looked over the top of the magazine he was pretending to read. Chloe Broussard was far more fascinating than the glossy advertisements. Not to mention, perusing an article that detailed the many benefits of breakfast abed with a willing partner, whilst Chloe sat across from him, made the small confines uncomfortably warm.

Feed your partner berries to kick off your day of hedonistic pleasure.

As Chloe chewed on the end of her pen, a vision of her lips closing around his fingers burst to life in his mind. He scowled at the unbidden intrusion. Damnation, he had not expected *she who digs in dust* to be so delightfully feminine.

He studied the delicate lines of her profile. Long lashes that he could make out even across the distance separating them dusted high, regal cheekbones. A smooth jawline tapered to a chin that would fit neatly atop two of his fingers. Full lips promised softness. All features designed to torment a man. Her nose, however, made him chuckle inwardly. Or rather, the slightly crooked way it sat between her eyebrows. He found the flaw endearing. A perfect imperfection designed to remind him that though her veins ran with the blood of angels, she was still an earthly human.

Her lashes drooped for the second time. As they lingered on her cheeks, her chin dipped with exhaustion. She jerked upright, scrubbed at her eyes, and squinted at the screen.

"Chloe, how long have you been here today?" he asked quietly.

"Hm?" She blinked, then regained her composure and pushed aside her momentary surprise. "Here? I come in around five every morning."

Lucan frowned. "'Tis almost fourteen hours of work. You should rest."

Her soft chuckle floated over the whistling wind. "I have four months to excavate that feudal castle before my special license expires. I lost most of January to the weather. February isn't much better. If I take time to rest, we'll miss out on key findings."

She would not see the completion of her four months. Once she uncovered the Veronica, her life would change forever. But Lucan kept that knowledge to himself. Soon enough he would have to tell her. Presently, however, she faced little danger. He fell silent as her short nails clicked across the keys, her dedication to her work a trait he found immeasurably appealing. Few mortals he knew would put in such time when they could have easily sloughed off with good excuses.

What would she say when he informed her of her seraph's status? Would she, like the others, disavow her fate? A frown returned to tighten his brow. Nay, she might resist, but he would not force her circumstance upon her as Merrick and Farran had done. Would not force *himself* upon her. 'Twas a reason good manners existed, and he would court her as she deserved. Solicit her affections afore she learned her fate and the greater duty required. As long as Azazel's minions did not force him into conflict and fill his soul with more evil, he possessed time to wait.

A rattle at the window lifted the hairs along his forearms. He stiffened as the certain scent of death met his nose. 'Twas faint, little more than the odor of a rotting mouse beneath the floor planks, yet present all the same. The wind buffeted the tiny window behind him, and the foul aroma of decay intensified. With it came an overwhelming awareness of a hate-filled presence.

Mayhap he did not possess as much time as he believed.

Centuries of combating Azazel's dark creations triggered his warrior's instincts. Reflexively, he dropped his hand to his hip to grasp his holy sword. His fingers, however, closed over empty air, and Lucan muttered an inward curse. Demons lurked outside, and he had foolishly left his blade in the SUV. His first day with his seraph, and already he failed to protect her accordingly.

As if Chloe too sensed they were no longer alone, she glanced over her shoulder at the window. Her gaze dipped to his. A hesitant smile waivered on her lips. "Some wind, isn't it? Guess that storm's blowing in after all." She let out a sigh as she swiveled back to her computer. "Tomorrow we'll have to dig out again. I wish the damn tarps I ordered two weeks ago would get here."

Lucan narrowed his gaze, unable to stop the rush of

suspicion. The quiver in her voice betrayed her awareness of the demons. But why did she show no fear? No
concern at all about the malicious creatures waiting
beyond? 'Twas as if she expected them.

He squeezed his eyes shut to cease the mistrustful
racket of his thoughts. That she did not acknowledge
their unwelcome company should not surprise him. She
possessed no knowledge of his purpose. She had only
been informed he, Caradoc, and Gareth were the
Church's educated experts on holy relics. 'Twould be
foolishness to speak of dark spirits and evil beings to a
stranger. She would subject herself to condemnation.

His belly rumbled, reminding him he had not eaten
since dawn. Using it as an excuse, he pushed out of the
chair and crossed the short distance between them.
Hands braced on both sides of her desk, he leaned over
her chair and brought his face close to hers. The subtle
scent of warm vanilla and roses flooded into his awareness. His body tightened unexpectedly. At once, he was
too close. Too far away. He closed his eyes to ward off
the deep-rooted urge to press his mouth to the delicate
shell of her ear.

Inhaling a short breath, he steeled himself against
Chloe's powerful allure. "My belly protests its emptiness. Let us leave this place."

Her spine straightened like steel. She stared straight
at the screen. "I'm almost finished."

It took every ounce of willpower Lucan possessed to
not dip his chin to her shoulder. He backed away before
primal instinct overrode common sense. "You said the
same an hour ago. Come." Leaning forward he closed
her laptop. "Let us sup. I shall treat you to dinner."

A quiet laugh trilled in the back of her throat. She

turned with an equally soft smile. "You have the most unusual accent."

Satisfied he had won the battle, Lucan grinned. "A product of too many years in the Church's employ." He tugged her coat off the back of her chair and held it open for her to slide into.

She twisted close as she shrugged into her coat. So close his nerve endings rose, anticipating the satisfaction of contact. But just as quickly, Chloe escaped. "I'll just grab something out of the refrigerator in my room. I keep it stocked for nights like this."

He pursed his lips, not at all content with her obvious attempt to escape spending time with him. But before he could protest, Chloe used his earlier words against him.

"I'm exhausted, anyway."

Grumbling to himself, he reluctantly accepted her excuse. He would not push her tonight. Though the creatures beyond demanded he reevaluate his determination to take his time with her, he did not have to begin tonight. He picked up his coat and stuffed his arms inside. "Where are your keys? I will start your vehicle."

For one unexplainable moment, she looked like she would protest. Her brows narrowed. Her lips parted as if she sought to speak. But then, like a veil drawn over an open window, her expression smoothed. With a short, succinct nod, she fished a small collection of keys out of her desk drawer and lobbed them in his direction. "The silver Mercedes closest to the door."

Lucan caught them at his shoulder. He let himself out into the cold and firmly closed the door. Standing on the porch, he blocked out all thoughts of Chloe and attuned his senses to the forest around him. He could feel them, aye. Demons amidst the trees.

Yet they kept their distance. Proof they waited for the Veronica, not the woman within.

He breathed easier, certain tonight would not bring a battle he could not fight. Striking a brisk pace, he hurried to her car and let himself inside. The engine turned over easily, a quiet rumble in the dark. As he waited for the heater to catch, he adjusted the seat. Though Chloe was tall, he still felt like a cramped sardine. Particularly after a day and a half in the larger, more spacious Templar vehicle.

To his absolute frustration, however, the trailer opened and Chloe exited. He tensed, thrust open the door, and set a foot outside to meet her on the stairs. But before he could fully remove himself from the Mercedes, she jogged down the graveled path and yanked on the passenger's door.

Lucan slid back inside. "I would have walked you to the car."

"That's really not necessary." The light extinguished as she pulled the door shut. Huddling into her coat, she shivered. "You'd think with March around the corner it'd be getting warmer."

Easing onto the gas, Lucan navigated out of the parking space. "'Twill be another month or so. Have you not worked much in France?"

"No. I've spent most of my time in Egypt. I did a dig three years ago in China, but politics took a downturn and forced us out. Otherwise, I've been working on mummies and tombs."

He glanced sideways as he turned onto the narrow

country lane. Though he knew the Almighty brought
her to France, he sought casual conversation. "Why did
you choose Ornes and the le Goix castle?"

"Le Goix?" Interest sparked behind her eyes. "I didn't
know the castle had a name."

"Aye, indeed. 'Twas erected centuries ago by Alaric
le Goix. He was a servant of the Holy Order of the
Knights Templar. What you are removing from the
earth are the sacred relics he was charged to guard after the Inquisition condemned him as a heretic."

Chloe's thoughts skidded to a halt. Silently, she repeated
Lucan's words. *Charged to guard* after *he was condemned*. Wide-eyed, she stared at Lucan's shadowed
profile as the contradiction thundered in her head.

The Church had eradicated the Order. And yet, if Lucan was here, the Church had known all along Alaric le
Goix harbored sacred objects. Her words came out in a
rush. "You mean to tell me you knew?"

Lucan nodded. "Aye."

She blinked, dumbfounded. "How is that possible?
Why would the Church bury or hide things they could
keep safe? You've got a whole Vatican to hide them in."

On a heavy sigh, Lucan shook his head. "Not the
Church as you know it. Members *within*. Leaders."

Suspicious, Chloe squinted at him. "That's insane."

He arched an eyebrow. "You object when you have
spent your career focused on Egypt?"

The superiority of his tone made her grit her teeth.
"My early schooling was in medieval France, thank
you. I left Egypt when the regime changed and it became unsafe." Not exactly true—she'd left when it

became unsafe, but for entirely different reasons than political instability.

She frowned at Lucan again. "How would *you* know the Church's motives anyway? You're not a cardinal privy to the Vatican's secrets. You might be an expert in religious antiquities, but no more so than I'm an expert in Egyptian artifacts."

Lucan reached a hand into the collar of his heavy long-sleeved shirt and pulled out a medallion. In the dim glow from the dash, a half-dollar-sized silver disk dangled from his fingers. She leaned closer to inspect the object. Her fingers brushed against his, and his gaze skipped down to hers for a heartbeat before he let go and fastened his attention on the empty road.

Still warm from his skin, the medallion rested on her fingertips. What had once been scalloped edges were now worn smooth with only a few hills and valleys to reveal its former design. She brushed her thumb over a crudely engraved cross. Equal in size, the four beams flared on the ends in classic Templar fashion. Above and below the vertical bar read the Latin words *Milites Templi*.

"What is this?"

Lucan's hand wrapped around hers. There was something profoundly intimate about the press of his fingers. The way his large palm enveloped the back of her hand. A foreign spark of excitement rushed up her shoulder, rocketed down her spine, and lodged in her womb.

"'Tis a story meant for another day." He tucked her hand against the center console, guiding her back to her seat. "We have arrived."

Chloe looked up to find the sweeping facade of the Château des Monthairons and its four towering fairy-tale turrets, aglow against the night sky. She stared at the nineteenth-century castle, spellbound by both the majestic appearance and Lucan's mysterious medallion. Her heart tripped faster as supposition crept into her thoughts. Quite possibly she sat beside a descendant of the fabled Order. Perhaps even a member. Though she had never been swept away by the mystery of the Knights Templar, the link to history he might possess gave her chills.

But why, if he were associated with a society intent on staying secret, *why* would he reveal this to her? Because she dug among the remains of one of the members? Did that somehow make her worthy to share their knowledge?

As the Mercedes rolled to a halt, she furrowed her brow. Her mind prickled with the awareness Lucan had tried to tell her something. Something important that he expected her to understand. Something between the Church and the Knights Templar.

He gave her no time to consider the matter. Before she could realize he'd left the driver's seat, her door opened. He offered his hand.

Chloe stared at his palm, wanting nothing more than to slide her fingers into his and let this handsome man possess her thoughts. She lifted her gaze, her blood warming when her eyes locked with steely grays. The interest there was unmistakable. Compelling. It had been so long since a man had looked at her as if he had one thing, and only one thing, on his mind. And the heat behind his gaze left no misinterpretation to his meaning. If she'd let him, he'd be more than willing to help her remember what a man felt like.

Which would only open her to vulnerabilities she didn't have the strength to overcome. She'd never been able to distance herself from sex, and as long as she had to work with this man, she wouldn't get attached to him. Wouldn't let him have that much power over her and blind her to his intentions. Blake had done enough damage. To her heart and to her career. When he'd taken her findings, claimed them as his own, and climbed over her to rise to the top of their field, she'd vowed she'd never again tangle business with pleasure.

Never again.

She ignored Lucan's offered aid and pulled herself out of the car. As she approached the front steps, he walked at her side, a comforting presence she hated to admit. But it settled into her awareness that for the first time in too many years to count, she hadn't thought of the dark presence as she drove through the forest. Hadn't felt it.

In fact, for the first time since she'd set foot in France, she'd felt safe.

He opened the front door, held it while she entered. Silently, he walked beside her to the elegantly carved winding staircase. There he defied her deliberate attempt at distance and captured her hand. Lifting it to his mouth, he pressed a warm kiss to her knuckles. She grabbed at the smooth rail to steady the sudden weakness in her knees.

"You are certain you will not dine with me?"

Chloe swallowed hard. "N-no." She took a breath to steady her voice and covered her nervousness with a smile. "I really need to rest."

"Very well, milady." Slowly, Lucan lowered her hand. "I will see you on the morrow."

As he released her, his thumb again grazed the back of her wrist and set off the same stuttering racket behind her ribs. She held her breath, prayed he would turn around and leave before she did something foolish like trip up the stairs.

To her frustration, he refused to budge.

With no other option but to make her departure in front of him, she grabbed the rail and forced her feet to move. As the staircase curved, she made the mistake of looking over her shoulder. When he smiled, her toe caught the edge of the next tread. Barely catching herself before she toppled face first onto the flowery carpet runner, she cursed beneath her breath. Good lord, she was thirty—not fifteen. He was just a guy, just a colleague she neither wanted nor cared about. Getting dizzy because he smiled at her was nothing short of foolishness. Worse, now he knew he affected her.

She expelled the breath she'd been holding and ran the rest of the way to her room.

CHAPTER 3

Lucan's quest to cease the rumbling of his belly yielded three bags of chips and a Coke from a vending machine. Not precisely what he had envisioned, but the restaurant's wait list exceeded his patience tenfold and ordering dinner to his room was a luxury he could not justify. Breakfast would arrive soon enough.

He mounted the stairs snacks in hand, let himself inside his room, and sank into the overstuffed couch. Thoughts of Chloe ran rampant through his mind. Tonight he confided secrets he had told no one before. Though she had not made the immediate connection between the Templar Knights and the Church, he provided her the means to do so. He showed her the medallion he wore next to his heart that marked him as a servant of the Almighty. That he had done so left him uneasy.

'Twas her right to know, but nonetheless, entrusting a stranger with the Order's sacred history disturbed him. Mayhap 'twas the suspicion that plagued him; the constant war in his head between what he knew as fact and what the stain on his soul tried to make him believe. If he did not suffer Azazel's taint, mayhap confiding what he had tonight would hold a degree of comfort. Saints knew the burden weighed heavily at times.

And yet he could not escape the nagging sense of warning. The voice he could hear but could not name that cautioned the dark presence he had sensed directly tied Chloe to Azazel. It had followed them to the château, clung heavily even once they stepped within. She could not be ignorant to such a strong manifestation. The couple they had passed in the lobby visibly shied away. And 'twas Chloe's ambivalence that concerned him, not the demons in pursuit.

Demons he could justify to the Veronica, to Chloe's status as a seraph. But no mortal being accepted the closeness of darkness. Chloe, however, seemed immune.

Lucan dropped his head to the back of the couch and stared at the ceiling. Nay, he must be wrong. Mayhap she was so pure of soul she truly could not sense Azazel's nearness. Mayhap the Almighty shielded her.

Or mayhap he had become so accustomed to the unholy beings that he created their appearance in his head. 'Twas possible. When only a handful of nights, out of centuries of time, passed without an encounter, the expectation became ingrained. 'Twould not be a far cry from logic that he envisioned shadows in the corners.

Two heavy thumps on his door brought him upright and out of his thoughts. "Aye?"

"'Tis I." Caradoc's voice carried through the heavy barrier. As Lucan cracked the door open, Caradoc asked, "Am I interrupting?"

"Nay. Come in." On seeing the jagged cut beneath Caradoc's eye, Lucan frowned. "What befell you?"

With a noticeable wince, Caradoc took a seat in the armchair near the window. "Where is Chloe?"

The underlying urgency in his brother's voice set Lucan's instincts on high alert. He crumpled the empty bag of chips in his hand and tossed it onto the entry table. Returning to his place on the couch, he propped his elbows on his knees and frowned at Caradoc. "She is in her room. Why?"

"Azazel is here. His beasts, at least."

Horns of warning blared inside Lucan's head. He had not imagined the evil. And if it had made its presence known to Caradoc, 'twould not be long before its purpose with Chloe became clear. "When did you encounter them?"

Caradoc raked a hand through his hair. "As we left the site. Five miles down the lane, at the forest's edge. Three demons came upon the vehicle." His brows pulled toward the bridge of his nose. "They know *we* are here. And there are more in the forest."

"Aye," Lucan murmured. "I sensed them tonight." *And they are here as well.* He kept the thought to himself, unwilling to draw suspicion on Chloe. She was his responsibility. Until he knew her association with the darkness, he would not give his brothers reason to cast her aside.

Lucan picked at a mismatched thread in his jeans. "She will uncover the Veronica tomorrow."

"Aye, and when she does I fear what may happen. Gareth will not accompany us come morn. He sustained a significant injury to his calf."

"Gareth?" Lucan blinked. "Have you sent for Zerachiel?"

Caradoc shook his head. "Nay, he shall heal." A touch

of wistful quiet slipped into his voice. "Like the rest of the European members, his soul is full of vigor." Caradoc sat forward and grabbed a bag of chips from the center table. He jerked it open. "He will heal in a day's time. But he is too weak to be of use on the morrow."

The perfect combination for Azazel to move for the Veronica. Or Chloe. Lucan's gut clamped into a fierce knot. "This makes no sense, Caradoc. If 'tis the Veronica he desires, why has he made no move for it on his own? 'Twould not be difficult. He did so with the Sudarium."

"And made the world aware of his presence by destroying the cathedral. Azazel knows no limitations. Were he to attempt the Veronica on his own, he would find himself before Raphael's sword. He needs more power, more relics, to confront either Raphael or Mikhail."

Power he would attain when he united the Veronica and the Sudarium. Still, Lucan could not leave off the feeling Chloe played a role in this. That Azazel's delay had little to do with Raphael's formidable wrath and indeed revolved around the seraphs. Chloe in specific. Azazel was no idiot. He must know by now *she who digs in dust* was the woman who would unearth the sacred relic he coveted. Possessing her . . .

A rush of anger flooded through Lucan, surprising him with its fierceness. He had known her but a few hours.

But the story of what had happened to Iain's seraph lingered in all their minds. As well as the knowledge of all the other foul things Azazel could accomplish with a seraph as his slave.

A smile crept over Caradoc's face. "Enough of this.

We shall see what the morrow brings when it comes. Tell me, do you find Chloe to your liking?"

To his liking? *Liking* did not begin to describe the way his blood warmed when she stood too near. The way fire had lit in his veins when she leaned in close to inspect his medallion and her breath had caressed his cheek. Had he met her in the era of his birth, she would now be in his bed, and he would have had his fill of her, and then some. But he had also glimpsed her dedication to her profession, a devotion to duty he intimately related to. In the car, he caught a trace of insatiable curiosity that undoubtedly led her to the professional success she knew. Pride as well, and on her, the mortal vice 'twas more virtue. She wore it well. All of which made his inevitable pairing that much more appealing. She would not be a pretty object to set upon a shelf, but a respected mate he would be honored to share life with.

As if Caradoc heard his thoughts in the brief hesitancy of Lucan's response, he laughed softly. "Mayhap I shall find mine equally as pleasing." Although humor touched his words, the light in Caradoc's expression dimmed. He looked out the window, his thoughts retreating to the place and time Lucan knew he could not escape.

The time that brought him physical pain now, aches that intensified in a span of years far shorter than the rest of the Templar who battled the taint in their souls.

Lucan resisted the unfair supposition that Caradoc resented he had not been chosen for the next seraph. Though the question tugged at his mind, he refused to allow it to take root. Caradoc did not covet. Resentment did not reside in his true heart.

"Mayhap yours will fill the ache of Isabelle," Lucan murmured.

"Nay." Caradoc rose from the chair, his expression grim. As he did each time the subject of Isabelle arose, he sought escape. He abruptly crossed to the door. "I shall allow you to rest. Tomorrow, you must be prepared."

Lucan did not bother to respond. 'Twas no need to agree. The door pulled shut, and Lucan rested his feet atop the sturdy center table. Stretching, he reclined. Indeed, the morn would find him prepared to battle. But sunrise would bring more as well, for on the morrow he must attempt to draw Chloe closer. And whilst her eyes spoke words of interest, what tumbled off her lips forbade his efforts. Breaking through that invisible barrier required more strategic effort than any battle of swords.

In the quiet of her room, Chloe burrowed under the heavy layer of covers. The television emitted a soft light that helped ease her fear of the dark. She couldn't remember when she'd last slept in complete blackness. She'd tried once or twice, particularly when Blake complained. Even then, with his strength to blanket her, she'd shivered when the rattling on the windows began.

Strange, he hadn't ever noticed it. Now and then he commented on the wind, but he'd never been aware that the sound didn't come from branches against glass. *They* were out there. They tapped to let her know she couldn't escape.

She pulled the blankets up to her chin and huddled deeper into the warm cocoon. Beyond the closed blinds, the racket took on more insistence. Chloe shot an arm from beneath the covers, grabbed the small dagger on her nightstand, and jerked her arm under the heavy canopy once more. She clutched the blessed weapon in both hands and lifted her gaze to the elaborate mural of angels on the ceiling. For this reason, this tiny bit of comfort, she'd chosen this room. Her gaze riveted on the archangel Gabriel who held a white lily in his hands.

"Gabriel, I call upon you to keep me safe," she whispered into the dark.

Taught to her by a demonologist the first year she'd noticed the presence, the litany fell off Chloe's lips. Each syllable unraveled the knot of fear around her heart. Tomorrow, she'd replace the sage and the bits of quartz in the windowsills. Julian would ridicule her, but she'd make some time this week to find a spiritual cleanser and pay to have her room washed free of negative energy.

None of the measures would last long. But she might gain a full night's sleep before the demons could regain strength enough to override her efforts.

How she wished she'd listened to the native people of Bahariya who warned if she walked among the bones in the Valley of the Dead, she wouldn't leave as she'd entered. But she'd been so young and naive then. So determined to make a name for herself within the Egyptology community. The remains she discovered, the artifacts she placed, all elevated her position among her peers. In hindsight, however, having her papers published internationally and her name recognized among her mentors didn't justify the sacrifice.

If she'd heeded the warnings, or even bothered to wear the natives' gifts of warding, she could have climbed to the same heights professionally without the nightmares. She might not have accomplished all the things she took pride in, but at least she'd know peace.

Still gripping her dagger, she rolled onto her side, her back to the curtained windows. As she closed her eyes, Lucan's handsome face came to life. With the vision came the earlier contentment she'd experienced in the car. And though she knew she shouldn't entertain the notion of getting tangled up in him, she indulged in a bit of private fantasy. She comforted herself by imagining the feel of his strong arms holding her tight. Sheltering her from the things that wished her harm. His skin would be warm, his body smooth and tight.

She created a fantastic scene of the two of them standing before the lake beyond the château, bathed in moonlight. His long raven hair would gleam in the silver light, and when she ran her fingers through the straight lengths, they would tickle against her palm. His gray eyes held promise along with a touch of arrogant self-confidence. When he dipped his chin to touch his mouth to hers, she'd feel the warm caress all the way down to her toes.

Heaven above, one night with him would erase all thoughts of demons, darkness, and nightmares. And the fact she entertained the idea of crossing that line between colleagues and lovers scared her more than all the things she longed to escape.

She opened her eyes and stared into the brightly lit bathroom. This was no way to find sleep. Thinking about him only added to her agitation. Besides, she didn't dare trust him enough to let him slide beneath her sheets. He was an archaeologist, and therefore, her competitor. She'd learned the only person she could believe in was Julian. Beyond the fact he deferred to her and cared little about recognition for his work, he was her brother. The only man in this world who truly gave a damn about her success.

CHAPTER 4

Complete silence jolted Chloe from sleep. She snapped her eyes open, abandoning the illicit fantasy world of Lucan and his storm-gray eyes, and glanced around the room. The sliver of bright sunlight that poured through a gap in the heavy draperies brought her upright with a gasp. Panic launched her heart into double time as she squinted at the clock.

Eight o'clock. Crap! By now the student archaeologists would be onsite and her brother would be cursing her name. She hadn't overslept in a good five years.

"Oh God," she moaned. "Damn it!"

Throwing the covers back, she bounded out of bed. She should have been at the trailer two hours ago. If not three. Julian would have her head on a platter for delaying their start. Not to mention she'd look like an amateur to Lucan and his friends. Of all the things she'd learned about her field, women had to work harder, put in more hours, and never complain if they intended to be viewed as equals.

She stumbled across the bedroom to the bathroom for her cell phone and punched in her brother's number. His voice mail answered on the third ring.

"Hey, it's me. I'm on my way." She caught her reflection in the mirror and swiped a hand through her hair. "I'm sorry I'm late. Call me when you get this, and I'll tell you where to start."

Double damn—where the heck was he? For that matter, why hadn't he called when she failed to show up by seven?

She tossed her cell aside and picked up her hairbrush. Wincing, she yanked it through the nest of tangles that had become a common morning occurrence since she'd set foot in Ornes. That she'd managed to fall so deeply into slumber was an oddity in itself. She remembered clutching the dagger, waking once to thumping at the window, and then nothing—unlike her usual nightly routine where she woke up three or four times, the last almost always fifteen minutes before her alarm went off.

Which was why she hadn't set it. She'd become so accustomed to her internal clock, she hadn't touched the alarm in a week.

When her hair refused to cooperate, she gave up and stuffed it into a ponytail. Shower would have to wait until tonight. Makeup would wait too. It wasn't as if she intended to impress anyone, and the artifacts certainly wouldn't care if she looked like a walking zombie.

She splashed a bit of cold water on her face to shake off the last of sleep's embrace, snatched her cell phone, and rushed back into the bedroom for her clothes. Halfway across the room, she dialed Julian again.

When his recorded voice came through the line, she terminated the call and dropped the cell on her bed.

Weird.

Maybe he'd met up with a girl and he was running late too.

The thought spurred her into faster action. If Julian was holed up with a woman, then the rest of the team was in Ornes waiting for direction. Which meant Lucan, Caradoc, and Gareth were also sitting in the trailer— correction, sitting in their vehicles, since she had the keys—waiting.

She groaned again as she remembered the lecture she'd given Lucan. Lord above, she couldn't look any more like a hypocrite.

Rummaging quickly through her clothes, she grabbed jeans, a sage green shirt, and a heavy off-white sweater. She pulled everything on in record time, jammed her feet into her boots, and tried her brother for the third time.

Again, no answer.

Where in the hell was he? He never ignored his phone. The damn thing was permanently affixed to his back pocket. And the sheer volume of text messages he received daily was proof enough he didn't suffer from a loss of signal.

For good measure she typed in a quick message reiterating her imminent departure, and yanked her coat off the back of the chair. She jogged down the hall, around a sharp corner, and down the stairs.

In the lavish front hall, Chloe skidded to a stop.

Lucan lounged on an antique settee upholstered in rich velvet. One arm casually slung over the embellished back, he greeted her with a knowing grin. "Good morn."

Heat rushed into her cheeks. Ugh. Nothing like being caught red-handed. She'd banked on the short drive to create a plausible excuse for her tardiness. Resigned to the fact she couldn't hide her unplanned delay, she smoothed her hands down the tops of her jeans and took a deep breath. "Morning."

A quick glance around the lobby revealed he waited alone. She cocked her head and gave him a curious frown. "You're by yourself?"

"Aye. Caradoc went on an hour ago." Slowly, he stood. His gaze held hers too long, stirring to life all the images of her fantasy kiss. She looked away as her pulse accelerated and an embarrassing warmth slid into her veins. Men like this should not be allowed to greet women first thing in the morning. Especially women who were already late and hadn't put makeup on. All they accomplished was unbalancing thoughts.

Lucan held his hand out, palm up. She glanced at it, then back to his face, not understanding.

"Your keys, milady. I shall drive you."

"Really, I can drive myself." Probably better that way too. At least she'd have time to collect herself mentally before she had to spend time alone with him. Time alone with Lucan was nowhere on her list of things to do anyway.

He, however, clearly had different intentions. He waggled his fingers. "I am quite certain you are capable of driving yourself. But as I have no other means of getting to the site, you may as well allow me to drive." His grin broadened, and the light in his eyes took on a teasing glint. "'Twill allow you to enjoy the cup of coffee I suspect you need."

In truth, she despised driving. Not that she couldn't. Not that she didn't. But she lacked the patience for traffic and her lead foot had a habit of accumulating tickets. Come to think of it, she couldn't remember whether she'd turned the last ticket over to her attorney before leaving Tucson. With her luck, she probably had a warrant out for her arrest now.

She'd let Lucan drive. Sometimes practicality took precedence over pride. Or in her case, fear of being cooped up with a man who smelled like a heavenly combination of old-world spice and clean soap.

"All right, fine," she grumbled as she pulled the keys out of her pocket.

His fingers grazed over her palm as he closed them around the simple rubber keychain stamped with the car rental's logo. She could have almost considered the touch accidental if it weren't for the way he caught her fingertips for a fraction of a heartbeat.

Ignoring the ripple of excitement that made her pulse jump, she made a beeline for the long table of breakfast pastries and a freshly brewed pot of coffee. Dang it all, she needed to get a grip on her hormones. He was just a guy. One out of a dozen or more attractive men she'd met in her short stay in France. *They* hadn't set off her pulse. There was no excuse for him to do so either.

She poured a liberal cup, grabbed a blueberry Danish, and turned around to find Lucan standing at the end of the table, eyes glued on her, his lazy smile intact. Long dark hair hung loose about his shoulders, blending into the deep black of his cropped, aviator-style coat. The heavy garment fell open to reveal a deep red shirt beneath. Despite the layers, his powerful build showed.

Chloe groaned inwardly. Likely nothing could hide that broad expanse of muscle. Thank heavens it wasn't summer, and she didn't have to worry about his taking his shirt off beneath the hot sun. She'd have to change her rules with her students if it were.

She took a step forward, declining to start conversation. Surprising her completely, Lucan's hand settled into the small of her back. Casual. Yet familiar. Too familiar. She took a quick step to escape his unsettling nearness.

He widened his stride.

Silently cursing the fates, she accepted the fact she couldn't avoid contact without coming off rude, and allowed Lucan to guide her through the front door all the way down to the car. He stopped at the passenger's side to let her in, then rounded the front bumper as she eased into the seat.

In seconds, he had the car started and steered down the drive. As they turned onto the narrow road, Chloe realized he'd only mentioned Caradoc. "Where's your other friend? Gareth? Is that his name?"

"Aye, 'tis." He chuckled softly. "France is disagreeing with him."

Surprise lifted her eyebrows. "Oh? Did he eat something that made him sick?"

Another chuckle rumbled in Lucan's chest. He shook his head. "He overindulged."

Oh. Like Julian. She supposed she should have sensed Gareth shared an affinity for women. With the same boyish good looks her brother possessed, they were apt to fall at his feet. Add in Gareth's impressive physique, and Julian might have a real rival when it came to shopping the château's female guests. Precisely what she needed to make the rest of this dig memorable—two men to baby-sit.

At the thought of her brother, she fished her phone out and tried again. Still, no one answered. Dropping it back into her purse, she sighed. "I guess he's not the only one."

"Nay?"

"Yeah, Julian evidently had a night of it too." She forced a light laugh to hide her concern. *Why* wasn't he answering? Even when he did have women in his room, four calls in an hour would have had him responding. It just wasn't like him. He worried over her too much to ignore her calls.

She glanced out the window and filled the silence with random conversation. "Well, at least it didn't snow. Though it looks like it might at any minute."

"It shall before the day is through."

"I take it you caught the weather report?"

"Nay. I looked at the clouds." He grinned again, the light behind his unusual eyes playful.

Teasing her again. If she let it go to her head, she'd think he was flirting. Oh, who was she kidding? There was no question about it—he absolutely was flirting with her. And damned if she didn't like it. She'd forgotten how nice it could be to bask beneath a man's attentions. Sitting here like this, riding passenger beside Lucan while he navigated the Mercedes down the winding road that led to the dig site, took her back to the innocence of youth. Back before Blake's betrayal. Back when she believed in happily ever after and didn't have to worry about who might steal her work.

Reality settled on her shoulders, shadowing her mood. Lucan came on the Church's behalf. They wanted something. Something of substance. The bejeweled crosses and painted icons of saints weren't enough to warrant assigning three experts to represent their interests. One *maybe*. But even then, what her team had uncovered wasn't anything that couldn't be shipped to the rightful owners.

She regarded him thoughtfully. "Why are you here?"

Lucan's hands tightened on the wheel. For a passing moment he pursed his lips. In the next, he drew in a breath, then gave her a sideways glance. "Today you will unearth Veronica's Veil."

Chloe's brows lifted to her hair. Wide-eyed she blinked. "What?"

"Aye, you heard me. The cloth that mopped the brow of Christ. You shall uncover it today amongst le Goix's sacred charges."

In the back of her throat, a giggle threatened. She tried to stifle it by swallowing, but it burst free with a quick, hearty bark of laughter. "You can't be serious. *If* that legend is true, there's no way a cloth like that would survive centuries underground. The bugs would eat it to pieces."

Lucan turned into the gravel lot, his expression void of his earlier good humor. As he applied the brakes and rolled to a stop, he leveled her with a hard stare. "I assure you, milady, I do not jest." He gestured at the trailers and the excavation beyond. "'Tis the reason why everyone is gathered near the castle ruins."

Chloe looked up. Sure enough, five students, along with her brother and Caradoc, stood near the wall closest to the forest. Three knelt on the ground, laboring with their trowels and small brushes. A fourth held the digital camera poised at an angle that gave him a clear view of the area they'd concentrated on the last week. The last student leaned over the three on the ground, anxiety lighting his face.

Julian looked on, arms folded over his chest, his expression flat. But the slight lift he made to his toes and the way he tipped his head to see through the gathered heads betrayed his interest.

Caradoc remained the only one disinterested in what came out of the earth. His back to the crowd, he watched the trees.

The dark presence slammed into Chloe's awareness with so much force her breath caught. She gripped the door handle, unable to move. In all the time she'd felt the demons, they'd never plagued her during daylight hours.

A weight settled on her thigh, slowly drawing her from the grip of fear. She glanced down to find Lucan's hand on top of her leg. He stared at her as if he expected her to respond. As if he'd asked something she'd missed.

"I'm sorry, what?"

"I said, are you all right?" Laden with concern, his eyes searched her face.

"Yeah," she murmured. "I'm fine." *Just terrified of my own shadow.* To emphasize her lie and divert his attention, she pushed open her door with the retort, "Let's see if they've found this legendary cloth you seem to think exists."

"Know." He stepped outside and looked over the top of the car. "What I *know* exists, Chloe."

The conviction in his voice added to the chill in her veins. She huddled into her coat, unwilling to admit even to herself that a relic like the Veronica would warrant the presence of three of the Church's experts. Without another word, she trudged down the narrow gravel path.

When Lucan joined her, she barely felt the press of his hand against the small of her back.

CHAPTER 5

✝

Lucan caught Caradoc's knowing gaze over the top of Chloe's head. The grim set of his brother's jaw spoke all the words they dared not. *Be alert. Azazel might strike at any moment.*

He returned his attention to the rich soil the students dug in, and the knot in his gut wrenched down tighter. For nearly five hundred years the Veronica lay asleep beneath the earth, free from the hands of those who would bring it harm. Now, one small team of archaeologists who knew nothing about the dark means of Azazel would bring it out of its sheltering grave.

He glanced at the people surrounding him. Eagerness brightened the students' expressions as the young man with the small brush dusted bits of frozen earth off a golden corner. Three inches of the reliquary protruded from the ground, enough to tell anyone who witnessed the exposed edge that they uncovered something priceless. Beneath Lucan's palm, Chloe's back stiffened.

He followed the path of her gaze, lifting an eyebrow when she looked not at the excavation but at the dense forest beyond. Her wide eyes, coupled with the way she chewed on her lower lip, betrayed her unease. Visibly, she shivered. The same ashen color he had witnessed in the car paled her cheeks. Aye, indeed she *did* sense Azazel's dark presence. Could she hear the low murmuring within the thick trees as well? The voices that rose just beneath the shiver of tall branches? The sudden fierce urge to protect her battled with Lucan's natural suspicions. He stiffened against it, unaccustomed to such unexplainable contradictions.

"What do you think it is?" the young man holding the brush asked.

Another student moved in closer and pointed over his shoulder. "Brush off this corner, Tim. I think that's a face sculpted into the overlay. Maybe that'll tell us more."

As Tim diligently bent forward to follow the directive, the freckle-faced man with the camera spoke up. "Wait. Back off a minute. Let me get a picture of that. The last one was just the tip of the corner."

"Oh for Christ's sake, would you just dig out the damn thing? We haven't got all fucking day," a voice snapped from behind everyone.

The sharp bark was enough to draw Chloe's attention away from the forest and back to the happenings in front of her. She frowned at the blond man who bore a striking resemblance to her. "Julian, lay off. Hurrying will only risk damaging the artifact."

Julian's gaze cut to her. The severe set to his jaw was enough to reveal his annoyance. But what flashed behind his blue eyes set Lucan's nerves on edge. Malice glinted there. Not aggravation, not mere impatience with his sister's reprimand, but unadulterated hate. Enmity that vanished behind a flat, unemotional expression that smoothed over his face as he blinked. "Sorry, sis. Just a bit excited, I guess."

Chloe answered with a short nod. The smile she gave her brother, however, held no hint she shared whatever animosity had possessed him. Bright and warm, her eyes sparkled with familial love.

Odd. Lucan well knew discord between siblings. But experience taught him when one could look at the other with such obvious hate, 'twas not a simple one-sided misunderstanding. When emotions ran to such depths, good cause flowed between them. Yet Chloe's smile contradicted the obvious. Could she mayhap be ignorant of hidden resentment?

As alarm bells rang in his mind, visions of his brother's treachery took life. He witnessed again the lifeless forms of his father, mother, and young brother sprawled on the cold stone floor of Seacourt's great hall. They bathed in their own blood.

He closed his eyes to cease the flow of memories and breathed deeply. In that moment, all the taint of suspicion rose from the depths of his soul and centered on Chloe's brother. Every suspect act Lucan had accused Farran of, every ounce of mistrust he had harbored for his brother Tane, amounted to naught as he opened his eyes and stared at Julian Broussard.

"Look! It's an ankh. Chloe, this is up your alley," Tim exclaimed as he rocked back on his heels.

Spurred into motion by the calling of her name, Chloe edged free of Lucan's hand and climbed into the four-foot-deep hole to inspect the reliquary. Her melodic voice drifted to Lucan's ears, stirring an unfamiliar warmth in his veins. He held in a smile.

"Those are Egyptian marks, yes. This is Anubis standing over Osiris. It's a depiction of the first embalming. Here, let me see that trowel."

Though her voice held authority, her tone remained encouraging and kind as she related to her students. It also held a slight note of respect, as if she did not consider herself above those she educated, as so many in her field were apt to do. Lucan's own pride stirred.

As he listened to Chloe, he watched Julian. Impatience marked his tight mouth, crinkled the center of his brow. He shifted his weight and stuffed his hands into his pockets. For a few seconds he rocked back and forth from heels to toes, then he withdrew a cell phone, flipped it open, and passed his thumbs over the keys. A blink of light indicated a quick response from whomever he had messaged. Julian scanned the screen, slid the face over the keys, and jammed the phone back into his coat. "Chloe, can you speed this up? It's going to snow any minute. You can look at the box inside the trailer." Again irritation edged his voice.

Lucan moved to stand at Caradoc's side. Lowering his voice, he instructed, "Mind him carefully."

"Aye, he has behaved most strange all morn. It began when he instructed the students to dig. I gather they waited on Chloe's directive, as the man holding the camera protested they should wait for her arrival."

"How soon did he instruct them to begin?"

Caradoc's hazel eyes reflected the same unease that stirred in Lucan's blood. "Within moments of arriving."

Hardly time enough for anyone to assume Chloe was running behind. 'Twas as if Julian sought to omit Chloe from participating. And from what Gabriel had disclosed about the Broussards, 'twas most unnatural for Julian to take such a measure. Chloe had handpicked the team. Applied for and signed all the licenses. Her brother, per Gabriel, willingly deferred to her, his preference that of support, not leadership.

What then had brought them to odds?

A low hiss from within the trees behind them lifted the hairs on the back of Lucan's neck. He dropped his hand to his waist, reaching for the sword he did not bear. A firm bump against his elbow drew his attention. He looked down to find his forgotten blade in Caradoc's outstretched hand.

"'Tis no time to concern yourself with appearances. If she asks, tell her I retrieved it from the blacksmith's shop for you this morn."

Grateful that Caradoc had thought on the important matters, Lucan buckled the plain silver scabbard around his waist, and the ever-tightening knot of apprehension in his gut unwound by several degrees.

Excitement bubbled through Chloe as the front face of a two-foot-square, gold and silver overlaid trunk broke through the ground. The artistry, typical of the famous Mosan style, defied the imagination. Across the top and the facing side, masterful reliefs depicted religious iconology throughout different cultures, including the Egyptian scene of Osiris she'd first observed on the top right-hand corner. Beside it, dirt packed into the grooves around a stunning figure of Athena framed by two elaborate columns crowned with laurels. To the left of her, an oak tree, complete with intricate leaves, stretched massive roots beyond the goddess's feet. On the lid, the

Virgin Mary knelt in prayer. All four perfectly centered. All four surrounded by tiny jewels and hand-painted beads that had somehow escaped the wear of time.

"This has to be the work of Nicholas of Verdun," she murmured as she carefully etched the dirt away from the left-hand side. "But even his aren't so . . . perfect."

"It's like Michelangelo on a box. Only not," Tim commented from her right.

She chuckled at his summation. Of all the things Tim excelled in, vocabulary wasn't one. Sometimes it was hard to remember his skull housed a genius' brain. He'd go far in the field if this dig yielded anything important. All of them would.

"Hurry *up*, Chloe," Julian grumbled for the third time. "It's starting to snow."

Grinding her teeth together, she tamped down an exasperated retort. What the hell was *with* him anyway? He hadn't even said hello. In fact, the last three days he'd been almost intolerable on site. Pushing the team to dig, dig, dig—no other time had he particularly cared when they finished their work or how much they accomplished. As long as he got to visit new places, sample the wine and the local women, and add his name on a few papers to prove he'd done something useful, he didn't give a damn. One of the reasons she could trust him. The other—behind all his playboy attitudes, Julian revered his field of medieval culture and shared the same love she did for artifacts. He'd never take risks with priceless pieces of history.

Which made his current demands to hurry up that much more of a mystery.

She scraped away another clod of frozen soil and

slipped her fingers into the shallow crater along the trunk's edge. A firm tug loosened the box. She glanced over to Tim. "How's your side coming along?"

"Just . . ." With the tip of the trowel he flicked aside a large chunk. "Got it. Try now."

Chloe fitted her hand into the narrow crevice on the opposite side, and with gentle pressure wiggled the box side to side. Her training rebelled against the forced extraction. Any archaeologist would have her head for trying to pull the box free. She could be dislodging beads on the backside. Pulling loose parts she couldn't see.

But the thick flakes that sprinkled on her shoulders and face warned of a heavy snowfall. She couldn't risk this box to exposure, nor did she dare leave it sitting out for anyone who happened by to notice it sticking out of the ground. While this part of France saw few visitors this time of year, she didn't dare take that kind of risk with such a priceless artifact.

She hoped Lucan and Caradoc would feel the same and not argue with Julian's insistence she hurry. She couldn't deal with testosterone today. Not with the overwhelming presence in the trees. Demons were bad enough. A fight between opinionated men would only delay their efforts further.

Another shimmy, and the trunk pulled free. She toppled to her bottom, the heavy object thumping into her abdomen. She inwardly rolled her eyes. So far, in twenty-four hours, she'd tripped up the stairs, overslept, neglected her makeup, and now a box off-balanced her. To Lucan, she must look like a class-A idiot. Lord, what she'd give to go back to yesterday and start over.

With a sharp frown, she reminded herself she didn't

care what Lucan thought of her and struggled to her feet. By the time she gained her balance, Julian stood in front of her, his hands reaching for the trunk. "Here, I'll carry it inside." His fingers closed over hers.

Perturbed, she jerked away. "What is wrong with you? You know it's got to be cleaned, and *you* gave that task to Andy. Go in the trailer. Find something to do before you drive me crazy and I throw this at your head."

As she emerged from the pit, her gaze locked with Lucan's, and her breath caught. Deep and intense, his eyes filled with silent messages. Everything from praise, to understanding, and above all, desire, flooded into her. She shivered under his intense perusal. Good grief, how could one person say so much without ever opening his mouth? And how in the world could he know she *liked* the way his appreciation lit her up on the inside—for certainly the self-satisfied upturn of the corner of his mouth indicated he was all too aware of how he affected her.

She turned away before she did something else foolish, like step on the shovel four inches from the toe of her boot. "Tim, log the site measurements. Andy, finish up the pictures here, then join me inside. Chris, Jeff, and Kevin, get everything inside before those clouds break." She glanced at her brother, took in his annoyed grimace, and decided not to give him a duty.

Avoiding Lucan's heated stare, she started for the double-wide trailer that housed the large bathing tubs and the rest of their equipment. But as she stepped onto the pebbled path, Caradoc's voice drifted to her ears.

"Stay with her, Lucan. I will stay here and guard the others."

Anger blistered through her at what could only be a

muffled inference to their clear distrust of her and her team. What did they think she'd do—run off with their priceless treasure? Couldn't she just *enjoy* the find a bit before they started hashing out logistics and demanding she turn the relic over to its rightful state of ownership?

The sound of boots crunching behind her made her quicken her step. No way was she going to let these two think she hadn't heard that statement. If they mistrusted her ethics so much, she was done with professional courtesy. Let Julian handle the both of them. His current bad mood needed an outlet, and he'd certainly find the words to put Lucan and Caradoc in their place. Maybe even land a good insult or two. Things her tongue would fail as soon as she looked at the handsome, dark-haired Lucan again.

She nudged the trailer door open with her boot and stalked inside. Julian, however, thwarted the satisfying slam. He entered behind her, catching the door inches from the frame. Gingerly, she deposited the trunk onto one of the chrome-topped tables and switched on an overhead lamp.

"Open it," Julian urged as he bent over the opposite side of the table.

Resisting the urge to take the flat side of her palm to the side of his head, Chloe squinted at her brother. "Did you drink too much last night? Still drunk, maybe? We don't *open* anything until we have everything documented exactly as we found it."

He grumbled. Looking over the gilt top, he urged, "Let me see it, Chloe. Damn, it's the nicest thing we've found. You don't have to be so selfish with it."

She arched an eyebrow but pulled her hands away and splayed them in surrender. A fierce gleam brightened behind his blue eyes as he turned the trunk around to look at the front side. He traced the high relief figures, ran his hands down the smooth silver corners. "Perfect," he murmured beneath his breath.

"It's got to be a Nicholas of Verdun work."

"I know what it is," Julian snapped. As she recoiled, he softened his inconsiderate words with a smile. "Sorry. I had suspicions the minute we turned loose the corner. Feels like I've been waiting days to look at this."

She nodded, but studied the dark circles beneath his eyes, not yet ready to let go of a brimming argument. "You didn't answer your phone this morning. Had you, you might have had this box out of the ground earlier."

He gave her a nonchalant lift of his shoulders. "I left it in the hotel room. Fell asleep chatting with Miranda."

Chatting . . . *right*. She'd bet the golden box that chatting wasn't the extent of a late-night conversation with the girl back home in Tucson who Julian tended to fall back on when his current well ran dry. Their *arrangement* defied Chloe's concept of logic. Why any woman would be content with a sometimes lover, fully knowing she wasn't the only one to slide across his bed, she'd never understand.

"How is Miranda?"

A smirk twisted his mouth, confirming her suspicions. "Good."

Chloe rolled her eyes. "Next time you might try remembering other people use your phone for *work* purposes."

Nodding, he traced the outline of the Virgin Mary's face. "Don't scold. I wasn't the only one with a late night."

"What?"

Julian chuckled as he turned the box to examine the

left side. "You're never late to work. And you roll in with one of *them*. I saw the way he looked at you."

Chloe spluttered as she grasped the meaning of his insinuation. "You've got to be kidding. You think I spent the night with Lucan?"

"So that's his name, huh? Pretty name for a pretty face." He looked over the top of the trunk, his gaze full of meaning. "Be careful. I don't like him."

"You don't even know him." That she was defending the very man she'd just sworn off crossed her mind after she spit the words out. Catching herself, she snapped her mouth shut.

"Just saying. He reminds me of Blake. He's got that look in his eye. Next thing you know, he'll be in here wanting to see the relic. Mark my words, when he leaves with it, your name won't make the Vatican's reports."

Chloe's stomach did a slow upside-down roll. She swallowed down a lump that rose to the back of her throat and cleared her voice. For her sake, more than her brother's, she argued, "He's not that way."

Julian gave the box another quarter turn. "If you say so."

Annoyed with the turn of their discussion, she reached for the trunk. "Give me the artifact. I'll start cleaning it up while Andy's outside."

Resistance met her gentle pull. His mouth once again a tight line of annoyance, Julian scowled at her. "Turn it loose, sis. I want to open it."

The hair on the back of her neck lifted as he repositioned his hands and tugged the trunk closer to him. What in the world had gotten into him? She wrapped her arms around the heavy square of gold and silver and jerked it away. "I'm cleaning it. Sticking to protocol. Andy'll be happy with the camera."

Before Julian could argue, the trailer door banged open and Lucan stepped inside. Triumph gleamed behind the look Julian shot Chloe before he shouldered past Lucan and stormed out the door.

CHAPTER 6

Lucan slowly crossed to Chloe and the reliquary. Her stiff spine and abrupt about-face made it clear he was not welcome. She spun on the taps above a fiberglass bath with barely controlled fury. 'Twas time for this animosity, this unfeeling distance to come to an end. She must begin to understand they were destined for something larger, and she must come to trust him. Courting had its place, and whilst he would not pressure her, he would no longer stand idly by and allow her to keep him at arm's length. Now that she had the Veronica, Azazel would soon arrive. To believe otherwise would be stupid.

He set his hands on her shoulders and leaned in close enough that her shoulder blades brushed against his chest. The urge to wrap his arms around her and snug her into his embrace flooded him. But the tenseness in her torso warned she would not welcome such forwardness. Instead, he lowered his head toward her shoulder, close enough she could not mistake his murmur. "I am no ogre, Chloe. I do not bite."

She let out a derisive snort. "No, you just think I'm going to make off with your prize. Guard the others—you think I didn't hear him? Good God, I was less than three feet away." Frowning, she gestured at his sword. "Is that supposed to intimidate me? Where'd you come up with that anyway?"

Lucan cursed inwardly. Damnation, 'twas no wonder her gaze shot daggers when he entered. He must explain this to her, explain her purpose. But here, in a field trailer where anyone could interrupt the necessary conversation was not the place. Besides, here she had too many places she could run, should she revolt against the preordained.

He pressed his thumbs through her thick coat into her tense muscles and gave her shoulders a squeeze. Her subtle perfume tickled his nose as he inched his mouth closer to her cheek. "I am not here to chaperone your actions or intimidate. Caradoc gave me the blade this morn—I wear it to free my hands. You must trust me in this." Before her smooth skin rendered him senseless and he yielded to the urge to brush his lips across her cheek, he straightened. With gentle pressure, he turned her away from the bath to face the reliquary. "Come. Let me tell you about your find."

Allowing her to hesitate only long enough to turn off the faucets, he dropped his hand to capture her wrist and lead her toward the table. When she stood before him once again, he shucked his coat, then gave hers a tug. She obliged by unzipping it and shrugging it off. The heavy down coat fell into his hands. Lucan tossed both atop the table, then pulled the reliquary beneath the light. Bending over the polished chrome, he pointed to the painted ivory beads that created divine light behind the kneeling figure of Mary. "These were crafted by a name you would well know."

Contradictory to her earlier reserve, she chuckled. "Tim said they could pass for Michelangelo."

"Nay," he answered with a grin. "'Twas not a mortal's hand, but that of the archangel Gabriel."

At the disbelief that passed across her face, he gestured to a rack of metal drawers to her right. "Have you a small knife?"

With a perplexed frown she passed him a utility knife. He placed the tip beneath the edge of one of the ivory beads.

"What are you doing?" Chloe cried. "Stop! You'll destroy it."

Her concern for the relic warmed him in ways he could not explain. It spoke of respect, for the labors of their shared ancestors, for the truths it could reveal. But 'twas unnecessary. He would no more harm it than she would. He gave her a smile. "Shh," he chided as he popped one free from its golden bed. "'Tis meant for disbelievers." He closed the bead in his fist and reached for her hand.

"No," she protested with a fierce shake of her head. "I don't want to be part of this. You've just ruined an intact artifact."

"Chloe." He lifted his gaze, held hers steadily. "'Tis my artifact to ruin, is it not? Give me your hand."

Reluctantly, she opened her fingers. Lucan dropped the bead into her palm, then pressed her fingers closed and held her hand between both of his. "What do you feel?" he whispered.

As he held her gaze, her rich amber eyes filled with tears. He knew not what she experienced—the beads spoke to the hearts of man. Each sentiment that carried through their divine creation differed from one to another. He gave her hand a supportive squeeze, then released her.

When she shook her head, he did not press for answers. He scooped the bead from her trembling fingers and dropped it back into the surface of the reliquary. Gesturing at it, he grinned. "Try to pull it free."

Chloe's brow furrowed as she pried at the bead with her nail. It remained unmoving, anchored into its lavish bed. "How the . . ."

"Divinity."

She drew back and folded her arms over her chest. "That's impossible, Lucan."

"Is it? Did you not just hold the bead in your hand?"

"Yes, but . . ."

Lucan lifted his eyebrows, daring her to complete the sentence. When she did not, he pointed to the images of Anubis, Athena, and the oak tree. "'Tis the union of all faiths as one, the portrayal we all serve the same creator no matter how we worship. Each scene brings power to the reliquary. The magic of the angels completes the divine link. A bead may be removed once each year. To those most in need."

She lowered thick reddish lashes. "I hardly believe I'm most in need."

As a stray tear crept from the corner of her eye, Lucan's chest tightened. He leaned forward and caught the drop on the tip of his index finger. Holding it between them, he whispered, "These speak differently."

Color filled her ivory cheeks. Unwilling to embarrass her further, Lucan wiped the tear on his jeans and straightened. "Come, I will help you clean up the reliquary."

Her stubborn pride returned as she hefted the trunk off the table and carried it to the bath. "I can handle it."

Lucan rolled his eyes skyward and muttered a prayer for patience. He joined her at the fiberglass tub. "I am aware you are perfectly capable on your own. I wish to aid you."

"So you can supervise? Make sure I don't break it?"

His temper sparked, and he narrowed his eyes. "Saint's blood, did we not just cover this? 'Tis naught you can do to harm the reliquary, and I am unconcerned with your intentions." Taking a deep breath to calm his rising ire, he expelled it in one heavy sigh and lowered his voice. "'Tis time with you I desire, Chloe Broussard."

He heard the catch of her breath. Observed the tremor in her hand as she reached for the sprayer. "I'm afraid that's not possible, Lucan."

Pressing in closer to her side, he challenged the invisible boundary she set between them. His hip brushed hers. "Do you find my company so disagreeable?" Lowering his chin, he gave in to the desire to touch his lips to her shoulder. The light feminine scent of roses engulfed him, the effect one of dizzying pleasantness. He could not help but wonder if that heady scent would cling to her skin as it did to her hair. If 'twould gather between the soft valley of her breasts. His throat tightened at the forbidden thought, and his voice hoarsened. "Do your hands shake because you find me so unpleasant?"

A shiver rolled down her spine and into him. "No," she whispered.

"Then why?" Pushing her further, Lucan boldly pressed a lingering chaste kiss to the side of her neck. He near groaned at the warmth of her silken skin, the vibration of her pulse beneath his lips. God's teeth, she was no more immune to him than he to her. Their shared energies arced between them like a live current, inflaming his senses. 'Twas all he could do to resist setting his hands on her hips, turning her into his arms, and sampling the sweet flavor of her mouth. She belonged to him. He possessed that right . . .

Nay. Though she might come to accept him in time, if he pushed her too far now, she would fight him all the more. This joining of their lives must come at her choosing.

"Because." Her voice caught and she swallowed. When she spoke again, the tremor that had lingered in her hands revealed itself in her words. "Because Andy is about to walk through the door."

Christ's toes! Lucan swore beneath his breath as he backed up several paces and cleared his throat. "Aye." He chose a respectful, professional distance and leaned his hip against the washing tub. "Indeed."

The faintest hint of an amused smile scampered across her face. Her gaze swept down his body, and her eyes crinkled in wry humor as she observed the tightness of his jeans, evidence of the blatant effect she had upon him. When she lifted her eyes to his, he quirked an eyebrow, silently challenging her to deny her blood ran equally as warm.

Blushing, she shook her head and turned the light sprayer on the relic.

Lucan captured her hand, forcing her to look at him. "You must not share the secrets of the reliquary with anyone, Chloe."

"Why not? If it's what you claim, the world should know."

He shook his head. "'Tis not time for the world to know."

She opened her mouth to speak, but whatever she intended to say was silenced by the opening of the door. Glancing over his shoulder, she pulled her hand free and turned her focus on the relic. "Hey, Andy. Take off your coat. We're just about to see this thing shine."

"Sure thing, Chloe. Julian told me to tell you to call him when you're ready to open the trunk. He went on back to the hotel for something." He scratched his short dark hair. "He said he left his phone in the room."

Chloe laughed. "Yes, it seems he got a little carried away last night and left it behind. Told me he left it on his nightstand after a long conversation with Miranda."

Lucan tensed. He had witnessed Julian use the phone outside. Yet he had clearly told both his sister and Andy otherwise. Why would he lie about something so benign?

"Ooooh, Miranda." Andy snorted. "You'd think she'd get it through her head that Julian will never settle down." He tossed his coat onto the table alongside the others and approached Lucan with an amicable grin. "Andy Graves, pleased to meet you."

Lucan gripped his hand firmly and shook. "Lucan Seacourt, and the pleasure is mine."

If Julian set off Lucan's instinctual alarms, Andy soothed his unease. The young man's open, friendly expression invited conversation. Enforced the words he spoke. A man with few secrets, and those he might possess were naught to find alarming.

"So the Church sent you and Caradoc?" Andy propped a hip on the countertop and lifted his camera. As he clicked, he spoke. "Must be quite the privilege to have access to all those treasures in the Vatican's catacombs. I s'pect you've seen some fancy things." He shifted his angle, glanced over the top of the lens, then snapped another picture. "What's the story on the Sudarium of Oviedo? I heard someone took it from the cathedral in Spain. Any idea who?"

Lucan knew, but he dared not speak of the truth behind the attack. 'Twas not a matter for the public to know. No amount of faith, of prayer, or any other Christian practice could alter the fates or stop Azazel's intention to ascend to the Divine Throne.

Instead, he chose a half-truth. "Aye, 'twas taken. We work to retrieve it now. I can offer no more."

"That's cool." Andy set the camera in his lap and watched as Chloe gingerly turned the reliquary inside the basin. "Can you say anything about the priest who vanished? Last I saw on the news they had no leads but presumed he'd been killed in the collapse. Haven't caught a word of English news over here since we got here."

"Father Phanuel has not been found." Nor would he, lest a search party ventured into Azazel's realm. The archangel of judgment lived, according to Mikhail, but no order came from the heavens to reclaim him. Until such a time as the Almighty dictated a rescue, Phanuel would remain in Azazel's grasp.

"That's too bad. I hear the people of Oviedo really loved him."

"Aye," Lucan murmured.

"Andy," Chloe broke in quietly. "Maybe we should change the subject. He's a friend of Lucan's, I'm sure."

At her attempt to ease his discomfort, Lucan smiled. "'Tis all right. I knew of him, but many years have passed since I last shared his company." He nodded at the reliquary. "Are you finished with the washing?"

"Yes." She reached in to lift the trunk out.

Before her hands could close around the heavy relic, Lucan nudged her aside, picked it up, and set it on a nearby sifting screen. Water dripped through the wire mesh to pool on the tile floor. He spied a towel on a nearby rack and tossed it on top of the puddle, ignoring the scolding that lingered in Chloe's eyes. Capable of doing for herself she might be, but 'twas time she learned that since she was his seraph, he would not stand idly by when he could lend a hand. He had no qualms with women assuming the freedoms modern laws afforded them, but in his heart, he could not cast aside the ingrained lessons from his youth.

He suspected also that Chloe could benefit from a bit of spoiling.

Stepping back, he gave her the space to conduct her work. Though he had allowed her to presume his background lay in archaeology, the processes she went through now were beyond his comprehension. 'Twas best to stand aside and observe, lest he reveal too much too soon.

Whilst he watched, she and Andy turned the reliquary around and around, snapping photos, jotting down remarks in a notebook, and once or twice, she sketched an image onto the paper. Her idle chatter fascinated him. The knowledge of history she possessed, the bank of names that lingered in her head—'twas like observing a live encyclopedia. Her years before she became immersed in Egypt became clear, and he admired the way she taught in a casual manner, never once asserting superiority over her avid pupil. In return, Andy's questions came more freely.

Another awareness infringed on Lucan's thoughts, however, as the sun dropped from its noontime zenith and the faint gray light that filtered through the falling snow dimmed. The wind picked up, bringing with it the voices from the unholy void. Through the thin windows Lucan caught the hiss of excitement, the murmur of anticipation. And the demons' ominous presence chilled his very blood. Were it not for the fact Caradoc remained outside, a sentry Lucan could trust with his life, he would have expected the glass to shatter at any moment.

Why it did not confounded him. The Veronica sat in plain sight. 'Twas no reason for Azazel to not attempt to take it, for even with their holy swords, Lucan and Caradoc could not defeat the dark master. Lest . . .

He looked to Chloe, recalling how the presence clung to her.

Lest Azazel sought subtlety, unlike his strike on the Sudarium. If he had seduced her, lured her into his evil embrace, he would not draw attention to his designs. Until Chloe was oathed, he could infiltrate her mind with ease.

Grimacing, Lucan tried to dismiss the suspicion from his mind. He had witnessed her fear. Observed the way her expression turned to chalk when the demons stirred in the forest. If she were trapped by Azazel's seductive power, she would not fear his minions.

Still, Lucan could not completely overlook her acceptance of their presence, despite her fears. Mayhap she had been approached. Mayhap she weighed her options. The lord of darkness could be gloriously deceiving. And if he had chosen her as his target, he must also know she carried the seraph's blood.

Nay. He would not allow misgivings to take root. If Chloe had been marked for conquest, it only meant he must secure her vows more quickly. And he must do all he could to protect her in the meantime.

Chloe pushed her chair away from the worktable. "I think that's enough for today, Andy. My eyes are seeing triple. Julian will have to wait until tomorrow to satisfy his curiosity about the contents."

Andy drew back with surprise that mirrored Lucan's. "You aren't going to open it today?"

"No." Chloe rubbed at her eyes. "I didn't sleep well last night. My eyes are sore. I'll take it back to the château with me and lock it in the safe overnight. We'll work on it more tomorrow." She glanced out the window where snow fell in thick flakes. "Besides, the weather doesn't look so good. I think you all ought to head on back before the roads turn to crap."

"Okay. I'll go tell the crew to lock everything up tight. They were trying to cover the dig site when I came in."

Standing, Chloe grabbed her coat. "Go ahead and carry that thing out, would you? Put it in the back of the Mercedes."

Lucan stepped forward, knowing the effect his words would cause and hating what he must do. Yet 'twas necessary. He dared not allow Chloe to take the Veronica on her own. 'Twas too great a risk that harm would come not only to the relic but to her as well. "Andy, place the reliquary in the back of my SUV. 'Twill stay with Caradoc and me."

As expected, Chloe's delicate face hardened into lines of granite. Her gaze clashed with his, speaking oaths she would not dare to voice in front of her student.

To her credit, when Andy looked to her for confirmation, she deferred with a nod. But as the young man carted the relic out the door, her gaze narrowed to a sliver of fury.

Before she could unleash her temper, Lucan caught her wrist and dragged her into his arms. Using her shock to his advantage, he dropped his mouth to hers in a light, lingering kiss. "Dine with me, Chloe," he whispered against her lips. "Forget the Veronica, my obligations to the Church. See me for what I am . . . a man." He drew her lower lip between his, unable to resist a greater taste. God's teeth, her mouth was soft. Sweet like nectar. 'Twould be so easy to forget himself completely and coax her into the deep kiss he craved.

Her lips hesitantly clung to his for a staggering heartbeat that nearly knocked him to his knees.

Tamping down a groan of longing, Lucan released her mouth and sucked in a deep breath. He took a step back and braved the stormy emotions reflected in her rich amber gaze. "I am not your enemy. Say aye?"

CHAPTER 7

⸸

Chloe shook all the way down to her toes. *Say yes.* God above, how she wanted to. How she *ached* to explore the promise of his chaste kiss. Even now, as he stood a foot away and his mouth no longer touched hers, she could feel the moist heat of his breath. Her lips tingled from his gentle assault. And his eyes . . . Her stomach coiled in on itself as those stormy grays held hers, laden with all the suggestion of what dinner with Lucan would involve.

But saying yes meant letting him beyond her defenses. It meant crossing the line between colleague and lover and opening herself to a man she hardly knew. One whom Julian didn't trust. And Julian had sensed Blake's motives long before they became clear to her.

"No," she answered in a strained whisper. Tugging her hands free, she grabbed at her courage. She shook her head and added in a stronger voice, "No, Lucan. You just usurped my authority with my student. Despite your assurances you trust my intentions, you insulted me nonetheless." Pulling on her coat, she took a deep breath and attempted a final blow that would forever terminate any thought of a less than professional involvement. "No dinner tonight, no dinner tomorrow. No dinner ever."

"Chloe—"

She lifted her hand to silence his protest. "I don't want to hear it. You just kissed me without my permission. Consider yourself lucky I'm not planning on turning you in for sexual harassment."

Taking two purposeful steps toward the door, she glanced over her shoulder and met his frown with courage she didn't feel. "Now, you have *my* relic in your vehicle. As long as we are *here,* I'm in charge of its care. You can either transfer it to the Mercedes, or you can take me back to the hotel." She zipped her coat with more effort than necessary, nearly catching her chin. "When we do get there, that golden trunk is going in the safe in *my* room. Because, quite frankly, I don't trust *you.*"

The widening of his eyes told her he hadn't expected that remark. But Lucan refrained from comment and merely gestured at the door, inviting her to exit first. She pushed it open and stepped onto the snow-covered steps. When he exited behind her, she tugged her keys out and locked the double-wide. "So, what's it going to be?"

To her complete surprise, despite her lecture seconds earlier, he grabbed her by the hand and twined his fingers through hers. "Caradoc and I shall drive you."

She scowled at their locked palms. Tugging, she attempted to break free from his possessive hold.

He held fast.

She pulled harder. "I don't *want* to hold your hand, Lucan. Turn me loose."

As his boot crunched into a newly formed mound of

snow, he came to an abrupt halt and swiveled around as if she'd called him out. "If you are not careful, milady, you will force me to prove just how false your words are by kissing you without your permission once more."

Shocked, Chloe gasped. She opened her mouth, but words failed her. What the hell? Surely she hadn't heard him right. He hadn't just announced he'd assault her again.

A strange, completely unacceptable thrill slid through her veins. The first kiss had been so damnably nice. A second . . .

She stopped the thought by clamping her teeth into the inside of her cheek until she tasted blood. Good grief, what was the matter with her? She was starting to resemble the foolish Miranda.

"Do it and I'll—" The threat stopped on the tip of her tongue as Lucan's gaze flared with annoyance.

"You shall what?" He pushed his arm behind his back, forcing her to step closer to him. So close she had to tip her head back to meet his steely stare—no small feat given she stood five foot seven. "I shall tell you what you would do. You would yield, and you would enjoy every moment of it. Shall we test my theory?"

Heavens, his arrogance knew no boundaries. Why then didn't it piss her off? Why did that self-satisfied smirk do strange things to her belly and make her feel like someone had just tipped her upside down, whirled her around by her ankles, then set her on her feet?

Why the hell did she *like* it?

Because she was going crazy. Too many nights with too little sleep and she'd simply forgotten how to function. Either that, or she'd spent one too many nights alone.

"Aye, 'tis as I thought. You do not possess the courage." He turned on the ball of his foot and took a large stride toward the already running SUV.

Her pride flared at the insult. But she held her tongue. What could she say? That she did possess the courage? He'd call her on it and demand she prove her words. Which was exactly what she sought to avoid. No kissing Lucan.

Never again.

He opened the rear passenger's door for her, held it while she crawled inside. Half expecting he would claim the seat beside her, she blinked when he slammed the door shut and climbed into the front beside Caradoc.

"Chloe," Caradoc greeted through the rearview mirror.

She held his gaze and clung to his cordial smile like a life raft. Anything to avoid acknowledging what had just transpired beyond the doors. Besides, his light hazel eyes didn't hold arrogance. Doubtful he even knew the meaning of the word—or he'd left that phase of youth behind. Not to mention, he didn't look at her like he could see through her clothes.

Why oh why couldn't Lucan be like Caradoc—a little less handsome, though striking all the same? She'd have no problem telling Caradoc to go to hell. And if Lucan didn't have such compelling good looks, she suspected she'd find telling him the same quite a bit easier.

As Caradoc nosed the vehicle forward, she caught sight of her car and sense slammed into her. Seeing the promised relief from Lucan's presence clearly, she cried, "Wait! My car. I need my car."

Caradoc applied the brakes, slowing near her Mercedes.

"Nay," Lucan argued. He gestured at the road. "Drive on, Caradoc. We will take Chloe to the site come morn."

At her outraged squeak, he twisted in his seat. "We are having a bit of a disagreement about the safekeeping of the Veronica." The tip of his head, combined with his cocksure grin, dared her to argue. Dared her to spit out the real reason she wanted her car—that she was desperate to escape his presence before attraction got the better of her senses.

Oh, damn him. He could read her like a book and he'd only known her a short day. Not even that. Very well, two could place his game of emotional chicken. "Yes, we are. Lucan wants to closet the trunk away from the public. I, however, am adamantly opposed to the idea. I'm not going to be a *pawn* to the Church and let it dictate what the public does, or doesn't, have a right to know. That's not what archaeology's about."

Lucan's mouth tightened, and the hand on the passenger's seat cushion clenched into a tidy fist. But he failed to give her the argument she wanted. Instead, he acquiesced with a slow nod. "Very well, Chloe, I shall not fight you on your desire to store the reliquary in your safe. You may take it with my blessing." He reclined in his chair, his stare fixed out the front windshield. "Tomorrow it stays with me, and we shall endeavor to learn trust in one another."

Oh for all the vile things . . . He'd tricked her! Now, if she protested, she'd look like the nonsensical reactionary. And confound it all, he'd just admitted he didn't trust her. Grumbling, she crossed her arms over her chest and flopped back against her seat. "Fine," she grit out between clenched teeth.

"And tomorrow you shall dine with me."

"Don't push your luck."

The rest of the short ride to the château passed in silence. When they pulled into the long drive, Chloe bolted outside before the tires had completely stopped moving. It had been a long time since a man pushed her to give in to an argument in front of someone else, and she was more anxious to be free of both men. She jogged around to the back of the vehicle and waited for Caradoc to open the door.

When he did, Lucan appeared at her side. He shook off his coat and wrapped it around the box. Then, lifting it from the cargo bay floor, he placed it in her hands. "On the morrow then."

"I'll be up by five, no later."

"I shall be waiting in the lobby."

"Good night."

He nodded toward the front door. "Good night."

So why wasn't she moving? As that damnable dark eyebrow quirked once more, and his mouth twitched with amusement, Chloe expelled a harsh breath and stalked to the door.

Lucan's shoulders shook with silent laughter as he watched Chloe storm through the château's front entry. He rounded the back of the Templar vehicle to join Caradoc on the driver's side and shook his head. Pride would become her downfall. But today he had learned something far more important about his seraph. She did not trust him. Gaining that trust was a task he looked forward to.

"Dare I ask what that was all about?" Caradoc asked as they mounted the steps.

Lucan laughed more heartily. "Aye. My seraph does not wish to admit her body is in conflict with her mind."

Caradoc groaned aloud. "God's blood, I would not wish a seraph upon any brother. They are naught but trouble."

True enough, Lucan admitted. Though he would take his current circumstances over that of Merrick's or Farran's in a heartbeat. At least Chloe did not provoke noble knights to kidnapping, and he felt quite certain he would not lead her to her death. Trust was easily gained, particularly when the offering was sincere.

They stepped into the lavish front hall, and Caradoc paused at the foot of the stairs. "You do not concern yourself with her safety and that of the Veronica?"

Lucan chuckled again. "Nay. I intend to bunk with Gareth for the night. His room is across the hall from hers."

"Good then, we are heading there. Alaric requested we brief him over the phone. As Gareth will wish to know as well, I have arranged a conference call." Caradoc glanced down at his watch, the only remembrance of Isabelle he allowed himself. "We are to call in ten minutes."

As the hearty aromas from the restaurant wafted up the stairs to his nose, Lucan patted his belly. "I shall ring for service in the room. I cannot go another night without a meal."

At Gareth's door, Caradoc inserted a key, reminding Lucan he ought to do the same and request a copy of his for his brothers. He took note of the task and filed it away for the following morning. Inside, dressed in shorts, Gareth lounged on the couch, his injured leg propped atop the coffee table.

Lucan took a seat beside the phone. "How fares your injury?"

Gareth scowled. "'Tis but a minor annoyance." He rotated his knee to reveal an angry red scar spanning across his calf. "It has begun to itch."

A tinge of envy stirred at the base of Lucan's spine. Would that his injuries healed in such a short frame of time. By the looks of the jagged tear, it had cut to the bone. For those who did not share the strength of the European knights, an injury so severe would take a week to heal. Longer depending on the injured state of one's soul. If he had become so infected with the darkness, it could take a month. Little more than a mortal's rate of healing.

Lucan picked up the phone. "My belly protests its emptiness. I am ringing for food. Do either of you wish something?"

Both men shook their heads, plaguing Lucan with a touch of guilt. But when Gareth explained he had eaten within the hour, and Caradoc mentioned his preference to dine at a table, Lucan dialed the front desk. He indulged in roasted lobster and a steak. Enough food to make up for nearly two days without a decent meal. And though he hated to admit it, since Anne had rearranged the menus in the American temple, he had become accustomed to more refined dishes—unlike many of his brothers who protested the lack of simple stews that had once been standard fare.

When his order was placed, he folded his arms behind his head and sank into the soft cushions whilst Caradoc arranged the call.

"How is your seraph?" Gareth asked.

He answered with the only truth he knew. "She

pleases me." Immensely, but a man did not admit such. At least not if he cared to avoid the brand of *soft*.

A wry grin brightened Gareth's expression. "I noticed 'twas not a crone Gabriel paired you with."

He acknowledged the younger man's observation with a slow nod. No crone at all. Indeed, Chloe defined the very meaning of beautiful. Aye, if he were completely honest with himself, she possessed the kind of face a man would never tire of looking upon. Curves he could entertain himself with for days on end. And her soft mouth would provide hours of pleasure.

Were it not for the presence of demons he could not explain, he would fall upon his knees and swear his loyalty the next time he saw her. Regardless of her questions.

"Sir Caradoc, how good it is to hear from you. I have been awaiting your call. How fares . . . my homeland?"

The sound of Alaric le Goix's voice pulled Lucan from his thoughts. He sat forward to better hear the European commander.

In his typical fashion, Caradoc answered with complete honesty. "You would not wish to see it, Alaric. 'Tis naught but rubble."

A heavy sigh drifted through the line. "Aye, 'tis as I thought. You have found the Veronica and the seraph?"

"Aye," all three men answered in unison.

"And they are safe? Oaths intact?"

Caradoc looked to Lucan for the answer.

Lucan rubbed his hand down his thigh and shook his head. "No oaths have been spoken. The Veronica, however, is safe. The reliquary will be opened on the morrow."

"I wonder, Alaric," Caradoc said in a thoughtful tone,

"if you would seek consult from Raphael and find an explanation as to why Azazel's minions are so close but show no interest in the Veil. He needs it to decode the sacred language that will give him the power to merge the tears with the spear."

"I do not need to consult with Raphael." Alaric coughed, cleared his voice, then continued. "When I was charged with freeing the Veronica from Charles' troops in 1527, I left Rome and came to the temple. As the Veil's fate had spurred such concern, Raphael, Mikhail, and Gabriel added another divinity to the reliquary. The cloth itself is not protected, but as the seraphs' serpents can recognize intent and will not release themselves if those with ill intentions try to pry them free, the trunk will not open for those who are impure."

"Impure in which sense?" Gareth asked. "Our souls are not wholly pure."

"Nay, I do not mean tainted. Azazel's minions cannot access the cloth without aid. Once opened, the spell dissipates. But until then, he must rely on others."

Lucan's pulse jumped. That explained why the demons clung to Chloe. But it did not answer why they followed only her. He leaned closer to the phone. "Would whoever possessed the reliquary be in any greater danger than we had initially assumed?"

"Indeed," Alaric confirmed. "The divinity is not flawless. 'Tis not perfect like the torcs that identify the seraphs. They were created by the Almighty. What guards the reliquary was crafted by angels. It cannot read shades of gray. It knows only true evil. A ward would become a target, a token for Azazel to bend to his vile desires."

The confirmation of Lucan's suspicions shot ice

through his veins. Chloe leapt into his mind, erasing all thought of anything else. The story of Iain's seraph loomed in Lucan's memory. Chloe was in danger. Even now, as she rested in her room, Azazel or his foul creations could enter through her window. He stood up, his meal forgotten.

As if Caradoc read his mind, he held Lucan's gaze and asked, "Are we quite certain Azazel possesses no knowledge of Lucan's true purpose here?"

A hush descended on the room, and Alaric's answer came so quietly Lucan had to strain to hear it. "The knowledge has not been passed beyond those who are trusted. Merrick, myself, Farran, the three of you, and the archangels. Azazel found Iain's mate by following Gabriel, and he has never visited Lucan's intended. If Azazel knows, 'tis through some miracle."

Lucan released the breath he had not realized he held. Still, the deep-rooted need to verify Chloe's safety refused to release the fist around his lungs. With a curt nod, he abandoned the call and exited the room. Across the hall, the murmur of the television drifted through the door. He paused, searching his mind for an excuse. He could not very well confess he came to ensure her safety. Nor could he claim he wished to see her—she would turn him away before he finished the utterance.

However, he could use the reliquary. Claim he wished to tell her more about the craftsmanship. She would entertain a conversation if she believed she had knowledge to gain.

Decided, he rapped on her door.

CHAPTER 8

Chloe answered the door in her bathrobe. Despite the cotton sweatpants that protruded from the hem of the soft white terry and told Lucan she was not undressed beneath, his blood warmed at the sight. 'Twas too intimate a glimpse into her personal life to keep his mind from wandering down the path of when she might wear naught under that alluring wrap. Visions of tugging loose the belt and peeling away that layer of cotton peppered his thoughts.

"Lucan? What are you doing here?" She stood between the door and the frame, barring him from glimpsing her living quarters.

He swallowed to cure the sudden dryness of his throat and fumbled to recall the excuse he had created. "The reliquary. I wanted to discuss it with you."

An exasperated sigh tumbled from soft pink lips. She rolled her eyes and pushed her long auburn hair over her shoulder. "Can't this wait until tomorrow? I'm eating. I'm relaxing, and I'm not about to have people start whispering about what you're doing in my room."

"'Tis important." Perturbed, he gave her door a gentle push. It gave beneath his hand, allowing him to sidestep into her room. Her world engulfed him. Books piled on the coffee table, an array of colorful spines and different sized bindings. The topmost cover portrayed the lighted Egyptian Sphinx against a backdrop of night sky. Magazines scattered beside them, and beside those, her laptop sat quiet and dark.

Her clothes dangled over the backs of the furniture. On the armchair closest to the bed, he recognized the sweater she had worn today. Neat she was not. Yet comfort came with the clutter. 'Twas as if each bit had a purpose for resting where it fell. He could almost make out the path she had taken when she arrived. Sweater landed on the chair. Then boots beside the desk. Turtleneck on the edge of the bed. In the doorway to the bathroom, he found her jeans, one leg inside out. Her hairbrush sat on the stand beside the television, as if she had been brushing her hair when she turned on the set.

As he inhaled the soft perfume of roses, the scent of meat drifted to his awareness. His hunger returned with a vengeance, and his gaze tracked through the room until he located the source of the aroma. A tray sat before the loveseat, piled high with American fries and a sandwich that looked too large for her dainty mouth. One solitary glass of white wine stood beside the plate.

Giving her meal a wide berth, he took a seat on the edge of the armchair and looked to Chloe, who stood at the closed door, arms folded over her chest, chin lifted with a touch of stubbornness.

Lucan gestured at her meal. "Eat. Where is the reliquary?"

"In the safe." She returned to her tray. "Like I told you it would be." Popping a fry into her mouth, she chewed.

He did his best to ignore her food. But as she lifted the sandwich to her mouth, his stomach clamped down like steel, and he deliberately forced his eyes away. Saints' toes, he knew not which was worse—watching her, or watching her eat. He should not have neglected his dinner.

"So what did you want to tell me?" she asked around a mouthful.

The relic. Aye, he had not thought that far. Sifting through bits and pieces of his knowledge, he grasped for something important to tell her. The beads. He would tell her more about the beads. "Each of the beads is carved from ivory. It required a full two years to—" He stopped as she dunked her sandwich into a bowl of broth. His mouth watered. His stomach protested overloud.

Chloe paused, the sandwich a fraction away from her mouth. "You haven't eaten, have you?"

"I shall."

With a roll of her eyes and a soft chuckle, she set the sandwich on her plate, picked up a steak knife, and cut it in two. She beckoned him to the cushion beside her. "Here, I'll share."

"That is not necessary."

"Yes." She nodded. "It is. Because if you keep watching me like a starved wolf, you're going to ruin my dinner with guilt."

Chagrined, he felt heat touch his cheeks. He stood and took a seat at her side. "I apologize, milady. It seems in my hurry to join you in France, I have neglected to eat."

Her distance rolled away with a husky laugh. "How well I know that feeling. Here." She passed him half. "Help yourself to whatever else. Want me to order another glass of wine?"

Lucan could not silence a pleasant moan as he bit into the thick slices of roast beef. In answer to her question, he shook his head and closed his eyes, satisfied by the food alone. Too hungry for words, he lapsed into silence.

Reclining in the corner of her couch, her feet tucked beneath her hip, Chloe smiled at Lucan over the top of her wineglass. He sat across from her, his thigh inches from her toes, an identical glass in hand. What had begun as sandwiches turned into a four-course meal when Caradoc knocked at her door with Lucan's previously ordered meal. They split it too, and somewhere between lobster and steak, she'd requested the full bottle of wine from room service.

As they dined, they shared a comfortable closeness. Her earlier angst evaporated—maybe from the wine, maybe from the laughter. For beneath it all, as Lucan and she talked about the things they enjoyed, his sense of humor broke free. He teased freely, held her eyes a bit too long. As he did now, his glass lifted to his lips while he swallowed the sweet late harvest Riesling.

The intimacy of his quiet gaze didn't escape her. Somewhere during their extended meal, they had crossed a line. *She* had crossed a line. The man who sat beside her now was no longer Lucan her professional rival, but Lucan, the man he'd asked her to see. And what she saw, she liked. Immensely.

He still bore the same appearance that made her think of motorcycles and sneaking out of her parents' house as a teen. But beneath the wild long hair, the darkly chiseled features, and his knowing gray eyes, Lucan possessed a refined nature. He was the kind of man who understood the difference between Riesling and Viognier. Who could appreciate classical music as well as a good dose of rock and roll.

Beneath each fascinating layer, Chloe discovered something constant and unchanging. From the moment he had entered her room she'd felt safe. Even now, with the sun no more than a sliver on the horizon—the time the demons usually swamped her—she barely noticed the things beyond her windows. Though the wind blew, and now and again she caught the subtle hum of malicious energy, Lucan's presence cocooned her with the promise of safety.

"Tell me about Egypt." He nodded at the stack of historical references on her table. "Did you enjoy your time there?"

"Oh," she said on a sigh. "I love Egypt. I love the tombs. The art. Everything about it. Not so much the cities—but then I don't tend to spend a lot of time in them. Out there in the shifting sands, it's heaven. You never know when the next storm might reveal some piece of lost history."

"I was there many years ago. I remember quite well the heat and sand."

"Oh? What were you working on?"

Lucan shook his head. "'Twas a military contingent. A brief assignment to lead those who had gotten themselves into quite a predicament back home."

With all the stories of tourists captured and foreigners disappearing, his story didn't surprise her. It did, however, explain the uncanny feeling that he'd protect her.

That military training had a way of seeping into every day life.

"Were you in the service long?"

He set his empty glass aside and folded his arms behind his head. "Aye. Until this assignment, 'tis all I have known." Sitting forward, he flipped open the book on ancient tombs and thumbed to the first page of the Bahariya Oasis. "I remember this place. To avoid the enemy we were forced to hide in tombs. The art was amazing. We had to descend through the bottom of abandoned homes. 'Twas near impossible to cover our comings and reseal the floors."

Chloe's feet thumped to the floor as excitement tripped down her spine. He'd been to Bahariya. In the tombs. Possibly those she'd walked in—her work had included the demolition of several abandoned homes. "Do you understand hieroglyphics?"

"Aye. A bit of them. Though I am certain your knowledge exceeds mine."

She chewed on her lower lip, debating. If she showed him the image she'd copied, would he ask questions she couldn't answer? Or would he assume it was simple curiosity? She shrugged off the worry, too anxious to find someone who might have seen the sigil that had doomed her. Standing, she went to her desk and withdrew a time-crinkled notebook. She flipped it open to the photograph she'd pasted inside and set it on the table beneath his nose. She tapped the curious picture of the jackal-like Wepwawet. "Have you seen this before?"

A shiver rolled through her as she looked once again at the glyph she knew by heart. The grayish head identified him clearly as the Egyptian deity who led the dead through the underworld. But where typical depictions of Wepwawet showed him holding an ankh in one hand and a spear in another, in this one, he clutched a sword and a strange winged head. On discovering the glyph deep within a shaman's tomb, she'd first thought it to be a false reproduction—the sword had yet to become the weapon known today during the era the tomb was crafted. Yet her team had the paint sampled, proving it predated Alexander's conquest by several centuries.

Lucan visibly stiffened. He shook his head slowly and murmured a quiet, "Nay." But when he lifted his gaze to hers, his eyes flickered with words he didn't say. He *had* seen it, damn it.

"What does it mean?" she pressed.

"Where did you find it?"

She shook her head and perched on the edge of the couch. If he didn't trust her enough to reveal the meaning, she wouldn't tell him why she wanted to know. Not to mention, if she spouted off about demons following her and curses, he'd probably laugh—as both Julian and Blake had. "I didn't find it. I was told I would encounter something meant for my eyes alone in the unfinished antechamber. That glyph was the only sigil present." And she'd known nothing but fear since that fateful afternoon.

Lucan's gaze bored into her. "Who told you of it?"

She shrugged, ignoring the way the intense light behind his stare sent another shiver rolling to her toes. "Just a guy." Under no circumstances would she tell him—or any other human being for that matter—that she'd heard the voice plain as day in the tunnel, the same voice of the native man in the oasis, but it had come out of nowhere. She'd turned around, expecting to see his weathered face, only to find darkness, her

team farther back, quietly at work documenting fu-
nerary items. She'd been alone in that tunnel when
some*thing* had spoken to her. The same something had
attached to her and refused to let go.

Chloe collected the notebook and returned it to her
desk. As she passed the small window, the all-too-
familiar *tap-tap* clanged in her head. She cast a nervous glance to Lucan, but he turned the pages in her
book, unaware they had unwelcome guests.

He looked up as she neared the loveseat. "Chloe, this
afternoon . . ." His gaze searched her face, uncertain.

Chuckling, she waved a dismissive hand. "Don't
worry about it. Julian and I argue in public too. I evidently have a way of provoking people."

"Nay. I am not speaking of that. The reliquary—I
meant it when I said you should mention naught of its
divinity. If it fell into the wrong hands, or the wrong
people should learn you possess it, your life could be in
great danger."

She almost laughed. If he only knew the greater
threat that haunted her. Men, guns, kidnappings, and
death threats didn't hold a candle to true evil. Instead,
she merely shrugged her shoulders. "I'm willing to risk
my safety if it reveals the secrets of our past."

He reached between them and caught her hand. Sincerity softened the insistent lines of his expression.
"You possess the Veronica, a sacred relic that belongs
to the Church. I cannot allow you to harm yourself, or
the cloth. I must return it."

When she pulled on her arm, annoyance driving her
to distance herself from the warmth of his fingers, he
refused to let go. She stared at the soundless television,
determined to ignore his argument. As an archaeologist

he should understand the need to educate the public. The purpose was the very foundation of their profession.

"Chloe."

His quiet voice urged her eyes back to his.

"I will make you a promise. When I return it, I will do everything in my power to establish a sacred resting place for such an important item. A place where it can be viewed, its story can be told, and 'tis safe from thieves and those who would wish to use it for corruption."

For one endless moment, Chloe couldn't breathe. Compromise, she hadn't anticipated. But what he offered was exactly what she desired—*if* the relic proved to be what he claimed. She didn't know how to respond to such a generous offer. Didn't know how to look away from his mesmerizing gray eyes that revealed such honesty she could feel his words in her soul. He meant it. He really meant it.

So had Blake, at one time.

She shook off the spell and frowned. "What if it isn't the Veronica? What if it's just another cloth, or what if nothing's inside at all?"

A smile lifted the corners of his mouth. "'Tis not, but should it be, you may do what you will with both the reliquary and the contents. We could open it tonight and solve those questions."

"Don't be silly. There are *processes*. Protocols I established with my team to ensure every relic was treated the same way." Her frown deepened as she remembered her students and her brother. "This isn't just about me and you. Julian wants to witness the opening. Andy's excited about it also. I have a whole team that came here in the middle of winter, hoping to find something of significance. Now we have. I won't cut them out. And

I won't jeopardize the integrity of my hard work among my professional peers either."

"I shall respect that." His thumb stroked over the back of her palm, stirring to life all the awareness she so desperately wanted to ignore. Tingles raced up to her shoulder. Her pulse stuttered. In the core of her soul, something wholly unfamiliar awakened to that gentle back-and-forth motion.

"Will you trust I shall reveal the cloth when the time is appropriate?" His eyes said something else, a plea she didn't dare consider: *Will you trust me?*

She glanced down at their joined hands, the warmth of his palm as enticing as water after a hot day amid the Egyptian sands. Strong fingers. A grip meant to soothe, yet prominent evidence of the power in his hands. Altogether masculine. Wholly appealing.

Against her will, her fingers tightened around his. She nearly sighed at the delight of holding on to him. They sat in her room, avoiding the subject of their earlier kiss. It had been so long . . . Did she dare take a leap of faith and believe in what he offered? His words *and* the physical pleasure?

No, she couldn't. Not when they disagreed over an important artifact. As long as they stood at opposing corners, too much room existed for him to work toward his own purpose and hide his intentions. Trust couldn't be established on such rocky terms. And though he had sworn he'd expose the relic if it proved legitimate, he'd mentioned nothing about giving her team credit for the find.

"I think you'd better leave, Lucan," she whispered.

"Aye," he answered, equally as quiet.

He rose, bringing her to her feet alongside him. She

followed to the door, indulging in the simple pleasure of holding his hand a few minutes longer. But when he should have disentangled his fingers and reached for the handle, he turned sideways and lifted her chin with his opposite index finger. He shook loose her fingers, used that hand to sweep her hair away from her shoulder. Then with it, he captured the side of her face and brushed her cheek with that tantalizing sweep of his thumb.

She knew he was going to kiss her. Knew she ought to step back and stop him before he could dip his head. But though logic screamed at her to move, she stood stock still, barely breathing.

As light as a feather, his lips brushed over hers. His breath stirred the fine hairs on her face. Goose bumps broke over her skin, and Chloe pulled in a short breath to keep from stumbling against his chest. With an inward whimper, she parted her lips and invited him into the kiss.

Lucan's mouth settled over hers softly. His lips played a game of capture and release, each press longer than the one before, until he slid his hands into her hair and accepted she had no intentions of breaking free. Warm and enticing, the tip of his tongue slid along the seam of her lips and, caught up in the rush of heady bliss, Chloe touched hers to it. The rich flavor of the wine they'd shared lingered on his mouth. She drank it in as deeply as she had from her glass.

Pleasure ignited like fire, warming her from the inside out. She leaned into his body, twined her arms around his neck, and rose to her toes as he deepened their kiss. The velvety stroke of his tongue against hers took her to a place she had forgotten. An oasis where no harm came from pleasure and desire knew no punishment. She indulged, abandoning her fears in favor of the safety Lucan's nearness offered.

When his kiss took on more demand, she gave freely. Met the seeking thrust of his tongue with equal greed. Satisfaction rumbled in the back of his throat, eliciting her into a soft moan. God, it had been so long since she'd been kissed like this. Maybe she hadn't ever been . . . Not so thoroughly. Not so incredibly. No, she'd never before felt like if the kiss ended, something inside her would crack into pieces.

She pressed in closer, and his hand slid down her back. His arms encircled her. The hardness of his breath mirrored her own. Warmth flowed between them where their bodies connected, drawing her deeper into the magic of the moment. Her womb tightened, and moisture gathered between her legs, stark evidence of how she'd starved her body.

Lucan's fingers pressed against the small of her back, urging her hips into his. She took a wobbly step forward, aligning their bodies from shoulders to toes. But when her belly flattened against the hard length of his arousal, Lucan sucked in a sharp breath and abruptly terminated the kiss.

He took a step back. Slowly, he released her from the protective circle of his arms. With one hand, he turned the door handle. His mouth danced once more across hers, chaste and soft. "Good night, Chloe."

"Good night," she whispered as he stepped into the hall.

CHAPTER 9

L ucan let himself inside Gareth's room and made his way through the dark to the empty sofa. He said a quiet prayer on finding Gareth sprawled across the bed, snoring quietly. Conversation was the last thing he wished to encounter after what had transpired on the threshold of Chloe's room.

Damnation, he had not intended one kiss to go so far. If it had not been for the fierce surge of white heat that shot stars through his mind when her body nestled against his swollen shaft, he would have taken her there on the floor. He was not opposed to such a notion— floor, bed, wall, couch, where mattered little. 'Twas the timing that concerned him. The hesitancy in her amber eyes before she yielded to the kiss. If she were not fully ready for something so simple, she would not embrace their inevitable joining. Her body would, aye. But she would regret waking from the haze of desire.

When he took her, and aye, he would, 'twould be to both her heart and her body that he brought pleasure.

He pulled off his boots and stretched out on the cushions. 'Twas also the matter of the glyph he must negotiate before he could consider a deeper involvement with Chloe. Oaths and vows aside, what she showed him tonight concerned him far more than the demons that collected in her shadow. The two paired hand in hand, but Chloe carried the mark of Azazel.

Someone in Egypt branded her for the dark lord.

Centuries had passed since he last witnessed the mark of Saladin's most faithful. So much time he thought to never look upon the glyph again. Yet tonight, he discovered it in his seraph.

Her hesitancy to accept a fair agreement regarding the Veronica added to the burden of his mind. Her resistance, combined with the demons and Alaric's words, only increased his suspicions that Azazel had already approached Chloe. Lucan could find no other reason for the mounting list of oddities about his intended mate.

Her on-and-off demeanor. Her fierce arguments that he did not trust her. Her insistence to guard the Veronica on her own, her refusal to open the reliquary with anyone else present—all acts that united her with the unholy one.

Add into the mix that unlike the previous pairings of Templar and seraphs, he could find no real obstacle to overcome, and as much as he wished to deny it, he could not turn away from the very likely possibility Chloe had been seduced by evil and worked to find a means of turning over the Veil. His presence, along with Caradoc's and Gareth's, made what she had been tasked with difficult. For if she chose to surrender the relic whilst they were present, she would fail.

She would not perish, but she would fail, and restoring her from Azazel's clutches might well erase what remained of her mind.

God's teeth—could he be part of a greater nightmare?

Tossing an elbow over his eyes, he groaned. Nay, he was missing something. He must be. If Chloe's soul housed darkness, his would recognize it. As his spirit balked each time he confronted Azazel's minions and stirred each time he crossed their vile path, he would feel darkness within her when he stood at her side.

Though his body had most assuredly awakened, tonight the darkness slumbered.

Lucan squeezed his temple between thumb and middle finger to drown out the noise. For the first time in a great many years, he questioned his ability to succeed in the Almighty's design. If he could not sift through fact and fiction and separate suspicion from what he recognized as truth, he could not hope to gain her oath. He would fail, and the prophecy would shatter.

One undeniable fact stood apart from the rest—he could not approach her about her Nephilim blood until he knew the meaning of the glyph. If he confided her status as a seraph, and she did indeed serve Azazel, the dark lord would have his new Lilith in a heartbeat. Azazel would steal Chloe away, use her body for his pleasure and her healing spirit for his destruction. All the light she carried would assume his taint, and in so doing, grant her phenomenal power. She would become Azazel's ally. His lover. His *mate*.

Christ, but Lucan did not know which way to proceed. If she were pure, presenting her with the seraphs' torc protected her.

Lucan flopped onto his side in search of comfort he

would not find. Wide awake, he stared out the window, listening for trouble through the walls.

He would have to wait. Bide his time and observe her carefully. She could not hide a dark purpose if he became her constant companion. Azazel could not reach her either. In protecting her, Lucan would die, but she would come to understand the danger she faced. The temple could offer her protection after his demise. Mayhap even find her another eventual mate.

A steady *thump-thump* drew Chloe from pleasant dreams. She opened her eyes, half expecting to find Lucan beside her in the bed, then blushed as her gaze fell on the empty pillow. No warm body at her side. Just in her imagination.

But man, oh man, he was every bit as incredible in her dreams as he'd been in her doorway. Giving in to a goofy smile, she sank deep into the pillows and pretended not to notice the *scritch-scratching* on her window pane. She never should have allowed him to kiss her. She'd known it would mess with her head. Now she ached in all the places that she'd convinced herself didn't exist. Restlessness infused her blood. Her breasts felt heavy, her skin too tight.

She tossed and turned and finally let out a frustrated sigh. "Damn," she muttered.

Another heavy thump brought her upright in bed. Cocking her head, she eyed the door. She leaned over and switched on the light. As light filled her room, the dark presence registered in the forefront of her mind. From beyond the window it bore down on her like iron weights, so thick and suffocating she couldn't bring herself to look for fear she'd see the beast through the drawn draperies. The hairs along her arms lifted. Her chest constricted, making normal breath impossible.

"Is someone there?" she called out.

"It's me, open the damn door, I've been knocking for twenty minutes. People are starting to peek in the hall," Julian answered with a touch of exasperation.

Twenty minutes? Good grief, she must have been out like a rock. Relief, however, accompanied the sound of her brother's voice, and she tossed the covers back to shuffle to the door. The chain lock rattled in the quiet, followed by the click of the heavy dead bolt. Chloe yawned as she opened the door.

Julian marched past her, looking like he'd shared the same restless slumber. His short blond hair stuck out at odd angles. Though fully dressed, his shirt was unbuttoned halfway down his chest and his belt buckle jangled at his waist. She dropped her gaze to his feet, observing he hadn't tied the laces on his boots either. "Julian, is something wrong?"

He pushed long fingers through his hair and shook his head. A frown marred the high line of his brow, a sure signal something was eating at him. But the way his eyes darted around the room, as if he feared someone waited for him in the shadows, aroused Chloe's concern. Something was most definitely wrong with her brother. Had he fought with Miranda? Gone home with the wrong girl and run into her boyfriend? Husband maybe?

"What is it, Julian?"

"I can't sleep. I keep thinking about that trunk. Keep seeing it in my head."

The trunk? For the love of Mary, he'd woken her up in the middle of the night about the *relic*? Chloe gritted her teeth and called on her patience. "Can't this wait until morning?"

"No!" He shook his head violently. "Let's open it, Chloe. Now. We can surprise the team tomorrow. Hell, we can even pretend we know nothing when we get there. But let's open it. I'll go crazy if I don't find out what's inside."

Dumbfounded, Chloe squinted at her brother. "You've been drinking."

"No, I swear I'm sober." He held up both hands in defense. Jumped on one foot. "See. Look. No wobbling." In a burst of unexpected energy, he rushed to her and caught her hands between them. "Let's open it, sis. What if it's filled with gold?"

One long, slow blink didn't change the situation as she'd hoped. Julian didn't disappear, and she didn't wake up to find this weird tirade of his had been a dream. She shook her hands free. "Go back to bed, Julian. For that matter maybe you ought to go find a stiff drink and unwind."

"Let me see it, sis?" he pleaded quietly. "Just once more. I can't stop thinking about it."

For a moment, she entertained the idea of pulling the relic out of her safe just for the sake of appeasing him so he'd go away. But as the notion surfaced, she dismissed it just as quickly. If she showed him the relic, in his current zealousness, she'd have to spend another hour disarming his ideas of opening the trunk. She went to the door instead. Holding it open, she pointed into the hall. "Out. Go back to bed, Julian. We'll talk about the relic in the morning."

"But—"

"Out," she insisted a bit louder. "I'm not doing this tonight. I'm tired, and I want to go back to sleep."

She braced for his scowl. Anticipated a rush of angry words. Julian's temper could put hers to shame when something really upset him. If she were lucky, he'd vent and blow, and then tomorrow they could talk about this rationally. If she weren't lucky, his attitude would cling to him throughout the next day, and God only knew how many others.

Instead, he merely stared at her, his expression flat, void of all emotion. His eyes locked with hers, but those blues that were usually so full of warm light darkened to a dull lifeless shade of near black. He looked beyond her, as if he saw something on the distant wall.

Vacant.

"Julian?"

As if someone snapped fingers in front of his face, his eyes focused on her. "Yeah?"

"Are you okay?"

"Fine." He forked his fingers through his hair again and gave her a half smile. "Tired. Tomorrow?"

"Yeah, tomorrow." She tipped her head toward the open door. "Get out of here. I need my beauty rest."

With a curt nod, opposed to the grin she expected, he strode into the hall. Chloe eased the door shut, locked it, then leaned her weight into it. Evidently they were both losing their grip on reality. Julian couldn't sleep over a fabulous relic, and she'd crossed boundaries with Lucan. The next thing she'd know, Andy would start hitting on women.

The light dimmed as a low wind whistled around her windows. Outside, the scratching raked across the glass like nails on a chalkboard. Chloe stiffened. When would it stop? What did it take to have one decent night's sleep? Drawing in a deep breath, she pushed away from the door and turned around.

As she looked to the curtained window, the glass shook with an earthquake's force. Chloe dove for a small red satchel on the opposite side of the bed. The curtains shimmied, whipped against her hand.

"Damn you, go back to the hell you spawned from," she muttered as her fingers curled around the crushed velvet. Sitting up, she jerked the drawstrings open and stuffed her hand inside. She grabbed a stick of sage incense, a stick of vanilla, and a small butane lighter. Lighting them both, she swallowed hard and swung her legs off the side of the bed nearest the window.

The racket grew ominous. A spine-tingling *crack* issued from the glass. Chloe steeled herself against the overwhelming malice that enveloped her. She took a step closer, drew in a deep breath. As she exhaled, she recited the words she'd used on only one previous occasion.

"In the name of the Almighty, I banish you from this place. Go now, you cannot bring me harm." Sweeping her hand before her body, she waved the purifying smoke toward the glass. "Mighty Gabriel, hear these words, protect me with your sacred might."

Beyond, something let out a low, hollow moan.

The curtains stilled. An eerie calm descended on the room. Her hands shook as she set the incense across the mouth of a wineglass and collapsed onto her bed. Huddled into a ball, she pulled a bracelet of blue beads from the pouch and slipped it around her wrist.

Then, she allowed her tears to fall.

CHAPTER 10

Darkness surrounded Julian. Closeted away in his bottom-floor room, he sat in the chair near the window and grasped at the last bits of sanity he possessed. Tonight he had nearly attacked his sister. Would have, if she hadn't spoken his name and pulled him out of the depths of the abyss that engulfed his mind. For what, he couldn't recall. Or perhaps he had never known in the first place.

It knew. This beast that fed off his soul knew precisely why it had gone to Chloe's room in the middle of the night.

He, however, only recalled the struggle for power, the sheer effort required to keep *it* at bay. Most days he failed. When he felt his strength weaken and the beast began to dominate, he retreated far from Chloe. Something about her enraged the demon. No . . . Enraged wasn't right. It only ever felt rage when she thwarted its plans. His sister *aroused* the demon. As if it recognized something about her and yearned to draw her into its arms.

His arms.

Fuck, he didn't know anymore. His arms, its arms— good God, what would it be like to embrace his *sister* as a woman?

His stomach roiled at the thought. But deep inside, something else stirred to life. It pulled at his mind, urging him to surrender. To accept his fate and his certain death. He pushed back on the presence, desperate to maintain some small fragment of what he once had been.

Movement helped. As did light. He stood up and flicked on the lamp. On his way back to his chair, he passed the wide dresser mirror and paused to study his reflection. Outwardly, he looked the same. Then again, that shouldn't surprise him. He had witnessed the crafting of this illusion. Hell, he'd given them the prototype.

He turned and looked over his bare shoulder at the two long scars that ran between his shoulder blades and across his ribs. Even this form bore the scars they had put upon his body. Strange, he could no longer recall the pain. He remembered the face. The voice. But how it felt to have claws dig between his ribs, he couldn't recall.

More evidence he was rapidly losing his tenacious hold on his soul.

A smile crossed his face as the beast latched on to his thoughts. His weakness pleased the demon. With it came power. The complete ability to move as it desired and follow the dark laws that governed its existence.

Julian struggled to smear the smile away. When his efforts only produced a slight downturn at the corners of his mouth, turning his expression into a grotesque sneer, he turned from the mirror and retreated to his chair.

It wanted the relic. Yes, that's right—he was supposed to convince his sister to give him the relic. That was the reason he'd been implanted alongside the demon. But Chloe and her protocols refused to budge. If she didn't cave soon, he'd have no control over what might happen.

And if she spent more time with that man whom the demon despised, Julian couldn't guarantee how much longer he could hold on. Each time the dark-haired representative of the Church drew near her, the demon threatened to break free.

His name is Lucan of Seacourt.

Julian ground his teeth together as the hollow voice mingled with his unconscious. It knew things he couldn't comprehend. Things that, when it spoke of them, he found himself unable to resist the call of darkness. And now, as the demon conjured an image of Lucan, Julian's hands began to tingle with the need to kill.

He glanced down at his fingers to witness the dark claws emerge. He let them break through—controlling the demon when it desired its natural form defied his meek ability. Besides, the battle tonight had taken its toll. He'd lost more energy by leaving Chloe and the relic than he had these last several weeks. And he couldn't deny that at times the thought of giving up completely offered comfort. If he didn't have to worry about Chloe, he would. But his love for her and all the years he'd protected her forced him to hang on.

Somehow he must make her turn over that trunk.

Declan.

The name whispered into his awareness. Yes, Declan and the Kerzu. He'd been advised to contact the man if Chloe gave him too much trouble. Maybe he would have an idea how to convince her.

He reached across to the table and picked up his phone. The number flashed on his outgoing calls list, but he couldn't recall ever speaking to the man before. He'd talked to Miranda. That night, he'd never forget. Five years he'd known her. Slept with her. Done everything a man and woman could, except give her his heart, though she had given hers freely. When she'd done what she should have years ago and finally told him to get lost, he'd wanted to weep. The demon, however, rejoiced.

Julian pressed the connect key.

"Aye?" a thick Scottish brogue answered on the first ring. "I dinna expect to hear from you so soon."

"I don't know what to do," Julian confessed.

"Does she ken what you want?"

"I think so. Should I tell her why?"

"Nay!" Declan softened his voice. "My brothers are with her?"

"Always."

"Then nay, you mustna confide our purpose. If she has listened to their words, she wilna believe naught of yours. She will think you deceive. Take heart, believe in Leofric's purpose of restoring the Templar code."

Julian let out a sigh and asked in a quieter voice, "How do I deceive my *sister*?"

"'Tisna easy, I ken." Declan's voice assumed genuine sympathy. "It becomes easier. When the day of judgment arrives, you will be proud of the things you have done. In this, you will find strength."

Silence passed across the line. Through the receiver, Julian recognized the closing of a heavy door.

"A question for you."

"Yeah?"

"Does the lass show a particular affinity for either of my brothers?"

Affinity? Shit, he could hardly remember his own name let alone what Chloe did all day. "I don't know. Why?"

"'Tis curiosity. Inform me if you learn of such."

"All right. But why?"

"'Twould mean she carries the blood of angels. A blessing to be certain. But if she is to pair with a knight, their joining must be pure. They canna be allowed to sin before oaths are taken."

Julian squeezed his eyes shut tight and attempted to make sense of Declan's words. The demon, however, surged to the surface making it impossible to decipher the Scot's meaning. Julian grimaced with the effort of chaining the beast back. A physical pain burst inside his head, and he dropped the phone. Clutching at his temples, he doubled over, gasping for air.

"Not now," he ground out through clenched teeth. "Let. Me. Go."

Slowly, the unholy presence retreated, allowing Julian the ability to reach for the phone. When he brought it to his ear, the line filled with silence. "Declan?"

A rapid beeping signaled the Scot had disconnected.

In a fit of satisfying temper, Julian chucked the phone across the room. It thumped into the wall, then clattered across the wood floor. He stood, went to the window, and pulled the drapes open wide. Outside, snowflakes drifted across a darkened landscape. The trees beyond caught the faint reflection of the château's exterior lights, illuminating leafless branches into eerie skeletons.

He searched the barren trunks for signs of the

creatures that shared his purpose. When he spied a pair of yellow-green eyes, unexplainable peace enveloped him. He knew their presence ought to disgust him. But he couldn't find the revulsion he'd first known. Those creatures, though they followed a different set of orders, comforted him with the knowledge he wasn't alone in this misbegotten quest.

Moreover, they marked Chloe. Where she went, they followed. As long as he could locate them, he'd always be able to find his sister. As for the knights—all Julian needed to do was prey upon her fears. Her mistrust of men ran so deep that too seemed easy. A few insinuations. A handful of suggestions about the men's characters, and Chloe would run from all of them.

If it meant keeping her safe, he'd see to that.

He didn't give a damn about oaths or sin or any number of the bits and pieces of information that flitted through his thoughts. But he'd fight to the end to keep Chloe out of this hellish game of unholy chess. He would die their pawn. Before he did, however, he'd ensure his sister knew the freedom of a queen.

CHAPTER II

✝

Chloe woke at dawn, not that she had slept well after the demons threatened entry. With a dull winter sun as her protection, she went to the window and pulled the drapes open to inspect the glass. Frowning, she traced a short nail down a jagged crack that ran from the left top corner to two-thirds of the way to the center. She drew away with a whispered oath and pulled the blinds closed.

Once before they'd attacked with such force, but even then, they hadn't done true harm. They'd made enough noise to scare her out of her skin and send her on the search for a demonologist to teach her how to ward them off, but they hadn't broken glass. Now what? Reverend Tobias hadn't told her what to do if they got through—they'd certainly made it possible to do so. One firm press on the pane, and that glass would break out.

She picked up the phone and punched in the concierge's extension. When he answered, she forced a smile on her face to hide the quivering under her skin.

"*Bonjour,* Monsieur Léglise, this is Chloe Broussard, room twenty-four."

"*Bonjour,* Mademoiselle Broussard, how may I serve you?"

"Something broke my window last night. Would you be able to put in for repairs?"

"*Quoi?*" He coughed. "*Pardon,* I mean—my apologies, mademoiselle. I was aware of no disturbances through the night. *Oui,* I shall put in the request, but it may be a day or two before a replacement can be finished. Do you require another room?"

"No, no, the glass is still intact." She shook her head and squashed the long line of burned ashes in the basin of the wineglass with the end of the incense stick. "A good storm would ruin it though. I can wait a day or two."

"Are you certain?"

"Yes. I really don't want to move my things. A day or two will be fine." She hoped. If her ward held, a day or two wouldn't make a difference. But much longer, and they'd return. As they always did.

"Very well. I will put in the request. Will it inconvenience you if we enter to take measurements?"

"No, that's fine. I'll be working most of today."

His voice brightened. "*Merci,* mademoiselle. Again, my deepest regrets. I will have your window restored soon."

"*Merci,*" she murmured before she dropped the phone back into its cradle.

She'd have to make sure to take the time today and find a spiritualist in Verdun who could aid her. Someone who really understood magic and could do something permanent. Problem was, she suspected she wasn't dealing with the same demon. If she were, it couldn't return again and again, and the magical incantation would hold longer.

She pulled open the desk drawer, withdrew the phone book, and stuffed it inside her leather bag. No one would be open this early. She'd look closer to lunchtime. Meanwhile, she'd shower. The hot water would soothe her nerves and hopefully take the stiffness out of her neck.

Trudging into the bathroom, she flipped on the light and started the water. While it heated, she gathered her robe and brushed her teeth. Then she stepped beneath the spray, sighing as she leaned against the tiled wall. She couldn't tolerate much more of this. Eight years was long enough—an eternity of running from demons would cut her lifespan in half.

But eight years had also told her there wasn't much she could do. Except, perhaps, find the man who'd somehow cursed her. And she'd tried that too. She'd visited every religious leader she could find, from voodoo priestesses to demonologists to Catholic priests. Every one of them swore *she* wasn't cursed, wasn't possessed, or whatever they personally called it. They offered temporary aid. Helped when it became too much. Gave her the bracelet to keep the beasts off her physical body, and wished her well.

This was her lot. For whatever reason, she'd been doomed to a life of fear.

Gathering her resolve, she stood up and lathered her hair. Maybe she wasn't doomed. Lucan knew about the glyph. Nothing in the world would convince her he hadn't recognized it. And for some absurd reason, when he was near, she didn't feel like at any minute something might leap out of the dark and attack her. This was indeed progress. Maybe he had the answers.

Maybe he was her salvation.

She cringed at the thought. One kiss, and here she was fantasizing about happily-ever-afters. Even if they could get past their professional and ethical differences, even if she could learn to trust him, one night of demons, and he'd take off like a rocket.

Besides, now wasn't the time to indulge in personal pursuits. The relic put her on the edge of incredible professional success. If she'd found Veronica's Veil, the next several years would demand a significant amount of her time—public appearances, papers and presentations, meetings with museum curators and a whole list of student applicants, additional job offers, and collegiate lectures.

She couldn't allow Lucan to distract her. Maybe when they finished in Ornes they could explore this attraction, but not until she had closed up the site and resolved the matter of what to do with the relic. Until then, she'd shield herself behind Julian. His dislike for Lucan would make it easy to keep her distance.

When Chloe didn't arrive in the château's front hall by six, the fist around Lucan's heart closed more tightly and worry took root. Mayhap she was in trouble. Injured somehow. Or worse . . .

He took the stairs two at a time, all the way to the third floor, and stalked to her door where he rapped on the thick wood. He counted to five before he leaned closer to listen for sounds of life behind the barrier.

Distantly, he made out a faint rustle.

Lucan knocked more insistently.

"Just a minute," she called from within.

Relief swamped him like a physical caress. His

shoulders sagged as he expelled a long hard breath. Not harmed. Just running behind.

The door cracked open, sending a whiff of flowery perfume through the narrow opening. She peered out with a frown, then drew back as if she had expected someone else. "Lucan?"

"Aye. When you did not . . ." He hesitated. When she did not what? Arrive in the lobby he had worried? He could not admit such. 'Twould make him look weak. A man who knew a woman only but a few days did not fret like a hen over her safety.

He shook his head. "I thought to drive you to Ornes. That we might take the reliquary together."

Her amber gaze narrowed for a heartbeat, and he cursed himself for once again sparking her ire. He grasped at words in attempts to sooth her obvious annoyance. "Your car is still at the site. Caradoc went on ahead with Tim and Andy."

She pursed her lips, then let out an exasperated mutter. Clearly she did not believe him. But she stepped aside and opened the door for him to enter. "Oh, come in. Stop making up excuses. If it means that much to you, we'll ride together."

'Twas then he noticed her wet hair. It clung to her face, dripped over the swell of her terry-covered breasts. Droplets of water streaked down her cheeks and lingered on the hand she lifted to push the wet auburn lengths away from her eyes.

In her other hand, she clutched her unbelted robe tight. Her hurry to don the garment was evident in the way it draped off one shoulder. She turned around, and Lucan's heart seized. A mark on her right shoulder blade stood out against her glistening skin. Small, brownish in color, it took the form of a miniature heart. Not false art, but natural to her birth.

His mark. The emblem that matched the one he despised on his backside and branded her as his seraph.

God's teeth, his blood rushed through his veins with a typhoon's power. His heart thundered in his ears. In a hidden portion of his soul, something fierce and wholly indescribable leapt to dangerous life.

He caught himself reaching out to touch her seraph's confirmation, then jerked his hand away, seconds before he made contact with her skin. His fingers grazed the edge of her robe. Lucan froze. Holding his breath, he waited for her to notice.

She picked her clothes off the foot of the bed and continued into the bathroom.

When the door closed, he sank to the edge of the bed, shaken. If he had needed more proof than Gabriel's words, he had just witnessed it. Chloe belonged to him. Not Caradoc, not Gareth, not any other knight who suffered the immortal curse. The Almighty chose her for him alone.

As he chose Lucan for her.

Lucan's hands trembled as he pushed them through his hair. He had known. Had believed. But seeing the evidence with his own eyes robbed him of the ability to take a normal breath. For the first time in his life, duty became meaningless, the oaths of brotherhood insignificant. As he looked around her room, letting her engulf his senses, he wanted naught more than to discover all he could about the woman. What did she drink on waking—water, coffee, something altogether different? When she readied for bed, did she unwind with a hot bath? Or were morning showers her preference?

The squeak of the bathroom door pulled his gaze to her entry. Dressed in jeans and a long-sleeved navy blue shirt, she emerged. Her hair was dry now, and the clean lengths hung to the middle of her back, shining like the angels had kissed it.

Mayhap they had.

His body tensed as she drew nearer to the bed. She poured into his awareness, suffocating all thoughts but those of her. Of what he would like to do to her. Experience with her. His hands itched to slide through her hair as they had the night before. He craved the taste of her sweet mouth. If he could but draw her close, sample the honeyed flavor, take them back to the night before. Here, where her bed sat beneath him. Where he could lay her back against the pillows and slowly peel away those clothes.

God's blood, he ached to touch her.

Even her melodic voice set him on edge.

"I think I'm ready. If you'll grab that bag there, I'll get the trunk." She gestured at a supple leather satchel carelessly tossed into the chair.

Stifling down the fierceness of his wayward thoughts, Lucan pulled his gaze from hers and looked where she indicated. Work. He must think on work. He could not forget the reliquary. Nor the darkness that surrounded Chloe. Even now, as the first bright sun in days poured into the room, he recognized the subtle presence in the trees beyond the château's manicured lawns.

He could not allow himself to become consumed with her until he gained the knowledge of what Azazel's demons meant. Too much lay at risk. The Veronica. The Almighty's battle.

Chloe's life.

He pulled himself together and stood. Before he could reach for her bag, she went to the small safe in the corner of the room. Kneeling before it, she punched in the electronic code. As Lucan collected her satchel, Chloe pulled the reliquary—still wrapped in his coat—from within.

A strange sense of pride infused him. She had not even disturbed his makeshift covering. True to her word, she left the relic untouched.

"Would you like me to carry it?"

"I can get—"

She stopped at the lifting of his eyebrow, realizing he knew full well she could carry the artifact and that had not been the intent of his question. A blush crept into her cheeks, and she dipped her chin in a quick nod. "I'm sorry. I'm just used to doing for myself."

"Aye. I see." Grinning, he took the trunk from her and tucked it beneath his arm. He passed her the satchel. "You should allow yourself to enjoy a man's company."

At once, he regretted the teasing remark. Her amber eyes flashed to burnt umber. The shared remembrance of the night before passed between them as those rich depths locked with his. Temptation rose with the brief parting of her lips. Intensified as she moistened them with the tip of her tongue. Became intolerable when she swallowed and her gaze dropped to his mouth.

Lucan tamped down an anguished groan and turned away. He strode to the door, unwilling to spend another moment in this room where the most prominent piece of furniture was the queen-size bed. Saints above, how one woman could so distract him, he could not explain. 'Twas not as if he had honored the code of chastity through the years. He took his pleasure as he required.

And though brief encounters in the night offered physical relief, fulfillment did not come with the release of pent-up lust. A woman's embrace did not provide escape. He would enjoy Chloe, aye, but 'twas no reason for this uncontrolled desire.

Holding the door open, he allowed her to enter the hall first, and she proceeded toward the stairs. His eyes betrayed his will and fastened on the trimness of her waist, the subtle sway of her hips. Unbound, her hair danced against her shirt in a matched cadence. Lucan ground his teeth together.

Today he would experience hell. Of that, he was certain. Odd, he had never imagined Azazel's realm could include a mobile trailer in the middle of a forgotten French town. But as certainly as he knew his own name, he knew the hours that lay ahead would be far worse than any battle against a demon or any strike from a fallen Templar's unholy blade.

Yet 'twas necessary. He would only discover the demons' purpose by immersing himself in her. Spending each minute he could in her company. Which meant somehow he must find the ability to concentrate on something other than her supple curves and how he longed to explore each tempting inch of her creamy skin.

Aye, Gabriel had indeed tasked him with a trial. One mayhap more damning than either Merrick's or Farran's. They at least did not have to discern whether their seraph already belonged to Azazel.

CHAPTER 12

A t the bottom of the stairwell, the scent of bacon hit Chloe square in the gut. Her stomach protested her intention to skip breakfast with a rumble. Her gaze slid to Lucan. Spending more time with this man would be dangerous. Yet he was right, she had no way to get to the site unless she wanted to take a taxi.

He glanced at her, puzzlement written in the slight crease of his brow. He didn't speak, but the question lurked in his quiet gaze—why were they standing in the middle of the front foyer?

"What time is it?" she asked.

Lucan looked behind her at the concierge's desk. "'Tis almost six thirty. Why do you ask?"

Chloe gave herself a mental kick. She wasn't seriously entertaining the idea of having breakfast with him, was she? One meal had caused trouble enough.

On the other hand, she had to work with this man. God only knew when he might decide the site held nothing more of interest to the Church, and so far they'd started out on all the wrong feet. While she was being bitchy and territorial, he'd gone out of his way to be amicable and approachable. Maybe if she opened her mind and met him halfway, as he kept trying to encourage, working with him wouldn't be so bad.

Last night hadn't been bad by any measure of the word. They'd actually gotten along . . . even if things took a drastically unexpected turn.

She tipped her head and caught his gaze. "Are you hungry?"

A flicker of surprise passed behind Lucan's eyes. It vanished in a heartbeat, replaced by a warm, genuine smile. "I could eat."

God she loved it when he smiled.

Stop thinking like that. It's a professional, working breakfast. Nothing else. It couldn't be anything else—she didn't trust him enough. Exactly why she needed to do this. She had to try, had to get out of the mindset he was out to usurp her work.

She returned his smile. "Let's do that. My treat."

Again, surprise registered for a brief moment before he nodded. "Very well then." He tucked the reliquary under his arm more securely and gestured at the restaurant. "After you, milady."

Chloe crossed the hall and seated herself at an empty table. Lucan took the chair opposite, with the reliquary positioned on the chair between them. She pushed down the nagging voice of reason that insisted Julian would be angry over her late arrival and determined to enjoy this morning. What was it Lucan had said? Enjoy the company of a man? She wouldn't go that far, but she did intend to enjoy a bit of downtime with him. Just for a little while.

The waiter slipped two menus on the corner of their table. *"Bonjour."*

"Good morning," Chloe answered in chorus with Lucan.

"May I start you with some fresh juice this morning? Coffee perhaps?"

"Coffee, if you please," Lucan replied, catching Chloe's gaze for a moment.

Her cheeks flushed beneath the warmth in his eyes and cut her gaze to the waiter. "Me too, please."

"Very well then, I shall bring them right out. Do you need a few minutes?"

"Aye."

The young man disappeared, his stride full of efficient purpose. Chloe took a deep breath and set the menu aside. The château's eggs Benedict beat any she'd had in years. She searched the depths of her mind for a conversation topic.

Lucan, however, beat her to words. "Tell me more of your time in Egypt?"

She could. She could go on about the rare pottery they'd discovered, about the absolutely perfect preservation of the mummies, or the incredible colors of the artwork on the walls. She could take the easy way out and fill up an entire thirty minutes or so with fantastic tales about her years in the desert . . . but she didn't want to talk about her job. Not right now. Her job always put them at odds.

Instead, Chloe reached across the table and laid her hand over his. Words popped out before she could wrest them under control. "Let's leave work out of this."

No doubt about it, those dark compelling eyes filled with momentary shock. As if he had never given consideration that she might actually take his suggestion to heart. As if her attempting to relate to him was the last thought that had ever crossed his mind.

A slow, heart-stopping smile spread across his mouth. He turned his hand over, his fingers loosely weaving between hers. Warmth skittered down Chloe's spine. Instinct demanded she retract her hand, tuck it into her lap where it was safe. Where he couldn't threaten her defenses. *Try, Chloe, try. Don't you dare chicken out.*

She blinked long and slow, pulled in a steadying breath, and left her palm resting against his. "What was the last movie you saw?"

Lucan laughed as he shook his head. "I do not have much opportunity to view movies. What did you last see?"

Well, that was a terrible place to start a conversation— it had been at least two years since she'd seen a movie. She couldn't even remember which one it was. Grinning, Chloe shook her head. "Me neither. I was hoping you'd bring me up to speed."

Those dark eyes glittered with mirth, and ever so slightly, Lucan's fingers tightened against hers. "Let us attempt this again. Tell me of you, Chloe. Tell me what 'twas like to grow up with Julian."

A flash memory of Julian hiding a frog in her sleeping bag when they'd gone on a family vacation burst to life, and Chloe laughed. "He was a pain in the rear. Still is. I think he'll be eternally twelve. It was his life's mission to make me scream, squeal, cry, and want to pull out his hair."

Lucan's grin deepened. "Scream?"

The memory took on vivid color, playing out in slow motion, and Chloe started there. "The last family vacation we took, I was nine and he eleven. Our parents took us camping at Yellowstone. We'd spent the day doing different things. Dad and he went fishing. Mom and I went on a nature hike."

She closed her eyes, reliving the last true happy summer they'd spent together. When she opened them again, Lucan's attentive gaze encouraged her to let down her walls. He wanted to know. Truly wanted to hear something mundane from her.

"We ate fish around a campfire. Julian and Dad took a little bit longer to dispose of our trash than they ought to have. Julian came back first, panting and frantic, swearing Dad had been attacked by a bear—he knew I was terrified they'd find our camp." She laughed again, shaking her head at her brother and father's antics. "He had Mom and me in a complete fit of worry, scouting the trees, calling out for Dad, chasing after snapping branches. I guess Dad didn't ever think Mom would take it seriously. I'm not really sure what got into his head, but he and Julian were like two little kids all the time."

The waiter interrupted her story long enough to set a carafe of coffee down and take their order. When he left again, Lucan squeezed Chloe's hand. His unsettling dark eyes pulled her into the simple quaintness of a normal conversation with a man she enjoyed. A man who made her heart tap a little too fast. She shifted their hands so their fingers joined more completely and resumed her story.

"Anyway, about the time Mom was ready to hunt down a park ranger, Dad jumped up from behind their tent, growling and doing his best to impersonate a bear. I've never seen Mom so angry with him. Julian and I went to our tent while they argued. He was adamant that I trade sleeping bags with him."

Lucan's thumb brushed against her wrist. A delightful shiver seized her, and she tripped over her tongue. To cover her startled reaction, she took a long drink of coffee, ordered her pulse to return to normal, and shifted position in her chair. Oh, this was so wrong. She was going down the entirely opposite path than what she'd intended.

But it was so nice too . . .

"What happened?" Lucan asked, grinning.

"I refused." She chuckled, seeing the horrified look on Julian's face as if it had happened yesterday. "I climbed into my own, only to find the biggest, slimiest frog I'd ever seen tucked into the bottom of my bag. I left the tent screaming, which stopped our parents' argument, and they found a new target—my poor brother."

"I expect they were not pleased."

"Well no, they weren't. But you have to understand that my family was a little odd. Mom and Dad never punished us like normal kids. Instead of spankings or groundings, they paid us back in kind." Chloe set her mug down, her heart tugging as she remembered her parents. She didn't know much about Lucan, but she sensed he would have instantly taken to her father. Her mother would have loved him—if he cut his hair.

"The next day, Mom and Dad convinced Julian that there was a snake in the campsite." Chloe smirked. "Dad found some old snakeskin and set it on his pillow when he wasn't looking. He made a point of showing it to me first. They had him jumping at everything. He was so scared he begged to sleep with them."

* * *

Laughter slipped free as Lucan pictured the vacation Chloe described. She spoke so fondly of her family. A feeling he had once shared as well, and reliving her happiness eased the ever-present ache that lingered in his heart. This side of Chloe, this unexpected normal side of the consummate professional, enchanted him. He could see her in youth, happy, free from the worry of her work, and he began to understand how close she was to her brother.

"You said it was your last family vacation?"

Chloe's smile dimmed. She nodded, her gaze skipping to the contents of her coffee mug. "Dad was diagnosed with prostate cancer that winter. He didn't make it to the following summer."

Lucan's heart turned over. So young—at least he had been a man when his father met death. The sadness that reflected in her eyes even now struck him with the urge to fold her into his arms, hold her close, and absorb that sorrow. Clearly she adored her father.

"Julian took care of me when Mom couldn't," Chloe continued wistfully. "She had a heart attack and died my senior year of high school. Julian moved back home from college and didn't move out until a few years ago. I know you've seen us bickering at each other here, but it's not usually that way. We're very close."

'Twas no wonder. They had depended on one another. More than any sibling pair might. And those close bonds explained how they had come to work in the same field, why Mikhail had said they were inseparable. Damnation, life had been unfair to her. He opened his mouth to offer some means of consolation, but words stuck in the back of his throat as Chloe picked up their joined hands.

His gaze followed hers, looking to where their fingers intertwined. The sight of her nails tucked between his knuckles slammed a fist into his gut. He could not recall when a simple touch had felt so intimate.

With her other hand, she traced a lazy pattern over the back of his wrist. Thoughtfulness filled her expression, words he would sever limbs to hear. "Chloe?" he asked quietly.

She chuckled. "I don't know why I told you all that."

"I am glad you did." He drew the side of his thumb down the length of hers. "Tell me more about your father."

As if some unseen dam gave, Chloe opened herself. As she talked, Lucan listened intently. But 'twas what she did not speak that told him far more. Moments of hesitation revealed she did not often share this side of her. The pinkening of her cheeks now and then said the conversation made her uncomfortable on some level, and yet she continued each time he prompted.

What grabbed his heart and twisted it into a knot, however, was the gentleness she exposed. She had helped care for her dying father. Donated significant money to prostate cancer research. Her mother had fallen apart after her father's death, and 'twas Chloe who became the nurturer, despite her claims that Julian looked after them. Chloe who assumed a parental role with her brother, even as she depended on him.

Chloe who had pursued her career with zest and passion so Julian, who did not share her dedication to their work, never suffered.

The discovery filled Lucan with an emotion he could not describe. More than admiration. More than compassion. A feeling that eluded him, but somehow pulled the conflicted portions of his soul into peace.

This nearness to her, however, drove him out of his mind. The more he learned, the more he found himself wishing he could escape the close quarters of the restaurant. For he began to fear that if her fingers did not stop sliding over his skin, and her eyes did not cease to communicate the desire he tasted in her kiss the night before, he would forget himself, lean across the table, and take possession of her mouth once more.

"Good grief," Chloe exclaimed. "We've been here almost an hour."

Her hand pulled free of his, striking Lucan with deep regret. He curled his fingers into his palm and slowly clenched a loose fist. His skin tingled where they had connected.

"I'm sorry," she apologized. She hastily signed her name on the credit slip that had been sitting on the corner of the table for quite some time. "I didn't mean to make us late. We should get going."

Lucan glanced at his plate, the food significantly untouched. Neither had he realized time had sped by so quickly. He pushed his breakfast aside and gulped down the remainder of his cold coffee. "Aye, we should."

It required all of his self-restraint to resist clasping her hand as she slid from her chair. He tucked the reliquary beneath his arm, careful to ensure his coat still kept it concealed. Her perfume tickled his nose as she walked in front of him, and he clenched his teeth against the sudden rush of heat that infused his blood. God's teeth, she was torture he could not get enough of.

CHAPTER 13

✟

Lucan breathed easier as he parked in front of the field trailers and stepped into the cold winter morn. Here, although Chloe would be present, he would have the benefit of her students' distraction. They would demand her time, allowing him to distance himself from the melodic ring of her voice. He could watch, study, and think.

Or so he hoped.

Never before had nine short miles seemed so eternally long. Chloe vanished behind the walls she kept around her the moment they seated themselves in the car. She fell into silence whilst he struggled against the need to reach across the center console and reclaim contact with her hand. She kept it in her lap, however, forbidding the contact he craved. And yet, despite the awkwardness that descended upon them, Lucan sensed something deeper than mere conversation transpired in the restaurant. Whatever it was, Chloe now sought distance.

As she joined him in the snow, he secured the reliquary beneath his arm and mounted the stairs. Inside,
Andy, Tim, and Julian gathered around a computer
screen, reviewing the photographs Andy had taken the
day before. Caradoc and Gareth sipped coffee in the
corner near the other three young men who had gathered in front of a small television to watch cartoons.

Chloe noticed the bright animation at the same time
Lucan did. Her laugh came short and quick. "Aren't
you three a bit old for French reruns of Bugs Bunny?"

A freckled young man whose name Lucan had not
caught leaned forward and turned the television off. "Just
waiting on you, boss. What's on the agenda today?"

Lucan set the reliquary on the chrome-topped table
and pulled up a tall stool beside Gareth whilst Chloe
carefully unwrapped her treasure. She grinned over
the top of the lid at the freckled man. "We're going to
open this after a while. First though, I want you three
and Tim to go over to the lab and get the box of things
we set aside for Lucan and his friends. Then, while I'm
going over those findings, I want all of you to hit the
shovels and start getting the snow out of that hole."

A chorus of good-natured grumbles accompanied
the squeaking of leather as the young men abandoned
the long couch. On the way to the door, Tim pulled a
shovel off the wall. "I'll start on that. See you guys there
in a bit."

Caradoc leaned over Gareth's knees and lowered
his voice. He looked to Lucan. "Do you wish to stay in
here?"

Lucan nodded, but a movement in the corner of his
eyes pulled his attention back to Chloe and her brother.

Standing at her side, Julian edged between her and the reliquary. His hands caressed the beaded surface.

"Back off," Chloe hissed softly. She jammed an elbow into Julian's side and shot him a disapproving scowl.

"Gareth, you stay here as well," Caradoc continued. "Take the artifacts she has already discovered and load them into the truck. When you are finished with those relics, return them to Raphael. I will stay with the team outside."

Gareth gave Caradoc a most displeased frown but downed his coffee and accepted the order with a curt nod. Lucan could not fault him for being annoyed. They had been sent to guard. Fight if necessary. Messenger boy was not part of Gareth's role.

Although Gareth's sword would be a welcome addition should Azazel's minions make themselves known, Lucan could not deny he preferred to have the younger knight out of his sight. Gareth served as a constant reminder of the younger generation. The men who had come after the original Templar first took up arms against the demons. The men who had inherited lands the founding fathers—such as Lucan and Caradoc— had been forced to leave behind. Although they too suffered the eventual loss of homelands, what they had enjoyed at Lucan's sacrifice, and the inescapable reminders of their stronger souls, made working beside the European Templar Knights difficult.

His plans outlined, Caradoc swiftly exited. As he marched through the door, however, his sword caught against the frame, making Lucan painfully aware he had once again left his in the rear of the SUV. Saints' teeth, he could not wait to have this business of Chloe's demons over with and his secrets bared. Then he could outfit himself appropriately without worry of what conversations might arise should she observe he wore a sword.

As the door swung shut, it abruptly changed course and thunked into the wall. Kevin and the other two students filed through, each carrying a three-by-three foot cardboard box that they carefully set beside the reliquary.

"Thanks," Chloe commented with a cordial smile. "Take a pail of hot water out too—you can melt off some of the ice, or use it to get what the shovels can't. We'll deal with the frozen mud as we need to."

"I'll get it," Andy chimed as he slid off the stool closest to the reliquary.

The way her students jumped to do what she asked spoke of their deep respect for her, and Lucan felt a smile pull at his mouth. Had she not disclosed all the things she had at breakfast, he would still have seen the kindness in her smile and hear the gentle note in her instructions. But he had heard, and he indeed learned secrets about Chloe Broussard, which made the way she interacted with her students even more revealing. He saw the nurturer, the counselor, the mature woman who wanted her pupils to succeed. She would do whatever it required to see that happen as well.

Whilst Lucan watched the students work, the feeling he was being watched set his nerves on edge. He looked up, away from the collection on the table, and found Julian staring. His gaze narrowed with contempt.

Lucan stiffened. Well he knew that gleam to Chloe's brother's eyes. More than once he had witnessed it seconds before his sword speared into an opponent's chest. It held one meaning, and one meaning only—*enemy*.

Because he had spent time with Chloe? Surely Julian could not be aware of the time they had shared in her room. Then again, mayhap Chloe had sought his counsel. Informed him of what had transpired. 'Twould not be so uncommon given their closeness. Did he then seek to protect her?

"Lucan?" Chloe called. "Do you want to see these?"

"Aye." He dismissed the trouble of Julian and slid off his perch.

"Chloe, let's get the damn reliquary open first. You can go over those things later. Hell, take them back to the château and do it after dark. I want to see what's in the golden box."

Chloe curled her fingers around the table's edge and straightened her shoulders. Deep creases crinkled the corners of her mouth as she slowly, deliberately, turned to address her brother. Through clenched teeth she ground out, "I'm the project manager, Julian. Enough."

Lucan met Gareth's lifted eyebrows and answered his silent inquiry with a shrug. He could not offer an explanation for the discord between brother and sister. But the exchange sparked his curiosity as well. The annoyance Julian had shown Chloe the morning before returned to Lucan's memory. Chloe acknowledged they were bickering, mayhap something significant divided them after all. A possibility that increased his concern tenfold. He knew firsthand how little family bonds could matter when siblings were intent on possessing something bequeathed to the other. How easy it was for them to hide their intentions behind carefully crafted words. To strike when least suspected.

Chloe's palm fell over his arm, drawing him back into the conversation. In her other hand she held a silver cross embedded with rubies. Across the horizontal beam, an elegant script read *Christo et Ecclesiae*, "For Christ and for the Church."

Lucan could not help but smile. "Aye." He reached over her and carefully pried the top section of the vertical beam open. Inside laid a tiny sliver of wood. "'Tis a piece of the True Cross. Carried in battle across the sands of the Holy Land."

Gareth gave him a look that questioned Lucan's judgment in revealing such things outside the Temple walls. Lucan shrugged it off. Chloe was entitled to the secrets. A piece of the True Cross meant little—it could not aid Azazel's lofty goals.

However, questions lurked in Chloe's eyes. How did he know this? Did he speak the truth? Her gaze dropped to the silver chain around his neck. Did his knowledge have something to do with the medallion he had shown her?

"You believe that ridiculousness?" Julian snorted from behind them. "The True Cross? Oh, come on, how would anyone in the middle ages even *know* whether it was real or not? It's probably nothing more than a rumor. One of those false icons that ran so rampant in the Church."

As if someone touched her with a hot poker, Chloe's spine snapped straight. She whipped around to face her brother. "Julian, I don't know what the hell's the matter with you, but you need to get a grip. *Now.* Or you can leave."

Julian's mouth twisted into a vicious sneer. "You would buy into it. Give you a pretty face, and you'll believe anything. Let's get to the trunk. It's more interesting than bits of glass pasted onto more glass and stories about chunks of wood."

Equal anger flashed behind Chloe's amber stare. She drew in a breath, held it, then exhaled hard.

Before she could spew her temper, Lucan shifted his arm so he could clasp her fingers and gave them a reassuring squeeze. Leaning close to her shoulder he murmured, "Let it go. 'Tis a tale for later." Saints' teeth, touching her satisfied his soul.

Surprising him, she did as he suggested and presented her back to her brother. With a subtle dip of her chin and a faint blush, she set the cross down and reached inside the cardboard box again.

Lucan looked over her head as she talked and caught Julian glaring at the back of his sister's head. Deep down in Lucan's gut, a similar anger sparked. Aye, indeed, Julian bore Chloe ill intentions. Why, Lucan could not fathom. Yet he did not attribute this to the centuries of suspicion that lived inside his soul. The evidence was plain. Julian, however, did not seem to understand that to get to Chloe, he must first get through Lucan.

Julian's gaze shifted to Lucan. His upper lip curled in what could only be described as a snarl.

Mayhap he understood after all.

Chloe watched as Gareth carted the last of the three boxes out the door. To her right, Lucan sat on a stool, one foot casually propped against the wooden rungs. On her left, her brother mirrored Lucan's position. But casual didn't fit her brother's posture. It reeked of mockery. Stunk of misplaced testosterone.

Lucan's relaxed expression didn't fool her either. He just managed to hide his animosity a hell of a lot better. Like he had practice doing so, where her brother had never known a day of temperance.

The tension that spanned them crackled like dried wood on a fire. Thick enough that she didn't need a knife to cut it. Her finger would do the trick. Maybe even just a hard breath.

But she could honestly say Julian deserved every bit of animosity he received. He'd egged on Lucan and Gareth at every opportunity. As if he was trying to drag them into a fight. One he'd lose, no doubt. Particularly if he'd managed to get beneath Gareth's skin as well as he had Lucan's. In truth, though, Julian aimed his barbs squarely at Lucan, not so much the younger Church representative.

Oddly, Chloe found herself siding against her brother for the first time since they'd been kids. Lucan's quiet, yet obvious, aggression strangely calmed her own. That he could contain himself, unlike Julian, increased her growing respect for him. It didn't hurt either that he'd just spent a good three hours enrapturing her mind with tales about the various pieces her team had collected over the last several weeks.

Whether he spoke the truth or not, the legends he recited fascinated her. Pieces of the True Cross. Bits of saints' bones. Fantastical objects made to hold them all. How and why they had been carried across the lands. Everything he said reinforced her opinion that he knew his field, and knew it well.

The fragile trust she had begun to embrace over breakfast wavered. All the more reason to mistrust him with the contents inside the last remaining piece—the golden trunk.

She glanced across the table at the five expressions that glowed with anxiousness. Anxiety she too felt, though for entirely different reasons. In the depths of her heart, she knew what she'd find inside the reliquary. She'd never admit it aloud, but after surreptitiously checking the beads to see if one might break free, and finding them unmovable, she couldn't find any other explanation for the surreal, otherworldly experience she'd encountered when she held the bead.

Veronica's Veil. Christ's existence at last proved beyond a doubt. The revered scientist Dr. Noelle Keane, whom Chloe had worked with on research many times, put those wheels into motion with the official carbon dating of the Sudarium of Oviedo. But since her disappearance, along with the Sudarium's, the Christian community lacked a crucial piece of evidence to celebrate the fact. Now, at last, Chloe would bring something useful to the world. People everywhere would rejoice, and she'd see to it the cloth sat on public display in a museum.

No matter how Lucan fought the notion.

"Damn it, Chloe, get on with it," Julian snapped. "We're all here. Open the trunk."

The shift of Caradoc's hand gave her pause. She followed the motion, observing as he wrapped his fingers around the hilt of a sword. Chloe blinked. Who wore a sword in public? And where had he gotten it—she hadn't noticed it before.

As if he sensed her questions, Caradoc gave her a warm smile. "Proceed, if you will?"

"Yeah." Weird. Just . . . weird.

She took a deep breath and reached for the lid. Digging her nails into the thin seam between lid and body, she pulled.

The top held fast.

"'Tis locked," Lucan murmured.

Chloe tried again, annoyed he'd made the observation first. When the lid refused to budge more than a fraction of an inch, she gestured at the metal rack of shelves. "Chris, see if you can find the ice pick in there. Maybe we can jimmy this lock."

While he rummaged, her heartbeat accelerated. She squirmed in her chair, anxiety possessing her as well. Beside her, Lucan chuckled. He dropped his hand beneath the table and gave her thigh a gentle squeeze. Warmth tingled up her leg. She shifted, expecting him to move that hand and relieve her of the pleasant discomfort. Instead, his palm rested heavy and unmoving, a blessed torment that made concentrating on the ice pick Chris passed across the table, and inserting it into the tiny keyhole, exceedingly difficult.

Lock picking had never been her forte. On one or two occasions she'd had to fiddle around with a pick until rusted old mechanisms broke free. But all of those events included a simple lever type of lock where all she had to do was press the bottom up or down to release the weight. In the reliquary's case, however, the designer made the mechanism more complex. She fumbled around inside the keyhole, scraping the ice pick's point against aged metal, accomplishing nothing.

As frustration set in, Lucan's hand left her thigh to close over hers. He stood up, bent around her, and enveloped her with his body. His chest molded into her back. His arms framed her shoulders. And his cheek tucked so close to the side of her face she could feel his warmth. Her gaze shifted as he turned her wrist, and she glanced sideways at high cheekbones, the touch of dark stubble that told her he hadn't shaved that morning. Damn, oh, damn. If she turned her head a fraction . . . If he did the same . . .

She swallowed hard and jerked her eyes away from the handsome outline of high cheekbones, long eyelashes, and tender lips she remembered all too well.

The lock gave with a faint *click*. Lucan straightened, taking the heavenly feel of his body with him. He released her hand, took the ice pick from her fingers, and passed it back to Chris.

A whole new sense of anticipation launched through Chloe. For a fleeting moment she forgot the way Lucan turned her mind into a pretzel. She reached for the gilt lid and lifted.

The ageless scent of earth escaped into the air. Hesitantly she pushed out of her chair, bending over to peer inside, as did all the other heads that gathered close. Nestled in the bottom, a length of delicate, yellowed muslin lay in a neatly folded square. Chloe's breath came out in a hard rush. The Veronica. Chills rippled down her spine.

"Let me see that." Julian's bare hand shot beneath her nose.

She slapped his wrist aside with more venom than she'd meant and drove his hand into the hard silver and gold edge. He drew back with a muffled oath. His scowl wielded daggers.

"What the hell?" she cried. "Damn it, Julian, you could transfer contact DNA without gloves. Where has your freaking brain gone? God, it's like this thing has possessed you." She drew in a deep breath and with more calm, motioned Andy and his camera close. "Get a few pictures of this. There's something weighing down the cloth—see it? Before we disturb it, I want it documented."

Dutifully he clicked away while she pulled on a pair of thin latex gloves. When he stepped back, indicating he'd finished, she dipped her hand inside and removed the chunk of metal atop the fabric. Her throat closed as she stared at the heavy bit in her palm.

Just like the medallion Lucan's dark gray shirt hid from view, this one bore the same engraving. The same *Milites Templi* above and below the cross's vertical beam. She looked to him, met the knowing in his steel-gray eyes. Unable to digest the meaning in front of her brother and her students, she set the coin-size medal aside. As she reached in once more, her gaze briefly touched with Caradoc's. There too, she recognized the same shared secret that reflected in Lucan's eyes.

While Chris laid a protective covering across the table, Chloe forced her brain to let go of the questions that leapt to life and reached into the reliquary for the cloth. Gingerly she unfolded it. Spread it on the covered table. Andy moved in to snap more photographs. The crowd gathered closer.

Chloe's fingers traced the brown stains embedded into the material. She knew what she touched. But the magnificence mystified her.

"What do you think it is, boss?" Kevin asked quietly.

Chloe looked up. Her students' expressions shone with curious intrigue. Julian's eyes gleamed, the age of the material not lost on him. But Lucan and Caradoc stood at ease. Only mild interest touched the corners of their eyes. Where everyone else stared at the fabric, the two representatives of the Church watched the people.

In that instant Chloe realized she, Lucan, and Caradoc were the only people who knew what lay beneath her fingertips. The discovery hit her with so much force she shivered. On its heels came the startling knowledge Lucan and Caradoc remained silent, though they were perfectly able to answer Kevin's question.

Lucan's question echoed in her mind—*Will you trust I shall reveal the cloth when the time is appropriate?* The same inquiry resided in his silent stare now.

Trust, no. But she would wait for solid evidence that her team could put together and reach the conclusion. She shook her head at Kevin. "The only way to know is to begin by dating it. If we establish what period it came from, we'll have a starting place." She nodded at the metal drawers. "Chris hand me a razor blade. I'll try to separate a few fibers out of this frayed corner. We'll ship it off to the lab."

"Let me see it, Chloe," Julian urged.

Lucan placed his hand on the cloth and leaned his weight into his arm. "Our scientist shall handle the carbon dating."

Chloe blinked at him. Do what? Their eyes clashed. In that instant, every last ounce of shaky trust Chloe had given him shattered. "This is my discovery. I'll have my normal lab date it. Get your bare hand off before you damage it."

With a firm shake of his head that left no room for argument, Lucan gently nudged her out of the way and folded the cloth. Depositing it back into the trunk he answered, "Nay. 'Tis the Church's property. 'Twill be dated by our representatives." He closed the gold lid.

Chloe shot out of her seat, knocking the stool over backward. "That wasn't part of the agreement! You're supposed to observe. Verify we follow protocol and take whatever we discover as rightfully belonging to the Church back to the Vatican. At no time did the letters I received mention you could take things away before we discovered what they were!"

Undaunted, Lucan passed the reliquary to Caradoc. He looked to her, firm warning etched into the tight lines of his face. "Then you were misinformed. I will not argue this with you. The relic returns with us."

She opened her mouth to spill the numerous curses and insults that rose in her throat. But before she could spout a single one of them, Lucan and Caradoc stalked out the door, leaving her no option but to clench her hands at her sides and bite back a frustrated scream.

CHAPTER 14

$\dagger$

C hloe clamped her teeth together and drew in a deep breath. Embarrassed in front of her students. Damn Lucan. The least he could have done was called her aside. He had to have known she'd want to date what was inside the reliquary—why hadn't he warned her privately he intended to have the Church's specialists date the damn thing?

She grabbed for her composure to keep from chasing after him and creating a greater scene. The stunt in front of her team already defied all the lessons she'd tried to instill in her students about the politics of archaeology and how to approach stubborn officials who tried to impede progress.

"Tim, would you oversee the closing of the site? Make sure we have everything inside—the shovels, whatever you all used. Andy, head on back and start downloading those photographs. I want to send them over to Cambridge and see if Dr. Hildenbrough has any thoughts."

Her students shuffled to life, grabbing coats and mufflers before filing out the door.

Chloe sank onto her stool and drummed her nails on the table. "Stupid jerk. I can't *believe* he just did that."

"Welcome to the Church." Julian snorted. "I told you he was in this for his own means."

Frowning, Chloe ignored his self-satisfied smirk. "He could have warned me. But in front of the team? Good God, Julian, who does that kind of stuff? That's completely unprofessional."

"Oh, come off it, sis. What else do you expect from an organization that's kept the truth from humanity for thousands of years? You think he doesn't know what it is?" He slapped his hand on the table. "I'll guaran-damn-tee he knows *exactly* what it is, and they don't want *you* finding out."

Stiffening, she gave him a sideways glance. That didn't make sense. Lucan had already *told* her what it was. "Why would you think that?"

Julian gave her a dumbfounded look. "Wake up, Chloe! He didn't give a shit about anything in those boxes that you showed him. But the minute you started talking about dating the cloth, he shut you down. If you think he has any intention of sharing what he *might* find out with you, your head's in the clouds. I doubt he has any intention of having the thing dated." He leaned back on the stool and rested an elbow on the counter behind him. "He'll probably leave with the damn thing tonight. We won't see him again. Mark my words that box is what they came here for. He knew you'd find it. They got what they wanted, used your efforts to do so, and they, along with the box, will disappear for another couple hundred years."

A sickening feeling crept through her veins. What if Julian was right? She hardly knew Lucan. And he *had* known what she would find. He'd predicted she'd uncover it the very day they did. She'd played right into his hands. Fallen victim to his pretty words and damn near handed the relic over to him without a single protest.

"He does know things," she murmured.

Julian's boots hit the floor like lead. "What has he told you?"

She should tell him. Her brother had worked at her side, struggled financially along with her, and devoted himself to their shared careers. If anyone deserved to know what Lucan had disclosed, it was Julian.

At the same time, she couldn't forget Lucan's promise to do everything he could to bring the relic to the public. The pleading nature behind his eyes that begged for her trust. He'd seemed so sincere. Why would he go to such lengths just to lie?

And he'd told her far more than he should have if he wanted her to stay in the dark. He'd taken her into confidence. Not Julian. Not anyone else on the team. *Her.*

She shook her head, unable to bring herself to tell Julian about the Veronica. "Nothing about the relic. But I showed him the picture of that glyph in Egypt."

Julian leaned forward with interest. His eyes shone dark, the same creepy way they had when he'd barged into her room. "What did he say?"

The nagging feeling something wasn't right forced her off her stool. Julian only ever laughed about the glyph. Not once in the last eight years had he entertained a conversation about what had happened to her in that ancient tomb. She moved to the other side of the table, putting it between her brother and herself. "Nothing exactly. But I could tell by his body language he's seen it. He asked a bunch of questions."

"And you told him?"

She shrugged. "Nothing." No, they hadn't gotten much further than that. They'd gone back to the Veronica, then she'd kissed him silly.

"I wouldn't advise doing so."

All the years of suffering his ridicule came out with one sharp question. "Why? Because he might laugh at me?" She let out a soft, derisive snort. "That wouldn't make him much different than you, would it?"

"I'm nothing like he is."

That was true. No two men could be more different.

From the SUV's passenger seat, Lucan stared at the trailer's front door, waiting for Chloe to exit. His hand kept nervous time on his knee as the minutes drew out. He had embarrassed her, and he was not fool enough to believe there would not be hell to pay for his heavy-handed tactic. But naught would have made him allow Julian to touch the cloth. He was too eager. Too . . . interested. And the way his eyes gleamed when he looked upon the fragile fabric made great horns of alarm blare in Lucan's head.

"Tell her," Caradoc urged from behind the driver's wheel. "Tell her what she is and be done with it. You two may resolve your differences in the Temple."

Lucan shook his head. "Nay," he murmured.

"You take risks you should not, brother. She is safe within the Temple walls. Naught can harm her whilst you work to obtain her oath."

"*She* is the risk," he confessed with a heavy sigh.

"Have you not noticed the constant presence of Azazel's minions? They follow *her*."

More quietly, Caradoc responded, "Then you were wise to take the reliquary from her."

"I took *it* from Julian. She has held possession of the Veronica for a full day. If the demons sought to take it from her, they would have already done so. 'Tis the why, in the fact they have not, that concerns me."

His brother twisted in the seat, his frown deep and dark. "You think Azazel has seduced her?"

Lucan expelled a harsh breath. "I do not know. But she has been given Saladin's glyph of unholy passage. I thought never to see it again, and she produced it from her notes. With the demons so close, and their refusal to take the Veil, I cannot help but wonder."

"'Tis only one way to discover the truth, brother. Ask." He gestured at Lucan's chest. "You have shown her your medallion. I saw the recognition pass across her face. You have entrusted her with secrets—tell her all of them. Allow her to explain."

'Twas a concept easy for Caradoc, who did not suffer the taint of suspicion. He could not fathom the difficulties Lucan struggled to overcome. Whatever Chloe might explain, his mind would turn in circles until he could not logic between truth, possibility, and lie. He sighed again. "'Tis too easy for her to create a plausible fiction. I lack the judgment, Caradoc."

Understanding filled his brother's quiet stare. He acknowledged the inescapable truth with a slow nod. "You must build trust. Begin on common ground. Give her absolute faith on one small thing, and you shall earn her secrets."

Something in common—Lucan nearly laughed aloud. The only interest they shared was the Veronica. And yet he could no more turn it over to her for safekeeping than he could bring himself to give her the seraphs' torc.

His thoughts skidded to a halt as another idea surfaced. The Veronica *could* work to his advantage. He didn't need to give it to her. Just a small piece would work. He kicked open his door and jumped out into the snow. "I will see you at the château." As an afterthought, he tossed his room key onto the leather seat. "Put the reliquary in my safe. The code is the same as the Temple gates. Come back in an hour."

He slammed the door and bounded up the trailer's steps. As he reached for the handle, the door swung open. Julian stormed out, nearly colliding into Lucan's chest. He shouldered past Lucan with an indistinguishable mutter and stalked toward the students gathered at the excavation site.

Lucan let himself in, absorbing the heavy tension in the long room. Brother and sister had argued. About what? The relic? He looked to Chloe and stiffened beneath her icy glare.

"Get out," she instructed calmly. "This is *my* trailer, and I don't want you in it."

"Nay, I shall not." He reached behind him and locked the door. Slowly, deliberately, he took off his coat and laid it over the back of a nearby chair. "I did not come back to fight with you."

"No? Just what exactly did you expect? I'd welcome you with joy? For God's sake, Lucan, you made me look like an idiot!"

Crossing the room, he reached for her hands. When she pulled them away, he grabbed again, and succeeded in capturing her wrists. "I am sorry for the way I handled something necessary. But I came back inside to offer a compromise."

She threw her shoulders to the side, jerking hard for her freedom. He held fast, determined her anger would not divide them further. They had made progress this morning. He would not have that so easily reversed. "Chloe," he said more softly. "Cease. Listen to what I have to say."

"I don't *care* what you have to say. That's my discovery, and I'm not going to have you waltz off with it. I've dug through frozen ground, dodged snowstorms, and nearly froze my fingers off for two months! I deserve to know the truth behind that cloth."

"Aye, you do."

Her slow blink said she had not expected him to agree. She ceased struggling and squinted with mistrust. "Then why are you trying to stop me from finding it out?"

"I am not." Lucan used steady pressure on her wrists to guide her to the stool and urge her to sit. When she plopped onto the vinyl seat, he released her wrists in favor of her shoulders. "I will tell you whatever you wish to know about the Veronica. You need but ask. Meanwhile, you will have your sample to send to your laboratory. We will collect it together."

The tenseness of her shoulders eased beneath his palms. She furrowed her brows, confusion clouding her amber eyes. "Then what was that all about? Why turn into a jerk when you could have said all that earlier?"

He chuckled softly as he slid his hands along the length of her upper arms. "I am not always rational. You will have to forgive me for my mortal flaws." He leaned in closer, drawn to the heavenly call of her mouth. His lips touched hers briefly, before he remembered himself and stood up straight. "I will keep the reliquary whilst we await the findings from both our scientists. You may help me lock it away. You may set the code on the safe. That way, we are both protected. You may not get into my room without my key; I may not access the reliquary without your code." Lowering his voice to a whisper he asked, "If I agree to trust you, will you trust me?"

Her frown deepened. "That doesn't make sense, Lucan. All I have to do is tell the château you're on my team and my records are inside your room. I have the documentation to prove it."

A smile lifted the corners of his mouth. "All I must do is call the concierge and inform him I have forgotten the code to the safe. 'Tis in my room. 'Tis about trust, Chloe. I want yours."

As he had hoped, his smile lit hers. Faint, but present nonetheless, it brightened her eyes. Spread hesitantly onto her soft lips. She agreed with an equally hesitant nod.

Stepping back, he slid his hands down her arms to once again capture her hands. With a gentle tug, he pulled her to her feet. "Will you show me what you've found in the site? I should like to see the remains of le Goix's castle."

The tenseness returned to her spine as she glanced toward the windows and the fading sun beyond. "I don't know. It's getting dark. Everybody's packing up. We should probably wait until tomorrow."

To his consternation, her hesitancy spread to him. He eyed her warily. "Is there a reason you do not wish to show me the excavation?" A reason such as the demons that lurked in the woods? Mayhap she feared he would notice them and make the rightful assumption they had something to do with her.

"No, no," she hurried to assure. "I'll show you anything you want to see in that hole or around what's left of the walls. Just not . . . tonight. We'll run out of daylight before you can see it all."

Fear vibrated in her voice, registered behind the widening of her eyes. Lucan drew back at the poignant truth Chloe *feared* something. Something she refused to explain. Could it be the presence of Azazel? Or was it something greater—such as a promise to turn over a relic and fear of what might happen now that she had failed?

He looked out the window she stared at, observing the darkening sky. In an hour, night would descend upon them. If the demons chose to attack, they would do so then. But for the next sixty minutes, he had time to push her before he needed to worry about his lack of a holy sword. By nightfall, he intended to know exactly what had her so scared.

"Oh, come now, milady," he chided with a grin. "You are beginning to sound like you are afraid of the dark." He gave her fingers a squeeze. "As you said to your team—are you not a bit too old for such?"

A deep blush infused her cheeks as she looked to her feet. The tremor that rolled down her spine vibrated against his palm, and for a heartbeat, Lucan felt guilt over forcing her to confront what she so clearly wished to avoid. Yet he would only discover what caused this fear by pushing the boundaries. The possibility he might learn the truth about the dark presence that surrounded her was too great to yield to sympathy.

"Okay," Chloe whispered.

CHAPTER 15

A s the last car left the gravel drive, Chloe wrapped
her arms around herself tight and looked straight
ahead at the graying ruins. Beyond the jumble of toppled stone and clods of earth that a long-ago mortar
shell scattered, the thick deciduous forest loomed dark
and foreboding. Within it, the presence waited.

She kept her shoulders straight, determined not to
give Lucan any more reason to suspect why she didn't
want to be outside near the tall trees. His teasing remark
about her fear of the dark had already cut deep. More
evidence that, like every other man she knew, he'd find
her demons laughable. And after last night, she couldn't
begin to find humor in the subject.

Not that she ever had, but the attack last night put
things on a whole new level. Never mind the fact she'd
lost all opportunity to find a spiritualist this afternoon.
She'd have to risk her room, and its broken window,
again tonight. Hopefully, the ward would last. Hopefully, it would work a second time.

They drew nearer to the base of what had once been a feudal castle, and Lucan squatted before the square-cut stone blocks. He passed a reverent hand over the pitted surface and bowed his head as if he offered a prayer for all who had once lived within the walls. Knowing his expertise revolved around the Middle Ages and the practices therein, she allowed him the freedom to explore as he desired. What she could offer about what they'd found, he surely could put to shame.

She glanced to the trees with a shudder. It overwhelmed her out here. Gave her the feeling that if she stepped too close, they'd snatch her in. A shadow moved within, creeping through the high branches, and she glanced away before she could put a face with the creatures that gathered at her window. She didn't want to know what they looked like. They'd plague her in her dreams then. And those few bits of escape when she slept, no matter how short they were, were too precious to sacrifice.

"Chloe," Lucan called softly. Hand extended for hers, he beckoned her to join him before the ruins.

She slid her palm against his, more grateful for the contact than she'd ever let on. The warmth of his hand traveled up her arm to quiet the frantic drum of her heart.

He drew her close to his side, sheltering her with his very nearness, but didn't look at her as he asked, "What is it you are afraid of?"

Demons. It sounded ridiculous even to her ears, and she knew the truth. She shook her head. "We found out about this place because thieves stumbled onto a gold goblet here. Right about where you're standing. One of them was murdered in the forest when they left. The other turned himself in after his friend died at his feet."

His fingers slipped through hers, twining their hands together intimately. Chloe gained strength from his firm hold. He turned and guided her hand to his hip. He caught her other hand, did the same. When her palms rested on his belt loops, he slid his arms around her waist. One half step brought his body close to hers. "I will keep you safe, Chloe," he murmured as he gazed into her eyes. He dipped his head to brush his cheek against hers. "I promise I will keep you safe."

She closed her eyes, longing to believe him. He used the right words, the confident comforting tone of voice. No one had offered anything of the sort, not even her brother. And yet, little could truly convince her. Lucan had no idea what he spoke of. No clue what lurked there in the trees. He couldn't defend her any more than she could protect herself. No one could.

Desperate to hold on to the promise of safety, she turned her face in search of his mouth. He gave it without hesitation. Their breaths mingled in the cold, and then the velvety stroke of his tongue against hers warded off the winter chill, along with the ice in her veins. Softly, slowly, he drew her into a protective bubble. The presence in the woods faded into nothingness. All the nights she'd lain awake in horror disappeared into the recesses of her mind. She stood in Lucan's arms, his strong body a shield to all her fears, his mouth a heavenly oasis where no trouble could cloud blue skies.

All too soon he drew the kiss to a lingering close and folded her tightly into his arms. His breath rasped against the top of her head, stirring her hair. Beneath her cheek, his heart drummed hard. "You are a temptation of the greatest kind, Chloe Broussard." With a light chuckle, he let her go and stepped away. "Now, tell me what you know of this mark."

He tapped a large stone block near his thigh where a detailed sword had been engraved into the stone. Nearly a foot in length, the point touched the earth her team had yet to disturb. In the center of the blade, a circular emblem contained what Egyptologists called the Eye of Horus, and conspiracy theorists called the All-Seeing Eye.

"That's pretty obvious." Chloe stepped forward to trace the emblem as she spoke. "It's a long sword. In the middle is a wreath of what looks like laurels, though the carving is a bit crude. And in the center of that is the Eye of Horus. Egyptians believed Horus was the sun and moon. One eye, as only one shone at a time. There are dozens of legends relating to him."

"Aye." Lucan grinned. "Have you questioned why this mark would be present here?"

She had. Many times. And along with wondering why Horus was present in medieval France, she'd tried to figure out the sigil next to the sword—a small shield carved with a large sun and two crossed swords.

Chloe traced the engraved stone. "The best I can think of is someone came along and carved it much later. The sword is the only real medieval representation. But the engraving is really a bit too defined and precise for that period."

Amusement lit Lucan's eyes as he shook his head. Twisting, he pointed to a large stone chunk that rose from the ground five feet away on the other side of the path. The side closest to the forest. "Step over there. Then tell me what you see."

With a gulp, Chloe looked to the forest. Slowly, she shook her head. "I'd rather not. I'll use my imagination."

"Chloe," Lucan protested, a touch of exasperation in his voice. "Did I not tell you I would keep you safe? Now go, look at the difference."

Letting out a grumble that made her distaste known, she trudged closer to the forest. When she stood next to the block of stone, she turned to look where Lucan stood. To her surprise, the carving took on a completely different design. Only the sharp edges of the long blade scarred the surface from a distance, with the sword's hilt and point fading into mere shadows. The crown of laurels with its closely carved mess of leaves took on a solid appearance, forming a rather plain circle. And within it, the Eye of Horus was no more than a large irregularly shaped blob.

She blinked, shook her head in disbelief, and looked again.

Not a sword, but the Masonic point within a circle. Holy crap! How could she have missed something so obvious? She'd walked past that portion of a wall at least fifty times, if not more.

All concerns about the forest and the creatures within it fled her mind as she hurried back to Lucan. "How did you know that? Why is that *here*?"

He merely smiled and tapped the center emblem once again. "Laurels you said? What if I were to tell you 'twas briars?"

A chill raced down her spine as she looked to where the point of the sword met the ground. Though the earth lay undisturbed and flat beneath the tilted portion of a crumbled wall, two feet away, a crater marked the place they had uncovered the Veronica. If it were physically possible to straighten the toppled stone, the sword would point directly to the hole.

Too coincidental to be anything but deliberate.

"It's a marker," she exhaled.

Lucan confirmed with a slow nod. "You will find the same on any place significant to the Templar. 'Twas a design instilled to guide those who pledged service to the safe harbors of their brethren during a time of persecution."

"That can't be that old. It's too . . . too perfect to be carved with anything but modern tools."

He quirked that damnable eyebrow. "Is it? Were the Templar not master masons as well? I would date these marks as early sixteenth century."

Chloe shook her head. She didn't know all the intricacies of medieval history, but she knew enough to know what he proposed couldn't be possible. "You can't mean that a society that vanished in the fourteenth century still existed two hundred years later. Someone would have said something or written down an encounter that survived through time. With all the research that's been done on the Order, someone would have discovered that."

"Lest they did not wish to be discovered." He gave her a look full of meaning. "Recall, 'twas not until the sixteenth century when education spread throughout Christendom."

Meaning, the majority of the populous would still record events with rudimentary pictures and markers like the sword.

Curiosity piqued, Chloe tapped the shield sigil beside the sword. "And this one? What is it? I've tried to figure it out at least a dozen times."

"That one you will not find in any reference books." Lucan set his fingertip beneath a rune in the top left corner. "'Tis an *A*. And this," he slid his finger to the opposite corner, "A *G*. Knowing what I have told you, what is the likely answer?"

Her brows tugged together, uncomfortable with where he was leading her. "Alaric le Goix?"

"Aye. And this . . ." He traced the outline of two crossed swords. "What would you suspect they represent?"

She couldn't bring herself to say it. What he spoke of was too fantastic to be true. If Alaric had been here after the Inquisition's persecution, the magnificent carving had to have been crafted in the 1300s. But no mark she'd ever witnessed, and no artifact she'd ever set her hands on, had such exact lines. For all intents and purposes, the shield Lucan was touching couldn't have been much older than a hundred years. If even that.

"That's just not possible. The Templar order was dissolved in 1312."

"If you were to tilt the swords, what would you have, Chloe?"

She squinted, unwilling to discover the answer, yet unable to curb her curiosity. Rotating the swords in her mind, she visualized the scene. They would sit at perfect right angles. The hilts would form the flared ends of horizontal bars. And as she looked closer, each point bore a hook that would also fashion it in a similar style—the same cross that hung around Lucan's neck.

"And this." Lucan tapped two raised hills beneath the sword hilts. "Represents knowledge. 'Tis either stone tablets placed side by side, or an open book—the meaning is the same."

He looked up briefly, gave her a warm smile, and tapped the final object on the shield, a detailed sunburst. "Do the Egyptians not refer to Ra as *hidden light*?"

Chloe's head began to pound with the effort of tying all Lucan's loose ends together. Knights Templar, Egypt, and hidden relics—why? None of it made sense, least of all how a man who only had access to historical documents could know such intricacies about an order of knights that people who'd spent decades studying couldn't answer.

"How, Lucan?"

"How what?"

She tossed her hands in the air exasperated. "How do you know all this? And what's it have to do with that medallion in the trunk that so neatly matches yours?" Pushing her hair away from her eyes, she frowned at him. "What exactly are you trying to tell me?"

The crunch of gravel beneath tires brought him to his feet. "I am not trying to tell you anything. 'Tis simple fact about objects you have discovered. All of which relate to the Veronica. Which," he gestured at the slowing SUV, "we must now collect samples from."

"No. I want to know what I'm missing. Where did you learn these things? I'm not an expert in the Middle Ages, but I've worked with plenty of men who were. My mentor is one. Julian as well. No one knows the things you claim."

For several never-ending seconds, his gaze searched her face as if he debated confiding something else. Then, his brows dipped ever so slightly, and he subtly shook his head. "By the time we have the dates on the cloth, all you wish to know, you shall." He caught her hand in his. "For now, 'tis time to leave. The sun sets."

She looked up at the sky, surprised the sun had set so quickly. Tiny stars pricked through the dull winter gray. Good grief, she'd been so consumed by his fascinating discussion on the engravings, she hadn't even noticed the descent of nightfall. He'd done it again—made her completely forget about her fears. Erased the presence of the demons.

But now, as she took in her surroundings and observed the utter quiet in the trees, the presence engulfed her with malice. A rustle in the shadows made her jump forward, dismissing all thoughts of protesting his suggestion they should leave.

Lucan escorted her to the waiting vehicle at a brisker pace than usual. He waited until she climbed into the backseat before locking her door for her and shutting it tight. He slid into the passenger's seat and acknowledged Caradoc with a short nod. "Let us depart this place."

Chloe couldn't think of any better instruction. She sank into her seat in an attempt to make herself small and unnoticeable to the demons that lurked in the dark. Maybe if they didn't see her, they wouldn't bother her. Maybe they'd forget their purpose, whatever it was, for one night.

Unrealistic, but she clung to the hope out of desperation. As long as she believed she might someday get a reprieve from her unwanted guests, she could keep the fear at manageable levels.

As she stared at the back of Caradoc's head, an idea surfaced. He too had witnessed the medallion in the reliquary. And he'd recognized it just as she had. Maybe she could learn something more from him.

"Caradoc, what's the meaning of that chunk of silver that was in the reliquary?"

Through the rearview mirror she caught his surprised blink. He looked up, meeting her curious gaze. "Do you know the Templar purpose?"

Excitement bubbled in her blood. Finally someone who sounded willing to tie together the loose ends. "No. Not exactly."

"Then 'tis not my story to tell."

Chloe sighed inwardly as her brief hope splintered. So much for answers. Evidently he too shared Lucan's nerve-wracking riddle-speak. Damn it. How was she supposed to document her findings, especially the Veil, when everyone around her seemed intent on keeping her in the dark?

Rolling her eyes, she dropped her head on the seat back and quietly groaned.

CHAPTER 16

✦

The walk to Lucan's room held far more intimacy than circumstance should have created. Though he didn't touch her, not even to place his hand on the small of her back, Chloe couldn't shake the surreal feeling that their conversation about sigils had been some kind of foreplay, and she walked toward the culmination of what they'd begun.

It didn't help matters that Lucan aroused her mind as well as her body. His allusions and inferred remarks about secrets of the past stimulated her in ways Blake had never come close to. And the subtle scent of cold outdoors that blended with Lucan's rich spice cologne stirred her neglected feminine soul.

Caradoc too had unwittingly contributed to her ever-increasing awareness of Lucan Seacourt. He looked at her with the flat indifference a man gives a woman he knows is unavailable. He spoke to her like she had already become a *buddy*. And the way he left their company with the remark he'd see them in the morning, a simple comment overall, came with the firm expectation he'd see them *together.*

All of which made stopping at Lucan's door, watching him insert his key, and entering behind him turn her stomach into a jumble of nerves. She avoided looking at him and sat on the edge of the couch. His room, as spacious as hers, held nearly the same components—a bed, a short sofa, a coffee table, a false wardrobe that housed the television, a desk, and a nightstand table. But unlike the Meuse Valley rooms on the top floor, where provincial flowers blended with modern themes, Lucan's first-floor chamber resembled the era in which the château had been built. From the intricate molding around the high ceiling and doorway to the bathroom, to the wainscoting and wooden floors, it was all a picture of nineteenth-century France, right down to the four-poster bed with gauzelike curtains gathered around hand-carved spindles. A little feminine for *him,* but nonetheless beautiful.

Caught up in studying the details, she didn't hear him approach until he took a seat beside her and set the trunk on the coffee table.

"Shall we?"

All too glad to get out of his room as quickly as she could, she nodded vigorously. As she wriggled out of her coat, Lucan spread out the veil. Their elbows bumped. He flashed her a grin that served to dissipate some of the tension not only in the room, but inside her as well. Too much time had passed since she'd experienced that simple, youthful lightness of heart. Way too many years.

Chloe leaned over the table as he did, content to let his

thigh rest against hers. He held her gaze warmly as he passed her a small, open pocket knife. "I shall allow you the honors of separating the fibers."

She accepted, holding onto his fingers a second longer than necessary, mesmerized by the bright light in his storm-gray eyes. When her heart thumped hard, and the room became uncomfortably warm, she focused on the Veil. Now wasn't the time to get caught up in Lucan. This was work, not pleasure. No matter how enticing that stolen kiss near the excavation site had been, she didn't intend to revisit it. Even if Lucan had extended a peace offering with this dual sampling, Julian's words still rang true. Lucan hadn't shown interest in the other relics. He'd known about the Veronica ahead of time, and he'd done all he could to ensure her complete silence.

Regardless of his reasons, that made him untrustworthy. At least when it came down to letting him inside her life. Until she could guarantee he wouldn't turn into another Blake, those few priceless kisses were all she intended to give him.

Brave, firm words—if she could convince her body to cooperate. With him so near his long dark hair brushed against her arm, her resolve threatened to crack.

As she picked at the cloth's frayed corner, time moved in slow motion. Every excruciating second dragged on longer than the one before, until her hands began to shake. Instead of concentrating on the tiny muslin fibers, her mind replayed each stolen kiss in vivid detail. The way his dark lashes dusted over his cheeks as he closed his eyes. The rasp of his breath against her cheek.

Chloe resisted the urge to let out a frustrated protest and pursed her lips. Damn, she never should have let two years pass without taking a man to bed. Maybe if she had, she wouldn't be so caught up in all things sexual and she might actually accomplish something worthwhile.

A fiber broke free from the tight weave, offering her relief. One down, one to go. Careful not to touch the sample with her bare hand, she used the point of the knife to nudge it aside and try for a second strand.

Feigning interest in Chloe's hands became a chore more difficult than fashioning metal links into shirts of chain. Lucan cared not about the bits of muslin she picked free—he already knew what they would reveal. But for her sake, for the guise he must maintain, he dared not let his disinterest become obvious. He would have to explain that her brother's behavior had forced him to create the farce in her trailer. A truth he suspected she would not wish to hear. Nor one she would believe.

He would not have believed it. Had not when Enid's cousin, his best friend, had warned that Lucan's very brother looked too long on the woman Lucan was to wed. Lucan had believed in his older brother. Looked up to him as well. 'Twas understood Malfred would inherit their father's larger holdings at Wynnewood and he, as the second son, would take on the smaller Seacourt upon wedding Enid. Naught would have made Lucan believe Malfred would murder their entire family for the sake of a simple maid's heart.

Siblings were not born to hate. Like he, Chloe would defend Julian no matter the cause.

She shifted position to better pick at the veil, and her thigh rubbed against his. He nearly jerked away at the shock of energy that coursed up his spine. God's teeth, 'twas ridiculous the power she wielded over him. Everything about her made his conviction to court her properly an exercise in absurdity. 'Twould seem at every opportunity it could find, his body betrayed his mind. If he did not find a means of expelling this desire, he would soon lose all objectivity.

"There, I think I've got it." Chloe leaned away from the table. "One for you, one for me. Do you have some sampling envelopes?"

Lucan cleared his throat, recalling the reason they had gathered in his room. "Nay. I did not think to bring any."

"I think I have some in my bag." She laughed and shook her head. "Guess that says a lot for my life if I'm constantly carrying supplies around in case I happen across something, doesn't it?"

Aye, indeed it did. It said she concentrated on her work far more than social pleasures. Which left room for the interpretation she did not make it habit to entertain herself with men. A slow burn spread through him.

Lucan scowled at the misplaced thought. But before he could comment, she twisted and leaned over the arm of the couch, granting him the most spectacular view of her shapely bottom. He sucked in a sharp breath and fisted a hand against the cushions to keep from hauling her into his lap. Damnation, suggesting they work in his room had been a mistake of the worst kind.

To his immense relief she sank back into the couch, two small paper envelopes in hand. "When I was a student, one of the archaeologists I worked under in Egypt reamed me for not being prepared. Embarrassed me in front of the whole team. From that afternoon on, I've always had rudimentary things in my bag."

As she talked, she packaged the two long fibers. "I think that should be good enough for the lab. Washington's never needed anything more. There's almost four inches per strand—they should be able to cut and sample it with that." She licked each flap, then pressed them closed.

With that innocent act, Lucan's composure shattered. Her sweet flavor rushed into his memory with a landslide's force, dominating all thought. He spiraled backward in time, to the place where he was a man of the sword, life depended on the outcome of the next battle, and pleasure was taken where it could be found. Chloe had been promised to him. He to her. She shared the same desire that heated his blood. He read it in her eyes, tasted it on her tongue. This attempt at chivalry was no more than a flirtatious dance he could endure no longer. He would go mad if he must take another false sidestep.

"May I use your restroom?" She smoothed her hands down the tops of her legs as she stood.

"Aye," he answered hoarsely. Lucan watched her go, his body as tight as stone. He grabbed at all the reasons he should resist one last time, then tossed them aside. Demons or no demons, he hungered for her.

As she passed in front of his knees, her perfume tickled his nose. He closed his eyes on a pained grimace. Beneath the denim of his jeans, he felt his cock swell. Aye, mad indeed. Mayhap he had already left sanity behind. Never before had such an innocent fragrance affected him so completely.

'Twas only one way to cure the rampant insistence of his body. Surrender.

She exited the bathroom with a curious tilt of her head. "You're awfully quiet tonight. Anxious about the samples?"

"Nay." He caught her hand, stopping her from passing before him once more. With a slight tug, he turned her so he could capture the other as well. Lacing his fingers through hers, he leaned back into the couch and pulled her forward until she placed one knee on the cushion next to his.

"Lucan," she protested with a soft laugh. "I don't think this is a good idea."

He kept pressure on her hands, drawing her so close her breasts brushed against his chest. "Nay," he murmured. " 'Tis not a good idea." As she landed in his lap, he caught her mouth with his. " 'Tis a magnificent idea," he whispered against her lips.

He ignored the stiffening of her body and nudged her lips apart to slide his tongue against hers. Sweet. So damnably sweet. And Saints' blood, she was not fighting him. Nay, she returned the seeking thrusts with the same urgency that flowed in his veins. The tension fled her limbs. Her soft breasts molded against his chest. A low murmur of pleasure bubbled in the back of her throat.

Lucan released her fingers and settled his hands on her waist. But the heat that ebbed from her body warmed him overmuch. He ran his hands over the sloping curve of her hips, down the backs of her thighs, then over her buttocks. Tightening his fingers into the firm flesh there, he urged her closer. Drew her hips flush with his and positioned her atop his swollen erection.

She settled against him with a soft moan. Instinct

drove him to satisfy that feminine sound, and he lifted his hips to press against her sensitive center. White-hot fire shot through his veins. He drew in a shuddering breath, broke the kiss, and looked into her eyes. Desire burned bright beneath lowered lashes.

Wordlessly, Lucan slid one palm over her ribs and cupped her breast. The cotton of her shirt was soft, but the flesh beneath far softer. He held her gaze as he rolled his thumb over her hardened nipple. She arched into his hand with a whispered gasp. The sound ricocheted through his head, vibrated down his spine, and tightened the fingers he held against her waist. Slowly, he rocked against her. She moved in time with the roll of his hips.

For several long moments they did no more than move together. But as Lucan's blood began to boil, and the swelling of his shaft became painful, he leaned forward and fastened his mouth to hers. Their kiss was feral. Full of untamed need. He fisted his hands into her hair and became lost in the satin of her lips, the nip of her teeth, and the subtle undulation of their bodies.

Yet as pleasure dominated his thoughts, he slowly began to recognize her little murmurs of satisfaction took on a new tone. That of protest. The hands that had roamed across his chest now pushed for freedom.

"Stop," she whispered between the catch of their lips.

Regret swamped him. Along with a hefty dose of shame. He had breeched boundaries. Let things go too far. Damnation! Where had his self-control gone? He had fair attacked her. 'Twas no wonder she wished to escape.

With one more fleeting press of his mouth, he reluctantly released her. She flew out of his lap as if she were afire. Her hands raked nervously through her hair, and she grabbed for her coat. "I have to go. I can't do this."

"Chloe—"

"No." She gave him a vigorous shake of her head as she stuffed her sample into her pocket. "Don't say anything. I have to go."

With that, she fled. The door slammed in her wake.

Lucan dropped his head to the back of the couch with a frustrated oath.

Chloe double-timed it to the stairs, anxious to be as far away from Lucan Seacourt as possible. Though, in truth, she wasn't running from him. She ran from herself. The way she lost every bit of sense when he touched her. How she couldn't seem to keep her body from seeking its own desires. Lucan reduced her to a frightening version of the naive young girl who couldn't read a warning painted in red on a white wall. Nothing like the level-headed woman who knew the cold, cruel realities of life that she'd become.

He made her feel. Woke her up and drew her out of the blissful void she'd carefully constructed. Reminded her that beneath all her protective layers she was nothing more than a simple woman, capable of a woman's weaknesses, and starved for a tiny morsel of that fabled emotion called love. Desperate for a bit of human closeness.

And terribly lonely in her black-and-white world of artifacts, dirt, and research.

Her heart clanged against her ribs as she reached the stairs and began the climb to her room. She slowed to take a deep breath and gather her composure.

So lonely she'd risk entanglement with a man who posed the same risks as Blake. She couldn't do that again. *Wouldn't.* Only fools refused to learn from mistakes.

But Lucan differed from Blake in so many ways it made remembering that they stood at polar odds professionally difficult to do. Blake had never willingly shared his knowledge—the first red flag she should have noticed. He'd never offered to share anything for that matter. Everything centered on what *he* wanted, *his* goals, *his* dreams. If hers differed, he made no attempt at compromise.

Blake had never made her feel appreciated either. Sure, sex had been good, but not a single one of his kisses held the underlying suggestion of emotional abandon that every one of Lucan's held. She'd never felt truly *desired* until Lucan took her in his arms and showed her how a man could lose himself in pleasure. And the heat in his intense eyes told her he took pleasure in her. Not just any woman. *Her.*

He had been every bit an equal participant in that terrifying encounter as she had. Wanted her as fiercely as she wanted him.

At the third-floor landing, Chloe's shoulders sagged, and she shook her head. Lucan's too-obvious desire scared her more than the half-distracted attention Blake gave to intimacy. If he could ignore her a little better, she could do the same, then sex with an incredibly hot guy wouldn't seem so daunting.

She put her key in the door and pushed. If Lucan's kiss didn't demand everything from her, she might not be afraid to give in. The subtle insistence for more, however, awakened all the possibilities of what might happen to her when he returned to Rome.

Chloe tripped over a book and froze. Her belongings

lay scattered over the floor. The dresser drawers stood open, bits of clothing hanging over the edge. Books, papers—all her journals from Egypt—littered the rug like confetti. Lampshades hung at odd angles. Her bed sat cockeyed to the wall.

On a hard swallow, Chloe slowly turned to survey the mess. Who had broken in? Why? *How?* The door was locked. She had the only key.

Her gaze skimmed over the safe, and terror raced down her spine. Three jagged scars gouged the thick steel, shredding it like paper. She stepped closer, knowing what she'd find, but unable to stop from looking. Kneeling before the safe, she traced the torn metal. Her mind refused to accept what lay before her eyes. Impossible. She had to be imagining things.

But as Chloe tucked her shaking hand back into her lap, she choked down a silent sob. Only one thing could score into metal like that. Claws. Great horrific claws.

She bolted to her feet and raced out of her room.

CHAPTER 17

✠

Chloe didn't give a damn about the many times Julian had laughed at her fears. She ran as fast as her legs would carry her for the one person she trusted without question. Down the stairs to the second floor, around the corner to the end of the hall where she banged on his door like the devil himself was on her tail.

"Julian!" She drummed her fist again.

When silence answered, she dropped her forehead to the aged wood and let out a sob. The one time she needed him more than anything, and he was off chasing skirts. Damn it! She sagged against the door, defeated. Demons broke through her ward. Trashed her room. *Touched* her belongings.

Little particles of ice beat through her heart, sending shivers coursing down her spine. Rivulets of fear spread through her veins until her hands trembled violently and she couldn't stop the tears from breaking free. They wanted her. Wanted the Veil. And she was helpless to stop it.

"Oh God, Julian, where are you?" she cried in a plaintive whisper. Safety lay behind his door. An escape from the nightmare, even if it was an illusion that would only last until he fell asleep and she was left with the dark.

The presence settled around her, driving her away from the door. She glanced over her shoulder, half afraid she'd find the creature standing in the hall. She couldn't stay here. For the first time since they'd attached to her, the demons had breeched a physical barrier. Standing in the empty hall left her open for attack. And God only knew what they might do to her.

If he even cared.

She stumbled blindly down the stairs, heading to the only other place she could think of—to Lucan. She didn't have to tell him about the demons, but maybe he could keep her company for a bit. Stay while she put her room back together and talk long enough so she could shove this night into an untouchable corner of her mind.

Stopping at his door, she wiped away her tears and lifted her chin. No crying. Not in front of him. She knocked tentatively.

He opened the door before her knuckles left the wood. One look at the concern etched around his eyes, and she knew he recognized something was wrong. He didn't stop to ask. Instead, he wrapped his arms around her and backed through the door, holding her close.

To Chloe's shame, the dam she'd built to withhold her tears broke. Clutching at his strong shoulders, she buried her face against his chest and sobbed.

"Shh," Lucan soothed as he stroked Chloe's long hair. "What troubles you?" Her trembling was enough to unsettle the most seasoned warrior. She shook so violently, he thought for a moment she might crumble to ash. He tightened his embrace and tucked his head into the crook of her shoulder to stifle the tremors. "Easy, Chloe, I am here," he murmured into her hair.

"Someone . . . broke in . . ."

The rest of her words trailed off with the shake of her head, but he did not need to hear them. Fighting back a fierce rush of protectiveness, he sidestepped out of her tight hold and tucked his arm around her shoulders to better escort her to the couch. There, he eased her coat off and guided her to sit beside him. He wrapped her in a gentle embrace and welcomed the way she burrowed into his chest.

For several long minutes he did naught more than hold her close and stroke her back. Life had not exposed him to this aspect of intimacy, this role of silent strength he had been thrust into, yet he found it agreeable. 'Twas oddly satisfying to absorb her tears, still the shaking of her body, and say naught at all.

But as her trembles gave way to the faint twitch of exhausted slumber, he nudged her upright. "You cannot sleep yet," he apologized softly. "We must deal with your room. Sit, and I shall inform the desk to call the gendarme."

"No, that's not necessary." Her gaze darted to the window, and she twisted her hands in her lap. "They were after the relic, which they didn't find."

Lucan lifted an eyebrow. She should desire the police. In particular if she suspected someone wanted the Veil. That she hesitated brought his thoughts immediately back to the dark presence that hounded her. In an attempt to gain answers, he urged her toward the logical.

"You do not want the gendarmerie to document the break-in? What if you are missing something else?"

Chloe shook her head as she slipped completely from his arms. "No. If I involve the inspectors, the story will gain publicity. It'll give more people reason to suspect we're on to something significant in Ornes, and then I'll have to worry about security at the site and increasing the odds of another break-in." She ran her fingers through her hair and rubbed her arms to ward off a chill. "Just come back with me and help me clean up a bit?"

Decent logic, but not sound enough. She held some piece of information back. Something that would make it plain why she found the idea of the inspectors unimportant. He would play her game. Discover for himself.

Lucan reached for the phone. "I will ask Caradoc to meet us there. Lest you object?"

"No, that's fine. I'm not sure what he can do, but that's fine."

He punched in the number, waited for Caradoc to answer. "'Tis I. Chloe's room was vandalized. Meet us there?"

"By whom?"

"I do not know. She suspects they desired the Veronica. I am taking her up to inspect it now."

"Is she harmed?"

He looked to her, picked up her hand, and ran his thumb over the meaty part of her palm. "Scared. But safe." He gave her fingers a gentle squeeze.

She returned the gesture with a faint smile.

"Aye, I will be there momentarily." He clicked off without delay.

Lucan rose to his feet, pulling Chloe along with him. She moved at a slower pace, as if the night had finally sucked the last ounce of energy from her bones. Defeat touched the corners of her eyes. Because she had been violated? Or because she had been punished for failing to deliver the Veronica?

He gave himself a mental shake. 'Twas not the time to question. She needed his aid, not his suspicion.

When she reached once more for her coat, he pulled it out of her hands. "Leave it for now."

Like a puppet controlled by strings, she nodded. No argument. No hesitation. So very unlike the stubborn woman he had come to know. It pained him to see her so.

With an inward sigh, he acknowledged 'twas naught he could do to restore her usual brightness and picked up his sword, expecting her to comment on the weapon. She said naught, did not even seem to notice as he belted it around his waist. In truth, her very demeanor suggested her mind was somewhere else, far from this room and the prospect of returning to hers.

Clutching her hand, he led her from his room. She tensed the moment they entered the hall. Frowning, Lucan hesitated. "Would you wish to stay within and have me bring something down for you?"

She gave a slight shake of her head and took a step toward the stairs. "I'll be fine. Let's just get this over with. I'll feel better with my room picked up and everything in its place."

He did not speak another word until they met Caradoc at her partly open door. The presence of demons hung thick like a low fog on a deserted country lane. In the air, the faint scent of decay lingered. He met Caradoc's knowing gaze that communicated he too sensed Azazel's nearness.

Instinct bade Lucan to protect Chloe, and he ushered her behind his back where if something lurked within, she would be safe from attack. One hand on the hilt of his sword, he followed Caradoc inside.

A quick survey of the chamber told him no demons waited, and he dropped his hand, along with hers. Chloe knelt before the scattered papers on the white rug. Uncertain what to do or how to aid, Lucan crossed to the crooked bed and scooted it perpendicular to the wall.

"Are you missing anything, Chloe?" Caradoc asked as he poked his head inside her bathroom.

"I don't know. I don't think so." She let out a hard breath that stirred the hair gathered around her face. Then, as if witnessing the mess took too great a toll, her shoulders bowed and she hid her face in her hands.

Silently, Lucan knelt at her side to pick up where she had left off on her chore. How he ached to comfort her, but he had learned enough about Chloe to realize she would not want Caradoc to witness this weakness. Her pride would take a horrific blow. Instead, he lowered his voice to avoid drawing Caradoc's attention to her distress. "Sit on the couch. We will do this."

"No." Sighing, she dragged her hands down her face. "I'll be fine. There's just so much to do."

Caradoc crossed the room and righted a toppled lamp. "Why do you think they wanted the Veronica? Does anyone possess a key to your door? Or know you possess the relic?"

As Lucan passed Chloe the stack of papers he had gathered, the color drained from her face. "Look at the safe," she whispered.

He looked beyond her shoulder to the far corner where the steel box sat. In that instant, Lucan understood why she did not want the authorities involved. The jagged claw marks that gouged the three-inch-thick door explained the lingering stench. She could not possibly misconstrue them.

Caradoc, however, missed her reaction and addressed the situation as if she were an uninformed mortal. "A fine axe blow."

Chloe reared back. "Axe? I don't know what kind of axes you've been using lately, but the ones I've seen don't leave that behind."

Her remark sealed Lucan's observation—she did indeed know something unnatural put the marks in the safe. But the *why* refused to show itself. Why did she know—did she suspect from the nature of the scars, or did she witness Azazel's attack, or did she even possess the forewarning his strike would occur?

Was she in fact baiting them mayhap?

"Tell me what happened, Chloe," he demanded a bit more harshly than he intended.

She blinked as if she found the question absurd. "I came up here, let myself in, and this is what I found."

"Your door was not ajar?" Bent over the safe, Caradoc inspected the damage.

"No. It was locked. And no one has a key." More quietly she added, "There's no one to give a key to."

"Not Julian?" Lucan asked.

She let out a soft laugh. "Hardly. I love my brother, but I also love my space. If he had a key, he'd be hanging out every minute he's not chasing women."

Caradoc read Lucan's mind and went to the window to inspect it for entry. On finding naught of significance, he drew away from the drawn curtains. "They had to come through the door. Who knows about the relic?"

"Just the team and the three of you."

Lucan abruptly stood. If 'twas the Veronica they sought, they would continue the hunt. The team knew he had taken the relic from the site. Chloe could well be staging a diversion to purchase the time necessary to break into his room.

"Come. 'Tis naught we can do here tonight. We shall finish righting your room on the morrow." He reached his hand out for hers.

She stared at his palm as if he had suddenly grown three extra fingers. A glimpse of her spirit broke through. "I can't go with you. I want my bed, my belongings. I need to shower, I've got reports to write—there's no way."

Folding his arms over his chest, Lucan met her wide eyes with a severe frown. "Nay. You will not stay here tonight."

To his immense relief, Caradoc slipped outside leaving them to argue in private. The door clicked closed behind him. Still kneeling, Chloe mirrored Lucan's position. "I will stay here. This is *my* room. They won't come back. They already know there's nothing in here; I don't have what they want. Besides, what would everyone think if I came waltzing out of yours in the morning?" When she glanced up at him, her brave words were shadowed by the fear that shone in her eyes. Clearly she did not mean what she said, but her stubbornness eluded him.

Mayhap she feared the acceptance of his invitation more—after the way she had run out of his room, he would not be surprised. "It matters little what others should think. 'Tis unsafe for you to remain here. If you wish to change your room on the morrow, then I will aid you. But tonight you will stay with me."

Her eyes glittered bright. "That's very convenient for you, isn't it?"

A spark of anger lit, threatening to push him into full temper. He had not offered out of selfishness. Had not even fully considered she would be near to him beyond the immediate matter of her safety. Her insinuation affronted his honor, and slights to such had warranted death for many men.

Moreover, it added strength to his suspicion she argued not the idea of leaving her room, but staying with him. Ridiculous, when he could protect her better than any wall or locked door. Lucan reigned in his rising anger. "I will not argue this with you, Chloe. Lest you wish me to carry you from this room, you will gather your belongings and cease your protests."

Her eyes clashed with his, and he prepared himself to prove his words. Regardless of her involvement with the break-in, he would not jeopardize her safety by leaving her here unattended. And he could not leave his own room empty all night either. Although indeed, he could gather the relic and bring it here, and further camp himself upon her couch, he could not justify the unnecessary effort. He also suspected that if he were to leave, she would not allow him entrance again tonight.

But Chloe must have sensed his resolve, for as she glanced around her room, the anger fled from her expression. Though she did not look pleased with the prospect, and her words came as if they required great effort, she admitted, "I guess staying here would be rather stupid."

He refrained from comment, certain his affirmation would only reignite her ire. Instead, he picked up her pillow and shook it free from the case. He offered the soft white linen to her. "This will serve to hold your things. Tell me how I may help."

She pushed the pillowcase aside, refusing it as she rose to her feet. "I'll come back in the morning. I only need a couple of things."

He waited by the door whilst she went about collecting a small red satchel from the open nightstand drawer, a vinyl bag from the bathroom, and the most alluring short sleeping gown he had ever witnessed.

Just how close she would be through the night slammed into his consciousness. He was too large for the small couch in his room, which meant they would share his bed. And she would lie within arms' distance, dressed in that tantalizing bit of satin.

CHAPTER 18

✝

Chloe stood in Lucan's bathroom, staring at her reflection. Shyness wasn't typically part of her makeup. But faced with the prospect of walking into the room where Lucan waited, a man she'd known less than a week, dressed only in her nightgown, left her more than a little self-conscious. She needed a few more inches to the hemline, a little more height to the neck. Long sleeves would go a long way too, as opposed to straps that weren't much wider than a tank top's and twice as loose.

For that matter, she wished she'd abandoned the personal luxury of spoiling herself when it came to sleep and adopted the habit of long pants and T-shirts. She wouldn't feel so . . . obvious. Like she'd picked this gown because she was sharing his room, when in reality, this was the most modest one she owned.

Damn.

She took the towel to her hair one last time and squeezed out the long lengths. At least with wet hair she didn't create the picture of seduction.

Despite her awkwardness, she couldn't deny he'd been right, and her earlier argument still embarrassed her. Staying in her room would have been stupid. Between the break-in and the episode at the window, she couldn't delude herself any longer. She wasn't safe. Wouldn't be until she figured out how to get rid of the demons. Permanently.

She only hoped they'd stay away tonight. That Lucan's presence would somehow hold them off. His protection, the safety she felt when he was near, was the only reason she hadn't insisted on getting another room altogether.

With a deep, fortifying breath, she looked in the mirror at the back of the door. When she'd entered the shower, the sound of the television drifted through the barrier. Now, quiet reigned beyond. Maybe he'd fallen asleep. If he had, she could climb under the covers and ignore her current state of undress.

Asleep or not, she couldn't procrastinate any longer. Already, she'd hidden away for almost an hour. *You're here because it's not safe to be alone.*

With the reminder to herself, she turned around and opened the door on the darkened room. Her gaze jumped to the bed. When she found Lucan there, not asleep but reading a magazine beneath the dim light of his bedside lamp, her stomach rolled into a knot. Propped against the pillows, legs stretched beneath the covers, the sight of him stifled her ability to breathe. His bare chest held more strength than she'd ever imagined. Thick corded muscles spanned across smooth, broad shoulders. A thin line of dark hair dusted between defined pectorals, then trailed over tight abs to disappear beneath the down comforter. He looked up, sending his long hair tumbling over his shoulders, and his gaze locked with hers.

A strange, unexpected thrill tripped down her spine at the bright appreciation that gleamed in his eyes. He took her in from head to toe with one quick, roaming glance, and a smile pulled at the corners of his mouth. Tipping his head to the side, he indicated the night-stand against the empty side of the bed. "I made you a cup of tea. I thought it might help you relax."

Under other circumstances, it would. But with such a splendid specimen of male beauty in the bed beside her, she'd be lucky to even choke it down. The thoughtful gesture, however, set off a tightening in her chest. "Thank you," she murmured.

With courage she didn't feel, she approached the bed, turned down the covers, and slid beneath. When she pulled the comforter up to her belly, she breathed a little easier. But as she reached for the steaming mug, she caught sight of her red bag on the coffee table several feet away. No way could she attempt sleep with it out of reach. The minute the lights went out she'd never be able to find it.

Annoyed with her forgetfulness, she tossed the covers aside and retrieved the tiny sack. Setting it on the table, she returned to the bed, tea in hand.

Her skin prickled with the heavy weight of Lucan's gaze. She drank from her mug, desperate to ignore the enticing scent of spice that wafted off his skin. Try as she might, however, he was simply too close to ignore. If she bent her knee, she'd touch his thigh. If she reached to adjust her pillow, her elbow would graze his thick bicep. Too much for her already strained senses.

Lucan tossed his magazine aside and scooted deeper beneath the covers. Twisting onto his side, he propped his head in his hand. "If you require sugar—"

"No, no. This is perfect." She took another drink to stop her hand from falling atop his where it rested between them.

He gave her another grin before he rolled onto his back and folded his arms beneath his head. "You are still angry with me?"

She couldn't help but laugh. "Why would you think that? I'm here, aren't I?"

"You are quiet. Your smile has disappeared."

A wave of warmth slid over her skin. He noticed the smallest things. Little things no one else would ever observe. He paid attention, more so than any man she'd ever known, including her brother, who prided himself on his ability to relate to women. "No," she answered quietly. "I'm not angry with you. It's just been a long day."

Like so many others.

Chloe set her mug aside, the last of her emotional energy having drained from her body. Escape lay in the man beside her. Freedom from the night, the demons, and the confusing collision of thoughts inside her head. She slid onto her side and tucked a hand beneath her cheek, facing him. As if he waited for her signal, he turned off the light. Darkness engulfed them, brightened only by the faint shine of the moon behind his tightly drawn curtains.

She took a deep breath and swallowed down a moment of awkwardness. "I'm sorry for arguing with you in my room. Thank you for letting me stay here."

He rolled over, his expression soft. Dropping his arm between their bodies, he covered the back of her hand with his palm. "Rest," he whispered. "You are safe with me."

What she would give for that to be true. If only he could fulfill that promise. She'd trade the rest of her lifetime for one full, uninterrupted night of sleep. For dreams that didn't wake her with nameless, faceless ghouls. If Lucan could take all those nightmares away, she'd never again question his intentions. Even if he vanished with morning's light, she'd treasure him for a lifetime.

Yet as the all-too-familiar tap-tapping began against the window pane, Chloe knew even this magnificent man couldn't chase away the creatures of the night.

He could, however, make her forget for a little while.

She brushed her fingertips over his soft mouth. His lips caught the pad of her index finger in a gentle kiss. He caressed it with the tip of his tongue.

A pleasant ache stirred in her womb, and Chloe shivered. With a smile, she ran her hand over his shoulder. He brought his to her hair and pushed the damp locks away from her face. His fingers settled against the back of her head. His gaze held hers, full of silent meaning.

They came together slowly, the touch of their lips soft and fleeting. The twining of their tongues languorous. Chloe didn't know who moved first, who shifted closer to the other, but the shock of Lucan's body molding against hers freed a pleasant gasp. He took advantage of the parting of her lips and deepened their kiss.

Warmth flooded through her. This was heaven. The insistence of his mouth, the firm but gentle way he bent her to his will. She ran her fingers along the length of his spine, savoring the feel of hard muscle and smooth, hot skin. Paradise.

The covers rustled as Lucan lifted to his elbow. A nudge of his mouth asked her to turn her head, and she yielded to his silent request. His lips scored along the side of her neck, sending goose bumps coursing down her arms. She shivered in the wake of delightful sensation and let out a soft murmur of pleasure.

"I like you here," he whispered against her collarbone. His teeth nipped, the flick of his tongue soothed. "In my bed. Overmuch."

"Overmuch?" she asked. "How can you like it too much?" Seeking to return the pleasure he gave to her, she rained kisses across the shoulder that supported his weight. Heaven above, his skin was just as warm beneath her mouth as it had been beneath her fingertips.

Lucan skated his hand down her exposed arm to her fingertips before dipping beneath the covers. His palm scraped over the flimsy satin of her gown, rising higher, over her abdomen, along her ribs. He cupped her breast in his palm and rubbed his thumb over her nipple. "Because," he answered hoarsely. He caught her lower lip between his, suckled, then eased away to look into her eyes. As he spoke, his fingers massaged her breast. "Your nearness plagues me with thoughts of all I wish to do to you."

God help her, the visual that surfaced with that raw confession was so sinfully erotic she couldn't hold in a low moan. She arched her back, pressing her breast more fully into his palm, and slipped her thigh between his. "Tell me," she whispered.

With a twist of his hips, he leveraged his weight and guided her onto her back. "Nay," he murmured against her mouth. Before she could catch and hold his kiss, his lips danced down her throat. Lower until his warm breath feathered across the swell of her breast. He traced a solitary finger over the low fabric of her gown, then pushed it aside. "I would rather show you." The tip of his tongue swirled around her exposed nipple. Slowly, he drew it into his mouth.

Chloe fastened her fingers into his hair and closed her eyes. Possessed by unexpected bliss, she bit down on her lower lip and pressed his head closer. Her womb contracted under the pull of his mouth. When he took her nipple between his teeth and gave it a tiny twist, she nearly came off the mattress. Moisture gathered between her legs, and she lifted her hips, desperate to feel more of him. All of him.

"Lucan," she murmured.

He released her nipple to whisper, "Aye?"

Before Chloe could find coherent words, he pulled down the fabric covering her opposite breast and treated it to the same excruciating caresses. She writhed against his body. He sank his hips into hers, pressed her into the mattress, and used his weight to hold her in place. Beneath cotton pants, the hard ridge of his erection nestled against her aching center, full of promise, yet an unbearable torment.

She scattered urgent kisses across his shoulder and clutched at his waist. "Take me away from all this," she whispered. "Make me forget, Lucan. Take today away."

The fire that blistered through Lucan's veins ebbed at her impassioned response. His body screamed against the effort of controlling himself, and he let her nipple slide from his mouth. She sought escape. Not a joining of their bodies and minds. A temporary relief.

Something he was not willing to share, no matter

how fiercely he craved her sweet feminine warmth. He wanted *her*. Not a mere physical release. He had experienced many of those, but never the full union between man and woman that came with the blending of far more than bodies. Deep down in an untouched portion of his soul, he knew she possessed the ability to bring him there. To draw from him not just his sterile seed, but something greater than he had given any woman. And he ached to surrender it to Chloe.

His body, however, was not so willing to cease as his mind. His hips sank hard into hers. His cock strained against the thin barrier of his sleeping pants. The feel of her feminine heat sent another shock of desire scalding through him. 'Twould be so easy to cast aside the foolish quest for a greater fulfillment, nudge their clothing aside, and thrust himself inside her, claiming what she offered.

He tempered the severe urge with a grimace. *Nay.* Ecstasy was not his to claim. Not this night.

Beneath him, Chloe squirmed. Eyes closed, she turned her head side to side. Her teeth pricked the soft fullness of her lower lip. Against the small of his back, the firm press of fingertips urged him to move. To ease the ache she shared.

That, he could do.

"I cannot be your escape, Chloe." Lowering his mouth to hers, he eased his weight off her body and stretched out along her side. "But I can give you what you desire." He gathered the hem of her thin gown in his hand and slid the material to her waist. His palm curved over the slope of her hip, cupped the weighty firmness of her bottom as she lifted her leg to set a foot on the mattress.

It required every bit of self-control he could summon,

and some he did not realize he possessed, to ignore the scrape of her nails across his chest. The seeking nature of her fingers as she fanned them over his abdomen. Then lower, until she caressed his swollen length. But before she could rob him of thought and free the willfulness of his body, he slipped his fingers beneath the thin band of her panties and eased them between her legs.

Chloe arched into his hand with a low moan. Her thighs fell apart, inviting his caress. Lucan ground his teeth together, determined to resist the silken promise of her damp inner folds, and stroked her hard feminine bud. He subtly eased his body away from her questing fingers.

"Please," Chloe whispered as she broke their kiss. "Let me touch you."

In the slight darkness, her gaze held his. He did not need the light to see the rich intensity of her amber eyes. He saw them each time he closed his own. Knew every burnished fleck of gold. He did not answer her breathless request. Instead, he dropped his mouth to the delicate hollow of her throat and eased one finger inside her slickened opening.

Chloe's nails dug into his shoulders as a gasp tore from her throat. Lucan withdrew, to slowly enter her again. Lacking the courage to witness her release wash across her expression, he closed his eyes and listened to the rasp of her breath. The soft mewl of pleasure that tumbled off her lips. Around his finger, her inner muscles contracted hard. He thrust once more, and Chloe came to a swift, fierce release. Her moist flesh pulsed around him, her hips bucked against his palm. From the recesses of her throat, a soft cry ripped free.

The sound shot down his spine, and his cock swelled

in answer. He dragged in a sharp breath, holding it as his body threatened to follow hers. God's blood, he was no saint, and the naive pursuit of something he quite possibly imagined seemed a quest of the most ridiculous kind. 'Twas a fool's endeavor. He would find less misery if he yielded to raw desire.

But Chloe's body relaxed, and the stinging pressure of her nails eased. She sank into the mattress with a soft sigh. The determination to deny his own needs became easier as he eased his hand from between her legs and wound his arm around her. Gathering her as close as he dared, he dusted a light kiss over her creamy shoulder. Through a tightened throat he whispered hoarsely, "Rest, my sweet."

She nestled close and tucked her cheek against his chest. "That doesn't seem fair."

His chuckle helped to ease the tightness of his lungs, and he allowed himself a faint smile. "My day has not been as exhausting." Giving her bottom a gentle squeeze he urged in a stronger voice, "Go to sleep. I will be here when you wake."

Trapped and helpless, Julian watched through the demon's eyes as it let itself into his room. The horror of what had occurred in Chloe's room brought the danger home. Those claws that could so easily shred metal would rip her into bits. The anger that fueled an onslaught onto her belongings could bring a hundred men to their knees. Powerless to stop the beast, Julian could do no more than shout protests that went unheard.

His weakening strength forbade him the ability to do anything the creature didn't insist upon. It grew in strength each day, its horrific spirit rapidly overtaking what they had allowed of Julian's to remain. Soon, he would watch his sister's suffering if he didn't find a way to escape before the beast captured her.

Julian didn't delude himself with thoughts of returning to save Chloe. His broken, battered body lay in a useless heap deep within the earth. It would never harbor his soul again. No, escape came with total surrender. Leave the demon to survive on its own, or fail. Whichever fate chose, he would yield and retreat once Chloe's fate no longer lay in question.

If the demon didn't overpower him first.

A figure in the corner near his bed stepped out of the shadows. Dressed in a long dark robe with a deep crimson cross across the front, he bowed his dark head with a touch of respect. "Julian."

The demon thrust Julian forth like a rock hurled off a cliff, forcing him to confront the stranger. A greater torture than merely observing. For although he'd be allowed to act, to speak, as soon as the stranger departed, the beast would cast Julian in chains, forcing him to bear witness as it drew on his thoughts and mimicked all the things that made him human.

"Yes?" Julian's voice echoed eerily in his head. It wasn't his own. Close, but all the same, nothing like his natural timbre.

"I am Eadgar, servant of Leofric, follower of the Kerzu's noble ways."

The Kerzu—Julian searched for an explanation to the familiar name. He knew it. Yet so many days rushed together that what happened hours before became difficult to remember. All he saw clearly anymore were the things that related to Chloe and the horrors. The vile, despicable horrors the demon reveled in. Each needless death gave it strength. The blood it bathed in when the château slept increased its determination. Things Julian had contributed to. Words that came from his mind, which the demon used on women to lure them into the dark.

The demon squeezed around his thoughts, forcing him to focus on the stranger. "What can I do for you?"

"I bear an important message. Leofric is aware of the relic. He bade me come and tell you 'tis of greater consequence than any other matter. You must reach it and claim it at all costs."

Risking the wrath of his controller, Julian shook his head. "My sister holds the relic. I'll see you get it, but I won't risk her safety."

Dark eyes glittered like shards of onyx. The lines of age around Eadgar's face deepened. "The woman is unimportant! She means naught. You must understand that mankind shall suffer if we fail. One woman is not worth the sacrifice of thousands."

"She's my *sister.*"

Eadgar lifted his hand in a dismissive wag of fingers. "She is not a seraph. She holds no purpose beyond uncovering the Veil. If she were indeed marked with the blood of angels, 'twould be a different matter entirely. For then she would become necessary." He narrowed his gaze. His voice took on a darker menace. "But she is not. And if you must kill her to fulfill the returning of the Veil, you will do so."

At the suggestion, the demon's unholy might enveloped Julian. It tugged at him, drawing him deeper into the recesses of evil, pulling him away until he snatched at the tattered threads of his humanity just to hold on to awareness a moment longer.

"I won't kill her," he protested feebly.

The man turned to the window, presenting Julian his back. "In battle, sometimes it becomes necessary for innocents to die." He looked over his shoulder, his expression laden with warning. Before Julian's eyes, weathered features softened. Youth smoothed the wrinkles of time, and beauty crept in to replace the scars along his hands. Where a middle-aged man had stood seconds before, a more robust, more attractive version took his place.

In that moment, Julian recognized the same surge of despicable power that surrounded him also radiated off the form near the foot of his bed. He opened his mouth to rage against the opposing beast, to condemn it in all the ways he could not condemn the creature that controlled his mind.

But the thing that mastered him shoved him aside, forbidding him the ability to voice a single thought.

Eadgar's voice rang with the same hollow emptiness Julian recognized as evil. "Should you find yourself unable to acquire the Veil, I will be more than happy to bend the woman to my wishes and see the task completed."

"It will be done," he heard his own voice answer.

CHAPTER 19

C hloe woke with a start. Lifting her head from the pillow, she leaned on her elbows and blinked at the dull gray light beyond dark green curtains she didn't recognize. She'd slept through the night. Unbelievable.

Momentarily disoriented, she looked over her shoulder at the sound of running water in the bathroom. In a blink, the previous day sifted through the fog of her memory to form a clear picture of her disastrous room and one humiliating attempt at seduction that ended with her release and Lucan seemingly unwilling to go through with anything further.

Ugh—what had she been thinking? No wonder he was up at the crack of dawn and in the shower. He'd offered her a place to sleep, and she'd turned a sweet gesture into something completely uncomfortable.

She scrambled out of bed and snatched yesterday's jeans off the couch. Stuffing her legs inside as quickly as she could, she sought to avoid the sudden stop of running water. As something metal clinked against the sink, she pulled off her nightgown and tugged on her shirt. When he exited, she'd be ready to leave. Ten minutes in her room, long enough to change her clothes since she'd showered last night, and she could flee to the site. Far away from the evidence of how she'd let things go too far and hadn't been thinking straight.

But damn, for a few minutes, she *had* forgotten everything. And oh, how she'd forgotten how pleasant a man's touch could be.

Heat infused her cheeks as she remembered all the rest of the embarrassing details. The pleading quality of her words. His quiet refusal. His deliberate caresses meant to satisfy her lust and nothing more. Like he honestly believed she *needed* an orgasm.

Chloe snorted to herself. She damn sure didn't need Lucan taking pity on her sexually starved body. She'd gone a long time. Longer wouldn't kill her.

The door opened to the bathroom, and Lucan stopped, one foot in the room. Though he'd donned jeans, he had yet to cover his magnificent chest with a shirt. Head tilted, he rubbed a towel through his long hair. Surprise passed across his face, as if he'd expected to find her still asleep. "I did not hear you rise. Would you like me to send for some coffee?"

No, she didn't want any more of his sympathetic consideration. "I'll wait till we go to the lobby. I want to go up to my room and change. And today I need to get to cataloguing Andy's pictures and get this sample sent to the lab in D.C. The team needs to continue with the excavation."

"Aye. I will take you upstairs in a moment."

Chloe picked up her coat and moved to the door. "That's not necessary. I'll be fine, it's daylight."

"Chloe."

The sharpness of his voice made it evident he wouldn't accept her objections. As he hadn't the night before. With a heavy sigh she dropped her hand. "What?" she snapped.

"Give me a moment to put on my boots, and I shall be ready."

Glancing over her shoulder, she observed he'd already put on a dark gray-blue pullover. In less time than it would have taken her to slide into her coat, he had his boots on and his jacket over his arm. He pushed open the door, held it while she exited.

The walk to her room seemed never-ending, the silence that spanned between them, intolerable. Her mind wouldn't let go of the uncomfortable turn of events the night before, and striking casual conversation didn't fit. Yet beneath all the awkward glances they shared, a deeper intimacy flowed that Chloe couldn't hope to ignore. She'd let him through the barriers, even if he hadn't reciprocated. Allowed him to cross that oppressive boundary of professional associate. He'd brought her to passion she hadn't experienced in so long she'd begun to forget the meaning of the word, and in the mere act of sleeping beside him, shared an indescribable closeness.

Deep within her, Chloe couldn't deny satisfaction thrummed. If she hadn't blundered everything, she might have allowed herself to enjoy the weighty feeling in her limbs. The lack of grit in her eyes that spoke of a full night's rest. She *had* found escape in Lucan, even if it differed than what she'd intended. For that alone, she owed him her gratitude.

At her door, she inserted the key quickly and hurried inside. "I'll just be a minute." Stepping over the clutter, she made her way to the bathroom and locked herself within. With Lucan out of sight, she leaned against the door frame and blew out a hard breath. Eight hours, she must face his nearness. A full day of working beside him—these few moments of solitude she intended to treasure.

Lucan sat on the arm of the couch and drew his first deep breath of the day. It helped a little to relax the tightness in his limbs—tension that had grown roots since he awakened to find Chloe tangled around him. He found he rather enjoyed sharing his bed with her. She did not distance herself in sleep, did not steal the covers, and she did not snore like a man. Nay, indeed, she slumbered as if she found equal contentment with his presence.

Although, whilst he took pleasure in the way she wound her legs through his and laid her head atop his chest, waking to such an innocent display of trust made it more difficult to recall why he had ceased their love play during the night. He was so stiff and sore he felt as if he had been thrust back to the days of battle amidst the desert sands. She may have found rest. He, however, had not.

A furious banging on her door brought a concerned frown to his face. He glanced at the bathroom to see if she would answer the beckoning. When the door remained firmly shut, Lucan went to answer the knock. He cracked open the door to find Julian on the opposite side.

Julian flattened a palm against the wood and barged inside before Lucan could offer a greeting. His eyes darted wildly around the room. "Where's the relic?"

The hair at the nape of Lucan's neck lifted. No word

of concern about his sister? No comment on the state of disarray surrounding him? He arched a mistrusting eyebrow. "'Tis safe."

Agitation flicked across Julian's expression. He passed a hand through his short hair and walked a tight circle. He stopped in front of Lucan. "What are the plans for it? Are we working with it in the field? I want to see the cloth again."

Though Lucan knew Chloe had no intention of taking the relic to the trailer, he did not trust Julian's overeager questions. He resumed his seat on the couch's arm and folded his arms across his chest. "I am not certain what Chloe intends to do with the relic, or the cloth inside."

The younger man whirled around and thrust an accusing finger at Lucan's chest. "You control what happens to the relic. Insist she bring it to the site. I must see the cloth. Today."

"Julian," Chloe scolded as she opened the bathroom door. "Would you knock it off? We'll handle the artifacts as usual. It's safe right now, and today we're going to document all the things we should have yesterday."

Julian stalked to where she stood by the dresser. "What about the cloth? We haven't done anything with it, other than take a couple pictures and unfold it. We need it present so we can document it appropriately too."

With every anxious word Julian uttered, Lucan's suspicions deepened. Excitement he could understand. To an uninformed archaeologist, the find was impressive. Rather like discovering an unopened sarcophagus hidden beneath Egypt's sands. But Julian's rapid-fire questions and veiled demands did not align with mere excitement. The urgency in his voice held a note of desperation. Like a guilty man, condemned to die, who pleaded for his family to be spared the same punishment.

"Chloe, please." Julian grabbed her shoulders and brought his face even with hers. "I *must* see the Veil again."

At that moment, Lucan realized Julian knew more than he let on. Lest Chloe had explained—and she had sworn she told no one—no one on her team knew they handled Veronica's Veil. But Julian had just referred to it specifically. Had Chloe lied? Did Julian know the same secrets she did?

"Julian, really, this is getting stale." Chloe picked up her coat and crossed to the door. "You know policy and procedure inside and out. Why would I deviate from it this time?"

"Because I'm your brother and this is our endeavor. We can change the rules now and then."

Chloe affected a sugary-sweet smile. "You are my brother, and I love you dearly, but we're not bending ethics on a whim." She looked over Julian's shoulder and lifted her eyebrows at Lucan. "Are you coming?"

As Lucan took a step forward, Julian's attention snapped to him. His gaze narrowed to a thin slit of light. Misplaced fury colored his expression with shades of red. He swung around and pointed an accusing finger at Chloe. "You've let him cloud your mind. You slept with him, and now you've become his pawn. Another person to do the Church's bidding. I can't believe you, Chloe—when are you going to learn a pretty face doesn't equal sincerity?"

At the sully to Chloe's honor, Lucan's spirit revolted. The fierce urge to stalk across the room and grab her brother by the throat possessed him. The way Chloe's eyes widened with hurt and disbelief made Lucan want to squeeze until Julian choked on his own tongue.

Though both urges sorely tempted, he did neither. He would converse with Julian privately, where the choice words he had to spew would not offend Chloe's sense of loyalty. With all the obstacles they had yet to overcome, he did not intend to throw more barriers between them by engaging her brother in the fight he requested.

Clamping a tight fist against his thigh, Lucan called on his self-control and held Chloe's gaze in silent support. "Shall I drive?"

"That's it!" Julian cried. "You have the relic, don't you? Chloe turned it over to you after you fed her full of lies."

Lucan cut a sideways glance to Julian. Another word and all the mountains between him and Chloe would not matter. He would strangle the man. Gladly.

She rescued her brother before Lucan could utter a single word.

"Let's go, Lucan, we have a lot of work to do." With a nod to her brother, she added, "It's time to leave my room."

On a furious hiss, Julian stormed into the hall. In his wrathful wake, Chloe visibly wilted. Her shoulders sagged, and the angry glint behind her gaze assumed the same inappropriate dullness of defeat she had borne the night before. Lucan placed his arm about her shoulders.

She wriggled out from beneath his attempt at comfort. Her voice hardened. "Let's go. It's not the first time we've argued. It won't be the last."

But the flash of shock Lucan had witnessed pass

across her face marked her words as bravado. They might have argued, but Julian crossed a line even Lucan could see. Chloe, however, determined to ignore it. As would he. He opened the door, held it while she ducked under his arm.

After mailing their samples at the front desk, Chloe hesitated near the doors.

"Is something amiss?" Lucan glanced around the wide foyer.

"Just . . ." She gave him an unsteady smile. "I'll meet you in the car. I need a minute." She backed away, turned toward the main floor bathroom.

Lucan left her to her business and ventured outside to start the vehicle. He warmed his hands before the heating vents, glanced in the rearview mirror. Disquiet stirred, misplaced worry he knew he should not feel but could not suffocate no matter how he tried.

She should have returned by now.

He reached for the door handle. As he pulled, the passenger door opened. Chloe ducked inside, bearing two paper coffee mugs. She offered him one.

Lucan blinked, first at the cup, then at her. After her earlier hurry to escape his presence, he had not anticipated such a kindness. He took the cup from her, all too aware of the spark that darted up his arm when their fingertips brushed. "Thank you," he murmured.

Her shy smile tugged at his heart. She looked away, fastened herself in, and drank from her cup. He did the same. To his surprise, sweetness met his tongue. Two sugars—she had remembered from their shared breakfast.

Lucan's heart rolled over. He could not have recalled

so precisely how she took her coffee, and yet she had paid attention. To him. To something as insignificant as two teaspoons of sugar.

He did not know what to do with that discovery.

Silence descended uncomfortably upon them as he drove. Lucan considered the possible reasons for Chloe's unspoken support of her brother's unacceptable behavior. He could not convince himself she had not heard the venom in Julian's accusations. Nor could he convince himself that she ignored it out of unconditional love. They shared secrets, 'twas plain to see. 'Twould be reasonable they shared confidences about their plans for the Veil as well. Only now, as Lucan compared her behavior with Julian's, he began to question who held the deeper, darker role. Chloe had yet to show the same aggressiveness about the relic. She did not make demands. Julian, on the other hand, was fair manic.

Lucan pulled into the parking area, his nerves more strained than they had been on waking. The pieces of this puzzle eluded him. Each time one came close to locking into place, it lacked the necessary contours. All he knew for certain was Azazel's presence lurked here. Somehow, the Broussards fit into the unholy design. And no matter how he tried, he could not be certain of Chloe's precise role.

She jumped out of the vehicle before he could fully open his door, but she slowed on the path to the office trailer when Caradoc bid her good morn. Lucan could not hear her words, yet the quizzical crinkling of her brow, combined with the thoughtful way Caradoc shook his head, told Lucan theirs was more than a simple exchange. He reached the pair in time to hear Caradoc apologize.

"I am sorry I cannot be of greater assistance."

The spray of gravel beneath tires drew their combined attention to the drive. Julian pulled in recklessly and slid to a halt beside the Templar SUV. He bolted out of the car and slammed the door. "Chloe!"

"Oh, for the love of God," she mumbled beneath her breath. Straightening her shoulders, she turned away from the trailer and hurried to join her brother.

Lucan's gaze remained on brother and sister, but he addressed Caradoc. "What did she ask you?"

"'Twas most strange. She wished to know if I knew of a spiritualist in Verdun."

A spiritualist? When she had two men who represented the Church on hand? Lucan frowned. It did not make sense. *She* did not make sense.

"When will Gareth return?"

"Tomorrow eve. Why do you ask?"

As Julian and Chloe approached, Lucan lowered his voice. "'Tis Julian. He behaves most odd."

A note of interest crept into Caradoc's voice. "Most odd how?"

Lucan's frown deepened into a tight scowl. In a hushed murmur he answered, "He reminds me of my brother."

Several seconds of silence passed between them. Caradoc knew the tale of patricide. He did not need Lucan to further explain—another reason the bonds of brotherhood tied them so closely together. They knew much about each other, as all the men who once served exclusively under Merrick did. That he did not need to offer more details comforted Lucan. A silence he would not exchange for anything.

Chloe and Julian passed them by, their heads bowed together in hushed whispers. At the steps to the trailer's door, Chloe threw her hands into the air, and Julian abruptly pivoted the opposite direction. He threw a glare at both Lucan and Caradoc as he stalked down the path toward the excavation site.

Lucan stiffened at the display, his mind automatically leaping to unfair conclusions. He shook his head, annoyed with his inability to objectively view his seraph and let out a sigh. "Be certain you pay Julian heed. I trust him no further than I can see him. And that is stretching my faith a great deal more generously than I care to admit. I suspect he plans to thwart our purpose here."

"Aye. I have wondered such myself."

CHAPTER 20

✝

C hloe stormed inside the trailer and hurled herself into her desk chair. Not only did Julian's insistence on working directly with the Veil push her to the ends of her patience, the mutterings she'd overheard between Lucan and Caradoc sent her plummeting over the edge. Thwart their purpose—how could Julian thwart their attempt to document and oversee the handling of any relics rightfully belonging to the Vatican?

Unless, as Julian claimed, Lucan had only told her enough information to gain her favor so he could follow through on something radically different. Maybe all his kindness *was* just an act. Lord knew she hadn't been able to see the real Blake until it was too late. Maybe, like her brother had insultingly pointed out, she'd let Lucan's pretty face sway her good judgment.

She let out a snort and dropped her head into her hands. No maybe about it—she *had* let him sway her good judgment. Nothing else could explain her wanton behavior last night. He'd drawn her in, and she'd been the fool to fall for sweet words and kind gestures.

Damn it, she didn't have time for this kind of distraction. With such a short time to complete her excavation, she needed to focus on artifacts. On sifting dirt and washing fragments of pottery, and analyzing the craftsmanship on the rocks to establish a concrete time reference. Not worry about men and what a kiss meant or didn't mean.

Dragging her hands down her face, she let out a heavy sigh. No time like the present to redirect her focus. She smacked the space bar on her laptop to bring it out of sleep mode. Her spreadsheet of relics, locations, and possible references faded into view. Along with it, a folder that contained Andy's photos popped open. She clicked on the first photograph, that of the reliquary half embedded in the frozen ground, and tossed open her notebook to enter the description of their findings.

As she set her pen to paper, the door opened. Lucan entered, giving her a polite nod as he took a seat in the chair directly behind her. Her heart jumped at the subtle fragrance of spice that accompanied his appearance.

Damn. It would be that much more difficult keeping her focus on work. For one full day she needed him out of her sight. Preferably near the excavation area, where he could bother everyone else with his overseeing and micromanaging.

To escape his nearness, she fled her chair and rummaged through the box of smaller discoveries on the distant countertop.

"Is there anything I can aid you with?" he asked quietly.

Chloe closed a fist around a man's heavy silver ring set with a large ruby. "I think you've done enough." She set the piece down and stuffed her hand back inside to fish for the dagger she remembered discovering.

A shadow fell over the countertop at her right. She stiffened, Lucan's unexpected presence fraying her nerves. Good grief, couldn't he take a hint? She didn't want him around. Not today. Not until she could control the way her body stood up and took notice each time he came within five feet of her.

"Chloe, I have done naught to deserve your anger. Can we not put this, whatever it is, aside and work together?"

She glanced up as the door opened again, and Julian marched back inside. He threw a glare her way, reminding her once again of his insinuations and beliefs about Lucan. They'd agreed he would keep his mouth shut in front of Lucan, but she didn't care to push his temper—it was already as out of sorts as hers. When his snapped, he didn't know the meaning of restraint. Judging by the way Lucan stiffened with Julian's arrival, it wouldn't take much to bring the both of them to blows. Not that she could blame Lucan—Julian crossed a line of unprofessionalism, not to mention basic respect. Frankly, he deserved a good fist to the jaw. Problem was, while Julian was by no means weak, Lucan's presence radiated experience. No doubt, he'd been involved in more than one fistfight, and she doubted he'd been on the losing end.

She lowered her voice to prevent Julian from overhearing. "Just go away." Gathering an armful of odds and ends, she crossed to the empty table at the front of the trailer and spread her collection across the plywood surface. Tension crackled in the air, every ounce of it directed at Lucan. Her brother's heavy stare dared him to make one wrong step so he could have the outlet he wanted for his frustrations, adding to the undercurrent between Lucan and herself.

Unable to look at either man, she stared unseeing at the metal trinkets and broken pottery fragments beneath her hands. Both wanted her loyalty, and for the life of her, she didn't know what to do, or whom to choose. She longed to believe Lucan wasn't capable of the deceit Julian claimed, but years of having no one but her brother to rely on prevented her from swearing off his protective instincts.

Add into the mix her humiliation about her own behavior, and all she ached to do was find the nearest hole she could crawl into and escape this mess.

"Chloe—"

She cut Lucan off with a sharp glower. "Just go. I'd like to work alone."

Lucan stared at Chloe's rigid shoulders, sensing that if he pushed her further she would unleash that anger on him. Yet he could not logic this abrupt change in her demeanor. Clearly he had upset her. How, he did not know. But whilst he would do naught to directly contribute to the obstacles already between them, he would not allow her ire to fester. He frowned at the back of her head. "We are all part of the same team now, Chloe. There is no need for this."

"Right. Sure we are." She snatched a notebook off the row of shelves behind her and jerked it open. Bending over the table, she picked up a small bronze cup.

Aware they had an audience, Lucan ground his teeth

together. He dared not mention the agreement they had struck regarding the Veronica in front of Julian. But he would not accept her insinuation their purposes differed. "What would make you think otherwise?"

"Oh, I don't know, maybe the way you've imposed your will every time I've turned around." She shrugged her shoulders, her voice becoming harsher. "Maybe the way you've taken control of my site and refused to let me make the decisions regarding the relics my team has uncovered." Turning, she met his frown with bitter accusation, and the meaning behind her words took a more intimate turn. "Maybe it has something to do with finding me at my weakest and then taking complete advantage of my vulnerabilities. Using pretty words to get me where you wanted me. You know—in your bed. Seems to me that's awfully one-sided."

He drew in a sharp breath to stifle the flaring of his temper. She believed he had manipulated her into his bed? God's teeth! 'Twas *he* who had stopped the physical act. If he had intended what she suggested, he would have stripped away her clothes and allowed his body the freedom it desired.

Infuriated by her unwarranted attack on his honor, he strode across the room, grabbed her elbow, and spun her about. All thoughts of Julian forgotten, he stared hard into her eyes. "Two of us were present, Chloe. As I recall 'twas you who put your lips to mine first, and I who put things to a stop."

Color flooded into her cheeks. Her eyes flashed like brittle pieces of glass. She jerked on her elbow, but Lucan held fast, denying her escape. She would confess to her own actions. He refused to become her scapegoat, to bear the burden of her choices and allow her to brand him as anything less than honorable. He gave her arm a jerk. "Do you think 'twas easy to say no? If I were so selfish in my pursuits, do you believe you would have slept the night through? That I would not have satisfied my hunger for you at your first offering?"

The crimson in her face intensified, and she averted her gaze. He tightened his grip on her arm, forcing her to look him in the eyes when she proclaimed his words lies. But to his surprise, when she reluctantly met his infuriated scowl, her expression softened with a touch of shame. Through her lowered lashes showed the faintest glimmer of desire. Passion she could not control, but did not want him to witness.

Understanding crashed down upon his shoulders like falling boulders. She did not mean her accusations. 'Twas all an attempt to cover her embarrassment. Embarrassment he had brought her by denying her the joining of their bodies.

He held her gaze, trapped by the sudden awareness of this unique glimpse of femininity. This vulnerability he had never imagined she could be capable of. And down deep inside, something wound into a fierce knot. Her quiet requests the previous night were not simple requests for escape as he had believed. She genuinely shared the same fierce yearning he did. He, however, had misconstrued the words she chose to admit acceptance of what flowed between them.

His retreating anger fed the warmth in his blood, and Lucan's gaze riveted on her soft mouth. "Tell me again, I sought my own pleasure, Chloe. That I gave you no consideration."

Drawn by a power greater than himself, he moved into the small space separating them. Her lips parted to answer. His body tensed with the fierce need to feel those silken lips move beneath his.

Julian shoved him aside before he could yield to the urge. "Take your hands off my sister. She asked you to leave."

Lucan breathed through flared nostrils, his jaw clenched so tightly he feared it might crack. Their scowls warred more ferociously than any clash of swords—a brother's protectiveness combating the fierceness of a preordained destiny. Once, Lucan would have cut a man in half for such a trespass on his person. For inserting himself in a situation that did not involve him. Although Chloe was his sister, Julian did not possess the right to interfere. Most especially with physical might.

Lucan took in the shorter-statured man. One hard blow to his jaw would drop him to the floor. 'Twould not take many more to render him unconscious. He could tear Julian to pieces with little effort.

And yet he could not bring himself to issue the first fist with Chloe standing at Julian's side. He clenched his hand so tight it cramped, and he turned away with a muffled oath. Three swift strides brought him to the door, which he jerked open, then stalked outside. Behind him, the door clanged on its hinges.

Caradoc leaned against the SUV, surveying the excavation from afar. He straightened as Lucan approached.

"I am leaving," Lucan gritted out. "At Chloe's request. See her safely returned to the château."

He did not wait for Caradoc to reply. Sliding behind the wheel, he turned the key, then backed onto the road. The drive passed in a blur of frustration and anger, darkening his mood to black as he reached Monthairons' vast manicured gardens. He stomped through the door and made for his room. Inside, he threw himself on the couch and slammed a fist into the plush arm. "Damnation!"

He could not fight both brother and sister, and as long as Julian possessed Chloe's ear, naught Lucan could say would make a difference. He must find a way of separating the both of them. Of allowing Caradoc and Gareth to observe Julian whilst he spent time alone with Chloe. But his endeavors of doing so amounted to wordplay. Each time he believed they had crossed some of the distance between them, and he could move on to further discover the truth behind her circumstances, he lost ground. Between the demons, her brother, and her own fears, Chloe kept him at an intolerable distance.

He was no closer to understanding the dark presence that followed on her heels than he had been the day they arrived.

Now he must deal with Julian's insertion into their affairs. Whatever conversation they had shared pushed Chloe further away. If Lucan were to ever accomplish the bond of seraphs, he must separate them from the relic. It divided them more surely than Azazel.

'Twas time to move forward. He needed to push Azazel's minions into revealing themselves, either as Chloe's ally or as her enemy.

But how?

Trust.

She drifted closer to him when he gave her what he himself desired. When he disclosed the truths he should not even consider sharing until he knew which side she fought for. Yet he knew that if he continued on this course, weeks could pass before Chloe took him into her confidence. All the while, his darkness would grow.

If he should happen to face one of Azazel's minions, he could lose what remained of his soul. He would become the very thing he sought to protect her from, and if he stood at her side when that occurred, he would become an even greater threat to her safety.

He had no choice but to risk more of the sacred purpose the Templar upheld. He must give her reason to believe him. In so doing, he would gain the trust she withheld.

Picardie held the answer. 'Twas close enough they could journey in a day and return to the château without rousing her suspicions that he sought baser physical gratification. There he would explain more of the past. Show her things that reinforced his claims about the Veronica.

In the meantime, he must repair this divide that lay between them now. To accomplish that, he would have to open himself and reveal the same vulnerabilities Chloe battled.

From the corner of his eye, he caught the wadded-up satin of her nightgown atop his bed. She would want her belongings. When she arrived to claim them, he would begin there.

With a deep, fortifying breath, he turned from the window and picked up the phone.

CHAPTER 21

†

As dark settled around the château, Chloe followed her brother inside the main hall. Getting rid of Lucan hadn't been as satisfying as she'd hoped. She'd spent all day distracted by his absence and worried about the ever-increasing tension between him and Julian. All told, she'd managed to correctly document five of Andy's photos, catalogue half a dozen small relics, and spend the majority of the afternoon staring out the window when Julian wasn't hawking over her and praising her for not cowing to Lucan's anger.

If she'd known she wouldn't have accomplished anything noteworthy, she'd have never let Lucan storm out the door. While his nearness disconcerted her, she might have at least benefited from his help and produced something of substance.

Now she had a day of nothing behind her and faced a never-ending night in her disrupted room.

She let out a sigh as they neared the staircase. "Hold on a minute, Julian, I need to see if the front desk can switch my room. I can't sleep in there with it all chaotic and knowing someone has a key."

He cocked his head as if she'd just spoken in French. "Do what?"

"Change my room."

"Don't be silly. You can stay with me a night or two. I'll even take the couch."

Chloe glanced up the stairs, debating. A night with Julian meant listening to more of his insistence that Lucan intended to discredit her. She'd heard enough of his ramblings to last the rest of their stay in France. The thought of going back to her room, however, made Julian's suggestion sound like heaven. She'd listen to endless hours of his rambling to escape the possibility of confronting the demons once again.

"Okay," she agreed with a sharp nod. "I need to get my things, and then I'll be down. Want to eat in? I bet they have your favorite, escargot."

"No, I'm not really hungry."

She did a double take and blinked. Julian not hungry? The man could eat an army out of camp if given an opportunity. And turning down escargot came dangerously close to the idea of his turning down a busty blonde who plopped her bare bottom in his lap.

Come to think of it, the fact he'd offered his room for more than one night bordered on unbelievable. He'd have to give up his privacy. Something he never did without protest. Endless protest at that.

Furrowing her brows, she set her hand on his arm. "Are you coming down with something?"

He chuckled. "Why would you ask that?"

"Because you haven't been yourself lately. It's like you've finally realized we're here to work, not play.

I don't think I've seen you with a girl in a couple of weeks."

His boyish grin and conspiratorial wink accompanied another low chuckle. "Oh, I've sampled the local fare. Just maybe not in the way you'd expect."

No way, nohow did she intend to ask for an explanation. What Julian did with the women she absolutely didn't want to know. His devil-may-care attitude about sex and dating made her glad he was her brother, so she couldn't possibly be on the receiving end of his escapades. If she had to put up with his ever-rotating schedule of partners, she'd likely strangle him to death. Why the ladies didn't seem to mind, she couldn't understand.

"Okay. I'll see you there then."

He rendered her speechless as he leaned over to plant a chaste kiss on her cheek. Someone had swapped brothers with her when she wasn't looking. Good grief, Julian hadn't kissed her since they were grade-school kids.

She watched him disappear up the winding stair before looking down the hall and offering up a silent prayer Lucan wouldn't make retrieving her things unbearable. At his door, Chloe lifted her hand to knock, then quickly dropped it before her knuckles could make contact. She didn't want to get into another argument, and she didn't really need her things.

No.

She wouldn't run from confrontation. Demons hadn't turned her into a total coward, and she wasn't about to let a simple man and his temper get under her skin. She raised her hand and rapped with purpose.

The door opened to a backdrop of low lights and soft music. Lucan stood before her, looking so magnificent that for a moment she forgot why she'd come. Long hair loose and free, it tumbled over his wide shoulders and contrasted against the white linen of his shirt. For the first time since she'd met him, he wore casual slacks, not jeans. And as she took him in, from the open buttons at his collar all the way down to the loafers on his feet, her heart tripped behind her ribs.

Good grief, *why* did he have to be her colleague? Why couldn't he be some stranger she'd met at the bar? A businessman working overseas, a tourist—anything but the man who shared equal interest in a piece of cloth from the first century.

"Good eve." He stepped aside, swinging the door open.

Chloe kept her gaze fastened on his face, determined not to investigate the cause of the dim lighting and soft music. If he had plans, she didn't want to know. Especially since he hadn't mentioned anything about her joining him. "I came to get my things."

"Come in. I expected you might. They are on the dresser."

Groaning inwardly, Chloe stepped inside the room. He'd gathered her meager belongings, a clear sign that the rich aroma of food and the bottle of chilled wine beside the table weren't meant for her. She hurried past the candlelit place settings for two and scooped her belongings into her arms.

When she turned around, she ran smack into Lucan's chest. Startled, she stumbled backward.

Lucan caught her by the elbows, a low chuckle rumbling in his chest. He held her steady until she regained her footing. Then, with a disturbingly warm smile, he gently plucked her things out of her grasp and set them behind him on the desk. "I also expected you should like to eat."

Glancing at the table once more, Chloe gulped. Seconds ago, the prospect he might have plans with someone else had stirred jealousy. Now, as the candles flickered in the shadowy light, and the quiet jazz filled her ears, apprehension bubbled in her veins. Wine, music, an intimate setting for two—this was by no means a casual affair. What if they ended up where they had last night? "I-I don't know, Lucan."

His broad smile scolded. "'Tis dinner, Chloe. No more, no less. Sit down and enjoy yourself." He slid his fingers beneath the shoulders of her open coat, removing her ability to protest as he pulled it off her arms. With a casual toss, it landed on the couch.

A couch that sat too close to a table set for two and a full bottle of Viognier. He took her by the elbow and guided her into a chair. Leaning close to her ear as he filled her wine glass, he murmured, *"Profitez de votre dîner."*

Enjoy your dinner. A chill drifted down Chloe's spine, leaving goose bumps in its wake. And dear Lord, the man spoke French like a primary language.

Lucan eased into the seat across from her and gestured at the silver dome covering her plate. "I ordered the sole meunière. I hope 'tis to your liking."

With an unsteady hand, Chloe lifted the lid on battered sole sprinkled with parsley atop a bed of wild rice, and a side of braised green beans. Her mouth watered as a hint of lemon wafted to her nose. Presented with one of the finest meals the château had to offer, her apprehensions yielded to the anxious twist of her belly. She set the cover aside and picked up her fork.

One bite of the butter-fried fish, and Chloe knew she'd discovered another side of heaven.

Over the rim of his wineglass, Lucan watched Chloe lift the last bite of her meal to her mouth. Despite the smudge of dirt on her cheek and the loose tendrils of hair that tumbled around her face, he found her more adorable than ever. One glass of wine, which she finished before she had eaten even half her meal, served to relax her. And in the following hour he had come to glimpse a different side of the stubborn archaeologist.

With a wistful sigh, she set her fork on her plate and leaned back in her chair. "Oh, Lucan, that was wonderful. Thank you."

Her smile pleased him more than it should. He found he could not deny she possessed a unique beauty. A classic elegance he had seldom witnessed in the modern women he had occasion to encounter. Looking at her now, as the warm light of candles glowed upon her skin, something down deep in his soul slowly turned in on itself. His blood warmed beneath the glimmer of her eyes. His chest felt tight, as if a large boulder rested squarely atop his sternum. And against his thigh, his cock stirred with awareness of the woman who sat across from him.

"Aye," he agreed quietly. "Shall we order dessert?"

"Oh, heavens no. I can't stuff another bite in—I'm too full." She lifted her glass and took a long drink.

What did he do now? Too many years had passed since he had cause to entertain a woman, and the lessons learned long ago were naught but a distant, vague memory. Yet with their meal completed, he risked the possibility she would take her leave.

He sifted through the occasions his father had entertained and those where he had conquered enemy holdings. Large banquets where men and women feasted until they could not lift themselves from the table and drank from tankards that never ran dry. What came after was debauchery Chloe would certainly not appreciate.

Distantly another memory rose. A time when their beloved king had paid visit to his father. With him came musicians. And the king's daughter demanded they dance. Lucan had not bothered to learn the steps, but the women fair squealed with joy at the opportunity to move their feet. What he recalled did not seem so very difficult.

He inclined his head toward the television where the music played. "Would you care to dance, Chloe?"

Her gaze held his, laughter brimming in her eyes. "I can't dance. I'm as bad as a mule trying to do ballet."

Lucan could not help himself—he laughed. Sitting forward, he set his wineglass on the table, rose to his feet, and extended his hand. "Mayhap then, we shall endeavor to learn together."

She hesitated for the briefest of heartbeats. But then her smile brightened, and she set her glass aside. Sliding her hand into his, she stood. "Don't be angry if I step on your toes."

"Nay," he answered as he drew her into his arms.

Standing in the small space between the portable dining table and the bed, they swayed together in time to the slow rhythmic melody of a saxophone. He turned her in a circle, his steps mere shuffles to prevent maligning her toes.

Silence settled between them, a comfortable lack of words that conveyed far more than any conversation.

Her body melded closer, each slight lift of her foot bringing her deeper into the circle of his arms, until at last she sated the erratic beat of his heart by laying her cheek against his chest. More profoundly content than he could ever remember being, Lucan tucked the top of her head beneath his chin and stroked the length of her back. She fit so perfectly against his body. Each gentle curve a matching counterpart to his harsher build. This moment he would carry with him a lifetime.

"You are more beautiful than any woman I have ever known," he whispered into her hair.

Her hand came up to settle over his heart. A light laugh accompanied the press of her fingers. "Careful or you'll have me believing that."

Lucan slid his hand into her auburn hair. It tumbled around his fingers like spun silk. "I want you to believe it." He curled his fingers against her scalp and massaged the nape of her neck. "I have never uttered anything more true." With a gentle pull, he tipped her head back to meet his gaze, hoping beyond all measure she would read the sincerity in his meaningful stare.

Her eyes searched his. Rich and bright, subtle chips of gold drew him into their questioning depths. The air that flowed between them warmed to uncomfortable limits, and Lucan ran his hands down her back to her bottom, where he gathered her flesh into his hands, seeking to fulfill the sudden need to be somehow closer. To feel her silken skin against his palms.

The innocent brush of her hips against his as she moved in time to the music sent a rush of pleasant heat scalding through his veins. His cock filled with want of her, and he closed his eyes to stifle a low groan. Instinctively, he dipped his head to capture her mouth.

Evading his kiss, Chloe turned her head and whispered against his cheek, "I don't understand."

His lips found the elegant line of her jaw, and he dusted kisses to the sensitive hollow at the base of her ear. "What is there to not understand? This want of you plagues my waking hours."

"But last night you said you didn't—"

"Nay." He drew back to look once more into those burnished amber depths. "I said I could not be your escape." Lifting her bottom, he brought her against the hard evidence of his desire. A shudder rolled down his spine, and his body undulated against hers. "I am more than willing to be your reality."

A delightful gasp tumbled from her parted lips as her hips returned the slow intimate caress. Lucan's body coiled like a whip against a shock of agonizing pleasure. Yet he did not move. He allowed the full meaning of his words to hang between them, waiting for her to answer. To give him the freedom to unleash the desire that roared through his blood and indulge in the magnificent gift of Chloe, his seraph, the one woman he would spend eternity serving.

She gave him liberty as she curled her fingers into the fabric of his shirt, and with a light tug sought the kiss she had thwarted. Every fiber of Lucan's body arced with live current. The desperate need to possess everything she offered at once brought his mouth crashing into hers.

Their kiss was feral and untamed. She buried her hands in his hair, her nails scraped against his scalp. And then it was too much, the stillness of their bodies unbearable, the hunger for warm bare skin overwhelming. He gathered her shirt in his hands at the same time her fingers sought the buttons on his. Hands and elbows tangled, becoming more hindrance than remedy. Frustrated beyond all measure, Lucan caught her wrists in one hand, trapped them behind her, and with a low groan pinned her against the sturdy bedpost.

Her back hit the wood with such force she let out a muffled squeak. Distantly aware he had hurt her, Lucan eased the assault of his mouth. On a relieved sigh, he sank his body into hers, grateful for a moment that she could not move. He dragged in a long, haggard breath and broke their kiss to nuzzle his cheek against hers. "Ah, Chloe, I ache for you."

He trailed his lips down the side of her throat, reveling in the way she tipped her head back and closed her eyes. Releasing her wrists, he held her in place with his chest long enough to slide his hands beneath her shirt and caress the smooth skin covering her ribs. When the fabric pulled tight, forbidding him the softness of her breasts, he leaned away to lift her shirt over her head.

No single ounce of shyness flickered in the brightness of her eyes. She held his gaze, made no attempt to move, seemingly aware he needed a moment to simply look at her. To admire the high swell of her breasts beneath a thin gauze of lace. To imagine the way her belly would flatten even more as she arched her back and took him deep inside her. To trail his finger along the waist of her jeans and release the row of buttons there.

"Lucan, I want to touch you," she whispered.

Aye.

The answer thundered in his head, but the tightness of his throat refused to let it escape. He stepped closer, his breath hard, his hands tight fists at his thighs. Time stood still as she freed the buttons on his shirt and slipped her slender fingers beneath. She pushed the fabric off his shoulders, dragged it down his arms, dropped it on the floor. And then her mouth touched his overheated skin, the scald of her lips both excruciating and gratifying. His heart clanged into his ribs. His shaft filled to painful limits.

Mimicking the way he had touched her, she glided her fingertips over his torso. The softness in her expression captivated him. In all the hundreds of years he had walked upon this earth, he had never witnessed such wonder touch a woman's eyes. That he could have such an effect rooted him in place with a tremor that ebbed down his spine.

He stood stock still, scarcely able to breathe as she released him from the confines of his trousers and took his swollen cock into his hand. Knowing he should not, but unable to help himself, he glanced down to witness her fingers wrapped around him. He pushed his hips forward, gliding through her gentle hold and staggered beneath an engulfing rush of ecstasy.

What remained of his control snapped. He caught her to him in a crushing embrace. No longer able to tolerate the barrier of their clothing, he shimmied her jeans off her hips. She followed the same unspoken command and undressed him.

Hands and mouth searching, Lucan guided her away from the bedpost. When the backs of her knees touched the mattress, he laid her on the bed. Lost to all that was Chloe, he surrendered to the one thing he wanted more than salvation and nudged her knees apart to nestle his straining erection against the thin fabric of her panties. One press of his hips teased aside the loose material, and he groaned against the warm, moist heat that touched his swollen head.

Yet through the bleary haze of all-consuming desire, he recognized a change in Chloe. The ardor left her kiss. Her hands explored more slowly, her touch light and hesitant. Where she had been eager and willing the night before, she lay beneath him barely moving.

Lucan raised his head and lifted to his elbows. "What troubles you, my sweet?"

"Nothing. I'm fine." Though she shook her head and offered him a smile, her voice lacked the same assurance.

He quirked an eyebrow.

"Really," she murmured as she slipped her fingers into his hair and pulled his mouth back to hers. "I'm good. It's just been awhile."

Though he was not quite convinced, he gave her what she desired.

CHAPTER 22

Chloe pleaded with her mind to shut up and participate in the tremendous ecstasy that rippled through her body. It had been so long. So unbelievably long. Lucan was the best candidate she could dream of to ease her draught. He was tender, handsome, and so delightfully thorough. She couldn't ask for a better lover. He didn't hurry her along for his own gratification. Took his time with gentle caresses. Used his mouth to make love to her before he allowed his body to dominate.

She'd like him to dominate her. Like him to do whatever it took to stop the nagging worry that if she allowed this to continue she'd never come back. Somewhere in the heights he took her to, she'd lose her safety net and plummet to a disastrous end.

She looped her arms around his neck and grasped at the flicker of desire that fringed her awareness. This was ridiculous. She had a hot, hard body and a mouth that knew how to give pleasure. No one else would hesitate.

Besides, as late as it was, the idea of going to Julian's

room and facing his inevitable interrogation turned her stomach. She didn't want to have to explain. Didn't want to hear his admonishment that she'd regret getting involved with Lucan.

Returning his kiss with renewed vigor, she arched her body closer to his.

But what if she couldn't return? What if making love to Lucan exposed her to the same devastating pain Blake inflicted?

"Chloe," Lucan whispered against her lips. He lifted to his elbows once more and studied her with a slight frown. "Where are you?"

She blinked. "Right here. What do you mean?" She knew damn well what he meant. But the fact he could sense her distance made her want to squirm. Again she confronted the unsettling awareness of how closely he paid attention.

"I mean . . ." He brushed the tip of his nose against hers. "Last night I enjoyed your full participation. You are far from here. From me. What troubles you?"

Heat infused her cheeks, and she said a silent prayer of thanks that the darkness shadowed her face. What was she supposed to say? That she'd scared herself out of a night of pleasure? That she was so afraid to sleep alone she'd do just about anything? No matter her response, he'd see her as a tease. He'd become angry. Kick her out on her rear, and she wouldn't blame him one bit.

"Really," she said with a soft laugh. "I'm a bit apprehensive. It's been . . . years."

For a heartbeat, the light in his eyes intensified. Good heavens, he liked that. Enjoyed the idea he would be the first in a long while. An unexplainable thrill raced down to her toes. But in the next heartbeat, his eyebrows furrowed, and the lines around his mouth tightened.

"Nay." He shook his head. " 'Tis something else. 'Tis in your eyes."

She nearly groaned aloud. No man on earth should be so observant. Nor should this one be able to read her so well. A heavy sigh slipped free. "I can't do this. I thought I could. I don't want to go to my room, Lucan, and I didn't want to invite myself to stay. I've been trying to convince myself it's okay . . ."

He reared back on his heels like she'd slapped him. "God's blood!"

She cringed beneath the oath that slipped through his teeth. Aware she'd just dug her own grave she wriggled off the bed and picked up her shirt.

Lucan snatched it out of her hands. With more force than necessary he hurled it across the room where it landed in front of the door. "Nay. You will stay if you wish."

Astounded, she could do no more than stare.

He rose to his feet, jerked open a dresser drawer, and yanked out a pair of long cotton pants. His expression tight, he pulled them on and eased them over his jutting erection. When he looked at her again, his eyes glinted in the soft candlelight. "When we lay together as man and woman—and we will, for there is too much passion between us—'twill not be because you have had to *convince* yourself 'tis what you wish."

He gestured at the bed before he moved to the bathroom door. "Sleep. I am in need of a shower."

The door thumped shut before she could utter a word of explanation. Groaning, Chloe flopped onto the pillows and tossed an elbow over her eyes. Great. Evidently abstinence had eroded her brain more than she'd realized. Only a fool would admit the truth she had. Who confessed that kind of honesty to a man?

Lucan braced his hands on the sink and leaned over the basin, willing his body to forget the idea of pleasure. His shoulders shook with the effort. His chest refused to expand. Convince herself? He would cut his own throat before he took her without her full and willing participation.

Convince herself. He smacked an open palm against the marble and shoved away from the sink. Why did she feel she could not just tell him she desired to rest her head on his pillow? He would have welcomed her company. Would not have uttered a single protest, and would have understood the unspoken message she did not desire intimacy.

Saints' toes, who had taught her she must hide behind false pretenses?

A tremor ran through his hands as a fresh burst of anger replaced the annoyance in his blood. Whoever had instilled that lesson, he would enjoy every minute of choking the life out of his lecherous body. When Chloe allowed Lucan to glimpse it, her spirit was much too precious to be stifled. Even her stubbornness, her fierce temper, he enjoyed. She should not have to chain herself so.

As the blood ebbed from his loins, he breathed more deeply and considered the larger concern that surfaced. She was willing to compromise herself to avoid her room. Did she fear another break-in? Did she, mayhap, *expect* the demon to return for the relic, and in so doing, once again find her without?

He eyed the back of the door, envisioning the woman who lay beyond. Now that his thoughts had retreated from the promise of ecstasy, he sensed the dark presence around him. Caught the faint stench of decay in his nose. They followed her here. Coincidence? Or mayhap strategy?

Was tonight a means of distracting him so she could free the Veronica for Azazel?

A chill rolled through him. Surely she could not be capable of such. She had no means of knowing he had planned dinner. She could not possibly stage the priceless moments where she had been an equal participant in the desire that they unleashed.

Nay. Chloe had not come to his room with the intent of deceit. He would not allow the darkness in his soul to convince him otherwise.

He turned the door handle and entered the sleeping quarters. Dressed only in her panties and her bra, Chloe lay atop the covers, curled into a tight ball. His heart turned over at the sight of her, and he closed his eyes against an unwelcome surge of feeling. When he had come to care for her, he could not say. But in that moment, as he observed the soft rise and fall of her shoulder and the protective way she sought to shield herself, he realized she had crept beneath his awareness and weaseled into the portion of his heart he sought to keep from her until he knew her purpose.

Aye, he cared for her more than he ought. And yet he found he did not so much mind the uncomfortable tightening of his chest or the stirring of his cock. 'Twas strangely pleasing to accept she held power over him. To acknowledge that when he took his oath, 'twould be more than words of loyalty and duty he uttered. He would mean every solemn word that bound them together eternally.

He bent over the table and extinguished the candles. Darkness descended, thick and opaque. For several long seconds he stood in the middle of the room, watching her shadowy form, debating whether he should wake her and offer the sleeping gown that lay on the couch.

Nay, he decided with a slow shake of his head. He would not rouse her. She would construe his meaning as he desired her to cover herself, when in truth he longed to peel off what remained of her clothes and indulge in the silken nature of her skin.

Soon enough, they would reach that precipice. But he would push her no further. The next time they came together, be it for a kiss or for the final consummation of desire, 'twould be at her prompting. Under her assurance she wanted to open her body to the will of his. Mayhap even her heart.

A noise from the window brought him out of his thoughts. He cocked his head, listening to the scratching on the glass. From the bed, a rustling stirred as Chloe burrowed deeper into the mattress. An almost inaudible whimper floated to his ears.

Fear. Even in sleep, she feared the presence.

His heart gave a pained little twist.

Frowning, he crossed to the safe and checked that he had locked the Veronica inside. Then he collected his sword from the corner behind the door and returned to the side of the bed nearest the window. He laid his holy blade on the floor beside the bed and eased atop the quilts. As he rolled onto his side to study Chloe's delicate face, he blinked on finding her eyes open.

"You are not asleep?"

"No," she whispered as she glanced at the window. "The wind . . ."

Not wind, and he recognized the lie for what it was. Yet he did not press for answers. In time she would come to freely speak the truth. He would wait until she was ready.

Extending his arm, he bade her welcome into his embrace. As if relieved by the prospect, she snuggled close. Lucan reached around her to tug the covers loose. "Lift," he instructed quietly.

She obeyed by raising her hips so he could pull the quilt from beneath her body. In one swift arc, he covered her, then shifted to better accommodate the nearness of her body. Chloe settled a warm palm against his chest and let out a contented sigh. "I feel safe here," she confessed.

He pulled his fingers through her long hair and pressed a kiss to the top of her head. "Aye, you are. Always, my sweet," he murmured. *I would give my soul for yours.*

"Lucan?"

"Hm."

"I didn't mean to offend you."

"Shh," he urged as he ran his palm down the length of her arm. "'Tis naught to discuss." Picking up her fingers, he laced his through hers and gave her hand a gentle squeeze. "Know you are welcome here. You need only make your wishes known."

Her nails scraped pleasantly across his chest. "That seems selfish when I know you'd like more."

Lucan released her hand and splayed his fingers over the curve of her hip. "In time you will want the same."

A shiver gripped her. It vibrated into him, and he

sucked in a sharp breath, unprepared for his honesty to
have such a physical effect.

She feathered a light kiss over his shoulder. "Sometimes I already do."

"Sleep," he instructed through a closing throat.
"Your words are a greater torment than the nearness of
your body."

"Kiss me, Lucan?"

Her whisper came so softly he doubted he heard her
correctly. But when she tipped her chin up, and her
wide eyes filled with apprehension, he knew his mind
did not play tricks. The fist around his heart clamped
like a vise, and he debated the logic in obeying her request. He did not trust himself to not fall victim to the
spell her sweet flavor wove. And yet he could not stomach the thought of denying her, of taking her back to the
humiliation he had caused her the night before.

Her fingertips drifted across his lips. Skated across
his cheek. "Please."

His will crumpled under her quiet plea. Groaning,
he dragged her close and settled his mouth on hers. The
tip of her tongue darted out to slide against his, filling
him with her heady flavor. Wine still lingered on her
mouth, more intoxicating than the fruity fermentation
in the glass. He became intoxicated by the velvety brush
and stroke and the warm caress of her breath against
his cheek.

In his arms, she wriggled closer. Her breasts stabbed
into his bare chest, her thigh slipped between his.
And though her nearness held innocence, his body
thrummed with awareness. 'Twould be so easy to
use this moment to his advantage. To slide his hand beneath the insignificant strap at her hips and slip his

fingertip between her womanly folds. Relaxed and unassuming, trusting he would take this joining of their lips no further, she would never anticipate his intimate caress until he had already coaxed her into willingness. From there, he could roll her onto her back and ease himself inside her waiting warmth before protest could rise in her mind.

Aye . . .'Twould be so easy . . .

As his cock filled with the prospect of imminent fulfillment, Lucan choked down another groan and tore his mouth from hers. In the quiet, their breaths rasped in harmony. The fall of her fingertips against his chest tortured worse than any hot pokers the Inquisition had once applied to his feet. His body strained with arousal. His heart beat so fiercely he feared 'twould bruise his ribs.

He loosened his embrace, desperate for a bit of distance. "I am not the saint you seem to think I am, Chloe."

"No," she murmured against his chest. "I know you aren't. You're a man." She trailed a fingertip down the center of his chest to his abdomen, then slowly retraced the path before settling her hand over his heart. "All man." More quietly, she whispered, "And I like you."

"Chloe," he ground out through clenched teeth. "I am warning you, cease. Else I will forget I desire something more than a mindless fuck. Which I could have twice-now had."

As he desired, she jumped at his harsh language and tucked her hand safely beneath her cheek. "Good night, Lucan."

He breathed a bit easier, but the roaring in his head left him silently swearing at the ceiling. God's teeth, if Picardie did not break down the last of her walls, she would break him into bits.

CHAPTER 23

✠

Lucan's warrior's instinct demanded he open his eyes. He lay still, surveying his surroundings with naught more than the movement of his eyes. Thick and foreboding, the unmistakable presence of Azazel hung in the air. It lifted the hairs on the back of his neck. The same tightness that infused his body each time he lifted his sword against the creatures of darkness crept into his muscles.

In the corner of his vision, he observed Chloe lay on her back, clutching the small red satchel she had brought from her room. Eyes wide, she stared at the ceiling. Her chest rose with shallow breaths, testament to her fear.

The stillness set off great horns of warning in his head. Something lurked. Watched. Waited to strike.

He inched his hand from beneath the covers, dropped it over the edge of the bed, and closed his fingers around cold, hard steel. Barely breathing, he lifted his sword atop his chest.

The door shuddered beneath a thunderous blow. As

if some terrific beast held fast to the handle, it banged and clattered on the hinges.

Lucan bolted from the bed. He drew his sword before his feet hit the floor. He charged around the foot of the bed, one hand out instructing Chloe to stay put. But as he opened his mouth to issue the order, she jumped to her feet and raced toward the deafening racket.

An icy blade of fear pierced his chest. "Chloe, stand back!" 'Twas not her fight. Whatever lay beyond that door would shred her to pieces. "Chloe!" He barked more loudly. God's teeth, he could not allow her to risk her life. Charging forward, he grabbed her elbow and hauled her away.

Tiny slivers of wood splintered off the door and peppered the floor.

Chloe twisted free with a fierce jerk of her head. "Let go!" She evaded his seeking fingers and rushed to the shivering slab of timber.

Anger took fear's place in Lucan's heart. He ground his teeth together and stalked after her. He had one hand on her shoulder and was seconds away from jerking her behind him when she dropped to her knees.

"For the love of the saints, Chloe, get back before you are harmed!"

When she refused to budge, he did the only thing he could think of. He placed himself between her and the door and lifted his sword, prepared to defend her should the barrier yield.

Behind him, a flame flickered in the dark. He glanced over his shoulder to find her with two sticks of incense in her hands and a lighter applied to the tips. "Damnation, Chloe, 'tis no time for perfumes. Get away."

She glanced up, perturbed. "Stop distracting me."

A shaking hand fanned the smoke toward his legs. Beyond to the door. To Lucan's immense frustration, she stood and took a step closer to the shivering wood.

As if whatever lay beyond sensed her nearness, the quaking intensified. On the nearby desk, the glass lampshade rattled on its brass supports. Lucan cast a wary glance at the doorknob. It held, but barely, each blow loosening the steel in its casing. He tightened his hold on his sword, lifted it a notch higher.

Chloe joined him at his side and held the incense toward the weakening barrier. In a strong voice that defied the wide whites of her eyes, she called, "In the name of the Almighty, I banish you from this place. Go now, you cannot bring me harm. Mighty Gabriel, hear these words, protect me with your sacred might." The words tumbled off her lips, fast and furious.

Beyond, a ghostly howl echoed.

Silence descended on them. The door stood motionless, as if it had never been touched. Lucan took a step backward, not trusting the stillness. When nothing happened, he slowly lowered his blade. For several heavy thumps of his heart, he stared at the wood, anticipating a renewed attack.

It did not come. Would not, he began to realize as he turned to witness Chloe closing up her satchel. The incense burned in a glass near the door, and Lucan hit the light switch.

Rage and fear warred for dominance over his confusion. She had foolishly risked her safety. Had her stunt failed, only the Almighty knew what fate she might have suffered. If Lucan would have conquered the beast, or if in attacking it, his soul would absorb the last bit of darkness to transform him into an equally horrific creature intent on sacrificing her to the unholy master's plan.

With an outward calm that disguised the trembling of his innards, he laid his sword on the back of the couch and lifted his gaze to Chloe's.

'Twas then he noticed she too attempted to disguise her emotions with a false hesitant smile. Her face paled to the color of death. Her wide eyes watered with unshed tears. Torn between offering her comfort and scolding her within an inch of her life, he tempered both urges with a deep, controlled breath.

Until he knew how she came by the knowledge of what lay beyond, and the adytum-keepers' words, he would do naught.

He gestured at the bed. "Sit. 'Tis time to talk."

Chloe bit down hard on her lower lip to stop her tears and sank onto the edge of the bed. Feeling exposed in only her bra and panties, she wrestled the quilt loose and pulled it about her shoulders. They'd come for her here. They'd interrupted her safe haven and forced her to admit no matter how she longed to believe Lucan could protect her, they could find her anywhere.

Would find her anywhere.

Shivers coursed up and down her spine, driving her deeper into the soft patchwork quilt's shelter. Lucan sat on the couch, elbows on his knees, his gaze firmly fastened on her. What would he say? When he finished laughing about demons and curses, would he toss her out on her ear with claims that someone merely wanted the Veronica?

She shifted, wanting more than anything to avoid this conversation. But she owed him an explanation.

She'd brought the danger to his door, hadn't bothered to warn him his own safety was in question, and tonight could have turned into a disaster.

The way he'd placed himself between her and the threat spoke of chivalry. Even that massive sword, however, couldn't protect him from the things beyond. He'd risked his life. She didn't dare belittle that daring gesture by telling him anything but the truth.

"Chloe," he urged with impatience.

"I'm sorry." She plucked at a loose string between a cream and lavender quilt square. "I should have said something. I'm sorry."

"Aye, you should have. So now you shall." His voice hardened with a touch of annoyance.

Unable to tolerate his certain ridicule, Chloe flopped onto her back and stared at the ceiling. "What do you want to know?"

"Everything you wish to explain."

"And if I don't want to explain anything?"

"'Tis not an option."

Of course not. She wouldn't get off that easy. But where to begin? With the declaration demons had just attacked his door? Or with the man in Egypt, the tiny little man with the odd-colored eyes?

"Start with how you know the adytum-keepers' words of warding."

Her brows furrowed. Adytum keepers? No keeper of anything had taught her the phrases. That wasn't the place to start anyway. Lucan might want to know, but without the beginning, any explanation about demonologists and priests amounted to nothing.

"Eight years ago I did my final excavation in the Bahariya Oasis. We found an unopened tomb that we were all very excited to discover. It turned out to be one of the greatest finds of my career. Eight rooms all connected and leading progressively deeper into the earth. Ten mummies—one in each alcove, two with children. All contained the complete treasures of a second-dynasty burial rite."

The couch creaked as Lucan shifted position. Footsteps on the wood floor made her investigate. She tipped her chin to discover him standing at the dinner table and refilling both of their wineglasses. Before he could turn around, she fixed her gaze on the ceiling again.

"Six weeks into what would become a full year of excavation, a man approached me in the oasis. He had the oddest bicolored eyes. One green, one a cloudy white. He swore to me I'd find something meant for me that day."

"Aye, you found the glyph you showed me earlier." The mattress gave as Lucan sat down next to her hip.

Chloe lifted her head. With a nod of thanks, she accepted his offered glass, scooted upright, and sipped. "What I didn't tell you . . ." She took a deep breath, hating what came next. Swirling her wine, she studied the tiny ripples on the surface. "I found a tunnel that day. It branched off from the fourth chamber and was partially hidden by a large urn. I couldn't resist the chance of finding something truly my own and crawled inside. The glyph was on the wall above my head. I wouldn't have noticed it if I hadn't heard that man's voice telling me to look up."

She shot him a furtive glance as she added, "Only no one was in the tunnel with me. My team was still working in the second chamber."

Anticipating his smirk, she braced herself for the

sarcastic retorts. Lucan merely stared at his wine, the tightening of his brow the only sign he'd even heard her fantastic claim. Otherwise, his impassive expression offered no hint to what he might be thinking.

Chloe continued, uncertain what to make of his silence. "Something followed me out of the tunnel. *Things* have been following me since. I can't see them. I don't know exactly what they are, but they aren't friendly. The night before my break-in, they tried to come through the window. Pretty much the same way they tried to come through your door."

She curled her free hand into the quilt and took a long drink. Her stomach twisted in on itself, the fermented fruit not sitting with her nerves. Setting the glass aside, she pulled her knees up to her chest and wrapped her arms around her legs. "I've talked to every spiritual leader in every religion I can think of, and no one has the answers. They all say the same thing—I'm not cursed. Not possessed. Yet I can't get rid of these things. The ward I used tonight was given to me by a demonologist in Tucson. It fends them off for a while."

At that, Lucan's eyebrows lifted a fraction. Wordlessly, he lifted his glass to his lips and finished off his wine. He set the empty glass on the nightstand and swiveled to face her. "'Tis all the story?"

She nodded. He hadn't laughed. Hadn't done so much as smile. Why? Why couldn't he be like everyone else? She knew how to deal with them. But this . . . This quiet lack of response disturbed her.

"I swear I'm not crazy."

"I would not presume such. You sought to send the attacker away then?"

Again, she answered with a short nod. His question,

however, reminded her of his sword. "What did you intend to do?"

A grin tugged at the corner of his mouth. With a nonchalant shrug he answered, "Kill it."

"Somehow, I don't think that will work," she murmured.

"Nay?"

Chloe stretched out her legs, relieved that she hadn't yet faced justifying herself. "Just a feeling I have. Like ghosts—I don't think you can really kill them." Hesitantly, she searched his gaze. She couldn't take the wondering any longer. Had to discover whether his reaction was politeness or whether he was truly receptive to the truth. "Do you believe me?" she asked quietly.

Lucan stretched out on his side and braced himself on one elbow. He laid his free hand atop her exposed foot. "I have no reason to doubt you."

Stunned, Chloe blinked. Her own brother cried off her claims as imaginings of her mind. Blake had done the same. Yet the man she'd known only a handful of days didn't attempt to discredit her story. "Why aren't you laughing?"

Repositioning himself so he lay diagonal across the bed, Lucan pulled his pillow beneath his head. "I work for the Church, Chloe. I have seen things that defy explanation." He dragged her pillow close to his and beckoned her to join him. "Share the quilt, 'tis chilly in here tonight."

Tears pricked Chloe's eyes as she stretched out alongside him. She'd never dreamed she might find someone who could understand. Someone who wouldn't condemn her or ridicule her fears. It was too good to be true.

He was too good to be true.

She snuggled close, inhaled the lingering spice of his cologne. He slid his arm around her waist and snugged her against his warm body. His fingers traced a lazy pattern across her skin.

"Were you really going to fight something with a sword?"

"Aye."

Curious, she peered up at his handsome face. "Where'd you learn that?"

Lucan's hand stilled at the small of her back. He should tell her now. With the proof she did not work for Azazel, he should confide all the secrets of his purpose and her fate. She gave him the opportunity, a perfect lead-in for the conversation they must inevitably have.

Yet he could not bring himself to tell her the truth. If she took it poorly, if she swore off his company, he could not protect her from the demons that plagued her. Next time, an attack might find her not so lucky. Worse, if he presented her with the seraphs' torc, and she dismissed his explanation and further revealed his words to anyone else, Azazel would strike like lightning.

Moreover, Chloe was not ready to accept *him*. Until she could open herself to the simple man, he would not ask her to embrace the not-so-simple immortal knight.

"'Twas a habit I picked up in youth." To veer her off the subject, he leaned over her to twist off the light near the bed. Sliding back beneath the quilt, he hauled her onto his chest and wound an arm tightly about her waist. Her contented sigh engulfed him. The splay of her fingertips against his skin stirred the ever-present warmth in his blood. 'Twas a mistake to hold her so close. To consume himself with the light fragrance of roses that clung to her hair and the feel of her silken skin sliding against his.

Yet 'twas the only way he knew of to silence her questions. This closeness distracted her as significantly as it distracted him.

He pulled his fingers through her long hair, enchanted by the way it tickled across his flesh. So soft. So glorious. Certain proof the blood of angels ran in her veins.

"Lucan? I'm sorry," she whispered.

"Nay. Do not be, my sweet."

'Twas he who should apologize for even considering Chloe could be aligned with Azazel.

CHAPTER 24

†

Morning brought the song of a lark and the first true signs of spring. Lucan opened his eyes to sunlight brighter than he had witnessed in many days. It streamed through the drawn curtains, peeking from the edges and illuminating the room with the promise of a beautiful day. Mayhap the Almighty chose to aid his plight, for 'twas perfect weather for a trip to Picardie.

Chloe was still draped atop his upper body, and her warmth soaked into him. She slept peacefully, as she had the night before. So deeply he hated to disturb her. But if he did not escape the temptation of soft breasts flush against his chest and long lithe legs tangled through his, he would indeed forget all the reasons he had not already indulged in the promised pleasure of her body.

Careful not to disturb her, he lifted her off and away, and slid from beneath the twisted quilt. He quietly pulled a shirt on and tightened the waistband of his cotton pants before retreating into the bathroom to shave away his whiskers. Whilst he attended to his morning routine, he stepped through his plans for the day, deciding what he would, and would not, tell her as they walked amongst the chapel ruins.

First, however, he must convince her to go. He could plan to show her the Seven Wonders of the World and 'twould do no good if he could not lure her away from the excavation in Ornes.

He turned the water off, patted his face dry, and returned to the bedroom where Chloe had not moved. Six in the morn—two hours to Picardie—he had time to retrieve a small breakfast.

With a backward glance over his shoulder, ensuring she still slept, he abandoned the room in favor of the small restaurant downstairs and its vast array of pastries. In the great front hall, he discovered Caradoc at a table near the window, coffee in hand, a plate of eggs and sausage before him. Lucan pulled out the chair and took a seat. "Morn."

"You seem in better spirits since yesterday," Caradoc observed.

"Bonjour, monsieur." A waiter greeted Lucan with a smile. "You shall join Monsieur Caradoc? What may I bring you?"

"Bonjour." Lucan felt the first true smile he had known in days cross his face. "I shall not be staying. But if it does not trouble you, I would like two cinnamon custard Danishes, two blueberry Danishes, and two coffees."

The waiter scribbled across a small tablet in his palm. "You will be taking them with you?"

"Aye."

"Oui, monsieur. I will have these for you shortly."

"Merci," Lucan answered as he pushed the lami-

nated menu aside. He folded his hands together on the table and answered Caradoc. "Aye. Much better spirits. Chloe is not a puppet of the unholy."

At the curious lift of Caradoc's eyebrows, Lucan explained the attack and Chloe's intent to ward off the demons. As he recited the tale, however, an unsettling discovery surfaced—Julian. In seeking to avoid her room, Chloe had not turned to her brother. And that brother, in fact, displayed more evidence he might be in league with Azazel than Chloe ever had. Lucan had not realized the obvious until Chloe's innocence became clear.

"Have you seen Julian since yesterday?" Lucan asked.

"Nay. He made an appearance in the lounge last eve, but disappeared soon after." Caradoc forked eggs into his mouth. He let out a satisfied grunt. "I had forgotten how nice breakfast could be until Anne and her menus reminded me. This, however, puts even her new cooks to shame."

Lucan gave the plate a disbelieving squint. "'Tis eggs."

Caradoc's gaze drifted out the window. More quietly he added, "'Tis Europe. And I have missed her."

Aye, they all missed their motherland. 'Twas where they had laid their roots, sowed their youthful oats, and spilled blood all in the name of leaders now forgotten. A simpler time, in many ways. But Lucan suspected 'twas more than nostalgia that put the sadness in his brother's eyes. More likely, 'twas the last time he had traveled to their homeland and met the dark-haired beauty called Isabelle.

Finding his seraph would do much to combat Caradoc's suffering. Lucan clapped Caradoc's shoulder, squeezed in reassurance. "We will search for yours when this business with the Veronica is over."

A veil passed over Caradoc's face, disguising whatever thoughts lurked in his head. He drank from his mug and summoned a brief smile. "You are off to Picardie with Chloe?"

Lucan blinked. He had told no one. "How did you know?"

Chuckling, Caradoc shook his head. "Mikhail informed me last eve when I told him the sample you collected was en route. He bade me to ask you to retrieve a package for me."

"Aye?" Lucan gave into a grin. "Mayhap the search begins soon."

"Nay. 'Tis research from Anne, regarding the final disposition of what was once known as Asterleigh."

"You seek to find those who own your holdings?"

Again, the grim lines pulled across Caradoc's face. "Nay," he answered quietly. "I seek to say good-bye. I shall not return to Europe again."

A chill drifted through Lucan at the pointed reference to their rapidly deteriorating souls. He had done his best to ignore his brother's pain, for with each day it became greater, and Caradoc drifted closer to transformation. But in his words, Lucan read resignation. The final acceptance his fate had reached a bitter end.

Unable to stomach the thought of losing one he was so close to, Lucan swallowed hard. "You do not know such. 'Tis still time enough to find your seraph."

Caradoc rose as the waiter wove his way through the tables, carrying Lucan's order. "I do not want her, Lucan. 'Tis unfair to ask her to heal what she cannot." He left the table as the waiter set down a small bag and two travel cups of coffee, leaving Lucan unable to follow.

Lucan paid for his order, determined not to allow Caradoc's morose mood to infect his good humor. He quickly fled the table and hurried back to his room. Inside, he smiled at the still-sleeping Chloe and set his things on the table near the door. A chuckle possessed him as he viewed the room from a distance. What remained of their dinner, the wineglasses near the bed, the tangled bedding itself—would that the night had turned out the way it surely would appear to the maid.

He crossed the room and crawled over Chloe to straddle her thighs with his knees. Bending over her, he touched his lips to hers. "'Tis morn, my sweet."

When she did not immediately stir, the devilish side of his nature reared its dark head. He trailed a solitary fingertip down her neck. Pushing the quilt aside, he delved deeper, traced the soft rise of her breast above the thin scrap of lace. Her breast tightened with goose bumps, the rosy nipple beneath the lace hardening into a stiff bud. He glanced up at her face, studied her for signs of wakefulness as he lowered his head and closed his mouth around the pert nub. The lace scraped against his tongue as he gently suckled.

Chloe stirred beneath him. She turned her head to the opposite side, shifted a leg. Her lips parted with a quiet murmur, but she did not open her eyes.

Lucan fought the rise of his own desire and tightened his fingers into the sheets at her shoulders, determined not to answer the call of arousal. Slowly, deliberately, he trailed the tip of his tongue to her opposite breast. He grazed his teeth over the covered nipple there, then closed his eyes and drew it between his lips. Her scent swamped his awareness. Light and flowery, it enticed more than the warmth that ebbed off her body. All feminine. All her.

If he could but change things. Transform this waking into a lover's impassioned embrace. Feel her arms slide around his waist and urge him to lower his body into hers . . .

Her fingers glided through his hair. Gentle pressure on his head pressed his mouth harder to her breast. "What are you doing?" Chloe murmured thickly.

Regretting that he must release her, he let her nipple slide from his lips and lifted his head with a playful grin. "'Tis time for you to leave my bed or stay in it through the day."

Her eyes widened in surprise, and she let out a husky laugh. Rocking back to his heels, he gathered her in his arms and drew her upright. "I brought you breakfast."

She gave him a scolding glance. "You're spoiling me."

"Aye, and I intend a full day of it." He retrieved their breakfast from the table, passed her a coffee, and deposited the bag in her lap. On observing her lack of clothing, he thought better of breakfast in bed and grabbed his shirt off the floor. Tossing it into her lap as well, he grinned. "Lest you wish a different sort of spoiling, 'tis best you dress."

Amber eyes widened with false innocence. "My lack of clothing bothers you?"

He grunted. "'Twould not under different circumstance."

"Circumstance like?" She slid her arms into the shirt and drank her coffee.

Lucan gave her a perturbed frown. "Do not play games. You well know what I speak of."

As if she had said naught at all, she plied open the bag and let out a squeak of delight. "Blueberry! My favorite!"

Her simple display of pleasure softened the growing tension in Lucan's body. Unable to help himself, he chuckled at her exuberance and perched on the edge of the mattress. Taking up one of the cinnamon Danishes, he asked, "How would you feel about a trip to Picardie today? I must go there to pick up a package for Caradoc."

"Today?" she asked around a mouthful. Shaking her head, she protested, "The sun's out, the site will thaw, and my team can get a lot of work done. I can't." She swallowed, waited a beat, and added, "But maybe we could sneak in a movie after."

The boon was tremendous, and Lucan bit back immediate acceptance. No matter how he would enjoy seeing his first movie with Chloe, he sought something more important. Something only Picardie could yield, and he had anticipated her argument. As such, he had anticipated the numerous ways to combat it. He took a bite, chewed, then countered, "'Tis one day. How long has it been since you have indulged in something unrelated to work?"

As expected, she hesitated. Chewing more slowly, she turned the Danish over as if she inspected it for flaws. "Awhile."

"And if I told you that in your excavation you will find naught of significance beyond the Veronica?"

With another sip of coffee, she swallowed. "How would you know?"

He shrugged, choosing to make no mention of Alaric le Goix's Templar past. "The Church has known about the site for centuries. All that is buried there is documented deep in the catacombs."

"Which blows my mind. I still don't understand why, if that relic is what you say it is, you've left it in the ground for so long and let it essentially disappear."

"In time, you will understand." He tore off a chunk of warm pastry and popped it into his mouth. "Will you accompany me?"

The fluffy Danish lodged in Chloe's throat. A day to forget about everything but a little bit of fun. With Lucan. Away from Julian's prying eyes and mistrusting remarks.

She'd like nothing more.

But a full day with Lucan was exactly what she sought to avoid. Particularly after the last several hours in his company. She needed time to think. Away from him, where she could sort her thoughts and figure out exactly what she wanted. Or didn't want. Already, the lines blurred. They slept like lovers. Talked like lovers. Touched like lovers. But they weren't. Not in the true sense. And she couldn't continue to lead him down a path when she didn't know the destination. She wanted him; she didn't want him—hot and cold a man would quickly lose patience with.

No, she didn't dare bail on her team for a few frivolous hours of play. She couldn't continue to play games with Lucan and keep him teetering on the edge. Maybe if he went without her, she might find the answers she needed.

"I'm sorry, Lucan. I can't. It's just not a good day to evade work."

"'Tis too bad," he commented with a one-shoulder shrug. Sliding off the bed, he set his coffee on the nightstand, then went to the dresser to pull out a pair of faded blue jeans. "I thought you might enjoy a day of freedom from the things that haunt you."

Her pastry halfway to her mouth, Chloe froze. Her gaze riveted on his broad shoulders. Freedom from the demons . . . Could he? She stopped the budding hope with a grimace. No, he couldn't. Eight years she'd suffered their presence. He couldn't just shoo them away in a matter of hours. "That's impossible. They never leave."

He caught her gaze in the mirror and held it. "'Tis possible. I promise. You will not notice them one bit."

His pledge was fantastic. Too fantastic to be true. Yet, a near-decade of torment refused to let go of the flickering hope that maybe he knew something all the others didn't. Maybe he had a charm to ward them off and *keep* them away. For that, she'd risk everything. "Okay."

The smile that spread across his face trumpeted victory. Damn it all, he'd known she wouldn't be able to resist. Once again, he'd said the right words, and she'd fallen right into his strategic trap. The man was good. Too good.

Grumbling to herself, she polished off the last of her Danish and took a gulp of her coffee. He understood her entirely too well. Time to solve that problem. "We need to set some ground rules though."

"Aye?"

Chloe nearly choked on her coffee as he shucked his sleeping pants without a care in the world. She squeezed her eyes shut, hoping to block the fabulous view before she couldn't forget it. No luck—fantastically tight buttocks and firm thighs appeared on the back of her

eyelids. Her heart jumped, and a delightful warmth
skittered through her veins.

Ground rules indeed.

Cracking open one eye, she found him fastening his
fly. Dimly it occurred that she hadn't seen boxers or
briefs come out of his drawer. But before she could
fully consider whether he'd had time to don them or
not, she shoved the thought aside.

"Yes. No touching and no kissing."

Lucan leaned a hip on the dresser and folded his
arms over his chest. A wry smile pulled at one corner
of his mouth. "I cannot promise such."

Chloe blinked rapidly. She opened her mouth to protest, to somehow cry foul, but words eluded her. At a
complete loss, she spluttered something unintelligible.

His chuckle sent a rush of heat to her cheeks. Amused.
What had gotten into him this morning? *This* was the
side of him she'd expected that first night, when he'd
caught her giving him an appreciative once-over. The
side that hinted at naughtiness. Nothing like the gentle-
man he'd been the last few days. Had last night changed
him? Given him the assumption more lay between
them?

"Chloe, do you intend to dress? Or will you sit there
all morning and fight for boundaries we have both already crossed?" He tugged a brick red shirt over his
head that did nothing to hide the definition in his well-
toned muscles. "I am spending the day with you, away
from all the stress of duty. I intend to enjoy myself."
Turning, he gave her a meaningful look. "I expect you
to do the same."

She told herself she slid from beneath the quilt without argument because her curiosity demanded she

discover whether he could indeed keep demons away, not because she liked the idea of not having to play by rules. Certainly not because the fleeting thought of Lucan smashing through all her protective barriers and forcing her to admit she wanted this thing between them held great appeal.

And absolutely not because the casual way he undressed in front of her suggested they already shared a deeper intimacy than she cared to admit.

She pulled on her clothes from the day before and rested her hands on her hips. "I need clean clothes and a shower."

"Clean clothes you shall have." He swept one hand toward the door, inviting her to go before him as he picked up their coats with the other. "Shower we do not have time for."

Great. An entire day with Lucan and she couldn't even clean up first. Muttering her displeasure, she yanked open the door.

In the hall, Lucan caught her by the wrist and dragged her to an abrupt halt. He turned her around so she had no choice but to look up at him and leaned in, his forehead inches from hers. "Cease your anger. I much prefer your smile." As his broke free, he tucked a lock of hair behind her ear. "'Tis too pretty to keep it hidden away."

To her shame, her resistance wobbled. No way could she resist compliments like that. Nor could she ignore the sincerity that warmed his gray eyes. With a sigh from the depths of her soul, she surrendered the annoyance that allowed her to keep him at a distance. "Fine," she whispered, hating that he could win her over with so little effort.

CHAPTER 25

✝

"What is it, exactly, that we're doing in Picardie?"

Navigating the winding road that ran through the French countryside and led to the region in question, Lucan chuckled to himself. He had wondered when Chloe would ask. For the last hour she had chattered about everything except where they were going and what they intended to do. Now, as the medieval hilltop town of Laon rose above the trees, she leaned forward to squint through the windshield.

"I have some errands to attend to in Laon."

"Oh." Curiosity satisfied, she fell back in her seat and resumed their previous discussion. "So I was thinking about this le Goix fellow. Since I'm excavating what is evidently his holdings, do you think we might uncover *him*?"

Lucan choked down a cough. "Nay." 'Twould be difficult since the man lived and breathed. Though Alaric would take great amusement in Chloe's deduction. He must remember to share this story.

"Damn," she muttered. "A real Templar knight would be quite the find. Kinda like that site in Languedoc a few years ago. Did you know about that? The knight found with all his regalia and a large collection of gold and relics?"

The unexpected memory hit Lucan with such force he could not find words. He tightened his grip on the wheel to squeeze the vivid remembrance of attack from his mind.

Chloe continued musing aloud, oblivious to his tense posture. "If le Goix was there with the Veil, that would prove without a doubt the Templars not only found sacred relics beneath the Temple Mount, but that they brought them back to Europe and hid them away."

"I knew of the grave," Lucan managed through a tight throat. That he had helped dig it, he would not confess. Nor would he share how the items buried with Gervais St. Soisson brought his early death. But the scene played in his mind as vividly as the day he had lost his brother in arms. Dark knights pouring from the trees, their ebony armor as black as the starless sky above. Horrific beings, transformed men who had once stood at his side. Their screams echoed in Lucan's head, despite the passing of centuries.

'Twas the first time he had battled the fallen Templar. He would never forget the brief flicker of remorse that had passed behind Gervais' eyes as his blood ran down Lucan's arm.

"I wonder who he was. What brought him to France— they didn't find architectural ruins like we have. He must not have lived there."

"He lived near Soisson."

"Oh?" Chloe's voice perked with keen interest. "I

didn't read any follow-up publications. Did they determine who he was?"

"Aye, Gervais St. Soisson. Born in the latter part of the twelfth century. He was—" Lucan caught himself before he admitted more than archaeological skills could uncover. Avoiding the explanation Gervais had been traveling to bid his family adieu, Lucan covered his slip of the tongue. "They suspect he was traveling when an accident befell him."

"Someone had to bury him, though. The villagers? That doesn't make sense. Anyone would have taken the treasures they found in the grave. Nor does it make sense that the Templar would bury him and leave both the treasure and his shield to identify him."

Lucan navigated a tight turn with clenched teeth. Whilst she merely mused aloud, her words sliced him into pieces. They had fought many battles together. Taken their immortal oaths side-by-side. Gervais rose to greatness, his honor and devotion more pure than many, even, sadly, Lucan's. All this Chloe should know. Her birth dictated that right. But tell her?

He ground his teeth together more harshly. Aye. Tell her. 'Twas why he brought her on this journey today—to share more of the truths and give her the ability to reconcile her find in Ornes with the Veronica and her immortal calling.

"Gervais attained the status of grand master within the Templar. You will not find his name in recorded history, his tenure was so short. Three days he held the position. On the third, he was attacked for the relics he carried." He frowned in attempts to block the memory from taking life once more. He could not tell her how he had stood less than a foot away as a dark knight speared Gervais through the heart. Nor could he elaborate on how he had held his brother close, listening to the last prayer rattle off his lips.

He swallowed, feeling once again the way Gervais' blood soaked into his clothes and wetted his skin. "His wounds were mortal. He was given an honorable burial, the relics left beneath the ground for protection—as with the Veronica."

How in the world could Lucan know such specifics? Chloe stared at him, wide-eyed. Although they dominated society, much of Templar life had been recorded. Never the secret meetings, never what occurred behind closed doors. But by nature of their organizational structure and the different heads of state that interacted with their leaders, the Templar leaders made it into history. Except for one, according to Lucan.

"That's crazy. An unknown grand master, buried relics—Lucan, how do you know all that?"

He kept his stare firmly affixed on the road. "I have made it my life to know the Templar."

His solemn tone of voice gave her goose bumps. An eeriness settled around her, much the same way it had the night before, when complete stillness pulled her from deep sleep.

All his knowledge quite frankly spooked her. But it did something else as well. It sparked her curiosity. Left her twisting between reality and speculation. And the more he said, the more she searched for holes in his theories.

Slanting a sideways glance his way, she did just that. "So why mark the grave? Why put a shield in it that says *I am Templar,* if the Order has just been persecuted by the Inquisition and they want to hide their relics? By nature of the beast, that's counterproductive."

He shifted in his seat, his discomfort pronounced in the deep crease between his eyebrows. "'Twas never their intent to disassociate. 'Twas more to protect the sacred knowledge they attained. As for Gervais—'twas a matter of honor to be buried as befitting his status."

Chloe chewed on humility. Years of studying Egyptians who were entombed with all their worldly possessions in preparation for a greater afterlife should have led her to that answer. Every culture in the world that celebrated its leaders honored them with lavish funeral rites. Alexander the Great named a damn city after his horse to honor its death. Burial with sword, shield, armor, and gold should come as no surprise.

Lucan filled the quiet, justifying the conclusion she'd reached. "In an era where survival depended on sword and armor, a great many men were put to rest with their most valued possessions. For Gervais, 'twas the sword and shield, for he possessed no sons to pass them on to in memoriam. The same would apply to me, and the sword I carry, were this the twelfth century."

"Yeah," she concurred with a nod. "That makes sense I suppose." At the mention of his sword, she glanced over her shoulder. It lay on the seat, silver scabbard shining in the sunlight. Until this moment she'd thought it some sort of reproduction. But as she studied the etchings in the scabbard and noted the same odd design of le Goix's wall carving, another chill gripped her. The protruding hilt also defied all possibility that it had been crafted in the last ten years. Hell, within the last century even. Despite the newish leather wrapped around the hilt, a deep engraved pattern in the rounded head of the pommel had worn smooth. Only a few faint scratches marked the place where an insignia sat. Steel didn't wear like that without a significant passage of time.

"Where did you get that sword again?" She looked at Lucan, gauging his honesty by his unchanging, flat expression. Not so much as a flinch darted over his handsome face. No help whatsoever.

"I inherited it."

A vague picture of Caradoc standing near the excavation pit, a similar sword dangling around his waist, flitted across her mind. "Caradoc has one too. Why?"

His jaw stiffened. He squinted, ever so slightly, at the road in front of them. Subtle signs, but proof all the same, that he didn't enjoy her line of questioning. Tough. She didn't enjoy this queasy feeling that came with the suspicion her excursion to Ornes held more secrets of history than just the finding of Veronica's Veil. "Lucan, that sword is too old and too perfect to be carried around casually. It should be in a museum. Why isn't it?"

He cleared his throat, repositioned his hands on the steering wheel, and gave her a brief glance. "Caradoc's history and ancestors have intertwined with mine through the centuries. We now work together, but we originate in a time when the swords were customary."

So they shared similar family heritages. Interesting how fate could lead people back together through coincidence. That explained why they both possessed swords, but it didn't say anything for why they *carried* them. And she wasn't inclined to let him slide around that question. "But why not keep them at home? I mean, last night, you looked like you intended to fight with that thing."

"Aye, I would have."

She let out a short laugh. "It would take years to learn how to fight with any real expertise." At his un-changing frown, she doubted her own convictions. Maybe not. Maybe Lucan's powerful build afforded him an advantage. Those hard pecs didn't come from sitting around on a couch, that's for sure. She squinted at him. "Wouldn't it?"

"It takes a great many years to master the broadsword, but 'tis not an impossible feat. Caradoc and I routinely practice. And you need not possess special licenses to carry a sword, like guns."

Chloe couldn't argue that sound logic. With strict airport security and differing European regulations that were too confusing to track from city to city, let alone country to country, even Julian left his prized pistol in his gun safe in Tucson. Still, something sounded off. Something she couldn't put her finger on, but the goose bumps that refused to smooth away reflected it.

"'Twould be an honor to teach you, if you should like to learn." He flashed a quick smile.

His unique accent rang a discordant chord in her head. Too harsh to be French, too resonating for stilted British. For anything else, it was too . . .

Archaic.

She shivered. Yes, archaic and formal. An accent that could pair all too neatly with the sword in the backseat. As if he had plucked it out of the very same chamber that had spawned the Veronica. Or maybe the formalities that accompanied the medallion around his neck.

Could he and Caradoc possibly be affiliated with a Masonic group that harbored the Templar secrets?

"How do you know so much about these relics, Lucan? What did you study that others haven't, or can't? Something in the bowels of the Church? Or does it have something to do with that hunk of silver around your neck?"

They rounded another bend, and houses replaced the dense surrounding greenery. No more than two hundred yards beyond, higher up the hillside, the sparse cottages conglomerated into a sprawling railway city, much like the size of the suburbs around Tucson. The first smile she'd witnessed in the last hour tugged at the corner of Lucan's mouth as he gestured at the aging buildings. "Save for a few years of my youth, I have always worked for the Church. There are many secrets in her cloisters." His smile broadened, lightening his eyes to the color of rain clouds. "Cease your questions, milady. You shall find answers soon enough."

With a short inclination of his head, he directed her attention to the massive thirteenth-century Porte d'Ardon arch. Chloe leaned forward in her seat and studied the ramparts that blockaded Laon and the two fat turrets on each side of the stone monstrosity. Awe stole the breath from her lungs. Living history. Unlike the majestic pyramids encapsulated by sand and the artifacts she pulled from the earth, these stone blocks defied the passing of time. As they had hundreds of years ago, people still strolled beneath the shaded passage to enter the heart of the city. Homes rose within the sheltered bailey, though these were crafted from brick, not thatch and mud as they once had been.

Here, the mark of the ancients brought her closer to the past. Put her on level footing with the peasants, the knights, the gentry who had reigned within. Reminded her she was not so far removed from the people and cultures she now studied.

Struck speechless, she stared out the window, her discomfort with Lucan's claims temporarily forgotten. Culture and charm radiated from the weathered edifices, a proud display of heritage the French revered. They made a sharp right, and Chloe's eyes widened. The infamous Cathedral de Laon stood at the end of the cobbled street.

Six tall towers reached skyward, each a perfect representation of Gothic architecture. High decorative arches beckoned visitors to enter. Perched on the gabled corners, ornately carved gargoyles monitored those who walked beneath. But what made Chloe's breath catch was the rose window that trapped the early morning sun and showered the surrounding stone with soft lavender.

"Oh, wow," she breathed.

"Aye. 'Tis beautiful. Though you would never know from looking at her, she is unfinished."

"Unfinished?" Chloe craned her neck as they passed into the sweeping shadows that darkened the street.

"The towers do not all match."

Sure enough, two stood out from the rest, lacking the top third of their siblings' height, including the needle-thin spires that grazed the clouds. But without knowing the flaw, the pairing was so precise it appeared intentional. "Are we going inside?"

"Only if we have time. We have more important things to see today."

A flicker of disappointment had Chloe sinking into her seat. Probably the most exciting site she'd seen in a good ten years, at least one that had absolutely nothing

to do with her work and could only be considered plea-
sure, and true to her luck, she'd miss the tour. Fine.
She'd make a point of coming back before she left
France.

But as they rounded the next turn, and Lucan steered
toward the curb, another stone edifice brought her upright in her seat once more. Although much smaller
than the grandiose cathedral, a stately bell tower atop a
rather plain square porch marked this building as a
place of worship. Simpler style. Devoid of the lavish fly-
ing buttresses, but still possessing carved modillions
beneath the roof's edge. Older, she determined with a
touch of curiosity.

Lucan shut the engine off, drawing her attention
away from the weathered blocks with their tricolor hues.

"What are we doing?"

The console chimed as he opened his door. "'Tis our
destination. The Chapel of the Knights Templar and its
forgotten cemetery."

Chloe blinked. She didn't know which word she feared
the most—cemetery, or the all-too-familiar Templar.

CHAPTER 26

T heir footsteps echoed hollowly on the broad pavers that led around the side of the quaint chapel and to the gardens beyond, where snow tipped manicured evergreen shrubs and gathered, untouched, on the clipped lawn. Chloe hugged Lucan's side, afraid to disturb the pristine blanket with a misstep, certain whoever had taken the trouble to shovel the walk would come rushing out with a string of French obscenities. The warmth of Lucan's hand against hers soaked in to soothe her apprehensions. As his touch always did.

With an inward sigh, she accepted all she'd been fighting so hard to deny. She *liked* him. Really liked him. Professional competitor, secretive historian—none of it made a difference when they were alone like this. Away from all the things that reminded her why she shouldn't give in to the way he lit her up from the inside out each time he turned those unsettling gray eyes her way.

"Where are we going?" she asked as he guided her

around a fork in the path and beneath the sweeping branches of a massive old oak.

"We will enter at the rear."

He stopped before a weathered wooden door reinforced with iron studs. She eyed the rusted hinges, certain if he tried to open the barrier it would either break loose and topple over, or remain firmly lodged shut. But Lucan didn't pull on the handle. He lifted the circular knocker and dropped it three times.

To Chloe's surprise, an answering knock sounded on the opposite side. Three times again. Each spaced in even intervals. She cocked an eyebrow as Lucan, and whoever stood on the other side, repeated the odd process.

Code? Church identification? Strange.

More strange was the six-foot-tall block of stone embedded in the buttress that swung inward. She glanced between the dark opening and the firmly shut door, then looked to Lucan for an explanation.

He tossed her a smug grin. "After you."

"Oh, hell no. I can't see in there. I'm not going to be the one to walk into cobwebs." And no way in the world was she going into that black abyss first. Too many things more terrifying than spiders could lurk inside. She'd left her beloved Egypt because of the things that lurked in the dark.

His laugh bounced off the high walls behind him. "Aye. I shall lead. Though I assure you, you will find no cobwebs. 'Tis Master Reginald's private entry." Ducking under the low hanging bulkhead, Lucan entered the darkened passage.

A tug on her hand insisted she follow. As her toes crossed the threshold between light and dark, however,

Chloe hesitated. With no light inside, not even a sliver of sun peeking through the massive stone blocks, her fears bolted to the surface.

"Chloe," Lucan encouraged with another gentle tug on her arm. "I made you a promise, did I not? 'Tis naught to fear in here."

"I'm coming," she hurried to cover her ridiculous anxiety. "Waiting for my eyes to adjust."

"And I am here." His fingers tightened against hers.

Chloe sank her teeth into her lower lip and took a deep breath. It was just a passage, one that, according to him, was regularly used. Even with the curse, she'd managed to work in underground tombs, and frequently without a light. Still, the encounter the night before had taken its toll, and no amount of logic could stop the hammering of her heart. She gripped Lucan's hand tightly and shuffled forward.

Lucan's fingers slid up to her elbow. His body heat drew nearer. Though his fingers were light against her skin, and he touched nothing else, she felt his presence as keenly as if he had slid an arm around her waist. She knew instinctively his chest sheltered her left shoulder. Felt the slight caress of his breath against her hair.

Drawing on the silent strength he offered, she felt her fear diminish. The shadows cloaked all but a faint beam of sunlight that filtered through the entry behind them and illuminated a descending stairwell. She squinted into the blackness ahead.

"I must shut this. Stay still. I am right behind you."

Chloe nodded.

The stone door rolled effortlessly closed, squelching the last bit of light. Lucan's hand settled on her shoulder. Warm and moist, his breath whispered over her cheek. At the light press of his lips, Chloe shivered. She summoned a laugh to fight off the nonsensical urge to twist into his arms and drown her fears in the velvet heat of his mouth. How long had it been since she'd kissed him? Six hours at most? It felt like years.

She breathed in the rich spice of his skin, and in the complete darkness that surrounded them, became aware of the warm body behind her. Odd how lack of sight intensified the rest of her senses. She could see more of this man now than she'd ever witnessed in the light. Not just his amazing physique, but what lay beneath the surface. His sincerity. The honesty in his words.

He interrupted the magical spell by moving past her. "Come. I should like to introduce you to Master Reginald. He should be arriving from the nave soon."

The nonsensical statement jarred her back to reality. Following his slow descent, she asked, "Arriving? Who opened the door?"

His low chuckle reverberated off the walls and scraped pleasantly over her skin. "'Tis operated from the nave. A lever in the wall behind a statue."

"Why?"

"Because, my sweet, there are things in this chamber only a privileged few may witness."

They came to an abrupt stop, and Chloe discovered the reason for the pitch black. Lucan put his shoulder against something that moved. A door, she realized, as it squeaked open and illuminated the stairwell with burnished orange light. He ushered her through the entry into a wide room adorned with ancient timber shelves and iron sconces in the walls. Torches, yes torches, brightened intricately carved stone and cast flickering shadows over a mosaic tile floor. A man sat at a plain wooden table against the far wall, bent over a leather-bound book, his long graying hair cloaking his face.

"Hello, Lucan," he said without looking up.

"Master Reginald." Lucan strode forward, dragging Chloe reluctantly away from a marble statue of an angel. "I have brought a guest."

"Aye, I was told to expect Miss Broussard." He shut the book and stood, his smile warm and welcoming. He extended a hand. "'Tis a pleasure to meet you, Chloe."

She blinked at his outstretched fingers. How could he possibly have known she'd be with Lucan? Lucan hadn't phoned anyone since she'd awakened, and she hadn't consented to come to Laon until midmorning. "B-but . . . How . . . ?" She blinked again.

Both men chuckled. Reginald clasped her fingers in his, lifted her hand, and brushed a kiss against her knuckles. "'Tis often prudent to forget the how and merely accept what is. I hope your journey was kind to you."

Journey? They'd driven almost two hours—hardly what she'd call a journey. She squinted at him, studying the deep crow's-feet at the corners of his eyes and the heavy smile lines around his mouth. Keen eyes held no trace of feeblemindedness, despite his aging features. And though his stubbly beard grew in with a generous amount of gray, the strength in his grip betrayed power beneath his dark clerical robes.

He released her hand, soft blue eyes lifting to hers. "You have come for knowledge, have you not?"

Chloe looked to Lucan, uncertain.

"Aye," he answered for her. "We would see the markers. And she would like to witness the relics."

"The relics?" It was Reginald's turn to show surprise. "I was not aware such permissions had been granted."

"She digs in dust, my friend. Her permissions are as ours."

Chloe shifted her weight while they talked about her as if she weren't present. As she looked on, the two men's gazes locked. Something passed between them, something silent and full of meaning she couldn't comprehend. Struck once more by Lucan's strange mannerisms and unique way of speech, the hair at the nape of her neck lifted. She rubbed her arms to ward off a sudden chill and gave Reginald a smile she hoped didn't reflect the topsy-turvy nature of her belly. "If it's too much trouble, really, I can do without."

"Nay." As if a greater force spurred him to life, Reginald hurried to a large crate in the far corner of the room. "'Tis no trouble at all. They are right here. Ready for your perusal." He dragged the crate away to the center of the room. "But let us start with the markers, shall we?"

"Aye," Lucan agreed.

Motioning them to follow, Reginald crossed to the back of the door they'd entered through. A gnarled finger tapped a deep etching in the stone. A carving that identically matched the unique sword engraved in the le Goix ruins. Chloe's eyes widened.

"Turn and look beyond you now," Reginald instructed.

Obediently, Chloe pivoted and discovered Lucan hadn't followed. Instead, he'd moved to the opposite wall. A torch in hand, he stood with his back pressed to the stone.

"Look above Lucan's head," Reginald murmured.

She lifted her gaze to where the bright light flickered on the white lime blocks. Deep shadows filled gaps in the mortar she hadn't observed before. They stretched to the ceiling in parallel lines spaced exactly a stone's width apart. Two feet down from the overhead support arch so typical of Templar design, the shadows spanned sideways. Chloe gasped. Her gaze skimmed down the wide length, anxious and hesitant all at once. She didn't want to look. Couldn't stop herself.

There, level with Lucan's head, the shadows soaked into a recessed circular design. She knew that if she moved closer, it too would bear the Eye of Horus. As did the one beneath Reginald's hand.

"Why?" she exhaled.

Lucan switched hands with the torch, turning the wall behind him into a plain block of stacked stone once more. "Where are you, Chloe? What is the name of this place?" he asked as he fitted the wooden handle back into its empty sconce.

She furrowed her brows, unable to follow his train of thought. "The Templar Chapel."

"Aye, indeed. And the marks you see identify it as such." He dusted his hands on his jeans. "They also designate this place as a holding for sacred relics. The same as le Goix." As he talked, he dragged two chairs to opposite ends of the two-foot-long crate Reginald had moved. "You will find Templar ruins throughout the world. But only those with markers contain the truths of the Church, and no common man will ever bear witness to them."

He beckoned to her with a lift of his hand. "Come see what was discovered beneath the Temple Mount."

Chloe's heart skidded to a stop. Legend after legend

claimed to know what the ancient Order found and what they did with their treasure. In a hundred years she never would have guessed she might learn the truth, let alone touch the artifacts. She looked to Lucan, afraid to believe, unable to accept the reality of his claims.

His solemn expression professed unyielding conviction. The light in his eyes, however, spoke to her soul. Laden with meaning, his unblinking stare made it impossible to deny his words. He was giving her this gift. This boon of knowledge that no other person outside of the Church would witness. Entrusting her with secrets that had been guarded for centuries.

The deeper meaning in his gaze penetrated her mind. *Trust me, as I trust you.*

He dipped his head toward the large crate. "Open the lid, Chloe."

No request for a promise she wouldn't reveal what lay inside. No warning that these were the Church's alone. Just the unfettered offering. Chills coursed down her spine as her heart twisted painfully. How could she doubt a man who gave without restraint? If he meant to usurp her efforts, he wouldn't bestow this honor on her. She could easily lead someone back here, release whatever sat inside this hide-covered crate to the world, if he did.

But he wouldn't. In the depths of her heart, she knew Lucan wouldn't climb over her to attain his own goals. He wasn't like Blake. He didn't even come close to resembling that leech.

Chloe reached between them and slipped her fingers into his. Yes, she could trust him. This didn't explain how he knew so much, or how he happened to discover all these buried secrets. He couldn't free her from the demons, or conquer that inevitable divide, but she could trust him until the demons forced them apart.

"Show me," she said with a smile.

He bent over and opened the lid with one hand, revealing several parchment scrolls tied together with a crimson ribbon. "These are testaments and accounts from the days the Almighty walked amongst man. They, and several other items, are scattered in the bellies of Templar holdings." Gently lifting out the bundle, he offered them to her. "Would you care to read? Master Reginald has left us to spend as much time as we desire."

She glanced up, surprised the older man had exited so quietly. Sure enough, the chamber was empty, save for the two of them. Curious, she slipped the tip of her finger beneath the scarlet silk and traced the fragile edge of the topmost scroll. Bits of parchment flaked off and crumbled, giving her pause. "I don't think I want to harm them."

Lucan shook his head. "They cannot be destroyed."

With a shaking hand, Chloe pushed a leather tie off one and gently unfurled it. Her breath caught as she scanned ancient handwriting, so precise, so meticulous it was astounding. But to her dismay, the words were unintelligible, a language she couldn't decipher.

"What language is this? Aramaic?"

Again, Lucan shook his head. "Aramaic is a language of men. These words came before. 'Tis the language of angels, Chloe."

The language of angels? Chloe blinked. Impossible.

He must have seen doubt pass over her face, for he leaned across the crate and pointed at the bottom of the parchment in her hands. "That one is signed by Gabriel." He touched one still in the cloth. "This bears Mikhail's signature."

How could it be? He was talking fantastic stories, and he wanted her to believe? Just because the name was indeed legible? Not wanting to spoil the afternoon with an argument, she slipped the ribbon back around the illegible document and passed it back to him. "Summarize for me?"

"Aye, if you wish." He set the scrolls back into the crate and shut the lid. "This particular collection contains accounts of the angels, the Nephilim in specific. Documented incidents where the fallen ones made mates out of mankind. Details about the stripping of their immortality and a recitation of the prophecy that their descendants would rise again when most needed."

"When most needed? Sounds a bit like Judgment Day."

He shook his head. "Nay, they are not the same. Those who carry the blood of angels possess power. The ability to overcome evil. Judgment Day is the judging of mankind."

Chloe frowned at the hidden etching on the wall behind him. "What's this have to do with that, other than the sword identifies this place as sacred?"

"The Templar discovered these things. Against the will of the Almighty."

"But why didn't they reveal them? They must have brought them to the Church, which yielded their immense power, and I suspect their demise as well. But why not share them with the world? Wouldn't that give them even more power? That would have prevented the

Inquisition and the burnings at the stake for heresy." Her frown deepened as another unsettling question surfaced. "And why keep them hidden now?"

"As I have mentioned before, there are those who would abuse the sacred knowledge. If placed in the wrong hands, 'twould have caused wars and persecution, changing all you know."

She gave him a doubtful look. No written word could have that much power or influence unless those documents, or others like them, disavowed the existence of Christ. Highly unlikely since the accounts here specifically pertained to the Almighty and his heavenly aides.

Lucan stood. "In time you will understand more. Let us enter the chapel itself."

Refusing to stand just yet, she stopped his about-face with a pull on his arm. "Wait. Does all this mean the Templar worked *for* the Church? Is that what you've been trying to tell me about the Veronica?"

Pride emanated from his wide smile. "You are very close. The Templar are servants to the Church."

Are. Her brain locked onto the present tense like neon paint thrown on a white canvas. "Are? Surely you don't believe the legends that the Templar still exist? That was hundreds of years ago. If they gathered in secret, by now someone would have spilled the beans."

Lucan's smile faltered, and a hint of sadness touched his eyes. Or maybe it was disappointment. She couldn't tell. Whatever it was, he didn't care for her challenge. As evidenced further by his clipped response. "Let us leave this place, Chloe. We have other things to accomplish before we must return to the château."

CHAPTER 27

‡

For the second time that day, Chloe fitted her hand into Lucan's of her own accord. A thrill slithered up her arm as his fingers twined with hers. He held on loosely, but with enough possessiveness in his grip to let her know he welcomed the casual link. Slowing his purposeful stride, he matched her pace and gave her the freedom to admire the masonry inside the nave.

Simple designs held a touch of bold elegance. Like the chamber below, the walls sported unlit torches and the floor bore the same mosaic of dark brown and beige tiles. Plain, but extraordinary at the same time.

"Did you find what you sought?" Master Reginald asked from behind a large desk near the front entry that served as a visitor's center.

To Chloe's dismay, Lucan disentangled his hand and left her to admire a life-size statue of a medieval lord alone. He joined Reginald at the dark mahogany desk. Bracing both palms on the polished surface, he leaned forward and lowered his voice. His dark hair tumbled over his shoulder, shielding his face, making her efforts to read his lips pointless.

She grunted inwardly as she realized what she was doing. She shouldn't be eavesdropping. His business was his. What he discussed with his coworkers, or even his friends, was none of her concern. Still, she couldn't stop the misplaced annoyance that niggled at the base of her skull. Until now, he'd included her on most everything. No, not *most*. When they were together, he didn't exclude her at all. So why now?

Bending her head, she looked out the corner of her eye through her own long locks and watched. The two men exchanged a hushed laugh. Lucan bobbed his head as if he agreed with whatever Reginald had said. Then, he picked up a pen and scribbled something on an open notebook. Reginald's smile grew to wolfish proportions as he again laughed. Only this time, he looked over Lucan's shoulder, straight at her.

Busted. *Damn*.

She sucked in a short breath. Held it. Forced her gaze to her feet. At least it was Reginald, not Lucan, who'd observed her not-so-subtle attempt at spying. She didn't have to spend the rest of the day with him.

The scrape of wood against the hard floor was too much to resist. She cut her gaze back to Lucan's broad shoulders in time to see him accept a package and stuff it under his arm. He thrust out a hand, shook with Reginald, and turned around.

Chloe reached out to touch the statue's face, feigning fascination with the artist's meticulous representation. Right down to the narrow band of metal around the nobleman's head, no detail went unobserved. The man's eyes even held a touch of supernatural life. As if he could see her, as clearly as she saw him.

Lucan's hand settled on her shoulder, startling her. "I have finished what I came for. Shall we go?"

"That was quick."

"'Twas just a package." He thumped the padded envelope beneath his arm. "'Twas left for Caradoc."

Caradoc? How strange. The château accepted mail. She squinted at Lucan. "Why not send it via mail? Shoot, how would anyone know you were going to be here anyway?" The minute she asked the question, she wanted to kick herself. Someone *had* known Lucan would be here today. Her too. And Reginald had avoided answering when she'd asked.

"'Tis more expedient when I am already here. 'Twould take another day or two to reach him via post."

Must be Church business. Or something related to the Veronica. Maybe an edict to pull it out from under her before their carbon dating samples could come back with any solid proof about the cloth.

She winced as the thought crept in. No. Lucan controlled the relic, not Caradoc. If the Church wanted it returned immediately, they'd contact him.

Shoving her doubt aside, she summoned the brightest smile she could muster. "Where are we off to next?"

"The cemetery and the woods beyond."

Determined not to revert to childish fears about ghosts in the graveyard, Chloe forbade any reaction but the lifting of her eyebrows. In a calm voice that surprised even her, she asked, "And what's out there?"

His grin teased. "Something you will want to see."

Before she could stop herself, she gave his bicep a

punch. "Jeez, stop with the riddles already. I thought we were going to enjoy ourselves. Yet you keep making me think."

The playful lift of his lips transformed into a wry smirk. He bent his head toward hers, brushed her hair off her shoulder with his knuckles. "If you would but hurry, you would find I have naught but enjoyment on my mind. Come outside so I may kiss you as I have wanted to all morn."

That was all it took to turn her legs into jelly and her stomach upside down. She set a palm against his chest to keep from stumbling forward. Damn, what was it about this man that could zap her senses so completely? One honest little confession, and she had visions of making out against the side of the chapel, the cold stone pressed against her back, his warm hands heating her skin.

"Lest," he murmured, "you have decided such would not be to your enjoyment."

"Not at all," Chloe said on an exhale. He was so close. Too close. All she had to do was lean forward . . .

As if he sensed her train of thought, he closed his hand around hers, lifted it off his chest, and stepped away. Still holding on to her, he led her through the octagonal sanctuary to the entrance to the porch, where Reginald bid them farewell with a lift of his hand. She waved in return, but Lucan's determined strides didn't leave time for words. Before she could blink, sunlight poured down on them, and Lucan turned her into his arms.

But instead of the harsh, passionate embrace her mind had conjured, he cupped her chin with his free hand and tipped her gaze to his. He studied her quietly. Then he slowly bent his head and brought his mouth to hers. Chloe closed her eyes.

Time stood still as his lips played against hers. His breath caressed her cheek, lifting her nerve endings until every fiber of her being awakened to his tender assault. He traced the seam of her mouth with the tip of his tongue, provoking a sigh from deep inside her soul. Oh this was nice. So very nice. But it wasn't enough. Too much distance spanned between them. She craved the taste of him. Parting her lips, she invited him to take whatever he wanted.

Lucan didn't hesitate. He slid his hand into the hair at the back of her neck and greedily accepted her offering. Slow, languorous strokes aroused the budding warmth of desire deep within her womb. The scrape of his short nails against her scalp, the way his fingers dug into her waist, spread pleasant heat through her body until she became oblivious to the chilly breeze that tickled his hair against the side of her face. But his mouth remained gentle, disobeying the insistence in his hands. A combination of contradicting pressure that filled Chloe with unexplainable urgency. She slipped her hands beneath his arms and curled her fingers into his shoulder blades. Rising to her toes, she pressed her breasts against his chest.

Lucan's hand slid from her waist to the center of her back. He splayed his fingers and held her in place. Their kiss intensified as their shared hunger for one another bubbled free. Light stubble grazed over her chin. His teeth nipped the tender flesh of her lower lip. A sweep of his tongue soothed the pleasant sting. Yes. This was what she wanted. What she needed. To have Lucan let go so she could indulge in abandon. To know he was as susceptible to her as she was to him.

A frustrated cry threatened to erupt as bliss crashed

to a sudden halt. Lucan eased the kiss to an agonizing close and brushed his thumb over her cheek. His chest heaved in time with hers. "Ah, Chloe, you make me forget myself."

She resisted the urge to thump a fist into his chest and forced out an unsteady chuckle. Reluctantly, she lowered herself to her heels. She nodded toward the thick trees on her left. "There was something you wanted to show me?"

The corner of Lucan's mouth quirked with mischief. "Aye, there are many things I wish to show you." He pressed a kiss to her forehead before releasing her. "But now is not the time, and here is not the place."

Her cheeks warmed at the erotic images that took root in her head. She fought to see beyond them, knowing that if she entertained the ideas, she'd only clam up again as she had the night before. Until she could go through with the physical act of sex, she wouldn't tease him, or herself.

"Show me what it is you wanted me to see. Then I think it's time for a cup of coffee." Anything that would put distance between them. Preferably a table amid a large crowd so she couldn't consider whether it was too cold to drag him behind one of those trees and *make* this the right time and place.

To her immense relief, Lucan ushered her down the narrow footpath, beyond a short row of cracked and pitted tombstones, to a slight break in the trees where cobbles gave way to loose rocks and hard-packed dirt. Caught up in the wonder of her conflicting emotions, she followed him beneath the overhanging skeleton branches into the dense forest.

The trail vanished at the base of a gnarled old elm.

There he turned right and passed behind a clump of overgrown evergreen shrubs. Chloe picked her way through the snow, stepping where he did, to avoid soaking her jeans.

Lucan looked over his shoulder, catching her mid–giant stride. He barked out a laugh, and gave her a shake of his head.

She froze, one foot stretched out twice the length of her normal step, the other twisted awkwardly behind her. "What?"

"Naught." He made an attempt to swallow his smile, but his mouth refused to obey. His lips twitched, and his eyes danced willfully. "I would not think one who dug in mud and sand would have such a fear of snow."

"I'm not dressed for work. My jeans are clean and these are my good . . ." She glanced down at her feet. Despite her efforts, the hem of her jeans darkened with wetness, and the fawn-colored toe of her suede boots was now a telltale shade of dirt-brown. So much for staying dry. She heaved a sigh. "Good shoes," she mumbled.

Her intentions foiled, she dragged her trailing leg forward and plunked it into a drift. "You could have warned me we'd be wading through drifts as deep as my calves."

Grumbling at him did nothing to erase his amused smirk. If anything, it deepened his chuckle. He turned and continued down the path, calling over his shoulder, "Would you prefer I carry you?"

That smirk goaded her. Struck by sheer mischief, she reached down, swept up a handful of snow, packed it as tightly as she could, and launched it at Lucan's broad shoulders. She missed by several inches. Wet, sticky snow exploded on the back of his head.

Chloe let out a squeak and froze, shocked at what she'd just done.

Lucan stumbled to a stop. God's teeth, she had not just . . .

Disbelieving, he turned to find her rooted in place, her hand over her mouth, eyes as wide as if she had just witnessed a demon. He blinked, dumbfounded, as he processed the reality that she had, indeed, smacked him in the head with a snowball.

"I'm sorry!" she blubbered as her own shock fell away. "Oh God, I'm so sorry. I didn't mean—"

Lucan swept up the largest handful of snow he could find and lobbed it across the narrow distance separating them. It struck her in the chest, at the base of her neck, sending chunks of wetness splattering into her face. At her stunned expression, his laughter burst free.

But he was unprepared for her to gather her senses and retaliate so quickly. He barely had time to duck behind a neighboring bush before her next missile sailed past the place where he had been standing.

When he returned fire over the top of the evergreen, a full-scale war began.

She took cover behind a thick tree trunk, her laughter joining his as they sought to claim victory over the other. The ground between them became no-man's-land, and had any of his brothers stumbled onto this scene, they would not have recovered from the shock of his childish antics. But Lucan had not played in eons. Not since his youngest brother had toddled on his heels, taunting Lucan away from chores at every opportunity. And the freedom he experienced, the jubilation that lighted his heart with each laughing squeal from her when he hit his mark, erased centuries of darkness from his soul.

Naught could have made their outing to Picardie more enjoyable or more memorable.

When he was quite thoroughly soaked, he edged around the bush, eyeing her reinforced position behind the tree. She held advantage—he could not clear the distance between them without leaving himself wide open. The laughter that refused to let him clear his head and breathe normally gave her additional superiority. He could not cease no matter how he tried.

'Twas nothing for it, 'twas time for his impish seraph to lose.

With one burst of speed, he shot across the open ground. She pelted him with every other stride. His thighs, his calves, his chest were all fair game. And his laughter rumbled louder. Hers rang through the air, giggles and shouts of triumph that satisfied more than any victory bellow.

But when he cleared the distance and darted behind her shelter, she let out a squeak and took off running. Lucan gave chase, lunging after her with a false growl. A deep bank of snow became her undoing, snagging her foot, catching her unprepared, and sending her stumbling.

He could not stop his own momentum. His fingers latched onto her arm in the same instant, propelling her forward though she had nowhere to go.

They fell together in the snow, amusement falling freely from their lips. He pinned her in place, set his elbows at her shoulders, and gazed down into her twinkling eyes. "Surrender," he ordered, grinning.

Beneath him she panted for breath. Another giggle

slid past her rosy lips, and she wrested her arms free to loop them about his neck. "You cheated."

Lucan scoffed. "I did no such thing. I merely sought to eliminate the threat." By the saints, in all his existence he had never witnessed a more beautiful sight. Her long hair clung to her head in places. Snowflakes glistened across her cheeks. And her eyes . . . the sparkle there erased all that divided them, showing him a glimpse of how life might be if naught placed them at odds. His heart swelled painfully.

As if the same depth of feeling crept over her, Chloe's smile dimmed. The light in her eyes shifted, teasing fading into . . . *affection*. Lucan's lungs knotted together as silence blanketed them. Her breath curled around him. Beneath him, the warmth of her body erased the wintry chill.

"Lucan?" she whispered.

"Aye?" His own voice hoarsened.

Chloe did not answer. Her eyes held his as the slight pressure of her fingertips increased against the back of his neck.

CHAPTER 28

✝

Chloe held her breath. Not that she could speak if she wanted to—the way Lucan was looking at her made her throat too tight for words. And the way she felt right now, tucked into his arms in a pile of snow, made thought impossible. All she knew was that she never wanted his smile to stop.

He dipped his head and every particle of her being tensed in anticipation. When his lips brushed hers, contentment flooded her senses. Despite all the logical reasons she shouldn't get tangled up in him, this felt right. His mouth gently taking hers. The sweep of his tongue as she parted her lips and opened to his kiss. The way one of his hands slid into her hair and his fingertips pressed against her scalp.

Not just right . . . incredible.

She didn't feel the cold, despite the fact her backside was soaked. No, she knew only the heavenly feel of his body weighing into hers, warming her somehow from the inside out. Barriers fell away as time stood still. Bit by bit she felt him battering through walls she no longer wanted to reinforce and creeping into her heart.

He laughed, he played, and yet there was no mistaking he was indeed a man, not a boy who knew nothing about life. He knew how to give pleasure, and moments ago she had witnessed how he received it as well. The simple kind, as well as the fiery desire that fringed his languorous kiss.

And oh, how she reveled in that tempered passion.

A crow screeched from a nearby tree, pulling Chloe down from the heights of happiness. It must have yanked Lucan back to sense as well, for he slowly drew his heart-stopping kiss to a close and lifted his head. Beneath his searing gaze, she shivered.

"Are you cold?" he whispered roughly.

"No," she answered just as quietly, hating to break the magical spell their game had woven around them. But all delight aside, they lay in the snow. Letting this go further was impossible. If not impossible, certainly it bordered on foolish. She gave him a regretful smile. "We should get up though."

"Aye." Lucan nodded with a deep sigh. "Aye, we should." He rolled off her and crouched, one hand extended to help her sit up.

She slid her palm into his, and they rose together. Lucan cleared his throat. "I had wanted to show you something, but perhaps we should return another day." He brushed a wet strand of her hair off the shoulder of her coat. "I do not wish for you to become ill."

"No. I'll be fine." Smiling, she tugged him forward, resuming the path they had started down, into a small clearing. "Show me."

He chuckled. "Look up."

Look where? She abruptly halted. Uncertain she'd heard him correctly, she turned around with a puzzled frown, nearly bumping into his chest. Startled, she let go of his hand and backed up. "What?"

Lucan pointed toward the blue sky overhead.

Chloe lifted her gaze. Her jaw dropped. Tucked beneath a pine's tall boughs, a twenty-foot-tall stone cross reached toward the heavens. Narrow as a telephone pole, its odd shape put the cross beam only a handful of inches from the very top. A good two to three feet below, a stone face stared into the distance. She moved closer, drawn to the curious totem.

"Holy cow. What is this?"

The snow crunched at her side as Lucan joined her. "Before I answer, can you tell me where you are?"

Of course she could. They were on a trail behind the church, which was only a handful of yards to the . . . Chloe blinked. Sure they'd been distracted with the snowball fight, but she'd been certain they entered this clearing from her right. Footsteps in the snow confirmed it. Looking at the trees alone, however, she'd have never picked out the direction they'd come. The branches wove together too intricately, each one joining the other, until they all looked the same. Every tree equal in height. Every trunk as thick as the next.

"If not for our footprints, you would not know, would you?"

"No," she answered, mystified. How did trees grow so perfectly in the middle of a forest? Even those planted by man would be subject to nature. And yet, not a single one of the tall pines looked a day younger than its neighbors.

"This," Lucan ran his hand down the narrow shaft,

"is another marker. Many years ago, a road ran through here. 'Twas a central route of passage to the chapel. If we were not standing in snow, you could still see the ruts of wagons in the earth there." He pointed behind them, at another row of trees that looked exactly the same as the ones before them.

Chloe lifted a disbelieving eyebrow. "How do you know a road ran through here? Wouldn't it be documented somewhere?"

"These things have a way of fading into time." He patted the stone beneath his hand. "This marked the way to the chapel. The face you see above looks down to promise safe passage." Gazing off in the direction of the trodden snow, he lowered his voice. "'Twas said amongst the Templar, *Seek the one who sees all and says naught, for there you shall find the sacred.*"

"Lucan . . ." Words failed her. She closed her mouth. He couldn't possibly know these things. Working for the Church afforded him access to a lot of secrets, but despite his claims, every historian in the world knew the Templar and the Church clashed violently. The people Lucan worked for now simply wouldn't possess knowledge of Templar prophecies. Or the meaning of a cryptic phrase.

He made a circle around the cross, gazing up at its high knob as if seeing it for the first time. "Once, many of these rose alongside the most prominent roads. Some stand still—this one, the one in Brittany, a few others buried in the forests. Where progress did not destroy them, time, and necessity, erased their meaning."

Her curiosity about his fantastic stories wouldn't allow her to let the subject die. "Necessity? What kind of necessity?"

"During the reign of the false papacy, when Philippe IV installed his personal pope, many things were protected."

She hugged her arms around her chest to ward off the sudden invasion of the cold. No employee of the Church talked about the wrongs they'd committed. All those stories lay under a rug somewhere, deliberately forgotten. She eyed his profile, unwilling to verify the obvious conclusion, and yet unable to stop the question from tumbling free. "Things like the relic my team discovered?"

"Aye."

The deeply meaningful look he gave her made her shiver more. Protected. It wasn't the first time he'd used the word, and she knew it wouldn't be the last. But protected from whom? The Church itself? Or the long-ago king of France? And why *keep* them hidden all this time?

His gaze softened with concern. "Are you cold?"

"No."

He looked beyond her, to the trees. "Is it the woods then? You have naught to worry over."

She became acutely aware of where she stood. Looking around, she took in the darker shadows of the forest beyond. In almost ten years, she couldn't recall a time when she hadn't sensed the demons just beyond her reach. Yet now, as she stood in the heart of a place she feared the most, she realized not once had she felt the foreboding presence of evil. Not here in the forest. Not in the chapel. Not on the drive. He'd done it. He'd really done it. He'd kept the demons away.

She let out a soft laugh. "No. Come to think of it, I haven't felt their presence at all. It's like . . . they're . . . gone."

His smile held no mockery. Genuine, it spread slowly across his face. "Aye. And they will stay away today, for we stand on consecrated ground. They cannot harm you here."

With one heavy *thump,* Chloe's heart came to a standstill. She stared at him, her breath lodged in her lungs. His conviction radiated out through his knowing gaze, echoed in his quiet words. He didn't dismiss her fears as things that went bump in the night, didn't belittle her beliefs. She'd treasured his reaction when she confessed, but hadn't really taken it for more than politeness.

Wonder slipped into her voice as she asked, "You *do* believe me, don't you? I mean . . . really *believe.*"

"Aye. Demons plague you. You would do well to stay away from the forest near Ornes."

Oh God. She'd wondered what it might be like to have someone *really* understand. But she'd never imagined the experience could be so all consuming. As she stood in the subtle gray light of his supportive gaze, tears rose and pooled in the corners of her eyes. She dipped her head to hide the unbidden display and drew in a deep, steadying breath.

When she exhaled, Lucan's arms wound around her waist. He drew her against his chest, his gentle embrace full of the strength she needed.

CHAPTER 29

✝

As twilight faded into deep shades of lavender, shadows stretched before the SUV's headlights. The forest rose around them, sentinels marking the way to the château around the bend. Wet from the snowball fight and continued outings through the Picardie countryside, Chloe pulled her coat around her tighter to trap the heater's blast. Her feet and ankles were icicles. Her hands tingled as they thawed.

Her mind, however, resembled overcooked spaghetti. Between all the information she'd learned that she tried to sift into logical order, she struggled to embrace the newfound contentment her afternoon with Lucan created. More correctly, she struggled to keep hold of all the reasons she *shouldn't* be so content with him. They hadn't just romped in the snow like children and talked about history. They walked quietly, holding hands as if it were the most natural thing in the world. They shared lunch, split a piece of chocolate cake. She'd even caught herself feeding him before she came to her senses and passed him the fork. More than anything, she'd come to see the man with his guard down, and she had allowed him to see the same. She'd been herself, work temporarily forgotten, the relic that kept them at odds shoved into a far corner of her mind.

And she'd liked it. Liked being with him. Thrived on his simple touch.

Yet the one person she trusted without question, her brother, suspected Lucan capable of the worst. They stood at opposing poles on what they believed regarding public knowledge of historical facts. And still, she couldn't move beyond the incredible fact he believed in her demons.

Worse, she didn't want to.

She wanted to embrace the simple gift of having someone understand what haunted her in the dark. Wanted to spend the rest of her days as content as she'd been today, not having to wonder whether she could trust him, or whether he'd turn out like Blake and rip her heart into pieces. Now, as the château's lights cast a warm glow on the distant trees, logic interfered to insist she was being foolish.

She *ought* to be annoyed with herself for shirking her responsibilities. Instead, she couldn't shake the faint smile that refused to leave and the lightness in her heart.

Nor could she ignore the other, very real discovery an afternoon with Lucan revealed. He'd made good on his word. Promised she wouldn't notice the demons, and she hadn't. Vowed she was safe with him—something she didn't just believe but felt in the depths of her soul. A sixth sense stood up demanding attention and screaming that Lucan would always keep her safe.

She slid her gaze sideways and caught him glancing at her. His grip tightened on her hand. "We are almost here. Would you like for me to aid you in the cleaning of your room?"

No. The answer rose to the back of her throat. She squelched it from breaking free by looking out the side window once again. No was too blunt. Too final. It left entirely too much room for him to unhesitatingly agree and leave her to right the mess, when what she really wanted was to spend the night with him again.

She sighed and looked up at the round silver moon. "That sounds like a lot of work. I think I'll take a bath instead."

There. Maybe that would spark his interest. Open the door for her to spit out a hesitant confession that she'd like to stay in his bed. If they could revisit what they'd started last night . . .

Her stomach hollowed out as the full reality of what she wanted thumped her in the gut. Him. All six foot-plus of his magnificent body touching hers and taking her off to an unforgettable place where long dark hair caressed like silk, perspiration slicked skin, and pleasure wasn't merely a feeling, but an odyssey to remember.

Lucan rounded the last curve, and the château sprawled out before them, aglow like Christmas and every bit as welcoming. As he eased down the long drive, bringing them closer to the moment she'd have to leave his company, Chloe cleared her throat. "I was thinking maybe a glass of wine after."

"Aye, wine will thaw you from the inside out."

She glanced at his face, searching for a clue to what might be going on inside his head. Unfortunately, his flat expression and relaxed features offered nothing.

"It's always better with company."

If he missed that not-so-subtle hint, he was dense. She watched for some reaction. Tensed as he remained outwardly calm, his hands relaxed, his profile unreadable. Damn. Surely he wouldn't make her spit it out in black and white. It wasn't as if she had a lot of practice at prompting this sort of thing. Why was this so hard, damn it?

He pulled into a vacant parking spot and shut the engine off, retracting his hand from hers. A faint *tick-click* emitted as the engine's hot metal met frigid air. Lucan's low baritone rasped over her skin. "Are you asking if you may stay?" As he twisted sideways, the blue dash lights illuminated his probing stare.

Chloe held his gaze. A tremor rolled through her body. Fear, anxiety, excitement—all three set off a terrible racket of nerves. Her throat too dry to form even a fumbling response, she answered with a slow nod.

Lucan reached across the center console and laid his hand on her thigh. "You have no need to dance around your questions. I already made it clear my room is yours if you desire." Casual. Noncommittal.

If she could kick him, she would.

He reached around to his back pocket and withdrew his room key. "Here. Let yourself in. I must take this package to Caradoc. You may bathe at your leisure."

Resigned to the fact she'd have to work harder if she intended for this night to end up differently than the last several, Chloe muttered beneath her breath, snatched the key out of his grasp, and exited the SUV. Lucan waited at the rear bumper with sword in hand. He guided her up to and through the front doors with a hand on the small of her back. Once inside, he escorted her to the stairs and kissed her on the cheek. "I will join you shortly."

She opened her mouth to tell him to hurry, then quickly snapped it shut. No, she didn't intend to come off as desperate. Good things came to those who waited, as her grandmother had been fond of saying. She'd bathe, unwind, and take the time his absence offered to get her nerves under control and her mind at peace with her longings. Not to mention, a little bit of surprise might go a long way.

"I'll be there." With a smile she hoped was as equally unreadable as his bland expression, she sauntered down the hall.

Lucan cursed the saints a hundred times over for the torture that lay ahead in the hours to come. Today had been torment enough. Another full night with Chloe tucked against his side and his shaft so swollen he could scarce move would turn him into a madman. He dared not refuse her and leave her unattended to face the perils that waited, yet he did not know how much longer he could tolerate this yearning. Sooner or later, his body would cease to care what regrets morn would bring. At the present course he was on, 'twould be sooner, rather than later.

He stiffened his shoulders to ward off his imaginings of Chloe contenting herself in his bathtub and squinted at Caradoc's door. Gareth would soon return, if he had not already. Mayhap Raphael bore news. Mayhap Alaric. News about the seraphs, Azazel, the relics—Lucan cared not as long as it prevented his thoughts from drifting to the woman in his room and the water she soaked in.

He rapped sharply. Waited as footsteps crossed the room beyond. The door opened confidently, as if Caradoc had been expecting him. "How did you fare at Picardie?"

Lucan entered Caradoc's tidy room and perched on the back of the couch. He passed Caradoc the sealed envelope. "'Twas eventful. She learned much." As had he. About her.

"Enough that you may say your oaths?" Package stuffed beneath his arm, Caradoc leaned against the closed door.

"Nay. She is coming to believe many things. But she is not prepared to accept what we are. The facts lay before her. She refuses to see them." Much to his consternation. If Chloe had made the final mental crossing, tonight would not be a certain exercise in self-restraint. They could say their oaths. He could share the rest of what her position demanded she understand. Then, they could . . .

The silence that descended on the room alerted Lucan that Caradoc waited for an answer to a question he had not heard. He glanced up from his hands to meet his brother's expectant look. "My apologies. What did you ask?"

"Master Reginald. Did he give you any difficulty in viewing the markers?"

Lucan shook his head. "I informed him who she was, and though he expressed surprise, he did not object. Where is Gareth?"

"I wait for him now. Trouble stirs at the forty-second gate. We must fight."

Fight. A way to keep distance from Chloe and exhaust himself until her nearness did not disturb his sleep. Lucan leaned forward. "Trouble? What has occurred?"

"'Tis open. Demons cross through freely."

Lucan slid off the couch to his feet and started for the door. "I shall inform Chloe we have business to attend to."

"Nay."

Caradoc's sharp response held authority. An order, not an argument. Lucan slowed to a stop and frowned at his brother. Commander replaced friend, the stern lines of his expression unbending. Still, Lucan could not bring himself to back down from their purpose without an objection. "I shall fight alongside you, as we are meant to do."

"Nay, you shall not. Your duty is here with Chloe and the relic. I will not risk your soul for a handful of demons and nytyms when your salvation is so near at hand."

Lucan bristled. They shared the same burden, all of them. He should not see pardon from duty when his brothers confronted the same risk. He narrowed his gaze. "And yours? Send Gareth then, if you are certain no dark knights await. A handful of demons and unintelligent nytyms he can easily slay. You do not need to risk your transformation either."

Caradoc's frown darkened by fathoms. His eyes glinted with harsh light. "Here, I am commander, Lucan. 'Tis not your place to question my decisions. You shall stay with Chloe, where you belong. Gareth and I shall close the gate."

Centuries of fighting alongside Caradoc told Lucan that further protest would fall on deaf ears. The man who stood as second in command of the American

Knights Templar would yield only to two—his commander, Merrick, and the archangel Mikhail. Lucan let out a disparaging sigh and pulled open the door. One foot in the hall, he stopped, unable to walk away without making his personal objections known. He would not allow Caradoc to embark on a self-inflicted death sentence with any guise of acceptance.

"You are also my brother, and I care not to lose you."

"Such things are out of our control," Caradoc murmured.

The weight of Caradoc's hand on the door forced Lucan to exit. Behind him, the chain lock scraped into place.

Caradoc took the envelope to the coffee table and dropped into the couch cushions. All he had once owned lay within this bulky package. Reduced from vast holdings that would make any man proud, all that remained were sales records, demolition documents, and a few photographs. Pictures that taunted more than the destruction of time. For he had taken them the last time he walked through his homeland. And in those remembrances lay his eternal pain.

He would be glad to escape it. The transformation of his soul into complete darkness at least offered the benefit of unfeeling. Two months ago, he had fought his inevitable demise. Swore that he could withstand the archangels' punishment until salvation found him. But the return to Europe shattered what remained of his resolve. He would never be free of the memories. He would never escape Isabelle.

And so he fought. 'Twas the only way to block the fire in his bones. Fight until he dropped to his knees.

Sleep so he could battle again. In both he found freedom from her.

He ripped open the envelope and shook out the contents. A stapled stack of papers dropped out. Four photographs fluttered to the wood surface. One landed face up. Caradoc stared at long golden blond hair and a face so lovely it could make the angels weep. Indigo eyes radiated indescribable love.

Grimacing, he turned the picture over. Not now. Later he would study the face he had never forgotten. The documents he could confront more easily.

As he picked up the stack of property records, a folded square of paper slipped from between the sheets. Curious, he set the others aside in favor of the slip that bore his name in Mikhail's lavish handwriting. He opened it, quickly scanned the message, and crushed it into his hand.

Damnation!

Sicily. Mikhail was pulling him out of France!

A sharp knock made him stifle budding rage. Annoyed by the interruption, Caradoc stormed to the door and yanked it open.

Gareth stood on the other side, looking hale and hearty as usual, the passing of centuries having done little to his youthful appearance. With a self-assured smile he let himself inside. "Shall we? I hunger for a bit of demon blood."

"Nay."

The younger man's smile vanished. He drew back in surprise. "Nay? The gate—"

"Speak with Mikhail about the bloody gate. He has forbidden me to fight." Caradoc's frustration rose to a head. He slammed his open palm against the wall. The sting of impact ricocheted up his arm, lessening his fury somewhat. Drawing in a deep breath, he braced his forearm on the wall and leaned his forehead against it. "Antonio Shapiro has died. Mikhail is sending me to oversee the estate auction and the relics in his possession."

"Shapiro?" Gareth asked with surprise. "I did not recall hearing his health failed him."

"It did not. Monsanato shot him."

A long, low whistle drifted across the room. "After thirty years he finally accomplished it. I suspect war will erupt in the streets."

"Aye." Caradoc hauled himself off the wall. "'Twill bring a change of power amongst the families." He fixed Gareth with a stern look. "You know what he harbors. 'Tis my duty to see it restored. Lady Anne has fallen ill, else Merrick would have been assigned the task. I depart on the morrow."

Gareth expelled a heavy sigh that mirrored the weightiness in Caradoc's heart. He accepted that he would fight alone with a curt nod. His hand gripped the sword belted around his waist. "Then I take my leave." He departed without haste.

When the door closed and Caradoc once again faced the quiet of his room, he sat down on the edge of his bed and raked a hand through his hair. Why could Mikhail not have sent Tane? He craved a chance to prove himself. Thirsted for the opportunity to right his wrongs. He would most assuredly leap at the chance to venture to Sicily and settle the affairs of a Mafia don.

Jesu, he did not desire this assignment. His duty was to fight. To combat Azazel's minions until his soul could take no more and the brother who stood at his side cut off his head. 'Twas not to mingle with the rich and disguise himself with airs whilst safeguarding a relic. Others could perform that duty more appropriately. He would have been content to stay in the shadows, offer support with his sword, and guard those chosen to bring the sacred tears home.

Alas, 'twas not his good fortune. He would go, as duty demanded. And he would count the days until he could once again return to the ways of demons and death.

CHAPTER 30

✦

Lucan flipped the channel on the television in search of a show that might drown out the splashing beyond the closed bathroom door. Each plunk of a washcloth strained his nerves. Each slosh as the water shifted conjured fantastic visions of Chloe's slick skin sliding through the bubbled surface. He ground his teeth together, shifted restlessly in his seat.

'Twas no use. Caradoc's unexpected determination to keep him from battle doomed him to disaster. He could no more keep his mind from Chloe than he could cease his lungs from drawing air.

The rush of water as she let down the drain redoubled his convictions. He would find a way to control these lusty thoughts, no matter the difficulty. He had gone centuries without suffering this disturbing reaction to a woman's nearness. He could survive a few short hours in Chloe's company before sleep took her.

When the bathroom door opened and a sliver of light poured out, Lucan held his breath. If she entered without clothes, 'twould be his undoing. He would have her here on the floor, if he must.

She stepped into the room wearing the flimsy ivory gown she had two nights previous, and Lucan nearly groaned aloud. With the bright light at her back, sloping curves silhouetted against the silk. His entire body coiled tight. Before he could fully appreciate the shadow of weighty breasts, a waist his hands could easily span, and long slender legs, his cock filled uncomfortably. God's teeth, the nightgown was more damning than if she had worn naught at all. Quickly, he jerked his gaze back to the television and feigned interest. In what, he could not say.

"That was quick," Chloe commented. The mattress sank as she sat on the edge.

"Aye." Too quick. Though he would not tell her such.

"Did Caradoc say anything about what the team did today?"

"Nay." Lucan gave himself a swift mental kick at the terseness in his voice. He swallowed through a thickening throat and tried for a friendlier tone. Forcing himself to look only on her face, he turned toward her. "He was leaving with Gareth. We did not speak long at all."

Chloe chuckled. "I guess I'll get my lecture tomorrow then."

"Lecture?"

Her eyes danced like burnished brass as she nodded. "The one my brother's going to give me. I haven't played hooky from work since college."

He gave her a disapproving frown. "'Twas not playing hooky. You learned things, did you not? Information you can apply to your research." Inclining his head at the window, he continued, "And other things as well."

"Yes," she murmured. A long slender hand picked absently at the fabric beneath her bent leg. With her quiet answer, her smile disappeared. She looked to the drawn curtains, and a touch of haunting sadness fringed her pretty face.

Lucan sat up on the couch. The one way he could keep his mind from barreling down a path of erotic fantasies had just presented itself. Conversation. Not insubstantial babble, but something meaningful that required actual thought. "Chloe, there is no need to fear the creatures in the night."

Her short laugh cut through the air like a bullwhip. "Right. You saw what they did last night. When does their strength override mine? What happens then?" Her soft mouth twisted cruelly. "I'll tell you what happens. That's when I'm the next dead body whose killer can't be found."

The sudden *tap-tap* on the window produced a bitter laugh. "See? Even they agree. That spell will wear itself out in time, and then I'm demon food."

Frowning, Lucan stood. 'Twas beyond time to broach the conversation of what she was and share the knowledge Master Reginald imparted. "'Tis not the spell, Chloe, but your belief in it. When your conviction falters, then aye, 'twill seem worthless to you." He stood at her side and reached for her hand. "The cure for this curse, as you call it, is within you."

She turned wide, disbelieving eyes up to him. "Within me? I don't understand."

"Come. Allow me to show you." He tugged on her hand, bringing her to her feet. But when he headed for the window, she sank her weight into her heels and resisted.

"No. I don't want to look out the window."

"Trust me, Chloe." Giving her no further opportunity to protest, Lucan tugged harder and positioned her in front of the curtains. He pinned her in place with his body, wrapped one arm around her waist, and reached for the pull string.

Chloe twisted against his imprisoning hold. Her nails dug into his arm. "Lucan, please. Don't."

"Shh. I am right here." He jerked on the string, throwing the curtains wide.

Chloe squeezed her eyes shut tight. Nothing on earth could make her look. Not curiosity. Not Lucan's reassuring words. Not even the hand of God. She refused to witness the creatures that haunted her dreams.

"Chloe," he coaxed near her ear.

She ducked her head to escape the warm caress of his breath. "No."

"Look, my sweet. 'Tis naught there. Just the gardens and the trees beyond."

She refused with a violent shake of her head. He couldn't be telling the truth. She'd just heard the thing. If she looked now, she'd stare straight into a grotesque face. "It just tapped on the window."

His fingers smoothed her hair. "'Tis not present. I would not lie to you." Warm lips touched the side of her face. Coaxing. Promising.

Begging her to believe in him.

She cracked open one eye and peeked through lowered lashes. Clear glass panes revealed a starry sky, not ghoulish faces or deadly claws. The breath she hadn't realized she was holding rushed out. Encouraged, she opened her other eye and straightened. Lucan's comforting nearness engulfed her in a heartbeat. His hard chest pillowed her back. Strong arms held her close. Sheltered. She indulged in the moment and rested her head on his shoulder as she stared out at a full, silver moon.

He leaned his head against hers. "You must learn to trust me, my sweet."

"I do. Well, most of the time."

A laugh rumbled in his chest. "Look to the trees. Tell me what you see."

Swallowing hard, Chloe dismissed the fear his suggestion provoked and dropped her gaze from the heavens to the thick forest. Shadows loomed thick and large. The tall pines formed a dense barrier she couldn't see more than two or three feet into. She shrugged. "Nothing."

"Look closer. Tell me when you can see eyes."

Eyes? Oh, heaven above, she didn't want to do this. If she had nightmares for the rest of her life, she'd never forgive Lucan. At the same time, she couldn't refuse. If what he said were true, if she somehow possessed an ability to ward off the creatures, she'd suffer whatever terror waited in the trees. She squinted at the distant, snow-tipped boughs, searched for a glimmer of light among the dark.

When two yellow-green specks appeared beneath the heavy canopy, she drew back with a gasp.

Lucan tightened his embrace, holding her more securely. "Ah, you see them, aye?"

"Yes. I think so. Yellow-green." She blinked rapidly, unable to believe the transformation within the trees. Where one pair of greenish lights glowed seconds earlier, now she saw three, and an eerier set of red-orange. A chill wafted down her spine. "Damn."

As if he had felt the tremor roll through her, Lucan rubbed her arms, restoring warmth to her frigid skin. "Remember what I said. You have the ability to ward them away."

"But how?"

He dipped his chin to her shoulder and tucked his arms around her waist once more. "They have seen you now. Let them approach. When they draw too close for your comfort, do not give in to fear."

"That's easy enough to say."

"Nay, you can do this, Chloe. Do not awaken the fear. Imagine, if you will, you can throw daggers with a stare. Will the injury upon them."

What he claimed sounded fantastic. But in his words, Chloe recognized the truth behind her protection spell. As the spiritual leaders she'd consulted had advised, faith brought the vastest power. If one did not believe in the words spoken, no ward would keep the demons away.

As she had taught herself to do years earlier, Chloe released her doubts and embraced the possibility. She watched the eyes drift closer and clump together as they gathered at the forest's edge. Shadows emerged from the trees, near enough she could recognize the varying shades of color, but distant enough she couldn't make out true forms.

Close enough, for this first night of new approaches.

Drawing in a deep breath, she focused on the solitary pair of red-orange orbs and did as Lucan requested. Instead of daggers, however, she imagined invisible laser beams coursing across the manicured gardens and searing a hole right between the glowing portals. She almost giggled as a mental picture of Cyclops took hold.

Across the way, the reddish eyes drifted behind the others.

Chloe leaned forward, unable to believe what she'd witnessed. Surely she was seeing things. This was too easy.

"Do you believe me now?" Lucan asked, a touch of arrogance in his voice.

Unconvinced the retreat wasn't just a product of circumstance, Chloe tried again, this time on a pair of yellow-greens that led the pack of approaching eerie lights. Only, when she focused on her target, she skipped the imagery and merely willed the creature to fall over dead.

It didn't. But it did scurry back into the trees.

Chloe turned in Lucan's arms and looked up at him in wonder. "How is that possible?"

A smile lifted the corners of his mouth. He raised a hand to tuck a straying lock of hair behind her ear. " 'Tis good to know you need not rely on props and prayers, aye?"

Good? He couldn't comprehend how liberated she felt. Eight years of searching, and this man, this stranger who had weaseled himself into her life against her will, handed her the cure on a silver platter. Priests couldn't. Rabbis couldn't. No religious leader she'd consulted had been able to release the curse. But Lucan had.

And in this moment, she felt more in control of her life than she had in a very long time.

She looped her arms around his neck and twisted fully around to face him. With a half step closer, she pressed her breasts against his chest. She eased to her toes, and beneath the fabric of her nightgown, her nipples pebbled as they scraped over his body. Her mouth a fraction away from his, she whispered, "Thank you."

Lucan's eyes clashed with hers, dark as storm clouds. She knew the look well. She'd witnessed it both nights she'd spent in this room. Desire. Raw need. For her.

Excitement thrummed all the way down to her toes. She took another shuffle-step closer and melded her hips against his at the same time she captured his mouth. He was there in an instant, greedily taking all she offered. His hands tightened at her waist, his fingertips biting in, pleasantly harsh.

Heavenly. The stroke of his tongue, the stinging nip of his teeth—everything combined into a blissful delight that pushed her to the edge of abandon. Her fingers curled into his shoulders to stop the sudden weakening of her knees, and Chloe held on, afraid if she let go she'd fall. Terrified if she continued, she'd drown in everything Lucan seemed so willing to give.

And yet nothing would steer her off this course. No fear, no relics, no cross-purposes. She wanted Lucan Seacourt, and she wouldn't let the ghosts of her past spoil the insurmountable feeling he stirred in her veins.

Caught up in the heat that coursed through her body, she slid her hands to his waist and pushed them beneath the loose hem of his cotton shirt. Her fingertips found warm taut skin that rippled beneath her inquisitive caress. Taking a step backward, she gave herself room to explore. The hard ridges of his abdomen gave way to an even harder chest. She flattened her palms over his nipples, skimmed her hands higher to splay her fingers over wide shoulders.

Lucan groaned softly, a sound that couldn't be

mistaken for anything other than approval. He closed his hands into the flimsy fabric of her gown, bunching it into his fists. But although his mouth bore fierce demand, the tenseness of his body spoke of restraint. His refusal to do away with her nightgown reinforced that suspicion.

When he abruptly terminated the kiss and distanced himself a good foot, Chloe wasn't surprised. She caught hold of his shirt and followed his retreat.

Lucan glanced at the bed, as if he could not bring himself to look at her. " 'Tis late—"

He had retreated far enough the backs of his knees confronted the coffee table. Chloe took full advantage of his thwarted escape. A slow smile spread across her face as she dipped one finger into the waistband of his jeans. "There are several hours left until morning." Her voice was little more than a whisper.

His gaze snapped to hers. His eyes glittered like live coals. One thumb absently brushed against her ribs. In his unblinking stare, she read the question he wouldn't ask. *Are you certain?*

She'd never been more sure. Lucan gave her strength. Offered her trust and demanded hers in return. He had crept into her heart. Coerced her into caring. Only one thing remained to distance them. Tonight, they would cross all those boundaries, and she would let him sink his teeth into her heart.

No. More. Fear.

She pressed the flat of her hand against the hard bulge of his jeans. His gaze flared white-hot as his breath caught audibly. With all the boldness she could summon, Chloe held his gaze and whispered, "I want to feel you within me."

Lucan exhaled, a combination of rushing air and a drawn-out groan. He caught her to him, crushed her against his body. His mouth claimed hers with savage hunger, pummeling through to shatter any trace of resistance she might have experienced.

Sharing his urgency, she pulled at his shirt. Urged him to give her the distance and freedom to drag it over his head. Instead, he reached behind his neck, and as if he lacked the patience of unclothing, doffed it in one quick yank.

Her nightgown followed in the shirt's wake. One impatient brush of his hands against her shoulders pushed the thin straps to her elbows where all she had to do was wriggle and the garment pooled at her ankles. She stepped out of it, moving back into the heavenly circle of his arms. As she pushed her hands up the broad expanse of muscle that was his chest, she brought her body into his and slid upward along the same trajectory as her hands, delighting in the electric shock of skin to skin.

He dominated her. Thick thighs enveloped hers. Strong arms bent her slightly backward so his teeth could graze her throat. He dipped her further, brought his mouth closer to her breast. A tremble shook her body as warm, moist air danced across her skin. And then his lips closed around her hardened nipple, and Chloe tottered in his embrace.

Sensing her inability to stand on her own two feet, Lucan urged her to her knees. Then backward further until the soft fibers of the rug met her skin. His kisses branded her flesh. Pulsed heat through her veins and tightened her womb. The satiny tickle of his hair as he leaned over her to suckle at her opposite breast teased.

She speared her fingers through his hair, pressed his head close, and arched her back against the tug of his mouth. "Lucan," she murmured on a shaky exhale.

A calloused hand scraped pleasantly down her ribs. Across her abdomen. Lower still to part the swollen folds of her feminine flesh. His thumb swirled across the sensitive nub there, and ecstasy shot through Chloe. She parted her thighs at the stroke of his fingers. Each caress matched the gentle tug of his mouth. Each stroke coaxed something deep within her closer to the surface. She writhed beneath him, lifted her hips into his palm. Her skin pebbled with goose bumps. Her breath came in short, hard gasps.

So close. So damnably close. She lifted up again, rubbed in countermotion to his hand. On the precipice of ecstasy, her womb contracted hard. Another press of his thumb, another languorous stroke, and she'd find relief from the unrelenting ache.

"Lucan, please . . ." She dug her nails into the rug, aware she begged, but unashamed. She had come to understand so much about him, even though she'd tried to keep him at a distance, and she knew he would relish the raw honesty of her spoken need. It seemed he wanted nothing but that from her. Nothing but the complete, unhindered truth. The kind of truth that only came with the trust he unrelentingly demanded.

He lifted his head, her nipple slipping from the wet heat of his mouth. In the dim light of the television, flecks of onyx glowed within his silvery gaze. Beautiful, fathomless eyes. She could get lost in them. Had already.

His lashes fluttered, threatening to close as he pushed one thick finger into her slickened opening. She closed hers before she could discover whether he did the same and arched off the rug. He pushed deep inside her, the friction setting of a percussion of pleasure like a match set to a chain of firecrackers. One by one, the nerve endings in her body ignited, each little snap building to an intensity that pounded through her. She twisted her head to the side, clamped her thighs together. To stop him. To encourage him.

Oh God.

The next slow push of his hand brought combustion. Release burst through her in a maelstrom of feeling. Tiny starbursts of light erupted behind her eyes. Weightlessness infused her limbs. For a moment, she felt as if she floated. In the next, she tumbled slowly off the high ledge she had so feared, and found herself sheltered in his protective embrace. His body blanketed hers, bringing her tenderly back to earth. His strong arms held her tightly.

"Chloe," he murmured as he cupped her face between his hands. The stroke of his thumbs demanded she open her eyes to look at him. When she did, his expression radiated tenderness moments before his lashes lowered and he gently took her mouth with his.

She twisted her head, terminating the kiss. "More, Lucan," she whispered. "I want more of you." And God help her, she knew in that moment, she would never get enough.

On a hoarse groan, he reached between their bodies, and released the buttons on his jeans.

CHAPTER 31

The flutter of Chloe's hands alongside his as she helped free him from the confines of his jeans electrified Lucan's skin. He was aware of her in ways he had never been aware of any woman. The scent of her arousal, the rasp of her breath, damnation, the brush of her hair against his elbow stirred some deeply foreign craving that only she could fulfill.

Cool air washed across his buttocks. A shake of his ankle removed the last of the denim. He was bare, and she lay stretched out on the floor beneath him. Ready. Willing. Waiting.

He ought to pick her up and take her to the bed. She deserved more than the hard floor and rug burn. And yet, naught would make his body obey. The need to be inside her, and quickly, beat through his veins like long-ago drums of war.

Kneeling between her legs, he bent his head to draw one rosy, taut nipple back into his mouth. He rolled his tongue around the hardened bud. Soft fingertips glided over his shoulders, and a quiet sigh of contentment slipped off her lips. Her hips lifted, grazing his, inviting him to descend and slide into her waiting warmth. He resisted. This was not about desire. Nay. Though the light in her eyes revealed she had surrendered her objections, he wanted more. *Must have* more.

Tonight he could not settle for simple pleasure, though 'twould be so damnably easy to do. He must elicit her complete, unyielding trust. For come morn, he would need it when he confided her status as a seraph.

And in truth, he ached for Chloe in ways he could not describe. Ways that went far deeper than the joining of flesh and the spilling of his seed. He could not abide this distance that spanned between them during the waking hours, and he would accept no more of it. Tonight, she would yield. As he yielded to her.

He released her breast and dusted kisses down the straight-line center of her body, to her navel. Her hands followed the contours of his arms, over his shoulders, along his biceps, down his forearms until her fingers lay atop his. He eased his weight to his elbows and took her hands. Contact. As much as possible. Saints' blood, *aye*.

Then he dropped his mouth on her warm, wet flesh. Her gasp tore through him like lightning, and she bucked up off the floor. His body answered, his cock stiffening further, though he had not believed such could be possible. He glanced up to look on her delicate face and nearly unraveled. Sweet sacred Mary, she was a fantasy come to life. Long auburn hair spilled on the white rug, a halo touched by fire. Rapture softened features that were already soft and inviting. Full pink lips swelled beneath the sharp press of her teeth.

He disentangled his hands, determined to hear the

cry she sought to silence, and gripped her hips, lifting her up into his mouth. Lapping at her sensitive feminine nub, he savored her sweet flavor. Reveled in her musky scent. She undulated in time with the steady, slow caress of his tongue.

"Oh, Lucan, that feels . . . good . . ." She exhaled unsteadily. "So good."

When her hands settled into his hair, Lucan sucked the sweet bud into his mouth. She keened as her nails scraped against his scalp. His pride swelled. He had broken through that barrier of restraint. Pulled from her a soul-deep sound that he knew she did not wish to give, but could not help herself. A precious, timeless cry he would carry in his memory for as long as he walked the earth.

As her flesh pulsed against his mouth, he withdrew from her intoxicating warmth and lifted his head, waiting for her to open her eyes and look at him. When she did, a question loomed on her face. But beyond the outward curiosity, something richer gleamed. Those dilated pupils held nothing back. He saw clear through to her heart, and what he found there, tightened his own to painful limits. Acceptance. Affection.

So deep was his reaction to the profound discovery, his lungs ceased to function for a frightening drum of several heavy heartbeats. But as she raised her hips to his and her moist flesh rubbed against the swollen head of his cock, his senses slammed back into him.

She pulled at his biceps, urging his body down to hers. "Make love to me, Lucan. Make me yours."

"Aye, my sweet." He took his hard shaft in his hand, aligned it with her slick opening. "From tonight forward, hold naught back from me, Chloe. Give me your word on this." His body trembled as he awaited her response.

A moment of fear passed across her face. She struggled for a tenacious smile, hesitatingly nodded her head. Her flesh clamped around the tip of his erection, begging him to embed himself inside her. Still, he resisted. He would have her words.

To elicit them, he would give her his. He held her gaze steady and willed her to believe in his sincerity. "I give to you my eternal loyalty."

Were they in different places, under different circumstances, he would have bent on one knee and pledged the words with the offering of his sword. But 'twas out of reach, and the gesture entirely unsuitable to the deeper intimacy flowing between them. Words would have to suffice. He only hoped she could understand the imperishable meaning. For in the utterance, he stood in service to her. He would be judged as she was, her safety his only responsibility. Even the oaths of brotherhood and the immortal Code came second unto her, and her alone.

Beneath him, Chloe shuddered. Tears pricked her eyes, adding a brighter sparkle to their already mesmerizing shine. "I'll fall in love with you."

Her whisper did not hold as much fear as it did promise. The tension fled his body, and with a low groan, Lucan pushed himself inside her warm sheath. God's teeth, she fit so perfectly around him. Each grip and squeeze of her flesh drew him deeper. Brought him into the depths of her body until he touched the mouth of her womb and staggered under the waves of ecstasy that crashed over him. No more divine haven existed. He could stay here a lifetime. Where her heat enveloped him and the steady thrum of her heart pulsed around him. Where he felt her unlike he had ever felt another.

Lowering his body onto hers, he hovered over her mouth. "I want you to, my sweet."

Before she could either agree or protest, he drew her into a hard kiss. Need surpassed all thoughts of gentleness. He had waited too long. Held back until his body refused to listen to another willful command. He knew he should give her a moment to recover, that as a virgin would need time to accommodate his body, her shy mind needed time to accept what had just passed between them. But damnation, he could not stop his hips from retreating and dragging his swollen cock through her tight, wet flesh.

He yielded to the timeless rhythm of lovers. With a hard thrust, he sank back into her. Buried himself to the hilt. "Ah, Chloe, you are more heavenly than I had imagined," he murmured against the corner of her mouth.

She turned her head to draw in a great gulp of air and lifted her hips. He sank deeper. Release clenched a tight fist around his chest, making it impossible to draw in a normal breath. Sweat broke over his body. His cock pulsed. His mind reeled. He pulled back, intending to give them both a moment. Yet her body clung to his, rising and lifting, chasing after pleasure that boiled just beneath the surface.

On a hoarse groan, Lucan gave up all attempts at restraint. He slammed into her, jarring her into the floor. She cried out, but as she lifted her legs and wrapped them around his waist, he realized the sound had naught to do with pain. Still, he could not abide the thought that tonight would leave her with any regrets. He slid his arms behind her and cradled her shoulders in his hands to prevent her body from rubbing too harshly against the course carpet fibers. Then he let go completely.

Her body moved in time with his, a matched rhythm to the piston of his hips. Her soft cries mingled with his low, satisfied murmurs. He thrust forward, dragged himself across the sensitive nub guaranteed to ignite her. Her inner walls clamped down hard. Lucan set his jaw. He would find release with her. Not before. Not after. Perfect synchronicity to match the perfection of their melded bodies.

His hard, steady strokes took on urgency. Chloe met him with equal abandon. Her hands grabbed onto his shoulders. Her legs tightened around his waist. "Oh God, Lucan. I'm going to—"

Her words strangled on a sharp cry as her body spasmed beneath him. He was there with her, need breaking to the surface and ecstasy ripping through his veins. His cock swelled and pulsed. Satisfaction poured through him, and along with it something deeper. Something richer.

Something akin to love.

Dropping his head to her shoulder, he sank into her, marking her with the spilling of his seed. Gradually, their bodies slowed. Their breathing stabilized. Lucan lifted on shaking arms to gaze into her amber eyes. Wonder lay in her wide-eyed stare. Tears crept down her cheeks.

And in that moment, Lucan realized 'twas not *akin* to love, but love itself. Though it seemed implausible, unbelievable in so many ways, he had lost his heart to Chloe. Something he had given no other woman in over nine hundred years of life.

Taking a deep steadying breath, he kissed the

dampness from her face and wrapped her in his embrace. "Shall we move to the bed?" he asked in a near whisper.

She let out an airy laugh. "I'm not sure I can move."

He could not stop a grin from spreading across his face. "You best be able to. I am not finished with you yet, Chloe Broussard."

Like a cat, she curled into his arms. Her nails scraped across the small of his back. "Mm. That sounds delightful."

Though he wanted naught more than to stay in the warm recesses of her tight sheath, he forced himself to leave the enticing heat and eased out of her body. As he rose to his feet, he brought her with him, then swung her into his arms. Three long strides took him to the bed, where he laid her down in the pillows and stretched out alongside her body. Pressing his lips to the hollow of her throat, he tasted the salt of her perspiration. "Come with me again, my sweet. I fear this hunger for you is yet unsatisfied."

"Let me help you with that." Smiling, Chloe turned into his embrace. She slipped her hand between them to rest over his cock. He swelled against the firm grip of her fingers, the equally firm slide of her palm.

God's blood, her touch gave him a sweeter glimpse of heaven than all the archangels combined. When morning came, 'twould be too soon.

Tane squared off with Merrick in the gray light of imminent dawn. Swords at the ready, he faced his commander, his body attuned to the fight. "One more time, aye?"

Merrick gave a sharp nod, his onyx eyes never leaving Tane's poised blade. "Aye. Then I must attend to Anne."

Slowly they circled one another. Mistrust flowed from Merrick into Tane. Four months, and though Merrick had agreed to allow Tane to return at his leisure, Merrick had not yet forgiven. Tane could not blame him for that. And so he challenged his commander to a round of practice, determined to prove himself in blades, if not in deed.

His fate hung in the outcome of the spar. If he lost, Merrick would deem him unworthy to accompany Caradoc to Sicily. If he won, he earned more than the assignment. He earned the chance to reclaim his honor.

Honor he was not so certain he deserved, and yet he craved all the same. He had wronged them all greatly by kidnapping Anne. Destroyed bonds of brotherhood that had withstood centuries of loss.

Merrick took a quick jab at Tane's left thigh. He drew his broadsword down sharp, blocking the crippling blow with a bone-jarring *clang*. The sound echoed through the indoor training yard as if they sparred in the long-ago tunnels beneath the Temple Mount that brought them to this immortal fate.

Bringing his arm up hard and fast, he thrust Merrick's blade aside. But the light of angels, the light Anne gave to her mate, made Merrick faster. He spun on his inside leg, arced his sword around his body, and slammed the flat side of it into Tane's shoulder. Had it been the sharp edge, as 'twould have been in battle, the forceful slice would have ripped through links of chain. As it was, the impact unbalanced Tane. He stumbled forward. Dropped to his knees.

Disgusted, he tossed his sword on the ground in

front of him. "'Tis an unfair advantage you possess, Merrick. That makes three of three."

A grin pulled at the corners of Merrick's mouth, but he did not set it free. Four months ago, he would have. Nay, 'twould take far longer to bring Merrick back to the state of laughter and companionship they had once known.

He did, however, offer Tane a respectful bow. "Aye, 'tis true. But 'tis why we are given the seraphs. I must take my leave. Your arm is sturdy, Tane. Do not be disheartened." Always the commander at heart, even the betrayal that lay between them would not deter Merrick from commending his men.

Tane did not believe the words. Yet again, he had failed. He watched Merrick leave, disgusted by his inability to stand toe-to-toe with one he had once matched. Sheathing his sword, he cursed the darkness in his soul. Had he not been plagued with such vile jealousy, mayhap the archangels would have seen fit to bless him with a seraph by now, and he too could experience the healing strength of their angelic light.

For now, he must content himself with once again being allowed to roam the Temple halls at will. And he must abide by the looks of reproach his brethren cast his way. Such was his punishment. Though 'twould have been a kinder fate had Mikhail seen fit to expel him from this earth.

He stormed to the door, only to have them open inward as he reached for the handle. Merrick ducked his head inside. "You will arrive in Sicily, two days hence. I shall inform Caradoc to meet you at the airport."

Tane blinked. He had failed the challenge. Why send him? He had not earned the reward.

As the door settled into its frame, he could not cease the quickening of his pulse. Though the reasoning eluded his grasp, he understood he had been offered the opportunity he requested on returning to the Temple at the beginning of the month. He would be allowed a greater duty. Although Caradoc would be present to oversee him, Merrick had extended a boon.

Tane ground his teeth together in determination. He would not fail. Despite the last words of a fallen brother that marked him as a betrayer, he would not bring the Templar to their knees. And in the assignment, he would, somehow, regain his brethren's respect.

Spirits lighter, he fled the training yard in time to catch a shadow slipping down the hall. He cocked his head at the fleeting glimpse of reddish hair. Squinted at the heavy Scottish accent that met his ears as the man spoke into his phone.

Declan.

Too long the Scot had lurked in shadows and distanced himself from those he was once closest to. All wondered what business he conducted in private, but none had the fortune to encounter him, he came and went so secretly.

Tane fell into step behind him, descending the stairs into the Temple's barracks. Declan did not look over his shoulder, though he would have to be deaf to not hear Tane's steady footfalls. He hurried onward, absorbed by the conversation he conducted. Words Tane could not make out through the distance that spanned between them.

He rounded the corner that led to the inner sanctum stairwell and stopped short. The hall stood empty. No sound drifted up from the cavernous stairwell. He squinted into the darkened recess. 'Twas only one way Declan could go—*down*.

Careful to keep his footsteps light, Tane descended the stairs, listening for the telltale brogue that would guide him to the man he sought. But at the foot of the long stairs, the sacred ceremonial chamber stood empty. One man knelt in prayer at the far side of the room, his cropped dark hair a contrast to Declan's shaggy red.

Damnation! Where had the man gone? He had not been so far behind him, he should have caught up to his wayward brother. And yet no sign gave any hint Declan had set foot in the heart of the temple.

Scowling, Tane leaned against the wall and folded his arms over his chest. He would wait. Declan could only pass through to the upper levels via these stairs. When he did, Tane would corner him and discover once and for all why their brother had chosen to skulk about in shadows. If Tane could succeed in this, he would once again know the full trust and support of not only Merrick, but Mikhail as well.

When the sound of footsteps descended beyond the hidden door, Declan slowly eased the lock into place, careful to keep it from clicking too loudly. He breathed easier and folded shut his phone. Too close. Tane had ventured too close.

He had not expected to stumble onto the betrayer. This close to dawn, the majority of the temple slept, the men's nocturnal schedules having exhausted them. But nay, Tane did not venture to the gates with the others. Instead, he sheltered himself inside the temple and trained in the yard under the guise of maintaining his skill. He avoided their calling. Which marked him as a weak link. One Declan must rightfully inform Leofric of.

He turned away from the door, conflicted. Revealing the failings of most of his brothers did not pose difficulty. But when it came to the five he had once fought side by side with, he could not bring himself to subject them to Leofric's punishment. Impeding their pursuits and placing roadblocks in their paths took courage enough. Yet he found 'twas easier on his conscience to attempt to thwart the failings of those he was closest to, than to callously report their misdeeds.

He had not disclosed even the recent trouble Lucan presented. He would rather confront Lucan directly, particularly in light of the fact the man assigned to the task—this Julian Broussard—could not succeed in his assignment. Stop Lucan from engaging in sin before the oaths were taken. A simple enough task. 'Twould only require distracting Lucan. But nay, Julian could not keep his eyes on Lucan long enough, it seemed. No doubt, Lucan had already stumbled.

If Declan could convince Leofric to allow him to journey to Europe, he could handle the matter himself.

He grumbled beneath his breath and struck off down the secret corridor that led to the meeting room where the Kerzu shared their plans and information. Inside, he found Leofric and Godric gathered around a small table. As he approached, Leofric shuffled a rolled scroll inside the gaping arm of his robe. "Declan. What brings you here at this hour?"

"I wish to inquire about the state of Eadgar's assignment in Ornes. How does he fare?"

Leofric reclined in his chair and folded his arms over his chest. "He has seen little progress. Though we suspect this Chloe may be a seraph. Eadgar awaits confirmation before he will act further."

"And if she isna? What will happen then?"

The leader of the Kerzu's mouth tightened into harsh, cruel lines. "'Tis not your place to question, Declan. Your assignment is to guide Julian through the acquisition of the relic. Once it has been restored where it belongs, you are finished with this duty."

Annoyance slid through Declan's veins. He had not given his oath to this cause of purifying the Templar to be treated as an insignificant servant. For too many years he had led men to meekly assume such a subservient position. Squinting at his commander, he challenged, "Send me. I ken I will succeed where Eadgar hasna."

"Nay. You are not ready."

"I am!"

"You will not go. Do not plague me further with these insignificant requests. When the time has come for you to leave the temple, you shall be notified."

Four months of working beneath Leofric's guidance warned Declan that further protest would fall on deaf ears. He held in a string of curses and checked the sudden urge to resign this post. Were it not for the knowledge that the work they conducted in secret would restore the Order to its true purpose once more, he would have. But the need to achieve one greatness before the darkness claimed him eternally forced Declan into silence. He turned away from Leofric, his fury in check, his emotions once more under control.

Opportunity would come soon enough, of this he was certain. A few more menial tasks, like this coaching of the ignorant Julian, and he would earn his place along with the right to do something truly admirable.

CHAPTER 32

✝

Chloe awakened to the gray light of dawn, feeling strangely alive and energetic. She ached in places she didn't know existed, and as she took stock of her well-used body, a smile crept across her face. *Lucan.* The memories of what he had done to her, the thorough way he'd made love to her through the night blossomed in her mind. Not once, not twice, but three times he had roused her to the heights of passion, then carried her over the edge, tumbling right along with her into the deep abyss that was sheer feeling. On her back. Sitting astride him. Stretched out side by side, her leg lifted over his hip . . . He knew his way around women, and now he knew his way around her. Inside and out.

The weighty feel of his arm at her hip and the warm press of his chest against her back stirred all that frenetic energy once more. She should have had her fill of him. Should be too exhausted to consider another robust round of mind-boggling sex. But with that physical joining, something deeper found satisfaction. The gaping empty hole inside her that had too long cried out for fulfillment closed tight. And God, how it felt good to let a man inside, not only physically, but emotionally. He had wrung from her all she had to give, and give it she'd done freely.

Now, as the day loomed before her and the explanations she'd have to give her brother, she ached for that contentment once more. She needed to find strength in Lucan. Courage to look her overprotective brother in the eye and fight off his suspicions.

The light brush of Lucan's fingertips against her bare belly suggested he was awake. The half-mast erection that nudged against her buttocks turned suggestion into fact. She wriggled her bottom closer, taking him between her thighs.

His mouth fastened onto the back of her neck.

"Mm. Good morning," she murmured, sliding her hand down to twine with his.

"Good morn."

His sleep-hoarsened whisper scraped over her shoulder seconds before his lips followed. She shivered at the warm caress and dragged his arm tighter about her waist, burrowing into the protective wall of his powerful chest. In no mood for conversation, and wanting nothing but the steady reminder that the man at her back was real, she brought their joined hands to her breast where she let go, and pressed his palm over the soft flesh there.

He gave her a gentle squeeze. Between her thighs, she felt him grow harder. The tip of his erection touched the very base of her opening, and she shifted her leg, pressed her body backward, taking him ever so slightly inside. Lying still, she allowed sexual awareness to engulf her. The heat in his body, in his swollen cock, spread slowly through her veins. Her pulse kicked up a beat. Moisture gathered between her legs.

"You are not sore?" The wash of his breath lifted the fine hairs at the nape of her neck. Her skin pricked with goose bumps. Beneath his tender fingertips, her nipples pebbled into tight, hard buds.

"Not enough to care." She angled her hips closer, drawing him farther inside her slickened sex.

Lucan's hand left her breast and glided down her body to slip between her legs. He toyed with the sensitive nub there. Pressed his thumb against it. Squeezed. She sucked in a sharp breath, let it out on a purr, and pushed backward into his body. He eased forward, slowly sliding into her swollen depths.

"You feel so good, Chloe. Do you feel me, as I feel you?"

Oh God, did she ever. Each hot, hard inch of him pressed into her innermost walls, all the way to the tip of her womb. Her muscles clamped around him. She clawed at the pillow beneath her cheek and managed a breathless, "Yes."

He stroked her clit as he eased away then thrust in inch by heavenly inch, his pace unhurried. Deliberate. His lips grazed over her shoulder. "When you come," he murmured, " 'tis as if naught else exists. I am part of you. I lose myself in you."

Devotion radiated off him like sunshine on a summer's day. She basked in it, warmed beneath the honesty in his heartfelt words. And those murmured confessions loosened the strings around her heart. It bloomed behind her ribs, swelling so fiercely she thought for a moment it might stop completely.

It kick-started with his next lazy thrust that brought her so tight against his body she began to understand what he meant. Part of her. Part of *him*. Like this, nothing stood between them. They moved as one. Felt as one. Shared the same needs and the same vulnerabilities. His heart thudded against her shoulder blades. His breath matched hers, hard and short. The tightness in his body spoke of the same restraint she exercised, both wanting to bring the other to equal passion and succumb to the same shattering end.

It wasn't a game of domination and conquest. No power struggle to see who could make the other crumble first. No, this was *loving*. Mutual consideration and the complete abandonment of personal gain. She'd told him she would fall in love with him. Damn it if she hadn't already.

"Yes," she murmured, agreeing in the only way she knew how. Though she wouldn't dare admit what she really answered—the inner acceptance that she had given all she possessed to this incredible man. She'd yielded her heart. Telling him, however, made the playing field uneven. In doing so, she threw power straight into his hands and gave him the ability to break her. In that one way, she would withhold. She'd say nothing of the emotion he provoked until he surrendered first. Nothing else offered protection.

She twisted her hips, the need for harder, faster, fevering her body. "Lucan. Please."

Lucan set his jaw against Chloe's plaintive plea. He would like naught else than to slam into her and drive her to the point of no return. 'Twas what she wanted. The utter eradication of soul-deep feeling, replaced by the carnal gratification of desire. He could not deny 'twas tempting.

Through the night, he had taken her relentlessly. Each time his body stirred, she was there to meet him, to welcome him. But each time he sought to draw their joining out, each time he strove to attune them body and mind, she pulled back and urged him into the place where need overruled all else.

Not this morning. He would have from her the ultimate surrender. Then, when they were so spent they could not breathe and feeling stole the strength from their limbs, he would confide what she was, elicit her seraph's oath, and return to her the same ties of binding.

'Twas only one way to provoke what he desired.

Twisting his weight into her, he rolled her onto her stomach, then slid his arms beneath and lifted her to her knees.

"Lucan, wait," she protested as she turned her head to look at him. Her eyes widened in surprise, as if she too understood that taking her this way stripped her of the last of her ability to resist.

Ignoring her protest, he gripped the graceful curve of her waist and thrust into her womanly depths with a hoarse groan. Her back arched. Her hips slammed back to meet his. A cry ripped from her throat.

"Feel me, Chloe," he urged. Bending over her, he planted kisses between her shoulder blades. "Inside you. Around you." He flicked the tip of his tongue out to trace the bumps of her spine. "Everywhere."

"Lucan . . ."

He draped his body around hers. Slid one hand beneath her to cup her breast. The other, he eased between her legs as he pumped once more. "I will never hurt you." The brush of his fingers against her moistened sex sent a spasm rolling through her body. Her hot wet walls clamped down around his cock, sending a shock of sheer ecstasy straight to the core of his being. He resisted the fierce call of her body. Ordered himself not to spill.

When he raked his teeth against the slope of her shoulder, she trembled. He shook with her, need rising to intolerable limits. Yet he knew she required more than his physical release. She required security that could not be found in the simple act of sex. Even if what flowed between them was not so simple. "I will not leave you," he whispered against her damp skin.

"Oh God, Lucan . . ." She pushed back, the fight leaving her body. Her arms relaxed, as did the rigid nature of her spine. Her hips gyrated against his.

Brushing his thumb over her sensitive bundle of nerves, Lucan slid home with the backward thrust of her body. She sagged to her elbows. He held her up, proving to her the only way he knew how, that she could depend on him when she was too weak to stand on her own. When fears dominated, he would be there. Always.

Forever.

Her hair spilled over the pillow as she turned her head once more. But this time, 'twas not to protest. Instead, she pressed a sweet, consenting kiss to the only part of his body she could reach, the small space of skin between his bicep and his shoulder.

The touch, so innocent and so light, spoke volumes. When she did not rear back upon him and urge him into a reckless pace, he knew he had attained what he most desired. Glorying in the profoundness of the moment, he glided in and out of her and let silence speak the words of love. He held the pace steady, determined to give her all the time she needed to accept and embrace what she let go.

Moments passed timelessly. The fall of their breaths was a harmonic chorus the angels could not mirror. Their sweat-slickened bodies entwined like the magic of the heavens. One heart. One mind. One soul. And yet, as intoxicating as it was, Lucan needed more. He needed to taste the affection that lay on the tip of her tongue. Needed to feel the silken glide of her arms as they looped around him and brought him into the pillowy softness of her skin.

Still keeping them joined, he rolled her onto her back. She lifted up as he lowered his body into hers, and her mouth claimed his in a sweet, thought-stopping kiss. Ecstasy blistered through his veins. His body tensed against the scald. Beneath him, she convulsed.

Lucan tore his mouth free. Lifting his head, he caught her hands and gazed down at her impassioned expression. When their eyes locked, and all that emotion he had sought to free poured out through her fathomless amber eyes, he lost the ability to function. Release crashed through him, drowning him in wave after wave of insurmountable pleasure. He shook with the force of it. Her slick sheath gripped and squeezed with the pulse of his cock, milking out his seed until he had naught left to spill.

Their voices mingled, a ragged exhale of the other's name, and Lucan collapsed into the only woman who could bring him salvation.

As he lay atop her, unmoving, he cradled her head to his shoulder and feathered kisses into her hair. The trembling of her body was so slight he would have missed it had he not been touching her everywhere. Against his bare skin, he felt the hot splash of tears.

He tightened his fingers against the back of her head and closed his eyes. "Shh. 'Tis all right, my sweet. 'Tis how it should be between us."

"No, it's not," she argued in a whisper. "I don't want to love you."

A smile pulled at the corner of his mouth, and he pressed another kiss to her hair. "Do you?"

The fist at his shoulder, and the firm pressure she used to push him away, said all he needed to hear. But when he refused to let her withdraw, she choked back a sob. Her mouth moved against his overheated skin. "Yes."

Letting her go, Lucan allowed her to fall back into the pillows. He braced himself on his hands and held her watery gaze. His heart beat like a drum, the hard racket threatening to crack through his ribs. "I have given my heart to no one," he murmured as he brushed his lips across hers. "Save you."

Shaken to the root of his being, he could not trust his own strength to keep him from toppling onto her and crushing her with his weight. He rolled to his side, gathered her in his arms, and took her with him. She curled against his chest, one long lean leg tucked securely between his. He took a deep breath. Allowed the truth to reverberate through his body.

Chloe turned the medallion around his neck between her fingers. "Tell me about this?"

Not now. She had heard too much already. He would not push her further until she had the time to believe that her confession of love would not bring her harm.

Yet he could not feign sleep and ignore her question. He must answer. Somehow.

She aided his dilemma. "It's Templar, isn't it?"

"Aye."

"Why do you have it?"

His brow creased with a tight frown. The words lay on the tip of his tongue. Her seraphs' torc rested in the drawer beside his bed. He could slide it onto her arm and speak the words. But without her solemn vow, 'twould be meaningless. *Nay*. Now was not the time.

"The Templar belongings should remain with those who know the secrets, who understand the Code."

"And you do?" she asked on a wide yawn.

"Aye."

"How?"

"'Twas taught to me." That much was true. When he had righted his family's murder by snuffing out his brother's life, he had turned to the noble Order. Merrick had taken him under his wing, taught him the Code, and the meaning of what it meant to wield a sacred sword. Though Lucan had never believed he would walk straight into the pits of hell and discover the holy knights fought the very existence of evil, not the heretics that plagued the roads to the Holy Lands.

"It must be nice." Exhaustion slurred her words. "Family secrets like that. My parents didn't believe in keeping things. They sold all the family stuff." She snuggled closer, let out a heavy sigh. "Maybe that's why I'm so committed to preserving relics." Her palm slid across his chest, and he felt the smile grace her mouth. "God, you're beautiful."

He couldn't stop a chuckle from slipping free. "Nay, 'tis you. Rest, Chloe."

"I can't. I have to get to the site."

"Nay, you can. I will wake you in a few hours."

For a moment, he expected her silence to bring protest. But when she twitched in his arms, he understood the reason she did not argue. He pulled his fingers through her hair and bathed in the warmth that ebbed into his side. A few more hours, and she would be his.

Eternally.

In the meantime, he must remove all reasons for her to escape the conversation they must have. When she woke, she would want to know how her team fared in her absence. What news they brought. The documents should arrive from both labs today, and he would need that scientific proof to verify his claims about the Veronica. With Chloe's business handled for the day, she would have no room to protest a few more hours away from her responsibilities. And if the Almighty chose to smile upon him, she would realize her responsibilities encompassed far more than the unearthing of ancient relics.

With great reluctance, he eased himself from the tangle of her legs and slid from the bed. Though his body screamed for the same relief of slumber, he pushed past the exhaustion in his limbs and quietly dressed. When he had donned both boots and sword, he grabbed his coat from the back of the couch and left the room.

CHAPTER 33

⸸

The drive to Ornes passed quickly in Lucan's current state of contentment. His eyelids sagged, reminding him he had naught but a handful of hours of sleep, but he would not exchange the exhaustion in his limbs for any amount of rest. The reward for his aches came with Chloe. She had given him more than he believed possible, though he would have killed himself in trying.

Already he could feel the effect her light had on his soul. The suspicion he fought for so many years no longer reared its head quite as easily. True, it stirred. But he had found the means to resist it. When their oaths were complete, he would know the healing his brothers celebrated. And he too would become a stronger ally on the field.

With Chloe's ability to combat mentally, like the other seraphs and their gifts, she too would become an invaluable asset. Though she could do little more than push the beasts away now, in time her power would grow. She would possess the ability to kill with a single telepathic thought. When that happened, his seraph would never again fear a solitary shadow.

They would stand together, a unified team, and eradicate Azazel's minions.

He nosed into the parking lot, feeling far more self-satisfied than he should. Arrogance bore foolishness, and he would be well served not to let a robust night between the sheets go to his head. He still had much to accomplish—including the very real possibility Chloe would resist. If not refuse.

He tempered his rising elation with a clenched fist to the steering wheel. Nay, he would not become consumed by possibility. Not until she freely bore the brand of seraphs and he could claim her words. While she would eventually be a formidable opponent of Azazel's, 'twould require time to accomplish her training. Meanwhile, he must achieve her oath to ensure naught could harm her.

Stepping out onto the frozen gravel, he observed the team's attention snap his way. From the hole near the toppled wall, all five students stood and looked toward the SUV. Julian stood at the edge of the site, arms folded over his chest. Even from this distance, Lucan could feel the man's disapproving frown.

Ignoring the censure that radiated off Chloe's brother, Lucan strode for the main trailer and let himself inside. The heater's blast hit him immediately, and he shrugged out of his coat. With a toss, he cast it on a nearby chair. A row of brass and a smear of dirt particles on the countertop caught his attention—the relics Chloe had inspected the last time he was here.

He moved to the tidy row and bent over the pieces.

Thick clods of mud still clung to a dagger's hilt, but the metal beneath bore no rust, no patina. A bright glint marked it as silver, and as Lucan pressed his thumb against the dirt, dislodging it, he found the unmistakable cross that marked it as Templar. Le Goix's dagger. Alongside his signet ring.

Lucan frowned. Why had his brother left such personal effects within the ground? He picked up the heavy silver ring inset with a blood-red ruby, and held it to the light to examine the engraving in the band. Though Lucan had long ago lost his on a forgotten battlefield, 'twas unlike le Goix to purposefully leave behind such an item. Indeed, however, the wide band bore his initials.

Why? Loss was one thing. But this deliberate placement near the reliquary marked abandonment, and no brother would abandon personal effects. 'Twas forbidden. 'Twas the very reason so few Templar artifacts made it to the public awareness.

He closed his fist around the ring and scowled at the dagger. Did the archangels know these things lay in rest here too? If not, would le Goix suffer their wrath?

Nay. They must know. All other things they swore would be discovered in the pit had been revealed. These two items, however, did not fall upon their list. And the rest of what did was as insignificant as the dirt it came from.

"What are you doing?"

Julian's harsh bark jolted Lucan out of his thoughts. His head snapped up, and he found the man scowling in the doorway. Agitation needled its way down Lucan's spine. He did not have the patience to deal with overprotective brothers and suspicious actions. His mind was not in good enough form to analyze Julian's ever-increasing odd behavior.

He set the ring on the counter. Later, he would broach the subject with Chloe and ask her if he might return the Templar items to their rightful owner. She would not relish the idea. But he was not averse to begging. These belonged in the Temple. If not on le Goix's person, then in the vast storerooms beneath.

"I came for a report on what was accomplished yesterday, and for the logs."

Julian took a step forward, fury gleaming in his eyes. "You'd know this, if you and my *sister* had decided to show up."

Grinding his teeth, Lucan swallowed a foul oath. No matter what he thought of Julian, the fact remained, he was Chloe's brother, which directly made the man Lucan's family. He could not stuff a fist between Julian's eyes no matter how he longed to do so. "We had more important matters to attend to."

The snort that issued from Julian's throat branded Lucan a liar. Julian's gaze pierced like the tip of the dagger at Lucan's elbow. "I can smell Chloe on you. You spent the day fucking."

Lucan bristled, his distaste for the man increasing by the minute. No brother referred to his sister in such a callous fashion if love lay between them. 'Twas words Lucan's own sibling might have used. And the cold hatred behind Julian's challenging stare fueled a rage Lucan could not explain. He cared little what this man thought of him. But he cared immensely about how Julian referred to Chloe. How he treated her. And since the day Lucan had arrived, he had witnessed naught but disrespect.

Driven by a force greater than himself, he grabbed Julian by the collar and hauled him against the wall. There he held him, his toes just touching the floor. "Your tongue runs too freely. 'Twould be a pleasure to my ears to crush your throat between my fingers."

Brief panic glimmered behind Julian's eyes before an enraged snarl ripped from his throat. He clawed at Lucan's arm with more strength than his body should possess.

Lucan tightened his hold, gave the man a shake. "Cease! Brother you may be, but I will not abide by your disrespect toward Chloe. You may call me out. Say all the foul things you wish about me. Another word that insults her, and I will cut that tongue out. Are we understood?"

Unable to speak through the pressure about his collar, Julian managed a short, succinct nod. His eyes warred with the agreement, however, and Lucan's instincts rose to high alert. From this day forth, he would have to watch Julian more closely. Centuries of battle explained that look, and men like Julian waited to attack when their targets were least suspecting.

He released his grip, allowing Julian to slide to his feet. But he did not step out of his space. "Where are the logs? I am taking them to Chloe."

"I'll g-get them." He rubbed at his throat. Swallowed. "T-Tim has something else in the pit, if you'd like to see it."

Convinced there would be no more insolence for the moment, Lucan stepped back. He cared little what else the team unearthed. But Chloe would wish to know. And the more he could tell her about what was occurring at her dig, the less she would protest about delaying her arrival. "Aye."

He stormed out the door, afraid if he waited a minute longer he would give in to the urge to pummel Julian senseless, simply for the pleasure of doing so. The cold hit him in the face, serving to temper his overwarm blood. He breathed it in deeply, let it flow through his veins. Feeling much more in control of his temper, he stalked to the pit and stood over Tim's crouched form.

"Morning, Lucan," Andy quipped, camera at the ready.

"Good morn. You have found something else?"

"Yeah. Check this out. What do you make of it?" Tim tapped his metal trowel against a square length of gold.

Lucan knew without bending over what the relic was. Another item bestowed upon the Templar, although this one did not bear the Order's mark. The same golden cross could be found in any knight's solitary quarters. 'Twas given to them on the time of joining, moments before they took their immortal pledge and the archangels cursed their soul.

Yet he bent to run his fingers through the loose dirt, feigning ignorance. With two gentle twists, he dislodged the cross and pulled the five-inch length from the dirt. "A cross."

"But why here? This was a castle, not a holy place."

Lucan's gaze drifted to the mark in the stone that identified the remains of le Goix's castle as far more, then back to Tim. "Did the people who lived here not have faith?"

Chagrin colored Tim's cheeks crimson. "D'oh. I should have known that." He paused, his face deepening an even darker red. "Sorry. Used to working in Egypt where ankhs and statues mark religion. I wasn't even thinking."

Lucan could not help but grin. He passed the cross to Tim as footsteps approached on the gravel. Standing, he turned to find Julian at the edge of the pit, a thick notebook in one arm, Lucan's coat in the other. He extended the latter with a forced smile. "You left this."

And he had brought it to speed departure along, Lucan had no doubt. He snatched the coat out of Julian's hands and shrugged it on. Climbing out of the shallow hole, he accepted the reluctant offering of the notebook. "If there are any questions, I am certain Chloe will contact you."

He strode past, as anxious to leave the site as Julian was to have him go. But Julian's voice brought him to a halt.

"The trunk, Lucan. What's going on with it? We all want to know."

Lucan stiffened as something else caught his attention. A distinct odor he had not smelled all morning.

The scent of rot.

Slowly, he turned. Every bit of his warrior's attention honed in on Chloe's brother. Faint, but present nonetheless, the foul odor wafted off his clothing. Muscles bunched, the instinct to kill as prominent as the sun in the cloudless sky above.

Though he could not explain how, or why, Lucan looked upon some dark creation of Azazel's foul design. One thought rose in his mind—*Chloe*.

Damnation! The one person she was closest to posed

the greatest threat. A threat he could not contain or eliminate with her entire team looking on.

He ground out an answer through clenched teeth. "The trunk will be dealt with when the time is right." Unwilling to waste any more time than necessary, he hurried to the SUV. Only one thing would ensure her safety. The oath. He must extract it now.

Chloe stretched beneath the covers, unable to tamp down her wide smile. She felt better than she had in years. A little achy, but nothing that the memories of Lucan's body gliding in and out of hers wouldn't soothe. Eyes closed, she reached an arm across her the bed to pet his strong arm. When nothing but the mattress, not even warm at that, met her groping fingers, she sat up and looked around.

Alone. Not even the sound of running water in the bathroom to indicate he was taking a shower.

A fission of dismay ebbed down to her toes. Damn. There was nothing worse than going to bed with a man and waking up without him. She loved the freedom to roll over, snuggle close, bask in a few thorough kisses before she had to haul herself out of bed and face a day of work.

Work. The thought crashed into her awareness like a hammer on glass. Ugh. Lucan had promised to wake her. Now, instead of facing down Julian's annoyance over a single missed day, she'd have to suck it up and take his lecture about sleeping in late too.

She looked to the clock to confirm the bright light filtering through the drawn curtains meant it was far later than her preferred six o'clock. Really, verifying was unnecessary. Just before she'd resigned herself to

Lucan's complete domination of her body and her mind, the bright neon blue digits heralded a quarter to six. She scolded herself anyway, when she read 8:15.

Time for a shower.

Unfolding her legs, she climbed out of bed and stumbled to the bathroom, where she turned on the water. A long look in the mirror made all the lack of sleep from the night before as obvious as daylight. Dark circles clung beneath her eyes. Long red creases across her cheek marked the place she'd crashed into oblivion.

Chloe stifled a giggle. She should be annoyed, not amused.

Still, it felt so damned wonderful to carry the secret knowledge that she'd given herself, several times over, to Lucan. Handsome Lucan with his gray eyes and long black hair. Intense Lucan, who refused to let her hide behind fear. Strong Lucan, who empowered her to confront the demons and gave her the gift of self-preservation. Good Lord, how could she have hoped to *not* love him? She'd been doomed the very day he walked into her trailer and lifted that taunting eyebrow, fully aware she found his imposingly large build amazing.

At the memory, she *did* giggle. He'd known all along. Dared her from the start to accept it. Pushed her until she had no choice but to cave.

Now, she wouldn't take any of it back. He'd done everything he could to prove himself to her. It was time to take a leap of faith and listen to her heart. Listen to *him*. Not her brother. Not the little nagging voice that urged her to be cautious and keep Lucan at a distance.

Nope. She was done with all of that. She'd cast it aside somewhere between his lifting her to her knees and when her confession of love slipped out. Now it was time to start concentrating on Lucan and returning to him what he gave so freely to her. She'd start the minute he returned. No matter how late she was to the site, she'd treat Lucan to breakfast and spend a bit of quality time with him before work demanded their mutual attention. Maybe breakfast in bed.

Yes, that's exactly what she'd do. She'd call room service and have breakfast ready for him when he returned. It wasn't much, but it was a start. A beginning.

She pushed the shower curtain back and stepped under the spray, knowing she ought to hurry but, for the first time since she'd set foot in Egypt's sands, unable to care. Work, relics, scrolls, and secrets—all she wanted to do was crawl back into that bed, wait for Lucan to return, and spend the rest of the afternoon learning everything she could about him. Not just his body, that she knew quite well. His flavor was salty. All male. Not a bit of him was small. Every square inch of his skin responded to her touch. And they fit together all too perfectly.

No, today she longed to learn about his past. About that ancestor who had once been part of the noble Knights Templar and all the secrets that had been passed down through generations. Truth be told, learning Lucan's family history held more excitement than the damned relic she knew would come back as what he claimed.

Lathering her hair, she hummed to herself. Two years of Blake hadn't made her feel this energized. Even on the nights that she had fallen into exhaustion after an especially vigorous round of sex, she hadn't felt this . . . this . . .

She frowned, searching for the word. Everything that came to mind felt trite. Like words stolen from someone else's fantasy, not hers. Still, she couldn't escape the haunting answer, no matter how unoriginal it might be. *Complete.* Lucan put all her missing stuffing back into holes she didn't know existed and stitched her fraying seams shut.

The soap ran from her hair to pool at her feet. While she bathed, hating the fact she washed him off her skin, she let the conditioner soak in. Her hands stilled as a terrifying prospect tugged at her mind.

Condoms. Dear God, not once in the course of the night had they used a bit of protection. Shit!

She stumbled as she reached for the towel bar to stop the sudden buzzing in her head. Oh no. This couldn't be good. When Blake had left, she'd been so certain she wasn't going to get mixed up with someone she'd stopped her shots. Declined the pill. And her cycle had been about two weeks ago.

Shit!

Lucan she could deal with. Even loving him. A baby? No way, no how. Not for another several years.

She pulled in a deep breath and stared at the shower tiles. Her mind ran in circles. She'd have to make a trip into Verdun and find a clinic. France had all kinds of morning-after solutions. This wasn't the end of the world. She'd suck up her embarrassment and ask Lucan to take her to the neighboring city. He surely wouldn't care. For that matter, he'd probably be relieved she thought of it so soon.

Feeling much more calm, she ducked her head under the shower and rinsed for the last time. As she reached for the faucets, she heard the bedroom door close. For an instant, disappointment pulled through her. So much for her breakfast idea.

In the next moment, her pulse picked up at the very knowledge he was in the nearby room. What he could do to her was simply mystifying. One glance, and her heart tripped into her ribs. One touch, and she turned into a puddle.

Another giggle broke free, and Chloe turned off the water.

CHAPTER 34

A ll thoughts of oaths and seraphs fled Lucan's mind as Chloe exited the bathroom. Fully naked, she greeted him with a smile that pulled his heart into his throat and turned his cock into hewn steel. Her long hair dripped at her waist. Water ran in rivulets over full, creamy breasts. And not a stitch of modesty clung to her as she waltzed across the room to welcome him with a kiss.

His arms wound around her waist, instinct driving him to urge her back to the bed and repeat last night. Saints' toes, a small portion of last night would satisfy. He cared not, as long as her lips remained on his and her body fit beneath him.

Chloe evidently had different designs. She eased out of his embrace, caught his hand, and led him to the couch. His baser nature rebelled. Not the couch. 'Twas too confining. Too short to do naught more than kneel between her legs.

But when she urged him to sit and planted her bare

bottom in his lap, the couch took on greater appeal. Aye, sitting would do just fine. He could wind her legs around his waist and suckle at her breast as he slid into her silken warmth.

He fitted his palm against the curve of her buttock, urging her leg into the position he desired.

She laughed, evading his seeking mouth. "We need to talk, Lucan. Stop before you remove my ability to think."

Think. Aye, he needed a good strong dose of logic as well. They had much to talk about. Although his cock might protest, he could not indulge when her brother was so near at hand. He must explain. Must demand her oath, whether she understood it fully or not.

Sobering, he tried to ignore the press of her body against his ready erection and focused on the movement of her lips.

"I need you to take me into Verdun today, please. Then we should get out to the site."

When that soft pink mouth only conjured visions of the way she had clamped her lips around his throbbing shaft, he groaned aloud and dropped his head to the back of the couch. He ran a frustrated hand through his hair. "Dress. I can focus on naught when you are like this."

Her giggle nearly undid him. The press of her hand against his chest had him sucking in a sharp breath. When she drifted that dangerous palm lower and flattened it over his all-too-willing member, he hissed.

"This is exactly what I'm talking about."

He gave her a perplexed look. "What is your meaning?"

To his dismay, her hand fell away. Color crept into her cheeks, and she lowered her head. Shy. He would have sworn she had moved beyond that.

"Chloe?"

"We haven't used any protection, and no matter how badly I want you—want this—I need to find a clinic. I wasn't exactly . . . prepared for you."

Oh aye, she had been more than prepared for him. He would wager she was now. But they spoke of two different meanings, and hers was more than clear. Sitting up, he let out a disparaging sigh. "Nay, 'tis no need. I cannot father children."

She blinked. "You've been . . . snipped?"

Regret he had never once expected to feel turned his stomach into a hard knot. But then, he had never expected he could care so much for one woman that the archangels' curse would matter. "Nay," he answered more quietly. "I am sterile." As the bitter confession made its way from the dregs of his soul, he found more strength in his voice. "I am healthy as well."

"Oh." Her wide eyes blinked once more, then she searched his face, as if she looked for something that would contradict his claims. "Are you certain? I mean, I've heard stories. Men who thought they were, and then—"

He placed a finger to her lips, silencing the questions he could not bear to hear. " 'Tis been confirmed, Chloe. A father I shall never be."

"Oh." This time, her quiet answer held a note of unmistakable dismay. His heart twisted at the touch of sorrow. He would have liked to someday honor what she apparently held so dear. But in time, she too would come to accept the loss of what they could never have. 'Twould not hold such poison when they had eons with each other.

Which reminded him of all else he needed to discuss with her. His desire now flat, he sat up fully and caught her hands in his. "I too wish to talk to you. I have been at the site." He inclined his head toward the table behind them. "Your logs from yesterday are there. And I observed something of interest."

"Really?" Curiosity replaced the dull light in her eyes. "What?"

"A dagger and a ring. Both are Templar. I would wish to have your permission to return them."

As he had anticipated, she tensed. Her mouth pursed, and her back turned as stiff as a board. "That's stealing."

"Nay. 'Tis only stealing if the object does not belong to you."

"But something like that doesn't belong to you *or* the Church. It's part of history, Lucan. It deserves to be shared with the people of the world. Even your ancestors would appreciate that."

Her emphatic position on something as relatively insignificant as a dagger and a ring said little for the way she would receive the rest of his news. 'Twould take every bit of patience he possessed to make her believe in who he was. What they both were. And pointing out that the birthmark on his buttocks matched the one on her shoulder and proclaimed something greater would accomplish naught more than another of her amused giggles.

"The Templar secrets are not meant to be shared with the world. 'Twas a reason they hid themselves away. A purpose that their existence reveals, and the artifacts you speak of link them to that purpose, *if* they are correctly traced."

"And so what?" She folded her arms over her bare breasts. "They are *dead*. Whatever drove them underground—politics, debts, heresy, you name it—no longer exists. You don't want them linked to the Church? Fine, we don't have to publish that they came from the same excavation plot. We can document the finding and quietly let the information slide."

"They are not dead."

His low response snapped her mouth closed. In the next heartbeat it fell open with a whispered, "What?"

Lucan pulled in a deep breath. 'Twas not how he had planned to start this conversation. He had intended to approach it more like an engagement. With the torc as an offering to a confession of unyielding love.

Nevertheless, he had said too much. He could not stop now. "The Holy Order of the Knights Templar is not dead. It exists. I am a part of it, not my ancestor."

He read her disbelief in the narrowing of her brow. Felt it in the absence of her hands, as she pulled them away from his body. Heard it in her short laugh.

Before she could completely vacate his lap, he caught her hands and held them tight. "I am a Templar knight, Chloe. And you are part of the Templar purpose. Of *my* purpose."

An insistent hammering on his door cut off the rest of his explanation. Lucan let out a harassed sigh and tipped his head back. "Begone!"

"Monsieur! Je suis désolé, il est important!"

At the concierge's frantic French, Lucan frowned. Important? Naught could be more important than this conversation.

The furious pounding, however, argued his belief. *"Monsieur!"*

Lucan eased Chloe off his lap and motioned for her to don the shirt he had worn the night before. As she pulled it over her head and quickly added her underwear, he crossed to the door. Harassed beyond imagination, he yanked it open to stare at the smaller, agitated man.

"Monsieur, I am so sorry. You did not answer soon enough. I could not stop—"

Two burly members of the gendarmerie shouldered the château's representative aside and barged into the room. Julian followed on their heels. He spared Chloe only a passing glance before he thrust a finger at Lucan's chest. "That's him. That's the man."

Before Lucan could do more than blink, the two gendarmes wrested his arms behind his back and hurtled him toward the door. He sank his weight into their determined push, thwarting their efforts to shove him into the hall. "Release me. I have done naught."

Behind him, Chloe cried, "Julian! What's going on?"

No sooner had the question broken through the air than Gareth appeared in the doorway. He took one look at Lucan, bound between the two guards, and scowled at Julian.

Confronted by not one, but two men who easily doubled them in size, the gendarmes evidently found it prudent to cease their insistent shoving at Lucan's back. Instead, they twisted his arms painfully toward his shoulder blades, forcing him to submit. He bit back a rush of anger and complied. Fighting would only give them further grounds.

"Julian!" Chloe latched on to her brother's arm. "Tell me what is going on!"

"I'll tell you what's going on." He shook off her hold to fling his hand at Lucan once again. "He's played you for a fool. I caught him in the trailer today looking at that signet ring and silver dagger. When he left, the ring went with him."

"You lie!" Lucan thundered. He surged forward to wrap his hands around Julian's neck, but the sharp twist of his arms stopped him in his tracks.

Chloe's eyes widened like saucers. Her lower lip quivered, and she looked between the two men. "You can't be serious, Julian. Lucan wouldn't steal. We were just talking about those items."

Saints' love her, she had faith in him. Lucan sagged at her words. This would end in moments, and when it did, 'twould be Julian who left in the guards' escort. When he managed to free himself from the jail, Lucan would be there to pound him back to the hell he had come from. God's teeth, could no one else smell the stench that rolled off him?

"Check his coat. He probably pocketed the damn thing. Though I wouldn't be surprised to find it empty either. We'll have to check his car."

Chloe hesitated, her gaze straying to the coat Lucan had carelessly flung over the back of the couch. A deep foreboding crept down his spine as he too looked at the leather. Julian had brought his coat out. 'Twas no gesture to hurry him away from the site. 'Twas blackmail. Lucan had no doubt that whatever trinket Julian claimed was missing would lie within his pocket.

Bloody Christ!

He struggled against his captors' hold, determined to break free and choke the life out of Julian. At least that would be a crime worth punishment. For when Chloe discovered a relic in his coat pocket, he would suffer far greater.

'Twas Gareth who dared to pick up the coat. He shoved his hand inside, his gaze locked on Lucan, conveying he understood the truth.

And the likely outcome.

Lucan knew the moment Gareth's hand touched the relic. His eyes closed a fraction. His jaw tensed. A breath of air hissed through clenched teeth.

It took all of Lucan's self-control not to bellow in rage as Gareth pulled his hand free and opened it to reveal le Goix's Templar ring. He stamped down the fury, turned pleading eyes on Chloe. Silently, he begged her to believe in all she knew about him. He had no reason to take the relic. He would have never touched it had she denied him permission to return it as he wanted to.

She watched him, her doubt etched into her ashen face. "Lucan?"

"I did not take it, Chloe. Why would I ask you about it, if I already possessed it?"

"Mademoiselle, what do you wish us to do?" asked the gendarme at Lucan's left.

Her eyes flickered, wavering between what she knew in her heart and what visible facts lay before her eyes. Praying to the only power he knew who could intervene and right this intolerable wrong. He held his breath. Waiting. Hoping.

The blissful world of happiness Chloe had known only a few minutes earlier slowly crumbled into pieces and crashed onto her shoulders. Standing between her brother and Lucan, she stared helplessly as the walls around her closed in. Both expected her to believe in them. Lucan's pleading stare demanded she remember his words. The promise he would never hurt her. His eyes hardened with each second that passed and she remained silent. Julian watched expectantly. His anger boiled to the surface, gleamed behind his eyes. The longer she stood quiet, the more triumph crept into his gaze.

Whom did she choose? Whom did she cast aside? Did she turn her back on the only flesh and blood she possessed, or did she walk away from the one man she wanted most?

"Chloe," Julian pressed. "He's not who he claims to be. Lucan Seacourt doesn't exist."

She whipped her head around to blink at her brother. "What?"

"I checked with the Church. They don't know anything about him, or him." He jabbed his thumb at Gareth. "They don't work for the Catholic diocese. And Lucan Seacourt died in the thirteenth century. Lucan *of* Seacourt. He's that man whose tomb they unearthed. His name was engraved in the shield they found."

Chloe gasped for air, but her lungs refused to fill. Lies? Oh God, it couldn't be true. She grabbed for the back of the couch as her knees went weak, unable to bring herself to look at Lucan and see the defiance in his eyes.

"You're lying," she whispered. Julian had to be. She'd touched Lucan. Given him entirely too much of herself for this to all be farce.

"I'm not. Pick up the phone. Here's the number." He thrust a piece of paper beneath her nose.

"Chloe, for the love of the saints, this is nonsense," Lucan protested. Resignation filtered into his voice. There could only be one reason for such a lack of conviction—guilt.

"Chloe, please listen to me. I just told you what I am."

A knight Templar . . . A story even more implausible than Julian's claims that Lucan had stolen the ring. But if he believed it . . . If he truly felt some tie to the extinct order, or even pledged membership to a legacy Masonic organization . . . Wouldn't that give him reason to possess the ring?

A sob rose to cut off her words. Shaking her head, she turned away from both brother and lover. Dead. Lucan of Seacourt was the knight in the grave. Damn it all, they had talked about him in the car! No wonder Lucan knew so much. He'd studied the discovery enough to mimic the role.

Oh, Lord in heaven, she couldn't be a bigger fool. She'd fallen right into his game. She would have surrendered the priceless relic without question. And he'd done exactly what Julian forewarned—used her.

"Arrest him," she choked out. "Just . . . get him out of here."

"Chloe!"

She grimaced at the harsh, unfriendly bellow. Let him protest. Let him rant. For that matter let him hate her. It would make forgetting him easier.

"Monsieur, you come with us."

The commotion behind her back told her Lucan wasn't making it easy to get him out of the room. She dug her nails into his couch and squeezed her eyes shut tight to block the hoarseness of his voice as he called out to her once again.

The door slammed shut. Julian's heavy hand settled on her shoulder. "I'm sorry, sis."

She shrugged his hand off. "Go. I don't want to see you either."

He gave her back an affectionate pat, and she felt him leave her side. A few seconds later, the door closed once more. Quieter this time.

The silence that remained was deafening.

CHAPTER 35

Lucan sank his head into his bound hands and raked his fingers against his scalp. Worry consumed him. With only Gareth to watch over Chloe, and her present state of disbelief, Julian could strike at any time. He could not fault her for believing her brother. Mayhap if he had been given a few more moments to tell her the truth, he would not be sitting on this hard bench, listening to the monotonous tick of an unseen clock, and feeling his life slip by with each passing second.

God's teeth, when he got free from here, he would rip that demon in half, regardless of his blood tie to Chloe. Her wrath would be immense, but 'twas a sacrifice Lucan was willing to make.

He dragged his hands down his face and leaned back, resting his head against the cinder-block wall. Beyond the bars of his cell, footsteps trekked down the sterile hall. The same pair of polished steel-toe boots with a slight heel he had heard intermittently for the last several hours.

His muscles twitched with restlessness. Chloe was out there. In danger. And the Almighty only knew what the person she trusted most had planned for her.

If he did not find a way out of this suffocating cell, he would go mad.

The clang of something hard against the bars drew him upright. A guard, no doubt the one whose shoes had worn a hole through Lucan's thoughts, peered in. *"Vous avez un visiteur."*

A visitor? Lucan frowned. Chloe mayhap? Could she have changed her mind?

As he pondered the possibility, a well-dressed man stepped from behind the gendarme. Long, golden hair tumbled freely about his wide shoulders and framed a face so beautiful, Lucan flinched.

Raphael. God's teeth, mayhap the Almighty had heard his pleas after all.

Lucan shot to his feet. Before he could speak a word, however, the archangel lifted one hand, palm out, indicating he should remain silent. He turned to the guard with a smile as brilliant as gold. A subtle light flowed from his fingertips, drawing the gendarme's attention to Raphael's flawless palm.

Lucan watched in fascination as the official's eyes widened. At the low chanting words that issued from Raphael's voice—spoken so softly Lucan could not make them out—the gendarme slowly nodded his head. The light dimmed. Raphael fell silent and lowered his hand.

"Monsieur, un erreur a été comise."

A mistake made? Saints' teeth, aye, 'twas one monster of a mistake. But the guard's statement perplexed him further. Lucan squinted expectantly, awaiting further explanation. It came as the gendarme inserted one key from a ring of several and twisted the cell lock. Opening the heavy barred door, he stepped inside and motioned for Lucan to approach.

Wary, Lucan looked over the guard's shoulder at Raphael. A slow nod of the archangel's head instructed he should obey the official's request. Lucan moved closer to the guard.

Pointing one stubby finger at the heavy handcuffs cutting into his wrists, the man instructed, *"Vos mains, s'il vous plaît."*

Understanding settled around Lucan. He lifted his hands toward the gendarme, complying with the request. The shorter man flipped through his multitude of keys, picked out a smaller, less obvious bit of metal, and thrust it into the hole at Lucan's wrist. With one quick flick of a scarred wrist, the handcuffs released. *"Vous êtes libre de partir."*

Free to go.

Lucan did not waste a moment as he hurried out of the cell and joined Raphael in the narrow corridor. "Thank you," he murmured beneath his breath.

"Say naught of it. Gareth told me of your predicament. Come." He grabbed Lucan's elbow and ushered him through the central processing room of the gendarmerie, across the lobby, and out the wide front doors. He did not stop until they had reached a silver SUV parked at the rear of the well-lighted lot. "You must take care not to be seen. I cannot follow behind you and alter the memories of all those who know of your arrest."

Glancing around, Lucan observed the fall of night. He had been inside several hours, but he had not anticipated to find the sun well beneath the horizon and the moon high in the sky. He must have been inside almost sixteen hours. He grabbed for the driver's door handle. "Chloe?" His voice held impatience.

"At the château. Gareth stands guard at her new door."

So she had been disgusted enough to flee his room. Lucan cringed. Still, for now, she remained unharmed.

He climbed behind the wheel and keyed the engine.

"If you must, Sir Lucan, bring her to the temple. Sometimes 'tis easier if you remove all exterior factors."

Lucan read between the polite phrasing, hearing the real meaning—*force her to comply*. He shut the door and dropped the gearshift into reverse. Naught would make him force Chloe. If he tried, he would never obtain the words the Templar, and the archangels, desperately required.

Unable to sit idle, he tapped his fingers against the wheel as Raphael backed away from the fender. Lucan could not recall a time when the archangels had intervened to such a degree. That the European master of combat unhesitatingly used divine power to influence Lucan's fate mystified him even more. By all rights, he should have been left in the cell to sort this out for himself. 'Twould not be the first time, nor would it be the last that a Templar found himself at the end of a short rope. Through the entire Inquisition the archangels remained silent. 'Twas not until the sentences had passed down, and they were forced to deal with burned bodies that would not die, that they stepped in and took the entire Order underground.

Why now? Why *him*?

As the golden specter shimmered, then slowly became one with the night, Lucan dismissed the questions. Why mattered not. Chloe's life depended on his expedient return. True, Gareth could keep her safe for a short time, but she would not allow him close enough to keep her out of Julian's clutches. Not when her brother implied Gareth spoke lies as well.

He sped down the empty highway, a death grip on the wheel. Time suspended as tree after tree passed. Urgency forced his foot to the floor, and he whipped around the curves like a high-speed train on well-oiled rails. He knew naught but one thing: he must reach Chloe before her brother could.

The château's roof emerged over the tops of the trees, and Lucan willed the SUV to move faster. Yet with the pedal pressed as far as it could go, the vehicle could not comply. The last several yards that led to the garden drive seemed to pass at a snail's pace; an intolerable crawl that left Lucan's nerves raw.

At last the château rose against the night sky. He zipped into a parking spot, shut off the engine, and flew out the door. In seconds he was inside. Several more, and he stood in his room, the torc in his hand. He stuffed it into his pocket, rushed back into the hall, then took the stairs two at a time. On the second floor, he paused only long enough to poke his head into the corridor and verify Gareth did not stand in the hall. Which left the third. The same floor she had occupied before the demons attacked.

He bolted off the landing and around the corner, into the narrow corridor. To Lucan's surprise, Gareth stood outside the door he had previously claimed as his own. Head cocked in curiosity, Lucan strode quickly toward his waiting brother.

A smirk broke across the younger man's face. He dipped his head in greeting. "Raphael indeed moved quickly. He was most concerned when I phoned."

Lucan frowned at the door, then at Gareth. "She is inside?"

Chuckling with immense amusement, Gareth nodded. "I vacated my room when I overheard her request another, to keep her close at hand. The hotel is otherwise full. Might I have your key?"

Fishing into his back pocket, Lucan produced the key to his room and passed it to his brother. "Leave me a place on the couch. I fear I shall need it."

Two golden eyebrows arched with surprise. "You do not think she will believe the truth?"

She would believe. 'Twas *when* she would believe that Lucan did not know. With Chloe, it could take weeks, if not months, for her to find faith in him once more. Time they did not have. He kept his thoughts to himself, unwilling to disclose her deep mistrusts and the confidences she had unwittingly shared in all she did not verbalize. "I will be late, I am certain."

Gareth shrugged off his concern. "I sleep like the dead." With the parting remark, the knight's grin returned, and he touched his knuckles to Lucan's shoulder. "Good luck, my brother. May your bed be warm, not cold this night."

Indeed. Lucan almost snorted. Frigid was far more likely.

Once Gareth was out of sight, and the hall once more empty, Lucan raised his fist to the door. It shuddered under his single, forceful knock.

"Julian?" Chloe called from within.

He did not answer, knowing if he announced his

presence, the barrier between them would not open. He would give her three seconds before he knocked again.

One . . .

From within, the noise from the television faded.

Two . . .

Light footsteps approached the door. The lock tumbled free. The brass handle turned.

Three . . .

As Chloe eased the door open a fraction, she let out a surprised squeak. Before she could slam the heavy wood shut, Lucan shouldered it open, barged inside, and quickly threw the lock. "We will talk. Now."

"Get out, Lucan."

"Nay. I shall not. We were speaking earlier, and I will finish what I have to say."

Stubborn defiance lifted her chin. Her eyes narrowed into angry slits. "You lied to me. I don't even know what name to call you. I don't want to see you."

Sheer arrogance drove him to an equally bitter retort. He leaned against the door, folded his arms across his chest, and stared at her. "Call me what you wish. Bastard. Traitor. Murderer—I have answered to them all. But in the year of our Lord 1097, I was christened Lucan. Second son to Richard, lord and master of Seacourt, as established by the letting from the abbey in 1080."

Chloe's eyes widened seconds before her brows furrowed in a severe frown and she scoffed. "And I'm the queen of Persia. Who are you?"

Undaunted, he held her stare. "Not of Persia. Of Seacourt, or what exists in memory. You are my mate, my bride, if you wish to look upon it so, and indeed, Chloe Broussard, you are my queen."

Her mocking laugh did little to hide the shock that registered behind her eyes. She shook her head and pointed at the door. "Just go. Leave me alone. You've done enough damage, no need to make it worse with more lies."

The barb stung. He had wounded her, but not of his own accord. Still he could not stop the needles that pricked his heart. Leaning forward, he caught her by the fingers and studied the back of her hand. He brushed his thumb over the soft flesh at the base of her palm. "Whatever you may think of me, 'tis one fact that shall not change." He lifted his gaze to hers, held it steady. "I am in love with you, and I will not leave until you hear me out."

He heard her breath catch. Witnessed the lowering of her lashes. Using her momentary weakness to his advantage, he asked, "Will you sit with me, or must we talk like this?"

She pulled her hand free, as if she could not stand the thought of touching him. "Fine. Sit. You have ten minutes."

He required hours, but he would take the offered ten. Grateful he did not have to try and explain with the door at his back and a gaping distance between them, he sat down on the couch. She glanced at the chair, piled high with her unpacked belongings. Then, with a mutter, she seated herself beside him. "Talk. The clock's ticking."

"I must ask one thing first."

"What?"

"Did you mean your words this morn? Or were they merely a product of the ecstasy we shared?"

Terror turned her complexion chalk white. Her eyes

darted about, resting everywhere but on his face. In her lap, her hands twisted into knots.

Lucan leaned toward her to cup her chin between thumb and forefinger. Gently, he turned her face back to his. "Tell me, Chloe," he whispered. "Did you yield to me your heart?"

The tears that pricked her wide eyes were answer enough. He dropped his hand away from her face. " 'Tis your heart I want you to listen with, for your mind will most certainly object to what I must impart."

She gave him silence. Permission to speak, but a complete lack of agreement. He let out a heavy sigh. "I have told you I am a Templar knight, and I have confided the year of my birth. Your brother was correct in two matters. First, my shield. I buried it with the man I spoke of, Gervais St. Soisson. I was there when he died. His shield shattered beneath the enemy's attack."

She recoiled with a grimace. "Stop."

"I will not." He grabbed her hand to thwart the distance she sought. "You know of the Templar. What you do not know is the purpose we serve. The demons you have seen—I exist to keep them, and others, out of the mortal realm. We are amidst a war, but I will share that with you in a moment."

Chloe let out a sound that resembled a whimper. Her shoulders sagged. Lucan cast off all apprehension and drew her against his side. He held her tight and stared at the silent images that flashed across the muted television.

"The second." He held his breath a moment, knowing this would affect her more than all the rest. 'Twas the single most likely reason to drive her away. For he had indeed misled her, and he could not get around that fact. "I do not work for the Church as you know it."

As expected, her spine stiffened. She tried to push away, to sit up and extract herself from his protective hold. He tightened his grip on her shoulder. "I work for the archangels. Mikhail is my superior. 'Twas Raphael who released me from the cell you sent me to. Gabriel, Uriel, Zerachiel, Phanuel, and others known to mankind for their roles in the creation of the world."

"You're insane," she whispered.

"Nay, I am not. Your heart knows this too."

She said naught, but the resistance against his hand diminished. Lucan relaxed with her. The worst of it over, the rest of what she must know would not bring them to battle. She would not accept it easily, but 'twas unrelated to any wrong he might have committed.

"My brother slaughtered my family to ensure he could obtain the woman, and the property, he wanted, though they were both beneath him. He was to inherit the larger, more prosperous lands, and upon our father's death, I would receive the smaller Seacourt. She was my betrothed, and her dowry pitiful compared to what my brother would receive with his agreed-upon pairing."

Lucan paused to draw in a breath. He frowned as the past played within his mind. "I would have surrendered the woman and Seacourt if I had known they meant so much. He chose a night when I was away to kill our father, our mother, and our youngest brother to ensure his desires could not be overruled. I returned, and he intended to see me to the grave as well. The last I saw of him was at the end of my sword. I went then to the Holy Lands and swore myself unto the Templar."

Memories rose to the surface, as vivid as if they had occurred yesterday. His introduction to Merrick. Time spent learning the Code and devoting himself to the purpose. The night he had learned the true calling of the Templar and stood before Gabriel willing to receive the curse of immortality, and along with it, the first touch of darkness that would torment him the rest of his days.

As the images scrolled through his head, he recited them to Chloe. Minutes passed, turned into hours. Beside him, she sat still as stone, taking in what he said, asking no questions and providing no further commentary. He showed her their matched birthmarks, told her of Gervais' death. Spared no detail as he described the horrific dark knight that had attacked his brother, and how he had witnessed the life drain from his eyes.

All of this, and more, she listened to. 'Twas not until he returned to the present, and the reason he now sat at her side, that she participated in the conversation.

"You are a descendant of the Nephilim, Chloe. In your veins, the blood of angels flows. In your soul, you harbor the light that will heal the taint inside mine. We were fated before the beginning of time. 'Twas not until Gabriel demanded I come here that I knew 'twas you I would spend eternity with."

"What?" she softly cried in disbelief.

"'Tis true, I swear to you. But the oath of loyalty I gave to you last eve has naught to do with any preordained pairing. It came from my heart. Although my soul needs you to survive, I, the man you see before you, cannot draw breath without you."

"Angels? Immortality? Lucan, you can't be serious!"

"Why else do you possess the ability to wound demons with mere thought? It is a seraph's gift—each of you possess specific, unique abilities."

Her frown returned, sharp creases that marked her

inability to explain the supernatural talent. He gave her silence to process the explanation. Sat with bated breath and waited for the furrows in her brow to smooth and acceptance to touch her eyes.

It did not come.

With a violent shake of her head, she abruptly stood. "Leave. I can't believe you expect me to buy into this."

"Chloe—"

"Go! I'm done being lied to!"

The determination in her face made further argument futile. His heart as heavy as if it had been cast in stone, he stood. "I will go. But 'tis one more thing I must tell you."

"What?" she snapped with impatience.

Lucan steeled himself against her certain fury and delved into the one subject she would never believe. "Your brother knows Azazel's touch. I will swear my life on it. You must say naught of this to him. To anyone. If you feared the demons, you do not wish to meet what will come if your status as a seraph reaches Azazel's minions." He added in a lower voice, "Not even I can protect you from the unholy one."

Chloe gritted her teeth so hard a tick pulsed at her temple. She glowered at him, her chest heaving with unspent fury. "Get. Out."

With naught else left to convince her, Lucan pulled the bronze arm torc from his pocket and set it on the table. "Show this to no one. When you are ready to wear it, you know where to find me." He gave her one last meaningful look, then quietly left the room.

CHAPTER 36

✝

Chloe's hands shook as she reached for the ringlet of bronze Lucan had left on the table. She sank into the couch, afraid her legs wouldn't hold her any longer. Immortality. Unholy beings. Angels?

Damn it!

How did anyone expect someone to believe that story? Because she had been haunted by demons and possessed an ability to keep them at bay? Good grief. Demons were one thing. What Lucan claimed was straight out of a sci-fi movie.

She turned the heavy armband over in her hands. He couldn't be over nine hundred years old. She'd made a playground out of his body, and there wasn't a wrinkle on any inch of that taut skin that would mark him a day over thirty-five.

And yet he knew things he shouldn't. Nothing would convince her that the secrets he shared in Picardie were anything but the truth. Or the facts about the engravings on le Goix's toppled wall. He couldn't glean all that from stories passed down through ancestors. They were too specific. Too detailed.

Too obscure.

Nine hundred years old.

She ran the tip of her nail over the double-headed serpent's scales. A greenish-red patina glimmered in the dim light, accenting the bright glint of each snake's ruby eyes. On their tiny heads, she found the one symbol she could go the rest of her life without seeing—the Templar cross.

How else do you explain . . .

How else *did* she explain? She'd gone her entire life without knowing she had a supernatural gift. Had consulted with countless religious leaders about the curse. Lucan came along, and he immediately knew the solution to the demons. He'd flat-out forced her to believe in him, and when she'd taken a leap of faith, he'd been right.

No everyday ordinary man would jump to that kind of conclusion. For God's sake, Blake and Julian laughed at her fear of the dark, and they were about as ordinary as a man could get.

I cannot draw breath without you.

Shivers gripped her as his voice echoed in her memory. Anyone could say *I love you.* Lucan took it further. Though he had admitted the simpler version, twice now, he had said so much more without the actual mention of love. Exactly how she felt about him, for *love* didn't encompass all the intense emotion. The word she had once feared now seemed far too ordinary.

As she toyed with the armband, the rubies winked like they shared some great secret and mocked the turmoil in her head. She ran her thumb over the roughened circumference. Old enough to rival some of the pieces she'd collected in the Egyptian tombs. And yet the crude artistry spoke of an even older age. Maybe this was just some piece that someone believed in. Like the ankh. A relic ancient people believed held power because of the symbols that it bore.

Maybe it wasn't.

What if he was right, and she was descended from the cast-out Nephilim?

She laughed softly. Good grief, she couldn't really be considering that possibility. It was absurd! Thirty years ago, she'd entered this world on the night of October 28, in a hospital in Tucson, Arizona. Her parents were Regina and Matthias Broussard, second-generation French Americans. They certainly hadn't been timeless or immortal. Unless cancer and heart attacks didn't apply to those two states of being.

But what if Lucan was right and she'd been chosen to spend eternity at his side?

She held the torc to the light and squinted at the serpents. Chloe of Seacourt—it had a nice ring. She'd never be the fairy-tale princess she'd yearned to become as a kid, but she could be Lucan's queen . . . at least figuratively. Tentatively, as if she tried the idea on as well as the trinket, she pulled her left arm out of her sweater and pushed the armband on. It fit snugly, just above the top of her bicep.

Lucan's bride . . . *Lady Chloe.*

A soft knock on her door made her jump. Embarrassed to be caught fantasizing about the impossible, she blushed and stuffed her arm back into her sweater. "Coming." It better not be Lucan. She'd kick him in the shins this time. Or Gareth. She couldn't deal with him either.

Her brother waited on the other side, concern etched into his expression. She swung the door wide, inviting him to enter.

"Are you okay? I saw Lucan in the hall."

"Oh God, Julian, I feel like such a fool." She fell into his outstretched arms and hung on tight. He held her, offering the familiar comfort she needed. If she'd listened to her brother, she wouldn't be in this predicament now. Thank heavens he wasn't the kind of person who'd rub in her lapse of judgment. He hadn't cared much for Blake either, but when Blake showed his true colors, Julian had never once made Chloe feel like she'd invited the heartache with her inability to see Blake for the bastard he was.

"I gave him everything. Fell in love. For this! God, I was so stupid."

"Don't beat yourself up about it." He patted the small of her back. "It's not your fault you're dumb about men."

Her cheek plastered against his shoulder, Chloe frowned. Dumb about men? Maybe she made mistakes, maybe she lacked clear judgment, but *dumb*? Not what one said to a heartbroken sister who needed comfort. And while Julian was a little rough around the edges, even he knew that.

She edged out of his hug and peered up at his face. Though he held her close, and made a good show of offering comfort, his expression held the blankness of boredom.

Boredom! Annoyance seeped into her veins, making her blood fizzle and pop. The fine hairs along her arms lifted in apprehension. Something was most definitely *not right* about her brother.

In the next heartbeat, however, his gaze dropped to

hers, full of all the compassionate warmth he'd shown moments ago. The endearing smile he gave her, along with the tightening of his arms, erased her apprehension. "Sorry," he apologized quietly. "I was just wondering how best to help you."

She stepped back, grateful she had at least one person in this world she could count on.

"Tell me everything." He led her to the couch where he urged her to sit.

She leaned back against the cushion. "I was saying I bought into everything he said. And when he's been caught, what does he say? Not, I'm sorry. Not, please forgive me." She let out a soft laugh. "No, he comes back with some ridiculous story about immortal Templar knights and seraphs." Leaning her head back, she looked up at her brother. "Can you believe that? He actually came back here and tried to tell me I was some descendant of an angel. Guess that explains your good looks, huh?"

"What?" Julian snapped forward to stare at her. "What did he say?"

His questions lacked the disbelief she'd given Lucan. His gaze bore into her in the most disturbing way. As if he looked all the way through her.

Or not at her at all.

She glanced over her shoulder, curious what captured his attention. But as she looked, his body followed hers. His expectant gaze set off the jangling of her nerves.

"What did he say?" Julian demanded more forcibly.

"H-he said I was . . ." *Tell no one.* Probably because they'd all realize he was crazy. She shrugged off Lucan's warning and her grin returned. "Some descendant of the Nephilim and could live forever."

When Julian reached between them and urgently

grabbed her hands, Chloe nearly jumped out of her seat. His grip was firm and tight. Painful where he pinched her knuckles together. "Hey, ease up. You're going to break my fingers."

"Did he give you anything?"

The anxiousness in her brother's voice gave Chloe pause.

Your brother knows Azazel's touch. Show this to no one.

For the umpteenth time she asked herself, what if Lucan was right? Pulling on her hands, she chose to play ignorant. "Give me anything?"

Julian tightened his grip and tugged on her arms so fiercely she had to lean in inches away from his face to ease the twist of her skin. "Ow, you're hurting me. Let go!"

"I asked you if he gave you anything."

"No, it was just some stupid story." She twisted with a grimace. "God, Julian, let go. What's wrong with you?"

Julian's uncharacteristic reaction did more to justify a stupid story than all of Lucan's carefully executed words.

He thrust her hands from his and abruptly stood. The blankness returned to his eyes. Though he looked straight at her, he didn't focus. Adding to her unease, the usual soft blue color of his eyes darkened to near black.

"Make sure you have the trunk tomorrow. Don't let him spend another minute with it."

Chloe blinked. The reliquary? Of all the goddamn things. Here she was in the middle of a crisis, and Julian wanted her to think about a relic they had yet to officially date?

With the measured precision of a formal guard, Julian turned crisply on one toe. He glanced down the length of his shoulder. Summoned an unnatural smile. "Good night, Chloe."

As the door firmly closed, icy fingers trailed down the length of her spine and curdled her blood. She huddled into the far corner of the couch, her arms wrapped around her knees, and stared wide-eyed at the drawn curtains. What the *fuck* was wrong with her brother?

Touched by Azazel.

Suddenly, the idea of being two floors away from Lucan seemed so very wrong.

Damn it all, she didn't know whom to trust anymore. Lucan came with fantastic stories. Julian was a different man from the one who'd left Tucson at her side.

No matter where she turned, big screaming, angry sirens of warning blared. No one was safe. No one offered security. Her rug had been ripped from beneath her, and the world she thought she understood tipped sideways on its axis.

Pain infiltrated all other awareness. It ravaged Julian from inside out, or maybe outside in—they'd become the same thing. Hadn't they? He could hardly keep his thoughts in line, let alone exercise the enormous amount of force required to override the beast that clawed at his soul, intent on ripping him into oblivion.

He let go, retreating to the safety of recessed shadows where the demon couldn't sense him. Stopping the thing from attacking Chloe had weakened him beyond the point where he could maintain control. For now, he would watch. Listen. Store what little energy he possessed for the next encounter. If he survived that long.

Looking out through eyes he no longer focused, he watched as his body entered the room he vaguely recalled renting when he'd arrived in January. Lights extinguished, he moved through the darkness with ease. But then, darkness was everywhere now. He no longer needed light. Shadows were second nature.

A man sat on his couch. The same man who had been here before. Eadgar. Declan's man. Or did Declan work for him? It didn't matter. They all commanded what he had become, and they all represented a threat to the only person worth the never-ending agony— Chloe.

Eadgar stood. "Julian, where is the Veil?"

"With the knight." Julian heard his voice answer, though he hadn't commanded it. No, the days of the beast requiring his presence to speak were long gone. It did as it desired, except for the rare occasion, like moments earlier, where Julian sensed Chloe was in danger and fought for control.

"I warned you before, if you did not produce it, I would."

"I have learned something you would find of interest."

Eadgar's harsh frown smoothed, his interest keen. "Do speak."

The beast sat, crossed one ankle over a knee. Julian looked down on the perfect facsimile of legs he knew by heart and choked back another pinprick of pain. What he would give again to walk. To know the freedom he'd once taken for granted.

"She's a seraph."

Though the response was short, and Julian didn't fully understand the meaning—he couldn't access the beast's mind as it could access his—what remained of his senses rose to high alert. Something deeper lay in the heavy words. Significance. And along with the utterance, he sensed the beast's unquenchable urge to kill.

Eadgar stalked to the small table near the window and turned on the lamp. The jerk of his arms, the snap of his wrist, all suggested he too shared the knowledge Julian lacked. He spun around, pinning the beast with a sharp squint. "Why did you not send for me upon immediately discovering this?"

"I only just learned it. Tonight she admitted Lucan confessed his immortality and her place amongst the Templar."

Julian had listened to Chloe's story. He'd wished like hell he could comfort her. Had tried for a few seconds before he'd been thrust aside and slammed into the corners where he could only watch and listen. Forced into mute idleness. Now he understood why. His sister's story, as absurd as it had sounded, was true. Why it mattered, he couldn't explain. But her status held importance.

It also put her in great danger.

Harm he not only felt emanating off the beast, along with its vile thirst for death, but also witnessed in the hard set to Eadgar's jaw and the beady glint of his eyes.

For several seconds, Eadgar did nothing but stare. His jaw worked soundlessly. His hands clenched and relaxed at his sides. Then, he expelled a harsh breath, and his voice cut through the thick silence. "I want them both. You will bring her, and the Veil. I will ensure you have aid."

No!

Julian surged forward, throwing every last ounce of strength he possessed into dominating the beast. Not

Chloe. Never his sister. He must stop this nonsense. Urge Chloe to go far from here. Back to Lucan if he could keep her safe.

He fought against the dark presence that engulfed him, striking out with blows that pummeled through him as much as they damaged his captor. The beast howled with rage, retaliated with the fury of a hundred men or more. And though they didn't battle physically, the stakes were the same. One of them would die tonight.

He gained control long enough to shout, "Stay the hell away from Chloe!"

Eadgar gave him an indifferent look and walked out the door.

As if someone had hurtled him into a stone wall, the beast grabbed hold and shoved Julian's spirit aside. Agony knifed through him. Blinded him. With sheer determination, he struggled toward the surface, desperate to emerge the victor and control this facsimile form. Chloe depended on him. He had to warn her. He knew what this creature was capable of, and if he did not stop it, his sister would believe *he* brought her harm.

Again, the foul creature thrust his presence aside, the clash more jarring than any high-speed collision. Long moments passed as their wills wrestled for ultimate power. Each grip of the dark presence squeezed off a little more of Julian's soul.

You can't have her!

Julian threw every last bit of strength he possessed at the vile being that dominated his spirit. In one relentless attack, he battered the despicable creature back. Beat on it like a madman until it shriveled into the same corner he'd sought refuge in. He took a moment to assess his surroundings. Stood and took a step toward the door, intent on warning Chloe to run like hell.

Then, with a combination of rage and might Julian had never witnessed, the beast surged out of its confined prison. It slammed into his soul like a sledgehammer.

A low guttural howl broke through the room, and Julian heard no more.

CHAPTER 37

A high-pitched ringing jarred Chloe from a fitful sleep. She jerked upright with a gasp. Bright sunlight poured through the window, slamming her eyelids back together with a groan.

The whining siren sounded again. From her left. Near the bed. The cause slowly connected in her foggy brain.

Telephone.

She dragged herself off the couch where she'd collapsed into a comatose-like slumber hours after Julian's departure. Long, mind-numbing hours where she couldn't bring herself to do more than huddle into a ball and sob until her eyes were as fat as golf balls and her throat resembled sandpaper.

Stumbling across the room, she caught the receiver as the god-awful wail issued for the third time. "Hello?" The hoarseness in her voice made her answer little more than a raspy whisper. She cleared her throat and tried again. "Hello?"

Lucan's rich baritone rumbled in her ear. "I have the results from our samples. I believe you would wish to see them."

Oh God. Not him. Not now. Why wouldn't he just go away? "Leave them at the front desk. I'll pick them up on the way to the site."

"Nay. I will not leave them with strangers. Dress. I am in the hall."

She spun around to stare at the door. "The hall?"

It was useless, the line buzzed in her ear. Damn it! She couldn't deal with him yet, wasn't ready to look him in the face and demote him to the status of co-worker. It'd take weeks to accomplish that, if it were even possible. If he'd just give her some space . . .

The light rapping on her door made space a fantasy. As determined as Lucan was, he'd stand out there all day. "Hold on," she muttered. She glanced down at her wrinkled shirt and twisted jeans, and groaned inwardly. The last thing she wanted Lucan to know was that he'd kept her up all night. She'd like him to believe she could just wash her hands and be done with him.

So much for that idea.

She rubbed her eyes and trudged across the room. Unwilling to give him the slightest clue her heart tripped at the thought of seeing him, she cracked the door open and stuck out her arm.

Lucan pushed on the door. Firm. Insistent.

Chloe stumbled back with a squeak and glared at him as he strode inside, looking every bit as if he believed he had the right to be here. His arrogance doubled her annoyance. "I don't *want* you here, Lucan. How hard is that to comprehend?"

Ignoring her, he made himself at home on the couch,

opened both envelopes, and spread the four pages of documentation across the coffee table. He studied the papers so intently that for a moment, Chloe thought he hadn't heard her. But in the next moment, he looked over the back of the couch and took her in with one sweeping gaze from head to toe.

"Aye," he murmured as he turned back around.

"Aye? What the hell is that supposed to mean?" Chloe came around to the front couch, indignant. "Why are you here? I don't need you to translate radiocarbon-dating reports for me. I've seen quite a few in my life."

He glanced up through his eyelashes, indifferent to her anger. "Aye, you speak falsely. You still wish to be near me as I wish to be near you."

She blinked. Opened her mouth to speak, only to find no words. How in the hell could he know that from simply looking at her? It might be obvious she hadn't slept well. But that only indicated she was upset. It had nothing to do with the fact her body cried out for him to take her in his arms, hold her close, and make this whole ugly mess go away.

She flounced down into the only open seat other than the bed—beside him. "If I look at this will you go away?"

"Nay. We have work to accomplish and agreements to come to regarding the Veronica."

Chloe cursed her bad luck, along with his steely determination. He wasn't going to make it easy to walk away. Then again, she shouldn't have expected he might. He hadn't made any of this easy from the day he'd arrived.

Sighing heavily, she leaned forward and picked up the envelope he'd sent to her preferred lab in Washington, D.C., where Dr. Noelle Keane had established the world's premier radiocarbon-dating facility. A shame she'd disappeared. She'd dated so many of Chloe's artifacts that Chloe felt she knew her personally and trusted her results implicitly. Whatever lay inside this envelope, she'd feel better about if the expert herself had dated the sample. Still, the facility's reputation couldn't be beat. She could be assured, regardless of who conducted the testing, the results were accurate.

She ripped open the flap and pulled out four sheets of paper similar to those Lucan had spread before them. Her chest tightened as she stared at the front page that documented what she had provided for testing. The next three pages would provide an analysis of the materials, regional comparisons to the organic and chemical compounds found in each tiny fiber. There would be a comparative analysis between the two strands, and on the very last page, she'd find what she already knew deep inside her heart. The Veil's age. As much as she longed for all Lucan's claims to be false, she knew it would place the sample close to the year A.D. 33, identifying it as originating in Judea.

Damn, this was a cruel, spiteful trick for God to play.

Trying to disguise the trembling of her hands, she set the documents in her lap and turned each page one at a time, letting them dangle over her knees. She skimmed the lines. Closed her eyes.

Silently swore every curse word she knew.

"This can't be right," she muttered as she tossed the paper onto the table.

Beside her, Lucan reclined with his arms behind his head. A self-satisfied smirk pulled at his full mouth and lightened his eyes. "Would you wish to review my findings? Or do you wish to argue the Veronica's existence more?"

Not yet ready to concede, she snatched up his results, reclined in the cushions, and perused the same data. Only, at the bottom of his document, something else caught her attention. Something more unbelievable than the relic that came out of a medieval archaeological site.

Scrawled across the bottom where the scientist of record signed, the customary neat tight script Chloe knew so well read *Noelle M. Keane*.

An additional note filled the last quarter of the page. *Lucan, have Chloe contact me if she has questions —N. K.*

Chloe rocketed forward. Her feet hit the floor with a *thump*. She flipped back to the front page, scouring it for the facility name. Nothing in the header. No address, no telephone number, no *nothing*. She turned wide eyes on Lucan. "Noelle?"

His smirk broadened into a wide grin. "Aye."

A thousand questions filled her mind. Where? How? What had happened to her? Chloe blinked rapidly as she tried to choose which one to ask first. She and the Egyptian Supreme Council of Antiquities had been waiting on data she'd sent directly to Noelle when Noelle disappeared. Then nothing. Their results didn't come. Phone calls went unanswered until Chloe finally received an evasive, "Dr. Keane's no longer with the facility." Internet searches yielded nothing—she'd tried like crazy to find where Noelle had taken another job just so she could continue to use her for field samples. Mutual professional associates hadn't heard a word. For all intents and purposes, it was as if Noelle had dropped off the face of the earth and given up on her life's work.

Lucan supplied answers before Chloe's tongue could function. Although his explanation left a little to be desired. "I trust you will wish to speak with her. 'Tis midnight in America. Noelle sleeps. We will phone her after we finish our business. Are you friends?"

"Just professionally," Chloe answered, bewildered.

Lucan snatched her hand and pulled her off the couch. He started for the door.

"Wait." Chloe pried at his fingers. "Where are we going?"

"You shall see."

Rooting her heels into the ground, she clawed at his hand. "I'm not going anywhere. Certainly not dressed like this. Turn me loose, Lucan. I'm finished with blindly following you around."

Thoroughly indifferent to her complaints, Lucan merely gave her a smile. "You look beautiful. As always."

Oh, damn. Now that was unfair. She tried to ignore the way his low voice made her stomach flutter. Looked away from his gaze before the intimate light in his eyes could melt the thin wall of ice she'd erected around her heart. But her legs gave up the protest, and she fell into silence as she followed him out the door.

At his room, Chloe waited in the hall, unwilling to confront the memories that would inevitably come if she stepped inside. Memories of all the passion they'd shared within those walls, along with the horrible confrontation and her request for his arrest. She couldn't face the combination. Could only deal with the here and now, and even that made her uneasy if she thought about it too long.

He took only a moment to retrieve the reliquary before he hurried her out the front doors to his SUV. There he let her inside, handed her the heavy trunk, and jogged around the front bumper to slide behind the wheel.

"Where are we going?" Chloe asked again as they nosed onto the main highway.

"To give you the proof you require." He glanced at her, then looked at her arm. "Do you have the serpents?"

With the question, she became aware of the band circling her bicep. Given her strange conversation with Julian and her crying jag, she'd forgotten all about the thing. Absently, she rubbed at it through her heavy sweater. "Yes."

Lucan said nothing, but she couldn't help but notice that the corners of his mouth lifted with the faintest hint of a smile.

She reclined her seat. He gave her silence, which she gratefully accepted. As they drove, her mind ran frantic circles. Noelle was a part of this. But what *was* this? Knights Templar, the Church, holy relics, seraphs— Lucan had told her so much, yet nothing that fit all the pieces together. No matter how much logic she put into his words, she couldn't move beyond the implausibility of it all. Moreover, if she chose to believe him, she'd have to not only accept all the unrealistic aspects, but accept her brother might not be her brother at all. That alone seemed like betrayal. Give up faith in Julian? Condemn him? In a hundred years she couldn't believe her brother had been touched by some unholy archangel.

Her gaze slid sideways to study Lucan's commanding build. Nine hundred years old? That would explain his unique accent. If he *were* a knight, that explained a lot of things. He didn't wear armor, but in every other sense he looked like one—slightly unkempt hair in the fact he didn't cut it. Strong body. The chivalrous way he saw to her needs first. His confidence. And that damnable arrogance that both annoyed her and turned her on like nothing else.

She twisted her head to look in the backseat and swallowed roughly when she spied his sword. That too fit the explanation. Possibly more than anything else. If she closed her eyes and recalled how naturally he wore it, she could easily see him in full armor.

But damn . . . No. It was impossible. There was something else he wasn't telling her. A missing link. Something that fit in between history and present day and explained all the lies. He *didn't* work for the Church. That much she knew. He'd even admitted it. And this nonsense with her brother was nothing more than testosterone. Lucan didn't like Julian, and Julian didn't like him. Both for the same reason—her.

The Veronica though . . . Scientific data proved it could very well be what Lucan claimed. While it could fit a lot of other parameters, and she might easily dismiss it as just another piece of cloth from the early era of Judaism, the idea that random cloths would survive centuries was a bit far-fetched. Cloth deteriorated unless someone took care to keep it safe. And someone would've had to have a damn good reason to keep a cloth through centuries. That those someones kept it in such an obviously holy case made all her desires to discover a more plausible explanation ridiculous.

"Lucan, I can't take this. Where are we going? And where's your friend Gareth?"

"Gareth already awaits us at our destination."

"And that is *where*?"

He took his eyes off the road long enough to reach across, meet her eyes, and give her hand a gentle squeeze. "To the European Temple of the Knights Templar."

A shiver filtered down her spine. Uncomfortable with the pleasant grip of his fingers, she pulled her hand away.

CHAPTER 38

✝

Four hours later, as the sun peeked over the high cliffs 46 miles northwest of Paris, Lucan brought the SUV to a stop at the closed gates to the château de La Roche-Guyon. He looked up at the keep perched at the peak of the cliff side and drew in a deep breath before he reached a hesitant hand across the console to awaken Chloe. As she stirred, he summoned the centuries-old facade he employed when it came to battle. Confidence. Outward calm. Show her naught of the nerves that shook his insides. But God's teeth, she did not make this easy.

"We are here," he murmured as her eyelashes lifted.

Scrubbing at her eyes, she brought the seat upright. She ducked her head to peek beneath the visor and stare up at the chalk-white mountain face and the château that lay at the base. "This is a temple?"

"In effect." He opened his door and motioned for her to do the same. When they stood in the parking lot, amidst the colorful cars belonging to the tourists lined up near the front entry, Lucan covered the reliquary with his coat and stuffed it beneath one arm. With his free hand, he took hers, in part to still his own disquiet, for touching her calmed the anxiety thrumming in his veins. The other—sheer pride. He would not have any man within question whom she rightfully belonged to, even if all knew he had journeyed across the sea to retrieve her.

"We will go in through the side."

She matched his quick pace, chin tucked against her chest to ward off the wind that rolled through the valley. Ahead, a brass-studded wooden door swung open in greeting. Gareth stood within.

Lucan pulled Chloe to a quick stop just inside the plain stone entry. "'Tis one thing you must know. Should any man offer you his sword, you need say naught when you return it. But we will use the tunnels in hopes of avoiding the distraction."

She blinked, then furrowed her brows. "Offer his sword?"

"'They are bound to swear loyalty to you." Before she could ask further questions he could not easily answer, Lucan gave Gareth a nod of readiness and struck off down an off-shooting corridor that wound behind the public-access buildings and the château proper to the chambers buried in the cliff.

He slowed, allowing Chloe to take in her surroundings at her leisure. Though he had long ago become accustomed to the sigils in the walls, the cipher that only those who upheld the Code could read, and the hand-tooled stone, he gave her time to trace her fingers along the chiseled marks. She studied. She admired. And yet she said naught. No single word slipped passed her lips until they had walked almost a mile and entered the vast central chamber of the inner sanctum.

Chloe stopped spellbound and gaped up at the mosaic ceiling and the elaborate arches carved into the natural rock. "Ho-ly . . ." She exhaled through her teeth.

"Aye, holy," Lucan agreed as he surveyed the works of the masters and allowed the presence of the divine to infiltrate his awareness. "Welcome to the temple, Chloe." He lowered his voice in reverence. " 'Twas built by the men who took their oaths just before I. Men whose hands were guided by the archangels. No more sacred place exists in this world. Not even the temple in America knows this greatness."

He watched as her eyes scanned over gold gilt reliefs and life-size statues of knights, gargoyles, and the angels themselves. Observed as a shiver possessed her and she inched closer to his side, as if the magnitude of it all was too much to take in at once. He tugged on her hand, drawing her down a wide hall off the circular nave. "You may look to your heart's content after we speak with Raphael."

Wide eyes rested on him for a painstaking heartbeat that stirred to life all the deep emotion he had tried to stifle. The urge to sweep her into his arms, haul her against his chest, and devour her parted lips until she could not believe in anything but the magic that flowed between them struck like a fist of stone. His chest swelled so painfully he thought his ribs might crack. Saints' blood, how could she not feel the same magnetic pull? How could she believe naught else but that they were fated? The very air crackled with the energy they shared.

Steeling himself against the uncomfortable tingling

of his skin, he set his hand on the heavy iron knocker and dropped it against the aged wood.

"Yes?" Raphael called from within.

"'Tis I, Lucan."

"Come in, Sir Lucan." Raphael's low voice drifted through the heavy wood. "Gareth, wait outside."

Lucan pushed the door wide, allowing a golden wash of light to spill into the hall. He escorted Chloe inside, his nerves as unsteady as his pulse. He feared the hope that this meeting might change her mind, yet he could not stamp it out of existence. More than the oath of seraphs and the healing of his soul, he longed for her acceptance of their love. Of him. The man who had come to at last find faith in something—her.

"Chloe Broussard." Raphael stood from a rich mahogany chair, hands outstretched to take hers. His lyrical voice resonated through his chamber, as if he had mayhap sung the greeting. "How I have waited for this day, when a seraph would stand within my temple. Mikhail quite gloats that he has seen the coming of two." A smile broke across his regal features to light his blue eyes with the crystalline sparkle of a deep tranquil pool. "Blessed am I to welcome the loveliest."

Chloe flushed so deep and hot, Lucan nearly laughed aloud. She dipped her head, her shyness setting in. But she allowed Raphael to take her hands, and as she found the courage to lift her gaze to his, Lucan knew the moment she had opened her mind to her seraph's status. She looked not on Raphael's face, but behind him, at the wall where the shadow of his majestic wings could be seen. With a gasp, she took a step backward and bumped into Lucan's chest. He set a hand on her shoul-

der to steady her resulting forward stumble and to offer
his silent support.

"Thank you for returning to me the Veronica." Raphael paid no heed to her reaction and bent his tall
frame to set a kiss upon her cheek. "I understand you
have questions concerning why we allowed it to remain
in the ground for so long and how it came to be there in
the first place?"

"Y-yes. I think." She tugged her hands free, turned
away from both Lucan and Raphael, and distanced herself by standing at the opposite end of the room, closer
to the door. As if she sought to flee, should the conversation become too uncomfortable.

"I think, 'tis best suited for you to hear it from the
man who was charged to protect the Veil originally."

Lucan stiffened, knowing this might well push Chloe
to the limits of her cooperation. Too much too soon, and
she had a habit of retreating to the safety of what she
believed she understood. Yet he could not argue with
Raphael. 'Twas his charge. His relic to guard, and his
man to command. So Lucan waited. Stiff as a board,
jaw clenched and fists tight against his thighs as the office door opened and Alaric le Goix stepped inside.

At once, Alaric drew his sword and dropped to a
knee before Chloe. He set the long blade before his
prostrated foot, laid his elbow on his bent knee, and
bowed deeply over it. "Milady. I am Alaric le Goix,
commander of the European Knights Templar, and I
pledge myself unto your service."

Chloe's eyes jumped to Lucan. In them, he read the
combination of disbelief, wonder, and confusion. But
'twas not his place to offer an explanation. Instead, he
encouraged her with a subtle nod of his head.

Tentatively, she reached down and picked up the heavy broadsword. Shaking arms extended, she offered him the weapon. Alaric wasted no time in collecting it, standing, and quickly sheathing it. As he did, he gave her the smile that had won over many a fair maiden in their earliest days, including his long-ago wife.

In that instant, Lucan came to understand Raphael's decision to introduce her to le Goix. No other man could present himself, nor their circumstances, with such grace. If anyone were to lift the burden of unease from her shoulders and make her feel at home, 'twould be the eloquent commander.

"I understand you have been exploring my home. I do wish you could have seen it in its glory. 'Twas a grand place to rear children once. The forest full of a day's adventure and the grounds safer than any keep within the province. We did not want for much there. Now, I fear 'tis naught but a ruin."

To her credit, Chloe smiled. She glanced at a nearby chair, then to Lucan once again. He gave her permission to sit with a slight gesture of his hand. He, however, remained with his back to the wall, one booted ankle crossed over the other.

Alaric pulled a stool out to sit across from her. "I would like to apologize for the trouble my ring created. You see, when I took the Veronica from Rome, to protect it from the brigands of Charles' barbaric army, I was injured." He extended his hand, palm up and splayed his fingers wide. Using the index finger of his opposite hand, he traced a deep scar that ran between the inside of his third and fourth fingers. "I foolishly grabbed a blade meant for my head. My hand swelled, and I left my ring with the reliquary, intending to re-

turn for it. I did not make it back before the castle toppled in an attack by troops from Lorraine, and I quite
forgot about my ring over time."

He chuckled. "Listen to me go on. I am sure you have
no desire to hear about my follies. Milady, may I offer
you a tour of this temple? There are all kinds of things
I am sure would catch your interest within."

"Um." Chloe twisted her hands in her lap.

"We have many other relics in these chambers of
stone, equal to the Veronica. Has Lucan told you the
importance of it and why Azazel covets it?"

For the first time since they had left the château, her
eyes sparked with interest. She shook her head. Leaned
imperceptibly forward.

"Azazel challenges the Almighty's throne. With eight
relics, he will obtain the power to ascend and claim that
holy station. He possesses the nails from the crucifix-
ion. They bear the power of the blood. He possesses the
Sudarium of Oviedo." He stood to open the reliquary
and withdrew the cloth. Gingerly unfolding it, he set it
across her knees so the dark stains were visible, and
tapped one large splotch. "If the Veronica is joined with
the Sudarium, it reveals not the face of Christ as many
would have you believe, but instead, the language of
Raphael and his brothers. The words unleash the power
to set Christ's tears into the Spear of Destiny, which
grants Azazel the right to claim and hold the holy
crown."

Chloe squeezed her eyes shut tight. Shook her head
as if she tried to shake off the news le Goix delivered.
When she opened them again, she frowned so deeply
her brows became one. "Maybe that tour would be nice
after all."

"Aye. As you wish." Alaric collected the cloth and passed it to Raphael. "Let us start then in the inner sanctum. We shall talk about this curse we all suffer, and the fates of those who crafted the walls."

As they headed for the door, Lucan stepped forward, intending to join them. But Alaric thwarted his designs with a halting lift of his hand. Chloe stepped through the doorway, and Alaric shook his head at Lucan. "I will look after her, Sir Knight, as if she were my own."

Every last particle of Lucan's being revolted at the idea of leaving Chloe's side. 'Twas his fate they discussed. His place to teach her the role she must fulfill. Yet, in his heart, he knew he was too close to her to succeed. He cared too much for her, and what they shared alone was enough to give her hesitation. Hating that he must accept what he did not wish to confront, he gritted his teeth and backed away.

CHAPTER 39

†

Darkness had fallen by the time Alaric escorted Chloe back to Raphael's office. With the heavy walls of stone around her, she couldn't see the night sky, but the hearty aroma of meat, potatoes, and fresh bread drifting through the corridors announced sunset.

Her hand tucked into the crook of Alaric's elbow, she followed along wordlessly. Silence fell between them, though he had talked most of the day. He explained the purpose of the Templar, much the same as Lucan had. He explained the seraphs, but where Lucan had shared only the most prominent information, Alaric told her of Anne and Noelle, of the threats they had overcome, of the fate that awaited the knights who weren't yet paired.

Her mind reeled with the knowledge he imparted. The facts that seemed so fantastical but could be backed by artifacts and documents he'd shared with her as well. Written accounts no mere human had seen, or ever would. Journals crafted by the archangels that held so much power, she felt the might within seep into her skin.

The final evidence she needed to be convinced of everything came with a brief phone call to Noelle. Alaric left her to talk in private, and though Noelle had been called away, Chloe heard enough to realize her wrongs.

And she'd been so very wrong.

Now, armed with the knowledge of centuries, she understood her purpose. Lucan's purpose. It was a bit surreal to think she'd descended from angels. That the Almighty chose her for this role long before she had ever taken her first breath. But the revelation also gave her strength she'd never before experienced. Beyond all the battling of demons and dark knights, she existed for one reason. Sure, Alaric could talk about how her oaths would aid the Templar cause, but all the justifications stopped with one. Lucan. She alone could heal him.

He'd known it from the day they'd met. He had bent over backward to prove himself to her, and she'd shoved him aside at the first rocky road they encountered. She'd allowed Julian to interfere with what her heart understood, and she'd wronged Lucan. Maybe even more so than his murderous brother had. At least *he* had possessed reason, no matter how thin it might have been. All she possessed was a handful of excuses and a whole lot of spinelessness.

Alaric knocked on the door to Raphael's office but opened it before anyone could bid him entrance. She stumbled in after him, feeling Lucan's presence and yet unable to look at him for fear, now that her eyes had been opened, she might see the hurt she'd caused. She looked to Raphael instead and gave herself a swift mental shake. An archangel. Good Lord. If someone

had told her she'd stand in the same room with one of
the angels of creation, she'd have laughed until she wet
her pants. Today, however, she'd met two. Raphael, and
the healer, Zerachiel. Incredible didn't define the experience. It came close, but . . .

A hand settled on her shoulder, the pressure familiar,
the gesture one she knew by heart. Her pulse ratcheted
up a notch as she caught Lucan's masculine scent. Hers.
His. She'd been so afraid of getting hurt that she'd seen
what she wanted to see. Heard what she chose to hear.
He ought to be thoroughly disgusted with her by now.

Raphael's smile touched her seconds before he looked
behind her, presumably at Lucan. "I believe 'tis time for
me to dine." He stood from his chair and grabbed a
thick cloak from an iron spike embedded into the wall.
"Alaric, come and share with me your news."

"Aye, sir." Alaric caught her by the wrist. Bending at
the waist, he slid his fingers down to clasp hers and
lifted the back of her hand to his lips. "A pleasure,
milady. I shall look forward to our next meeting."

It struck her then, as his eyes held hers for the
briefest of heartbeats, how similar Alaric and Lucan
were. Like le Goix, Lucan had treated her with charm,
chivalry, and manners more refined than any fraternity
boy's housemother could ever *think* of teaching. Lucan
changed though, as they'd spent more time together. He
became more bold, more assertive with her. A bit
more . . . primal.

She liked the change in him. As much as she liked
the change he brought to her. And although Alaric made
the afternoon pleasant, she much preferred Lucan's
self-assured smirks and mocking grins.

The door closed, and they were alone. Tension filled

the empty spaces Alaric and Raphael left behind. What to say? Where to start? She still had questions, specific things she'd deliberately left unasked because she wanted Lucan's answer, not Alaric's. She had oaths to say, vows to make. But before she could just turn around and spit out the words Alaric taught her, she needed to smooth things over. Somehow make up for the last day and a half.

Slowly, she turned. Gray eyes regarded her cautiously, as if Lucan also suffered the same doubt over what to say first. Chloe looked around, suddenly claustrophobic, despite the spacious enclosure. Too much stone. Cold, unfeeling rock. For this talk, this pledge of eternity, she needed something less constricting.

She gave Lucan a weak smile. "Do you think we could get some fresh air?"

"Aye," he murmured absently. "I could use a bit myself."

The bronze armband weighed heavily around her arm as Lucan led her through the torchlit passageways. Each echoing step made her more jittery, until they at last exited onto the street outside the château, her insides shook like a leaf on a blustery autumn day. Like that leaf, she held onto the last bit of normalcy with a fragile grip. In a few moments she'd surrender her hold. Tumble off the branch of security to begin anew. With luck, Lucan would still be there to catch her.

As they passed a stone bench in the public garden, Chloe dragged him to a stop and took a seat. Frowning, he glanced at a bench farther away, beyond an iron fence, as if he considered moving there. After a moment, he lowered himself down beside her and clasped his hands together in his lap. Staring off into the distance, he made no attempt to ease the crackling tension with conversation. Which meant she'd have to broach the subject.

She took a deep breath, fixed her gaze on an opposing fir. "You didn't tell me you were dying."

"Would it have made a difference? 'Tis more likely you would have dismissed it along with all else."

Okay, so she deserved the brittle edge in his voice. But if he really thought she wouldn't have given pause to a claim of death, he had to be stupid. She resisted the brimming smart remark and let her gaze slide sideways to study his profile. "How long do you have?"

Lucan clenched his hands together more tightly. 'Twas not the way he had envisioned her adventure through the temple would turn out. Pity, he did not desire. Nor would he have her give her oath for such. "Long enough."

Whether 'twould be long enough to gain her eternal favor, he could not be certain. So impassive was her expression, he could not guess at what thoughts ran through her head. Had Alaric made a difference? Did she now regret the fate he had brought her to? Mayhap even their meeting?

In all his existence, Lucan had never known such apprehension. Far greater than the worry of any battle with the heretics of old was his worry she would turn away. That her hours in the temple would not lead her into his arms, as he desired, but that Alaric had pushed them further apart. She possessed the right to refuse. 'Twas her choice as a mortal. But beyond the price he would pay with his soul, he could not bear the thought of a day spent away from her. One already pushed him to the edge of madness. He ached to fold her into his arms, taste the sweet honey of her kiss, and he ached for the feel of her, wrapped around him, holding him in the intimate way that only lovers could know.

He shifted uncomfortably, the stone bench as cold as the night air surrounding them. His gaze drifted again to the bench that sat on sacred ground behind the protected fence. Chloe kicked a toe into the hard earth and twisted it. Between them, silence hung like a thick, dark curtain. Seconds passed, turned into minutes. Unbearable, silent moments that filled Lucan with restlessness. He rose to his feet, unable to tolerate another breath of idleness. "We should move beyond the fence. 'Tis not—"

"I owe you an apology," Chloe murmured in a near whisper.

He halted, one foot in front of the other, ready to lead them to where they could talk safely. He stared at the ivory statue of a cherub and answered in an equally quiet voice, "You owe me naught."

From the corner of his eye, he observed the way she hung her head and twisted her hands. He took a step closer to the protective barrier. "Come, Chloe, we are not—"

"What is my role?"

Her question came so softly he almost did not hear her. Certain he had heard incorrectly, he turned around with a puzzled frown. "Pardon?"

Chloe looked up, her eyes full of quiet acceptance. "My role. My job. If I am this seraph, what am I supposed to do? Beyond this oath I'm required to say."

His heart drummed to a standstill. She believed. God's teeth, *she believed.*

He returned to the bench and clasped her hand. Her

fingers fit daintily against his larger palm. She made no attempt to withdraw. Though she did not tighten her grip either.

Lucan dropped to one knee. Held her gaze so there could be no mistaking his sincerity. "I do not know what the archangels might ask of us. Of you. You possess the gift to fight demons with your mind, and I expect you will be called to use that talent."

Her chin dropped, and her gaze returned to her feet. He closed his fingers around hers, lowering his voice. "If I were to write the rules, 'twould be only one, Chloe."

Hesitantly, her eyes lifted to his. "And it would say?"

Emotion clogged his throat as he ran his thumb over the back of her hand. "That every day passed as the one we shared two days hence, and every night, I would spend in your arms." He swallowed hard, cleared his voice. "I love you, Chloe. 'Tis all I wish from you as well."

Beneath the light of stars, her eyes glistened with a rush of tears. She choked out a laugh and tugged her hand from his. "You have that, Lucan of Seacourt. I couldn't take it back if I wanted to."

With a smile that made his heart take wings and soar, she shrugged out of her heavy wool coat. Sliding one arm up the large sleeve of her sweater, she fiddled with the armband beneath. Lucan's heart swelled to painful limits, and for a moment, he knew the fierce rush of nerves a groom experienced before his bride walked down the aisle. He had cared naught for Enid beyond the matter of fulfilling family duty. The wedding their families planned, though simple in comparison to the modern ceremonies, brought no anticipation. He had felt more excitement over the battle he would depart for the morning after than for the marriage itself.

But as Chloe eased the torc from beneath her clothing, a tremor ran down his spine. Though there would be no lavish ceremony, no church, the words they would speak to one another produced so much feeling he feared for a moment he too would weep. He reached for his sword. The scrape of metal as he pulled it free from its sheath rang in the quiet. Reverently, he laid it at Chloe's feet.

Bowing his head, he said naught. He had already pledged his loyalty in a way far more meaningful than this ceremonial offering of his blade.

Her fingers touched the polished steel. She picked it up, extending it toward him. *"Meus vitri, meus—"*

A boot flashed in front of Lucan's face. Steel clattered against the stone as his sword hurtled sideways. Another kick planted one heel in his chest, and Lucan toppled backward. As he scrambled to gain his footing, Chloe's scream pierced the night.

On his knees, he looked up to find Julian wedged between them, his sneer as vile as the odor that permeated the air. But his cruel expression did not hold Chloe's horrified stare. She looked beyond Lucan's shoulder, at a figure he could not see.

The clink of chain told him what she witnessed. A dark knight. Sent to collect her. To exterminate him. God's blood, Julian had followed them here!

Lucan rolled sideways, collecting his sword. As he sprang to his feet, he spun to confront his fallen brother and bellowed to Chloe, "Get beyond the fence!" Damnation, he should have insisted they move.

An onyx blade arced through the air, landing a

heavy blow on Lucan's forearm. Fire sizzled up his arm. Tingled all the way down his back. Gritting his teeth against the hot flow of blood, he took a step back. Without his armor, he dared not make another mistake. Though his brother, whomever he might be, now aided Azazel's army, he would recall the years of training. 'Twould be foolishness to judge the dark knight as anything less than formidable.

He ignored the burn in his shoulder and raised his sword to defend another strike. At his left, a howl broke out, drawing his attention to the demon that accompanied Julian and the fallen Templar. He shifted his gaze a fraction, in time to witness the creature lift jagged claws to the gaping wound across his face that Chloe had inflicted.

Despite her aid, her presence distracted him with worry. Whilst she stood so close, he could not focus on his opponent. 'Twas not him they desired, but her, and he must protect her at all costs. He backed up again, deliberately placing himself between her and the three unholy creatures. "Go, now, Chloe!"

Without waiting for her response, he sliced his broadsword across his body. It slid through the demon's arm as if the limb contained no more substance than a thin sheet of paper. Shadows dropped to the stone beneath their feet, and another ghostly howl rang through the air. Satisfaction burst inside Lucan. 'Twould take little to overpower the unholy shape shifter. He could not slay it first though, for in so doing, when he absorbed its evil taint, he would leave himself wide open for the knight to land a felling blow. Nay, he would cripple it. Devote himself to the larger threat of the knight, then finish them both off before the darkness could affect him.

Julian, he would deal with last. He remained Chloe's brother, regardless of the darkness that gripped him. If Lucan could spare the man's life and somehow restore him to the light, he would. For her.

The knight moved in, landing another heavy blow to Lucan's left thigh. Cold steel bit into his muscle. Lucan stumbled, barely catching himself on his good leg, before the demon raked its claws down his back. His bellow held both the sting of pain and rapidly building fury. Anger he allowed to flow through his veins and possess him. It gave him strength. The searing burn fueled his determination.

He summoned his resolve, blocked out the throbbing of his leg and the sticky wetness that seeped beneath his jeans, and planted his weight on his bad limb, giving him the force required to thrust his blade forward, into the knight's left hip. As his former brother barked in agony, Lucan took a sidestep that brought him into the knight's body. He threw his momentum into a downward cut that slashed through the onyx chain to rip open the knight's shoulder.

Behind him, the demon recognized advantage. Foul breath washed down the back of Lucan's neck as the beast dragged its daggerlike teeth across his shoulder. His shirt tore. Acid ran in long veins between his shoulder blades. He cried out. Arched his back to escape the assault.

Whilst his actions served to do just that, they left him open to a recovery attack from the knight. A ghostly voice rasped, "Victory is not yours to claim." No sooner had the words left the man's mouth than the tip of a sword pricked into Lucan's unprotected side.

Lucan twisted sideways before the blade could sink

in deep. With his attackers once more in front of him, he redoubled his efforts on the demon. Yellow teeth gnashed as Lucan advanced. He measured his steps, kept his approach well out of the path of the knight's reach. Like a falcon, he swept down on his prey. Blow after blow drove the monster to the stone floor. Claws ravaged the air near Lucan's shins. Hisses broke through its deadly teeth. Driven by the habits of a lifetime at war, Lucan blocked out the aching in his body and lifted his sword high.

He brought it down like a guillotine. Aiming at one shadowy arm, he severed it at the shoulder.

Before he could pull in a breath of recovery, the knight set upon him again. A mistimed blow glanced off the back of his hand and scraped down the length of his blade. He brought his broadsword up to his body with so much force he sent the knight stumbling backward. Advantage claimed, he pursued.

Nine hundred years of shared battles and enemies gave the two equal ability to anticipate the other's actions. No doubt he had sparred with this man on more than one occasion. He blocked when Lucan sliced. Evaded when he thrust. And parried with the skill of a soldier who had known a lifetime of victory.

Lucan's strength waned. His breath came hard and fast. But though his body tired, he witnessed the same effects take hold of his opponent. The knight's arm slowed. His timing faltered. When he thrust forward, 'twas with less vigor. Less precision.

And then he made a fatal mistake.

Sensing the toll the battle took on the knight, Lucan baited. He feinted to the right, aiming a false blow to the knight's vulnerable underside of his left shoulder.

His opponent bought into the distraction. Seeing Lucan in a weakened position, he dropped his shoulder. His right arm arced against the backdrop of the cliffs. A shadowy blade silhouetted in the moonlight.

With all the might he likely possessed, he took his blade in both hands and brought it toward Lucan's chest. Lucan moved faster. He threw himself forward, sinking his sword into the vulnerable area beneath the knight's arm and out through his back. Bone grated across the edge of Lucan's blade. Splintered near the point of exit.

He stuffed his foot into the knight's gut and shoved. His broadsword pulled free as his opponent careened backward. Chasing after, Lucan swung like a man possessed. His blade sang through the air. Thumped against the links of protective chain around the knight's neck. Then sank deeper.

In one swift follow-up slice, he severed the knight's head from its neck. Before the darkness could creep down the length of Lucan's blade, he whirled in a half circle. His sword arm swept before his body and slammed into the demon at his feet. The blade dug deep into the creature's abdomen, spilling its unholy essence. Its grotesque face contorted. Needle-thin teeth snapped together.

As death claimed the beast, darkness crept over Lucan's hand to sink into his veins and spread through his body. Fire seared through him, choking off an anguished groan. He staggered under the vile assault that threatened to steal his vision and knock him into unfeeling oblivion. Sword tip braced on the hard stone beneath his feet, he sank to one knee and clung to the pommel, willing himself not to faint.

He pulled in one shallow breath after another until the buzzing in his head ceased. When he no longer felt as if he might topple over face-first, and strength returned to still the shaking of his arms, he lifted his head, prepared to confront Julian. 'Twould take but one blow, severe enough to halt his retreat, but well placed to prevent his death. Then he would drag the man before the archangels, before even Chloe, and force her to recognize the threat her brother posed.

But as Lucan lifted his head, he found no trace of Julian.

Or Chloe.

No footsteps marred the snow between the side entrance and the garden. No Templar charged through the door as they should have if she had made it inside. He turned in a circle, scanning the gardens for some sign of her retreat.

At the sight of two pairs of footprints leading away from the garden to the thick trees beyond, his pulse quickened. It could not be. She would not leave with him. Not when she knew the truth and had accepted her predestined fate.

He squinted to examine the trail more closely. The narrower, leftmost set of tracks scuffed and blurred, as if she had not gone willingly. As if she had been dragged.

His heart lodged in the back of his throat. God's blood, he had failed her completely. What Azazel would do with her . . .

Lucan's veins filled with ice.

CHAPTER 40

†

Lucan ran through the tunnels, oblivious to the blood streaming down his arms and back. His boots pounded a frantic beat that matched the frenetic thump of his heart. Vision of Iain's seraph, and the horrifying things Azazel had done to her, played over and over in his head. Chloe laid out on a bed, opening her body to the unholy master's touch. Chloe embracing his seductive words.

Chloe crumpled on the ground, her heart still warm atop her chest.

And if she could not find the strength to refuse the lord of darkness, she would suffer a worse fate. Bearer of his evil offspring. Willing partner to all his vile desires. Lilith reborn, to reign at his immoral side.

Nay!

Lucan ran faster. He had fought demons, spent a lifetime at war, and had never known true fear. Now, terror coursed through his veins like poison, each clang of his heart spreading the infectious emotion. He burned with it. Broke out in a sweat.

He passed the mess where his brothers dined, their laughter rich and their conversation rumbling with warmth. Heads turned. A shout ricocheted over the din. "Lucan!"

Ignoring the call, he rounded a corner and descended deeper into the temple. Two pairs of boots joined the echo of his. He did not look back. Whoever followed would soon learn what propelled him blindly forward. Soon the entire Order would know he had allowed his heart to override sense and opened Chloe to this fate. If he had not entertained her suggestion to go outside, if he had kept her within these walls until her vows were completed, she would not now suffer.

If he had insisted they move beyond the fence . . .

At Raphael's chamber, he did not stop to knock. He shoved the door open with so much force it crashed into the stone wall, then shuddered on its hinges. "Chloe has been taken!"

The exclamation burst from his chest, and he doubled over, hands braced on his knees, panting. "Her brother . . . took her . . ."

Behind him, two men skidded to a stop. Their swords clanged against the door frame he blocked. He lifted his head, prepared for the inevitable lecture on his failings.

Raphael slowly extricated himself from behind a small desk. The journal he perused, he closed and set to the side. His gaze fell on Lucan, flat and unemotional. "Sir Knight, you bleed upon my floor. Take yourself to Zerachiel, then we shall speak."

Shock brought Lucan upright. Mend himself? He had not been wounded significantly enough to warrant the healer's touch. And he would not waste time with such nonsense whilst Chloe's life was in danger. "Did you not hear me? Chloe has been taken."

Raphael lifted a golden eyebrow in reproach. "Did you not hear *me*? You are to take yourself to the infirmary."

"Nay!" He strode forward and thumped a fist atop the archangel's desk. "I serve Mikhail. You cannot command me thus. Chloe's fate is of greater consequence!"

A moment of uncharacteristic anger darkened Raphael's beautiful face. His blue eyes clouded with sparks. Spots of color stained his cheeks. The air rippled as he undulated his disguised wings. Lucan stood his ground, his own fury equally tangible in the clench of his fingers, the tightness of his jaw. They stared at one another, each unwilling to bend, determined the other would yield.

Then, as if Lucan's words connected with Raphael's mind, the archangel turned his back to Lucan. "Alaric, enter," he murmured with the beckoning of his hand.

From the corner of his vision, Lucan observed le Goix step through the doorway. He moved to Lucan's side, his spine rigid, one hand resting on the hilt of his sword. "Aye?"

Behind his desk once more, Raphael bent over. When he stood again and turned to face the men, he held the reliquary in his hands. He dropped it on the desk and leaned his weight atop the lid. As he spoke, his gaze remained on le Goix. "Take Gareth and another of your choosing. Escort Sir Lucan to Zerachiel and see that his wounds are mended fully."

Anger morphed into fury as Lucan listened to the orders that circumvented the chain of command. He took a step forward, possessed by the urge to drive his fist into Raphael's teeth. Stuffing a wayward hand against his thigh, he checked himself, aware that to attempt such would be naught but foolish folly. Raphael could steal the breath from his lungs with the lift of a divine finger.

The archangel's gaze fell on him, laden with warning. "Do not forget yourself, Sir Knight." He pushed the reliquary to the edge of the desk. "*When* you have healed yourself so you can be of use, you will accompany Alaric and his men through the sixty-third gate, where you will exchange the Veronica for Chloe." Eyebrows lifted, he looked down his nose. "Lest, of course, you should find my *orders* disagreeable."

Chagrin squelched the burn of anger, and Lucan relaxed his fist. In the next heartbeat, the full meaning of Raphael's offering crashed upon him. Exchange the relic? Give Azazel the power he desired? He fumbled for words.

Alaric beat him to a cry of disbelief. "You cannot mean to hand over the key to the cipher!" He cast a sideways glance at Lucan. "My apologies, brother, I know Chloe means much to you. But our purpose is to prevent the acquisition at all costs."

Lucan nodded. The same conflict waged inside him. Whilst his heart leapt at the one means certain to see his seraph's return, the idea of surrendering a relic warred with the Order's very purpose. Sacrilege—'twas as if the archangel sought to play directly into the dark master's hands!

Raphael clasped his hands at his waist and rounded

the desk to stand before the two men. A dip of his head beckoned Gareth inside. He entered, his expression one of equal disbelief.

With a pinched frown, Raphael looked between them. "Need I remind you of Chloe's importance? If the prophecy is broken, the seraphs who remain shall be lost. All of you will fail. The war we wage becomes certain defeat, and the world we have sought to protect for so long will shrivel under eternal damnation." His gaze lingered on Lucan. "'Tis more than the matter of your salvation or the love you stand to lose. Were you not part of the prophecy, I would turn my back with the deepest of regrets. Chloe, however, is part of a greater fate. Your oaths more important than your personal pleasure."

He did not say the words that reflected in his eyes. But Lucan heard them anyway: *If you had considered the greater consequence and brought her here the night of your arrest, this would not be necessary.* Lucan bowed his head under the weight of the truth.

"Do you wish to remind me again who you report to, Lucan? Or do you wish to accept my orders?"

Eyes closed in silent apology, Lucan answered, "I will see Zerachiel."

"Good then. I trust you shall wish to depart for the catacombs as soon as possible. Since we are agreed, Alaric will remain with me whilst my brother sees to your wounds, and I shall instruct him further."

Dutifully, Lucan turned toward the door and gripped the thick iron handle.

"One other thing, Lucan of Seacourt."

He stilled.

"You will take care to mind the state of your soul.

My men do not suffer the same weaknesses as Mikhail's. Under my leadership, you will stay your sword, lest it becomes absolutely necessary to engage."

Ordered not to fight—again. Lucan squared his shoulders and marched through the door. He would accept many things from Raphael. But even Mikhail could not convince him to stay at the rear and watch others fight. All his life he had lived by the sword. To do naught else defied all he knew.

Chloe huddled in her dark corner, knees drawn to her chest, her swollen cheek gingerly resting on them. She ached from head to toe. The upturned side of her face itched with dried blood. But she dared not lift her hand and scratch, for that might remind Julian—or whoever he was—she was still here. Still alive, despite the fist he had pummeled into her temple.

She watched from the shadowy recesses of a cavern. Dimly, she recalled passing piles of bones. Skulls that leered from stacks of femurs. But her memories stopped at a dead-end in the tunnels, where her brother had turned to her, closed his fingers around her throat, and squeezed until her world went black.

She'd awakened here. Where she'd remained, God only knew how long.

The creature who had attacked her wasn't her brother, despite their identical appearance. No, Julian lay beside her, stretched out on the wet stone, his body frail, his skin the pallor of death. She inched a hand across the short distance that spanned between them and slid her fingers around his wrist. Faint and weak, his pulse still beat. Relief trickled through her.

Movement on the other side of the small cavern

froze her in place. She shifted her eyes to the *thing* that looked like her brother, sounded like her brother, yet somehow, wasn't. He spoke with a man in a black robe. A robe like so many others she'd seen in the Templar stronghold beneath the cliffs. It bore the mighty crimson cross that identified the knights, and Alaric had explained the men wore them for prayers. But this figure kept his head cloaked with a voluminous hood, unlike the men who had dropped to one knee and sworn their fealty.

Low and resonating, their words echoed off the walls. "You have done well, Julian. Exceeded Leofric's expectations. For this you will be rewarded."

The false Julian shrugged his shoulders. "It was easy with the knight nearby. Had I realized she was a seraph earlier, this wouldn't have drawn out so long."

Tell no one. Lucan's words echoed in Chloe's head. Damn it! He'd warned her. And she, because she'd been so convinced what he confided couldn't *possibly* be true, had laughed it off to her brother. Rather, who she thought was her brother. Whatever that *thing* was— she'd brought this all onto herself.

If she'd just believed what her heart said. If she'd trusted Lucan, as he'd asked so many times . . . A tear trickled down her bruised cheek to drip onto her knee. She'd had no reason to doubt Lucan. And yet the one thing she wanted the most, an eternity with a man who loved her, terrified her to the point she'd endangered them all.

Now, having accepted her status and purpose, she realized her trepidations caused far more damage than wounding Lucan. She'd risked the Order as a whole. The stench around her told her where she was—in the bowels of the earth, surrounded by evil beings she couldn't see but that looked on from the crevices in the damp rock.

The hooded man inclined his head toward her. "You should not have beaten her. Azazel will be most displeased that you have bruised his bride."

"It became a necessity. She scalded me." The creature extended his hand and pointed at something Chloe couldn't see on the back of his wrist.

Her eyes widened. She couldn't remember physically touching him. She'd pried at his wrist, but her fingers didn't possess half the strength his did. However, she distinctly remembered willing him to let her go. Had the ability Lucan taught her somehow affected him?

Excitement quickened her pulse. If she'd wounded that thing, that could only mean he was a demon. If he was like those creatures in the trees, she could overtake him. Get out of here, maybe, and get back to Lucan.

Eyeing the broad shoulders that perfectly impersonated her brother's, she drew in a shallow breath.

"Can we kill him now and be done with it? I grow sick of his presence." The creature jerked a thumb over his shoulder at Julian.

Chloe paused, her breath held. Reaching within herself as deep as she could, she tapped into the restless energy in her veins and envisioned channeling it into a solid mass.

"'Twould change naught. He will still be joined with you, even if the body expires." The hooded man clapped a hand on the impersonator's shoulder. "'Twill not be long now. His lungs scarce draw air."

Gradually, Chloe released her lungfuls of air and slanted her gaze back to her brother's limp form. Joined with the beast? She blinked. That *thing* was linked to her brother? Oh, good God! *How?*

"Oh, look!" Humor laced the creature's exclamation. "She's awake."

Realizing he could only be talking about her, Chloe flattened her back to the wall. Instinct ordered her to shrivel out of sight. To somehow blend into stone. But her efforts at making herself as small as possible failed.

The impersonator took four giant strides across the cavern and loomed over her. He glanced back at the man behind. "She reeks of goodness."

"Concern yourself not with that. Azazel will coerce it out of her, as you shall see when he comes."

The creature looked down at her, his sneer as vile as the fathomless dark eyes that studied her face. He lowered himself until his gaze leveled with hers and reached a hand out to trace the line of her jaw. "I'll get to watch him master her?"

Chloe recoiled as his hand stroked the length of her throat. Grimacing, she squeezed her eyes shut. Master her—oh hell no, not as long as she had anything to say about it. No one would.

"If you like. Though I expect you shall hear her moans throughout the realm tonight."

She swallowed hard, the implication clear. Revulsion balled her stomach into a tight knot, and Chloe twisted her head away from the creature's cold caress. "Get away from me."

He gripped her chin and wrenched her face back to his. "Watch your tongue. Azazel will care less for your insolence than I do." His thumb stroked her swollen lip.

"I'd much rather witness the mating of your body than the shredding of your heart."

Possessed by rage that knew no boundaries, she drew back from his hand and spit in his face. "Fuck you."

A low, sinister chuckle rumbled through the cavern. The creature stood, his eyes dancing with dark light. "No. I believe, more aptly, it's you who will be fucked."

Before Chloe could unleash the chain of curses that rose to the tip of her tongue, the creature drew his arm back. He snapped it forward with a hoarse laugh. Her head whipped sideways. Pain lanced the side of her face. A dull, unrelenting throb broke out behind her skull.

The second blow brought darkness.

CHAPTER 41

✟

Forced to the rear of the small group of men, Lucan held his sword in one hand and the reliquary tucked beneath his opposite arm. To his eternal dissatisfaction, Alaric took Raphael's orders to heart and charged him with the guarding of the Veronica, forbidding him the ability to fight except as a last recourse. With the bones of centuries of France's dead behind them, they stood before a jagged stone at the end of one quarried catacomb tunnel. The fetid stench of death poured through a gaping crack in the rock. Beyond, the pitch black of damnation waited.

Alaric lifted a gloved hand, motioning for the men to follow. He shouldered through the wide opening. One by one they slipped into a realm forbidden to mortals.

Within, Alaric struck a match. He set it to a cloth-wrapped torch and light blazed through the corridors. Living shadows shrunk back. A hushed buzz filled Lucan's ears as those who served Azazel spread news of the invasion.

In seconds, the foul beasts set upon them. Nytyms poured down the corridor, their high-pitched screams chilling. Forced to stand and watch, Lucan ground his teeth together as his brothers made quick work of the formless shadows. Like rats beat aside with heavy maces, they piled on the floor, squeaking out the last of their vile existence.

Stillness returned. Waiting. Watching.

The men moved forward as a collective unit. Their chain armor clinked. Boots echoed. Insignificant sounds that drew more attention than if they had announced their entry with a mighty horn. Lucan felt the presence everywhere, as if the very rock that surrounded them lived and breathed. He strained against the urge to break formation and charge ahead in search of Chloe. She was in here somewhere, mayhap already in Azazel's hands. He felt her too. A thin line of a substance he could not define wrapped around his heart and pulled tightly against his soul. Mayhap 'twas only his imagination, a product of hope he clung to. Mayhap 'twas something tangible, a bond instilled by the divine. He did not know. Yet he sensed he would know if death came upon her. He could believe naught else.

They descended deeper into the cavernous network. The air became colder, though it teemed with greater life. Hellfire and brimstone did not exist here. They would not descend to Azazel's kingdom, but skirt the edge.

Alaric drew to a stop. He swept the torch toward a mark on the wall, a deeply etched cross haloed by a crown of thorns. The mark Raphael told them to watch for.

He beckoned for Lucan to join him. Gareth and

Tomas parted, allowing Lucan to move to the front of the small formation. As he had been instructed, he placed the reliquary at his feet. "Julian!" His voice boomed into the dark. "You have wanted the Veronica! I bring it to you now. In exchange, I wish to set my eyes upon Chloe one last time."

All around them something stirred. Things they could not see. Things they could not hear. And yet the movement rustled Lucan's hair and his long surcoat. Beneath his chain, the ghostly caress lifted the hairs on his arms.

An angry wail pierced through the air. In the next heartbeat, shades invaded. Morphed into animalistic forms, teeth snapped and claws raked as they descended on Lucan and the knights. At the forefront of the group, he lifted his sword, prepared to cut the juvenile beasts to shreds.

Alaric shoved him aside. "Nay!"

Lucan found himself at the rear once more. "God's teeth, they are but simple creatures. Their taint will not affect me overmuch!"

Gareth possessed the gall to laugh. "Then do not feel compelled to aid, for they affect us less." With an arrogant grin, he surged into the fray, his sword a glint of silver as it glided effortlessly through the air.

With naught left to do but swear, Lucan cursed Gabriel and the rest of the archangels.

When the last shade sagged to a moaning end, Alaric lowered his sword. "We wait for Julian."

It took mere heartbeats for footsteps to echo in the oppressive black beyond. Lucan cocked his head, listening. One being approached. No clink of metal to identify a dark brother. No scrape of steel to reveal an unsheathed sword. He tensed. Where were the mighty fallen? 'Twas not right for Azazel's most powerful to trail behind. They should have already encountered several, not the failed attempts at powerful beasts Azazel sent their way. The more intelligent demons—they too lurked in shadows. Why?

He did not have time to debate the matter. At the edge of the flickering torchlight, Julian emerged. Raphael's wisdom reverberated in Lucan's head: *He is still part man, his follies the same. Appeal to his pride, and he will yield.*

Lucan pushed his way to the reliquary once more. He challenged Julian with a glare. "You have Chloe, but you failed to obtain the Veronica."

Julian folded his arms over his chest and flashed a cocksure grin. "An omission Azazel will forgive."

"Mayhap," Lucan allowed. "Would it not be a greater success to present both at the same time?"

Mistrust flashed across Julian's brow. His gaze narrowed. "You aren't here to hand over a relic. What do you want?"

Swallowing his pride and his warrior's hide, Lucan allowed true emotion to slip through his throat. "I wish to see her. To take my last breath at her side, if I must."

Slowly, Julian shook his head. "If you'd brought the relic by yourself I might believe you. But a man who's come to yield to Azazel wouldn't bring three others."

Alaric sheathed his sword and stepped forward. "We come only to ensure he is taken to her. We are prepared to leave when you have honored the request."

"Leave?" Julian barked out a laugh. "You won't be leaving here. Azazel knows you've arrived. In moments the knights will cut you into bits."

Lucan slid his gaze sideways, meeting Alaric's steely

gaze. Behind him, Lucan heard Gareth draw in a sharp breath. So the fallen Templar would come after all. Although they could fight a few, they must hurry. A full regiment of dark knights would quickly bring about their end.

He looked back to Julian, determined, and besieged the buried portion of his soul. "If we are all to perish here, what is the harm in allowing my request? You care for her as well—would you deny *her* the opportunity to say good-bye to one she loves?"

A moment of indecision passed over Julian's face. He looked between the men, as if gauging the wisdom of honoring Lucan's plea. For a terrifying moment, when he stiffened his shoulders and shrugged, Lucan thought Julian might walk away. That they would make one final stand here, and lose both Chloe and the Veil.

But in the next heartbeat, a wicked smile twisted Julian's mouth. "Very well. It'll amuse me to hear her grieve her lover's death."

Rage boiled through Lucan's veins. That a brother could wish such torture on his sister defined the very meaning of vile. If there had been any thought in his mind that decency remained in Julian, it had just shattered. Not an ounce of light remained in Chloe's brother's soul.

He scooped up the reliquary and strode to the edge of the light. As Julian reached for the golden chest, Lucan twisted away. "I will yield the Veil when I set my eyes upon her."

With a scowl, Julian strode into the darkness.

They hustled through the twisting maze of tunnels. Raphael bade Gareth to mark their way—whether he did, Lucan did not look to verify. 'Twas not worth the risk Julian might observe the chalk marks on the wall and see through their ruse.

Light interrupted the never-ending black. From an offshoot several feet ahead, it illuminated the corridor with faint orange. 'Twas there Julian led them, and there he stepped back to allow them entrance first.

Lucan's gaze swept across the far wall, his heart swelling as he spied Chloe in the corner. He dropped the reliquary at Julian's feet and rushed to kneel at her side. When he looked upon her battered face, fury fisted through him. "Chloe," he murmured. Gingerly, he reached out to trace the bruise beneath her eye.

Her lowered lashes lifted. Bleary eyes slowly focused. "Lucan," she said on an exhale. She grimaced with the effort of a smile. "Oh, Lucan, I'm so sorry."

"Shh." He bent forward and dusted a kiss atop the matted hair at her temple. Near her ear he whispered, "You will leave this place with me. I swear it to you."

The heavy clink of metal pushed him to his feet. He spun around in time to witness three dark knights step from the opposing corridor of black. In the distance, throaty shouts warned of the coming of several more. He dropped his hand to his sword, and a fist drilled into his cheek. Caught unawares by the blow, he staggered. A pair of robed arms broke his fall. But as he found his footing, a searing fire knifed into his ribs. Warm sticky wetness trickled down his side.

"Lucan!" Chloe cried.

Lucan glanced down his body. The hand that had caught him withdrew, taking with it the glint of a small metal blade. Another burn lanced through his body as the man palmed the ancient dagger. Lucan clutched at the rend in his flesh and gaped in disbelief. As his blood trickled through his fingers, he lifted his gaze to his unexpected attacker.

The sight of Templar robes and a face he recognized snapped him into sense. Blinded by fury, he drew his sword and lunged at Eadgar the Brave. Eight centuries they had stood side-by-side against Azazel. Now, though his brother did not wear the garb of fallen knights, they stood as enemies. Sworn to the same pledge. Divided by the very oaths that bound them together.

He ignored the burn along his left side and attacked with vengeance. Why his brother turned his back on the Order, he could not fathom. What drove Eadgar to ally with Azazel before his soul turned irrevocably, he could not explain. He did not care to try. Betrayal from within was worse than any beast Azazel might create.

As Lucan drove in hard and fast, his sword poised for Eadgar's throat, Julian set upon him from behind. Claws raked across Lucan's chain, shredding the shoulder of his surcoat. The distraction was enough to thwart his attack on Eadgar, and Lucan spun to confront his new attacker. His sword glided across his body, one deadly strike meant to cleave the demonic brother in half.

At the last possible moment, Julian twisted aside. The broadsword slid down his back, landing a glancing blow to his left thigh. Crimson stained through the light denim of his jeans, nonetheless. But the sight of blood was not enough for Lucan. This man would die. For what he had done to Chloe. For what he had done to him. Chloe's brother or not, his time upon this earth had come to an end.

He advanced, one eye on the skulking traitorous Templar who hovered near Chloe. Around him battle raged. Steel clanged against steel. Voices comingled in victory and defeat. The sounds drove him onward, blocked out all thought but one—*slay*.

He landed a strike to Julian's arm. Another on his shoulder. A lunge pricked Julian's opposite knee. Lacking any physical weapon, save for the unholy claws that emerged from his hands, Julian backed away from Lucan's relentless assault. His back hit the wall with so much force his breath expelled audibly. Defiance glinted in his glare.

Triumph roared through Lucan's veins. Gripping his sword in both hands, he lifted it high over his head. He would not only kill this despicable creature, but send his head rolling across the floor to join the one at Gareth's feet.

"Lucan, *stop*!"

Chloe's frantic scream filtered into his awareness. He hesitated and threw a questioning frown over his shoulder.

She clutched a body he had not observed before to her breast. "You're killing him!"

'Twas such an illogical concept, his arms faltered. The moment of indecision gave Eadgar advantage. From Lucan's right, he rushed in head-first. He shoved Lucan several steps backward, his sword now brandished, his rage equal. The sting of steel at his shoulder pushed Lucan beyond his confusion. Renewed in his purpose, he sucked in a deep breath, braced his weight on his left leg, and waited for Eadgar to strike.

In Eadgar's chaotic aggression, Lucan recognized the desperation of a man who cared naught for his own survival and who had become blinded by certain defeat. A caged animal. Strategy forgotten, he opened himself to folly.

Lucan took full advantage of the mistake. As Eadgar lunged into the wide arc of Lucan's blade, Lucan swept his sword from hip to ceiling. The blade plunged into Eadgar's gut. Momentum carried Lucan's arm higher, carving out a gaping hole in Eadgar's flesh. The unarmored knight's eyes widened. Bloody spittle trickled from the corner of his mouth as he rasped out a gasp.

Withdrawing his sword, Lucan dragged in a shallow breath. Eadgar toppled backward, where he lay upon the stone unmoving.

Silence invaded Lucan's awareness. His body burned like fire. Where the dagger had pricked him, his clothing stuck to his body. He lowered his sword and glanced around the cavern. Gareth, Alaric, and Tomas looked on. Strewn across the floor lay the lifeless bodies of their beheaded brethren. Where he had left Julian, the wall was empty. The reliquary was gone.

Lucan turned in search of Chloe. He found her in the same place, cradling the same still body to her breast. The aching in his side gave way to the overwhelming need to touch her. To kiss away her bruises and take from her the suffering she had survived. As he sank to his knees beside her, he dropped his sword. Drawing her into his arms, he held her close. Scattered frantic kisses through her hair.

She tipped her head up, and his mouth descended on hers. He released his fear, his pain, and his love in his kiss. Absorbed hers. As emotion swelled and threatened to overcome him, he slowly withdrew. Her lips clung to his; he savored the salty flavor of her tears.

"Lucan, we must hurry. Say your oath and be done with this!" Alaric urged.

As Lucan pulled away from Chloe's fierce hold, he

glanced at the man who's head lay on her thigh. A face of identical resemblance to the man he had known as Julian twisted with agony, though he bore no visible injury. Her brother. Not the thing possessed with evil, but the real man he had never met. How could such be possible?

Unable to dwell upon the matter, he shoved his hand into his pocket and produced Chloe's serpent torc. "Will you?" he murmured.

"Yes," she answered through her tears. "God, yes."

Lucan dropped the armlet of bronze onto his sword. It slid down the blade, coming to rest against his hand. He grimaced as throbbing broke through his body. Each beat of his heart pulsed torment across his ribs. Yet despite the pangs, he found the strength to whisper, *"Meus vires, meus mucro, meus immortalis animus, fio vestry."*

My strength, my sword, my immortal soul, becomes yours.

A smile pulled at the swollen corners of her battered mouth. She wrapped her hands around his. *"Meus vita, meus diligo, meus eternus lux lucis, fio vestry."*

My life, my love, my eternal light, becomes yours.

Between them, his sword flared with a blue-white light. Against their intertwined fingers, the serpents stirred. Elongating into one snake with two heads, it stretched out atop their hands. Two golden jaws opened to reveal small pointed teeth.

Lucan watched in fascination as one head attached itself to the small golden cross at the broadsword's point of balance. The other slithered to the identical mark embedded in the pommel and sank its teeth into the metal. With one slow undulation of its bronze body, it shook the patina from its scales, then lay still. Where he had naught but a plain pommel before, warped quillions formed an eternal barricade to the vile darkness he would spend immortality combating.

He gazed down into Chloe's wonder-filled eyes, and a new sensation filtered through his veins. The sting that accompanied each beat of his heart dulled. The hot flow that seeped down his ribs trickled to a stop. Warmth, unlike any he had experienced, slid through his body from head to toe.

With it came something else. Something more valuable than any gift of healing or protective guard.

Trust.

As he held Chloe's gaze, it sank into his soul. He knew then the freedom he had longed for. She would never betray him. And he would never again doubt the allegiance of her heart. In time, he would regain the same confidence in his brothers. As he would regain the light that had once filled his soul.

"Lucan," Gareth urged quietly.

At the louder sound of approaching knights, Lucan sheathed his sword, swept Chloe into his arms, and eased to his feet. "We must flee this place."

"Take him?" She pointed at her brother's battered body.

"Aye."

Lucan directed Gareth to carry Julian with a jerk of his head. When he had picked the man up, Lucan strode down the corridor behind Alaric, following the tiny white marks Gareth had drawn upon the wall.

CHAPTER 42

✠

A heavy hand settled on Chloe's shoulder. She smiled at the familiar weight. The silent offer of support she'd come to know so well. Turning over her shoulder, she looked up at Lucan and bathed in the warm light of his loving gaze.

"How is he?" he asked quietly.

She covered his hand with hers and turned back to the tiny bed her brother lay on. Two days of Zerachiel's healing touch and the cook's rich broth had restored color to his skin. But nothing had brought him from the place his mind lurked, and his breathing became more shallow with each passing hour.

"He's dying," she whispered. Tears pricked the corners of her eyes, as they had countless times since they'd returned to the temple. "Zerachiel said his soul was transferred to the demon's body. It is sucking his life away. He won't last much longer. But Zerachiel swears he is out of pain. That he'll die in comfort, and when he does, he will ascend to peace."

She couldn't ask for anything more. Her brother had suffered unfairly. But the knowledge he'd die without pain made her grief bearable.

Lucan too eased the ache in her heart. When she looked at him, when she went to sleep in his protective embrace, her sorrow ebbed. Though her own injuries had prevented the reunion her body craved, consolation came with the warmth of his skin, the stroke of his hand.

"Mayhap not."

He slid his fingers through her hair, stirring her innermost awareness of him. Her body tingled from the inside out. Her pulse quickened as it did each time he touched her. She tried to ignore the unsettling sensation and focus on his words. "What do you mean?"

"I spoke with Raphael. He comes now."

Just then the door to Julian's private healing room opened. The golden-haired archangel entered, his expression serene, his blue eyes alight with divine radiance. Hope burst inside her, and she turned pleading eyes on his beautiful face. "Can you do anything?"

Raphael drew in a deep breath and set his hand on Julian's shoulder. He lowered long lashes in concentration. After a few moments, he withdrew with a sharp frown. Chloe peered at him quizzically, but said nothing as he dragged a chair close to Julian's side and sat down.

On her shoulder, Lucan's grip tightened.

"My strength is with the sword," Raphael murmured. Folding his hands in his lap, he continued, "But I concur with Zerachiel's assessment. Julian's soul is damaged beyond repair." He looked to Lucan. "It is the same sort of affliction Gabriel and I beset upon you. You are possessed by darkness. Except, in your circumstance, the darkness does not think for itself. In

Julian's, the demon is possessed by him. He resides within a living, breathing entity, that has stripped him of control."

Chloe shriveled at the delivery. Fresh tears tracked down her cheeks, and she dropped her head to hide her heartbreak. Lucan rested his other hand on her shoulder, drawing her back against him.

"Zerachiel was not instructed in the curse. His purpose is to heal, not to wound."

She shook with the devastating news, and her heart broke all over again. A sob wrenched its way out of her throat.

"Chloe." Raphael reached across Julian's unmoving form and took her hand. "You must look beyond your heartbreak. Consider what Julian would most desire, for you have a decision to make."

She lifted her head with a prolonged blink. "Decision?"

"Aye. I can pull his soul back to this body. The vessel that harbors it now will cease to exist. But the demon will remain with Julian. Though I will grant him the strength to dominate the presence, it will always be a torment. A day shall not pass where he does not combat Azazel's dark desires. He will have to dedicate himself to the Templar purpose, for with this he will also gain immortality."

On a hard swallow, Chloe nodded in understanding.

Raphael's fingers gripped hers harder. "You must decide what your brother, not you, would want. If you let him go now, he will ascend to the heavens and know eternal peace. But if you believe he would wish to live, no matter the struggle, and that he is capable of keeping the beast within under control, I will grant my aid."

She gazed at her brother's handsome face. To ask her to decide was unfair. She couldn't guess at what Julian would choose. But he'd never shrunk from a challenge. Never ran away from anything that intimidated him. His zest for life, even if he tended to embrace it too much now and then, had inspired her on countless occasions.

As she studied his serene expression, she thought of the many things he'd sworn he would do before he died. Climb the Tibet mountains. Walk the Great Wall of China. Visit the Australian outback. All things he'd never accomplished but had talked about with such passion he'd made her own heart race with excitement.

A strange, displaced thought drifted to her mind. *Miranda*. One solitary word that as it echoed in her head, she knew what she must choose. She pulled her hand from Raphael's and wiped the tears from her cheeks. "Bring him back."

"Are you certain?"

No, she wasn't. But the voice in the back of her mind echoed Miranda's name again. She couldn't shake the gut-deep feeling that allowing Julian to die was wrong, even if living meant he'd never know peace. That Miranda would somehow suffer.

She gave Raphael a slow nod. "Bring him back."

A faint smile touched Raphael's eyes. "Go then. Leave me to my work."

Hesitantly, she stood. "Are you sure it'll work?"

His smile broadened as he looked between her and Lucan. "Aye. Go and embrace the life that flows between the both of you. You have had little time to celebrate the vows that bind you together. Tomorrow you shall speak with your brother."

Guilty pleasure seeped into her blood. The Veronica was gone. A gray cloud hung over the Order. The knights she passed in the halls wore the touch of defeat behind their cordial smiles. She had no right to know happiness when she had contributed to the Veil's loss and those around her knew only despair. And yet they had been given a gift in this time of darkness. A divine gift handed down by the Almighty, blessed by the archangels. She couldn't bring herself to feel shame.

And she hungered for time with Lucan to celebrate their vows. Now that her bruises were little more than purple spots and the swelling in her face had lessened so his kisses didn't hurt, nothing sounded more delightful. Knowing her brother wouldn't die while she was away allowed her the freedom to revel in the man and the love she treasured.

She slipped her hand into Lucan's. With a blush, she found the first genuine smile she'd experienced since her capture. He met her gaze, his gray eyes bright. Between them the undercurrent of desire flowed freely. His fingers twined through hers, and as Raphael bent over Julian, Lucan led her from the room.

In the hall, heedless of those who might pass by, Lucan dragged her against his chest. He captured her with an ardent kiss, the stroke of his tongue laden with urgency. His weight pressed her backward, until she came to a stop against the stone wall. On a sigh of surrender, Chloe looped her arms around his neck and welcomed the hard press of his hips.

His mouth softened. His hands settled at her waist. Slowly, he eased the kiss to a close and withdrew to stare into her eyes. "My love for you is as eternal as our lives," he whispered as he tucked a lock of her hair behind her ear.

Her heart swelled to painful limits and she rose to her toes. Subtly, she rolled her hips into his. "Take me to our room and prove it to me?"

Desire blazed behind his intense gaze. In one effortless sweep, he lifted her off her feet and tossed her knees over his arms. "Aye, milady. There is naught that would satisfy me more."